THE ARISTOCRATIC OUTLAW

"You are the oddest woman I have ever met," Damien stated in retaliation to her smile—to the alarming havoc it unleashed through his senses.

"And you, Mr. Sharpe, are the first outlaw *I* have met."

"Where did you hear that?" he asked in a lethally soft murmur. "No one calls a man an outlaw without having a bloody good reason, princess." He moved closer to her. "You know, don't you? You know all of it."

Kira's downcast gaze confirmed his suspicion. "I just wanted to know why you were so . . . why you were hurting so much," she said softly.

She could have landed an arrow into his chest and caused him less agony. He didn't need the exhilaration of her touch, the warmth of her gaze, and most of all, her truthful words slicing much too close to certain places inside him. Places he'd vowed nobody would ever see again.

"That's none of your bloody business," he retorted, feeling both anger and desire for her.

"For God's sake!" she cried. "No wonder nobody cares about you anymore. You won't let them!"

Dell Books by Annee Carter:

The Promise of Your Touch
A Fire in Heaven

Annee Carter

A Fire in Heaven

A Dell Book

Published by
Dell Publishing
a division of
Bantam Doubleday Dell Publishing Group, Inc.
1540 Broadway
New York, New York 10036

ISBN: 0-440-22297-4

Printed in the United States of America

Published simultaneously in Canada

March 1998

10 9 8 7 6 5 4 3 2 1

OPM

For the real untamed gypsy beauty
who has helped me see the magic in chimps and deer,
and even bugs!
A sister I am also privileged to call friend . . .
Susan Locke, you are a treasure beyond compare.
I love you.

One

*Run! no one would blame you. No one would care.
You don't belong here . . . you don't belong here. Run!*

The thought clung invitingly to Kira Sergenkov's mind,
warming her more than the cold muck attaching itself
around the rest of her body. "Fog" was what all these En-
glishmen kept calling the sludge, yet the stuff wasn't like
anything she'd seen before. The disparity, however, didn't
surprise her in the least. Nothing had been familiar in her
life for the last four weeks.

The mighty mausoleum of a house towering before her
didn't help matters, either.

The only building she'd ever seen that dared to rival this
place was the White House, home of President Tyler himself. But beyond the polished brick driveway and column-
framed entrance of *this* mansion, she reminded herself,
no president dwelled. No influential man made world-
changing decisions. A man had instead used this palace as a
hiding place.

A man who'd forsook the fact he ever had a daughter
named Kira.

Trepidation clogged her throat again. She was suddenly conscious of her faded walking boots, the missing tassels on her shawl, the wrinkled ribbons dangling from her bonnet. She swore the holes in her thin gloves grew as she reached a trembling hand to an unsmiling footman.

She was really here. Really about to meet *him*. Had she imagined this day, even in her most farfetched envisionings, but four weeks ago?

Four weeks . . . twenty-eight days that now represented the expanse between two lifetimes. But she shouldn't find *that* so hard to believe. It had taken a mere hour for the only life she'd known to burn to the ground. Another two days had successfully scattered the fire's other survivors—the last of the ragtag troupe she'd called family for eighteen years—to the four directions of the wind and then some.

And then the most bizarre shock of all had come: the father she'd thought dead was suddenly very alive, very much an English lord, and "requesting" her presence by his side.

Kira wondered what the child-abandoning coward would look like.

She would have to wait for an answer. Appearing at the mansion's door wasn't the looming London lord she expected but an imposing figure nonetheless. Even with its distinctly feminine outlines, the silhouette momentarily snatched Kira's breath away with its regal presence and commanding height.

"My lady Kira, I presume," the shadow issued in a tone that could have been pulled from the foreboding mists themselves.

Kira averted her gaze, certain she'd be more comfortable center stage at the Paris Opera. "H-how do you do," she stammered. When only a prolonged pause answered from the doorway, she grew even more painfully aware of how like a fish on land she appeared.

Of how like an outsider she felt.

She forced a breath past a chest suddenly full of a hundred knives, the blades all sharpened on memory's ruthless whetstone. But she hadn't learned to throw knives—literally *and* figuratively—at the age of five for nothing. Fury welled within her, summoning daggers of defiance. She jerked her spine straight and affixed her gaze back to the figure atop the entrance stairs.

Easy as pie, she inwardly congratulated herself. Oh, yes; she'd faced more intimidating strangers than this haughty housemaid before celebrating her tenth birthday. Growing up on the front seat of a circus performer's wagon showed a person many of life's more "unique" aspects, including the inclination of folks to turn a hateful eye at anything or anyone different from themselves.

And Kira, nervously fingering one of her unruly auburn curls, certainly knew what it was like to be different.

"Inside with you now," the figure at last bade, "before those threads give you a pneum, or worse."

The remark again rendered Kira irksomely conscious of her attire, which set off another flash of pride-filled indignance. She wasn't allowed half a moment to indulge the fury, however. It was barreled out of the way by an enthusiastic ball of sopping fur that hurdled into her legs. Equally sodden limbs gripped her knees, her waist, then her neck as the creature climbed her like a miniature palm tree. But she couldn't be angry at the invasion if she tried, especially as a five-fingered paw thumped the top of her head and blissful primate grunts resounded in her ear.

"Well, hello to you, too." She laughed, hugging the fur ball closer. She shut her eyes for the briefest of moments, believing the two of them were wrapped in Boston fog, instead; or perhaps an evening mist off a lake in the Carolinas, where Chico had deemed it best for the wagons to stop for the night.

"Dear God!"

Boston became London again, as Kira reopened her eyes and beheld the face of the maid for the first time. Obviously, flying fur balls were deemed cause enough to descend a few steps, even in England's goopy capital. From where the woman now stood, her features were clearly discernible.

In unthinking reaction, Kira kicked up both brows in shock. The woman's height had deceived her into expecting a mannish matron, but now she gazed at the epitome of the opposite. In a stylish dark-blue gown, with impeccably chiseled features and intricately coiffed hair, the woman was dipped from head to toe in proper English femininity—and at the moment, in proper English horror, as well.

"What—is—*that?*" A manicured hand extended in shaking shock, to which Kira replied with an amused grin.

"His name is Fred. I've had him since he was a baby. His own mama was accidentally killed." She pursed a momentary frown. "She was playing around on the trapeze, just as we'd told her *not* to."

"He . . . it's . . . a *monkey.*"

"Chimpanzee." Kira had no trouble adding ire to her expression. "Fred is a chimpanzee, not a monkey. I'll thank you to inform everyone of that."

But instead of compliance, Kira was struck with a stare of contempt. "I'll thank *you* to take that . . . *animal* to the barn. They can bathe it . . . then perhaps trim it, or something."

"They—won't—touch—him." Despite the menace of her glare, Kira railed at herself for allowing her vulnerability to show through about this. As if the threat of *her* fury would force someone to give Fred even the respect they'd afford their dog.

But Fred was different, too. *He'd* come to accept it a long time ago. Tarnation, the imp even flaunted his disparities.

Kira supposed that's why she'd threatened a bullet through the gut of anyone who'd tried to sell him off after the fire.

She supposed that's why she pulled him closer to her right now and continued leveling her determined stare along with her next words. "Fred will be staying with me," she stated calmly but firmly.

She wasn't surprised at the reacting gasp from the steps. "I think not!"

"I think so. He's my pet, and he goes everywhere with me."

"A *pet*, my lady, is a poodle, or—or a cat—"

"And I'm certain they're very nice pets, too."

"But—but a chimp—"

"Is infinitely more agreeable than a poodle and more affectionate than a cat. May we come in now?"

At first, only a pair of sighs answered the continuing serenity of her smile. When no other response came except the maid's militant pivot and subsequent retreat, Kira interpreted both actions as a victory. After a quick kiss to the top of Fred's head, she ascended the stairs with a dash more confidence than she'd had ten minutes ago.

The feeling was very short-lived.

Clean. As soon as she recovered enough from a blindingly up-close view of the chandelier, that word resonated as her first impression of the mansion. The butler who stepped forward to take her shawl was impeccably clean, his face betraying no surprise at the drab garment draped over his arm. The marble floor beneath her feet was gleamingly clean, actually mirroring each of her steps. And the pervading scents in the air were so clean, they hurt to breathe: lye, lemon, and bleach. There was no aroma of simmering soup in the kitchen, or freshly arranged flowers from the garden, or even the rain that seemed certain to form from the muck outside. Everything was clean and cold . . . and daunting.

Kira clutched Fred closer and wondered if her father might be Prince Edward himself.

She followed the maid past a stairway of oiled mahogany and into a perfectly arranged sitting room. As they entered, the woman addressed a pixie-faced maid who was finishing her duties before a fireplace at least five feet wide, bordered by the same marble they'd just crossed in the foyer.

"Emma," the woman directed, "we shall take tea and cider in here now and be seated for dinner in exactly one hour."

Kira pondered if that was when she'd at last meet her father. She also admitted she didn't anticipate that encounter as eagerly as she had an hour ago.

As her heart formed that thought, another voice surged through her senses, swirling into her mind through the mists of memory. *Be strong . . . oh, please be strong, my lipistok . . . my little rose petal. Be strong for me now.*

"Mama," Kira rasped into Fred's fur as the two maids discussed some dinner details. "Oh, Mama, I don't know if I *can* be strong!"

But the words came again, echoing through her soul now just as Mama had rasped them past smoke-filled lungs and a body crushed by the scenery flats she'd been trapped under. *There is so much ahead for you, Kira. The spirits and the saints have blessed me with this knowledge, even before tonight. You must believe this, lipistok. You must believe in your destiny. . . .*

But Kira had felt nothing destined about watching the

last breath leave Mama's body. She'd cursed destiny through scalding tears as her mother's heart ceased, joining her to the spirits of the earth in a continuation of life's eternal circle.

Saints, how she yearned to indulge those tears again! But now wasn't the time to surrender. Resolutely Kira leveled her chin as the older woman approached her again.

Fred picked that moment to squirm out of her arms and start exploring his new surroundings. As soon as he scampered off, the maid grabbed Kira's elbow and unceremoniously pulled her forward. On a surprisingly prissish gasp of her own, she fired, "I beg your—"

"Let's look at you properly." The woman issued the decree as if Kira's protest had been rendered in dog grunts. She peered down her skinny nose, directly at the corresponding part of Kira's face. "You've excellent features," she said with low reluctance. "Your face *is* mostly that of a Scottney, thank God. The exotic tilt to the eyes can be explained away easily enough. Or we might have Dr. Diedrich take a look at the problem. Perhaps he can stretch the skin back in some—"

"Perhaps he *cannot*." Kira jerked back, returning the woman's insult by raking *her* with a all-over scrutiny. "I want to see my father," she seethed. "Where the hell is he?"

The thin nose drew in fast air, becoming skinny as a bookkeeper's quill. "Young lady, you will refrain from spouting your American vulgarities in Scottney Manor!"

"Perhaps my father should tell me that. The father who 'requested' I cross the entire confounded ocean to get here, then remains scarce as a damn—"

"Lady Kira, I promise you I shall fill your mouth with lye myself, and posh to the fact you're my brother's by-blow heir!"

They gasped together—the maid, as she comprehended what she'd spewed, and Kira, as she gaped at the maid who wasn't the maid at all.

"You're . . ." she murmured. "You're . . ."

Though the woman looked like she'd rather jump into the North Sea in the middle of February, she dipped a brief curtsy. "I am Lady Aleece, sister to your father. And I—"

"You're my *aunt*." She knew she was spared an ear beating about interrupting her elders only because she cut off what was to be the woman's apology for calling her the English equivalent of a bastard. Still, only through a great effort did Kira refrain from throwing her arms around Lady Aleece in a hug. "I've never had an aunt before," she confessed softly. "Unless one counts Sheena, who liked to call herself my aunt. She was our troupe's contortionist. She let no one else but me handle her snakes—"

"Her s-snakes?"

"She said I had 'the touch.' Eventually she taught me how to feed them, too. She would say, 'Let Aunt Sheena show you how to feed a snake, leetle Keeerrra.'" She smiled then, as her deliberate use of Sheena's thick Ukraine accent flowed warm memories into her heart.

"You . . . haven't brought any pet *snakes* with you, have you?"

Aleece's trembling voice would, in another time or place, have brought on another amused grin. But not now. "The snakes are gone," Kira murmured huskily. "So is Sheena."

They're all *gone*, she thought with searing finality. They were all gone in one way or another, whether buried beneath the charred Virginia field upon which a colorful pavilion had stood, or vanished beyond the steam of trains that had taken them away to other lives . . . gone. She would never see any of them again. The horsemen, acrobats, and other exotic misfits of the Webber's Magnificent Menagerie and Circus would never love, laugh, live, or perform together again.

By the heavens themselves, she missed them. Yet like Sheena, they had all been *adopted* brothers, sisters, aunts, and uncles to her and Mama. Couldn't she find it in her heart to love her *real* family in the same way?

She promised herself she'd try.

With that resolution in mind, she worked her lips into a dutiful smile as Aleece approached with authoritative purpose once more. "Well, then. I promise you the curriculum *here* will not include any snakes; though I am confident you shall find your . . . education . . . both informative and enlightening."

The woman's all-too-careful phrasing sent Kira's eyebrows into curious arcs once more. "Education?" she repeated warily.

Her aunt's mouth pursed, deepening the crimps in her chin. When she confronted Kira's gaze, she did so with undeviating conviction. "Yes," she asserted, "your education. The responsibilities you must learn about the station you now hold."

"Responsibilities? My . . . station?"

"Why, yes, of course." They might as well have been talking about chuck-a-luck rules, so pragmatically did the woman press on. "The station you must fulfill to the letter, if we are to succeed at this outrageous plan at all."

"Plan?" Kira echoed with deeper confusion. She sounded like she'd spent one too many hours in the sun, but until four weeks ago, the only "stations" she'd had to know about were those where she waited for trains or steamers.

Fortunately, instead of disparaging her ignorance, Aleece angled a look at her bordering on motherly understanding. Yet when her aunt spoke, each word continued to resonate like an actress performing Lady Macbeth for the last time.

"You are not just a Sergenkov anymore, Kira. You are a *Scottney*. With this name comes centuries of honor, tradition, respect, and responsibility." Indeed, as if on cue, the woman raised a stately hand to the fireplace mantel, her profile forming a perfect cameo against the marblework there. "We are one of the most powerful families in the country. Our ancestors ate at Henry the Eighth's table and laughed at Shakespeare with Elizabeth the First. We survived with distinction through Cromwell and all four Georges; I personally attended Victoria's coronation seven years ago."

A distinct pause followed. "The . . . food must have been wonderful," Kira offered awkwardly, though it wasn't hard to lace the words with sincerity. A loud snarl of hunger emanated from her stomach.

Unfortunately, sincerity earned her nothing but another pursed grimace. "You are a part of a *legacy* now, Kira! This is something bigger, much bigger, than you've known in the little world of your circus."

She wouldn't let *that* go returned by a bit of casual banter. "That 'little world,'" Kira retorted tightly, "was plenty big enough for Nicholas Scottney."

"For a time, yes," came the disgustingly breezy reply. "Nicholas was young then, and easily lured by a pretty ankle and a mysterious lifestyle." Yet then came the cautious picking-my-words tone again. "Boys *will* be boys, my dear . . . and they do make their mistakes accordingly."

Kira bit down hard on the inside of her bottom lip, hoping the pain would obliterate the stinging stab to her heart. *You expected this,* her brain drilled at her. *You expected a comment like this at some time, so why are you letting it hurt so much?*

Her heart possessed no reply. Only a whirlwind of confusion filled her senses. She felt just like the first time she'd heard the truth of her identity, crouched on the floor beside Mama's cot . . . straining to hear her mother's last words. . . .

It was love, little rose petal, which brought you here . . . you must believe you were always loved! But your papa, in the end, he could not marry me freely, and I did not want him at a price. I refused to be known as his "kept woman," and you would not be known as his "accident."

Now God and all His angels and spirits have rewarded me for my honor. Nicholas has sent someone for you, to take you back to your papa. And you will become Lady Kira at last!

Indeed, here she was, living Mama's prediction to the syllable. But Mama's "gift" had been as normal in her life as sunrises and sunsets; she didn't concede a bit of perplexity at the fact she knew she'd be here a full month ago. And Aleece's words, though successfully striking their target in her heart, answered none of the questions in her head.

"What am I doing here?" she at last exploded with the biggest of those questions. "If I was Nicholas Scottney's 'mistake' eighteen years ago, what makes me so high and mighty good enough for him now?"

A thick silence stretched as her reply. It seemed, Kira concluded, she was not to receive an answer, though she suspected Aleece had it in her power to render one.

The pause was terminated by, of all people, Emma. After a hurried curtsy, the maid pronounced, "Dr. Diedrich has arrived, m'lady. Shall I show him in?"

Aleece responded eagerly. "Thank you, Emma. Yes, yes."

No, no! Kira's head railed. Though enough lightning bolts of shock had been hurled at her to form a summer's worth of storms over Georgia, she wasn't too dazed to remember Dr. Diedrich was called upon to do things like stretch faces. She backstepped behind the Renaissance-style settee, preparing to use the heavy furniture as weaponry if need be.

"Doctor," Aleece gushed at a man who bustled his portly frame into the room with harrumphing purpose, "thank you so much for coming, with the weather about to turn so foul upon us."

"It's my pleasure, my lady, and you know it." Diedrich had the most mushy British accent Kira had heard since arriving here. He flashed Aleece an equally outlandish wink. "Gave me a reason to brush up on the old Latin."

Aleece and he shared an all-too-enthusiastic laugh. Kira, without veering her stare from them, reached and pulled Fred to her side. Her pet cackled, yanking Diedrich's sights her direction. Though both his bushy eyebrows jumped, he betrayed no further horror at her pet's presence, winning him a degree of respect from Kira. But only one.

Diedrich broke into a friendly smile. She nervously returned the look, but the doctor had begun his thorough once-over of her. He concluded, surprisingly, with an energetic nod. "Her posture is commendable."

At that, Kira flashed Aleece a vindicated look. Her aunt only sighed wearily. "I suppose we are forced to thank the theatrical experience for that."

The inside of Kira's lip fell prey to another furious mangling. It was either do that or give in to the urge to tell this witless biddy "theatrical experience" meant she was raised in a circus, not a brothel. That the only "animal" she'd ever slept with was a pillow-stealing chimp. That she'd been raised by a dozen fathers more real than the man who'd sired, then abandoned her.

"Now, dearie—" Diedrich said in a businesslike tone. Kira found his voice a source of assurance—until he continued, "What of diseases?"

"Diseases?" Kira scowled, perplexed. "What of them?"

"Are you prone to chills?" the doctor clarified. "Allergies?"

"No." Kira now tensed defensively. "Why?"

"Have you had the pox?" the man pressed on. "Influenza?"

"No."

"Malaria? Diptheria? Typhoid?"

"No. No. No!"

"And your flows come regularly, I presume?"

She took no care to hide her astonishment at that. Apprehension surged so intensely through her that Fred hissed and bared his teeth at the physician, as well. "I beg your pardon?"

"Your flows," Aleece interjected, as if merely discussing ear bobs or hair aigrettes. "Your courses. Your monthlies. You . . . do know of what I speak, Kira?"

"Y-yes," she stammered. "Yes, of course I know, but—"

"And your cycle—it occurs regularly?"

"I—I really don't understand what this has to do—"

"And you *are* a virgin?"

"It's none of your damn business!"

The eruption felt good, despite how both Aleece and the doctor gaped as if she was the heathen who'd just giggled in church. "W-well," Diedrich finally muttered, "she is small, but healthy. *Most* healthy."

"Of course I am," Kira snapped. "But what does that have to do with anything?"

She didn't miss the brief but explicit glance shared by her aunt and the doctor. Nor did she misinterpret the bow Diedrich gave Aleece, as if he passed some invisible scepter to her. The woman accepted the deference with a great sweep of motion and a loud crunching of horsehair crinolines as she moved across the room to Kira. Firm determination was stamped on her every feature.

"Your health," Aleece stated, "has everything to do with bearing strong children."

"Ch-children?" Kira repeated in a disjointed stammer. Tarnation, would there be an end to the confusion she endured today?

"Yes." Aleece spoke melodically, as if explaining to a three-year-old why touching the stove was dangerous. "*Children*, Kira. As in Scottney descendants. The heirs to our line and our lands."

"And you think—" As comprehension sliced through, she found herself longing for the confusion again—with agonizing desperation. "You—you expect *me* to—"

She attempted to laugh at the ludicrous concept, but only Fred joined in her effort, flashing his teeth with gleeful abandon. Kira whirled from Aleece and Diedrich as a profound darkness descended on her heart, snuffing the last trace of idealistic hope she'd held there. Odd, so odd. She hadn't even known that hope was there until now, with its death. The recognition should have lessened her grief for it. Instead, she moved to a window seat overlooking a rain-drenched lawn, waited as Fred made himself comfortable in her lap, then watched three rebellious tears soak into his black-brown fur.

She'd been brought here not out of love or even curiosity. She was to be the Scottney clan's brood mare, and nothing more.

She suddenly wondered if P.T. Barnum needed any more freaks for his emporium.

"Kira."

A moment elapsed before Kira snapped her head up, realizing her name had not been invoked by Aleece this time. Nor the doctor.

Yet a man *had* murmured the greeting to her. A man who now stood watching her from a decorous distance of approximately four feet, not a wrinkle marring his tailored frock coat, satin paisley waistcoat, and perfectly cut trousers. Atop his loosely knotted tie, a face of "Scottney" features—balanced lips, aristocratic nose, high forehead—had aged to a handsome dignity and now gazed at her in unreadable stillness.

Except for his eyes. The man's eyes examined every inch of her while appearing to take in none of her, like a hawk assessing friend or foe, though confident he could be master of either.

Kira found herself evaluating *him* in the same mode. Friend or foe? Or both? She *knew* him . . . didn't she?

The curiosities drove her to step closer to the stranger. "Who are you?" she softly demanded.

The slightest movement ruffled the man's lips—as if he wanted to smile but couldn't. Or wouldn't. "My name is Nicholas Scottney. I am your father."

The words didn't surprise her. But they didn't fill her with the joy she'd fantasized about having in this moment, either. No, Nicholas Scottney's introduction inspired her to do only one thing.

Kira took another step forward, then slapped her father as hard as she could.

Two

"*D*EAR *LORD!*"

Aleece's gasp was joined by a bout of coughs from Diedrich's direction. The next instant, Kira found her shoulder caught beneath five white-knuckled talons.

"This is an outrage, young lady. An *outrage!* You shall—"

"She shall do nothing." Pinning Aleece with his hawk's eyes, Nicholas Scottney ordered with similar intent, "Let her go, Aleece."

"Nicholas!" she hissed. "You cannot mean to—"

"I *can* mean to." He actually released a rueful chuckle as he glanced back to Kira, rubbing his cheek. "I deserved it."

"Yes, you did," Kira retorted. Diedrich erupted in more spluttering coughs.

"Well," Aleece decreed then. "Then we have a problem, Nicholas. The girl is an urchin, just as I told you she would be."

"The *girl* is eighteen," Kira interjected then, "and wants you to stop speaking about her as if she's no more than the family bloodhound." She speared Nicholas with all the anguish in her gaze while adding "Even if you are breeding her like a second-rate bitch."

"*Nicholas!*"

"Aleece, don't start—"

"That is my point! Where *do* I start? How do you expect me to present her to the court at St. James, let alone around this city's finest ballrooms, with that beast around her neck and those profanities on her tongue? It shall take a small miracle to have her ready for presentation at all. And quite frankly, Nicholas, I'm not sure if I'm capable of the feat."

While her father drew in an exasperated breath, Kira released a relieved sigh. She knew no more about this "presentation" nonsense than she did the duties of her "station," but she was certain if either involved being called an urchin again by a pinch-nosed shrew, she wanted no part in the scheme. She wanted no part in this family at all.

She'd rather be an orphan than a brood mare.

Dr. Diedrich, however, was clearly of another viewpoint. "My dear lady," he said effusively, rushing over and scooping up Aleece's hand, "you are too blind to your own capabilities. I am certain if anybody in London is capable of miracles, it is you."

This time even the doctor's moonings didn't mollify the woman. "No, no." She moaned. "There's too much to be done, and we very well cannot do it *here*. Nearly everyone has returned to Town by now; a thousand eyes shall be on us if we so much as take a step in Piccadilly."

"Haven't you retained your staff at the Yorkshire property?" Diedrich queried.

Aleece slowly turned and beamed at the man. "Why . . . yes." Her smile actually lent a pretty charm to her face. "And Yorkshire shall give us all the space and privacy we need."

"Need for what?" Kira asked then, unable to ignore her

aunt's fervency—nor her own stomach's deepening queasiness.

"Yes," her father concurred. "Yes, Aleece; you're right."

"Need for *what?*" Kira pressed, bodily inserting herself into the conversation this time. "Will somebody tell *me* what in tarnation is being decided about my future, before I march out that hell-fired door and get on any boat I can find out of here?"

Three stunned stares swung and locked themselves upon her. Kira returned each scrutiny with unmitigated defiance of her own. Only Fred dared to at last interrupt the silence, whomping his hands together in applause at the ridiculous human circus playing itself out before him.

After a full minute passed, Nicholas closed his eyes. "Aleece," he murmured when he opened them, "I'd like a moment alone with my daughter." When his sister didn't budge, he added with pointed emphasis, "If you please."

Aleece managed a sanctimonious glare before motioning to Dr. Diedrich and letting him escort her from the room. She closed the door with a lady's version of a slam, of course.

Leaving Kira alone with the stranger who was her father.

Despite the room's velvet-upholstered stuffiness, Kira shivered. She sat down on the couch and opened her arms to Fred, silently apologizing to her pet for all the times she'd bemoaned his eager devotion, as he burrowed against her with blissful abandon.

"I know you must be upset and confused by all of this," her father finally began, turning and bracing both hands on the mantel.

"That's a good start," Kira returned. "You can add 'furious' and 'starving' to the list, too."

At that, her father did turn toward her. His gaze was active with bits of dark-gold light—the same look, Kira recognized, Mama would bestow on her when she'd done something pleasantly unexpected to earn her mother's pride. "Duly noted," he responded.

She gathered up Fred and cut a path back across the room again. "I'm your daughter, Lord Scottney," she pronounced as she did, "not your bookkeeper. You can no longer 'duly note' me into a category in one of your ledger books."

"Yes. I know."

"The hell you do."

So much more than that burned to be released from her heart and soul, but Kira's mind searched in vain for the words. The paths of her life, once so clear and simple to find, were now overgrown by vines of loneliness, clogged by brambles of confusion, shadowed by forests of grief. Would she ever find her way again?

This man didn't make the quest for that answer easy. "You truly are Rose's daughter," he stated with a gentle chuckle she did *not* expect. "So full of fire; so full of life . . ." His voice descended to a husky murmur as he looked into the fire. "Passionate about everything, even your anger."

Kira didn't want to see this aspect of her father. She told herself to look away from the clench of sorrow that started at his silver-touched temples and ended in the quivering fist at his side. She didn't want to think the only person in this mausoleum to understand her anguish was *him*.

Still, before she could swallow the words back, she murmured, "You *did* love her, didn't you?"

Her father's eyes slid shut. "I loved her."

"Then . . . why?" Kira raised her hands in a gesture of desperate supplication. "*Why* did you let her go?"

Why did you let her leave, knowing she carried your child inside her? Why did you let her tell that child you were dead?

Why did both of you hurt me like this? Why?

Nicholas's hand rose to wrap around the mantel's over-hang, as if he struggled for support. "Don't you think I tried to stop her?" A humorless laugh twisted his lips. "God, how I tried to stop her, Kira. I offered her a town house with servants in Mayfair, a monthly stipend better than most duchesses, a phaeton of her own, and the best tutors for you."

Kira took less than two seconds to issue her comeback to that. "She would have been miserable."

"Of course." Nicholas gave a fast shrug. "I know that now. I think I even knew it then. Your mother loved her gypsy life. That was why I bought her the new wagon and wrote up the promissory agreement that would see you and she well taken care of, no matter where you ventured in the country." As he grabbed a poker to jab angrily at the dwindling log, his features betrayed raw defeat. "But she ripped the document to shreds and said she had no intention of remaining in England at all."

"Of course she did," Kira returned without thinking—only then realizing the importance of doing so. *Oh, Mama, her heart cried then, why was it so hard for me to understand what you did? I've understood all along, haven't I? I've understood as easily as I breathe; as easily as your blood flows in my veins. You would have invited a devil spirit into your heart before selling that heart for a house or a phaeton or even a new wagon.*

"Your mother was a very proud woman," her father stated then, a good measure of the gentleness in his tone replaced by a tautly enunciated anger. "Because of it, she subjected herself and her child to a hard life in a foreign land." He grimaced once more. "A life that eventually killed her."

Kira's next words didn't even need two seconds to form.

"My mother," she bit out, "didn't want to be your whore, Lord Scottney. You can call it pride. I call it honor."

Her father cocked a sideways stare at her. "Honor is important to me, too, daughter. And I shall tell you something now that I never told your mother. Honor comes in many forms."

"Well, of *course* it does," she sallied in a mocking soprano. "How very silly of me to have forgotten, Papa dear. The greatest honor of them all is serving the great Scottney name, isn't it? Isn't that why you denied your gypsy whore and your bastard child the only two things they ever wanted from you, your love and your name?"

In answer to that, her father shoved himself from the mantel and advanced across the room. "Do you think I was *happy* about that choice?" Nicholas snarled, coming closer. "Do you think I *enjoyed* making it? If you do, then it's time you understood something, daughter dear."

Kira now stood, squaring her shoulders in preparation for the physical manifestation of the violence in his eyes. But her father halted, instead. His shoulders slackened. A long sigh poured off his lips.

"When your mother told me you were coming, I'd never known a moment of such joy," he confessed softly. "Yet I'd never known a moment of such terror. I was eighteen, Kira. *Eighteen*, the same age you are now, only without such a keen head on my shoulders. I had grown up with governesses and polo ponies; with benefactors in Parliament and estates at all corners of the country. I saw a full meal prepared for the first time in my life only when I spent my first night in your mother's wagon.

"Yes," he affirmed to her disbelieving gape, "it's true. Rose and her world were exhilarating to me, full of passions and freedoms I'd never known . . ."

His stare darkened in the moment before he bent to

offer a tentative hand of friendship to Fred, who'd finally loped over in shameless pursuit of attention. "But it didn't take long to know I could never be a part of that world, either," he continued. "My father clearly stated I'd be a Scottney only in name if I married Rose. And without my family's money or resources, what could I do? Could conjugating verbs in Latin put food on our table? Could dancing a perfect quadrille buy my baby medicine when she was ill?"

Kira listened to her father's explanation in deliberating silence. And, she admitted reluctantly, with increasing understanding. Her father had, in his own way, done the best with the limits set upon him. How many times had she been forced to do the same, making one costume work for four different scenes, or watching Mama turn beans into culinary delights for a week straight?

"I didn't know how to be a part of her world," he went on, "and she didn't know how to be a part of mine." Even the tug on his trouser leg from a newly devoted Fred didn't erase the searing pain from his eyes. "I made the wisest decision I could at the time, Kira. I'm not proud of it."

"But," she heard herself say, though her heart screamed at her tongue to stop, "you'd make the same choice all over again, wouldn't you?"

"Yes. I would make the same choice."

Kira thought herself prepared for that admission. Yet she felt herself stepping back, dipping her head to stay the sting behind her eyes even as her father stepped closer. Another frustrated snort escaped Nicholas.

"I've done my *best*, Kira," he said with a growl. "I've helped as I could, on the rare occasions your mother let me. If you'll just let me explain—"

"Then why don't you do that?" she snapped. "Because I'm truly at a loss for reasons why you've brought me here, Father. If things were so confounded fine the way they were, why did you summon me to provide a grandchild when one of your legitimate child—"

"There *are* no legitimate children," he cut her off with a vehement sword of a tone. Yet the next moment, his voice became a rasp again. "There are . . . no other children at all."

Curiosity clawed at Kira to press harder, but a noose of sympathy tightened around her throat. *Sympathy!* she thought, astounded. She actually felt *sorry* for the man responsible for putting her through this mess! Worse, an instinct deep in the pit of her belly told her Nicholas Scottney deserved that pity.

She forced those perturbing thoughts away with the next point of logic in her debate. "What about my dear Aunty Aleece? Why wasn't *she* ever offered the honor of providing your heir?"

This time her father took the backstep. "Aleece has no children, either," he stated past lips pressed so tight, his groomed mustache didn't move.

Kira sighed heavily. "So I am really the only one?"

"You are."

"The last hope for the great Scottney clan, is that it?"

Again her sarcasm barely produced a twitch in her father. "That is exactly 'it.' "

Beyond her control, her lips quirked into a laugh, anyway. *"Please,"* she quipped, "I was born in America, not China."

"Precisely" came Nicholas's easy agreement. Too easy. "You see, daughter," he continued, "there is a quaint little law we have here in England, a law under which the Scottney holdings fall. This law says that our estate *must* fall to a male blood heir of the Scottney line."

The answer doesn't matter, so don't ask the question, she

ordered herself. But the next moment, her lips formed the words, "And if there isn't a male blood heir?"

"That depends. Usually after the last living member of the family has died, the government divides up the holdings and sells them. Sometimes the government retains part of the holdings for its own uses. The other lands may fall into the hands of entrepreneurs, or even for the rail companies to destroy as they see fit."

Kira shrugged away the strange clamp of dread those facts dumped around her shoulders . . . and the even odder sense that she actually cared half a fig about her ancestors' land.

Her land.

"I'm sorry about your dilemma," she retorted. "But it's not my concern." She stepped past her father with impatient urgency and proceeded toward the door. "I just want to go home now."

She should have known Nicholas Scottney wouldn't let her go that simply. She should have anticipated the way he'd anticipate *her* words and how he'd gather a potent arsenal of persuasion to be ready at his bidding.

Just like the mercilessly quiet tone he hurled at her back now.

"Home . . . to your burned-out circus, you mean?"

Kira stopped. Bit hard on the insides of her lips. "I'm good at what I do, my lord," she stated, not pivoting by a toe in his direction. "I'm sure I can procur—"

"What? A position doing what, Kira, as an unmarried girl of eighteen without her own wagon or family? Will you be satisfied entering a show ring behind a horse instead of atop it? How long will you be able to fetch water, mend costumes, scoop hay . . . scoop dung?"

"As long as I have to." She clamped her teeth around every syllable. "If that is what I must do, then—"

"Then you'll be miserable, sweetling."

At that, she spun around. "I am *not* your sweetling."

"But you *are* my daughter." Nicholas flung the parry with the confidence of a rapier-wielding Frenchman. "And though I wasn't there to share every day of your life, I know you are meant to do much more than pitch hay."

Kira coiled her stance tighter, hostility curling its way around her every muscle. "You don't know anything about me."

"Oh, but Kira, I do."

"Stop it."

"You're a *Scottney*, daughter," he declared, voice rising with relish, as if his rapier had just found its mark in her heart. "You are a Scottney as much as you're a Sergenkov. *Look*"—he swept a hand toward the room's gilt-framed mirror—"your very face betrays you. Our blood courses in your veins!"

Kira jerked herself the opposite direction. "That doesn't mean I have to like it!"

"No." His voice plunged back to a composed murmur. "No, it does not mean you have to like it. But . . . it does mean you can take advantage of it."

At first, Kira said nothing. She squeezed shut her eyes, wondering why she suddenly felt like a maiden being enticed into the bathhouse by an unclean *bannik* spirit . . . yearning to resist, helpless to resist.

Surely enough, she opened her eyes and tilted a wary stare over her shoulder. "What in heaven's name does that mean?"

"Come walk with me in the garden, daughter," Nicholas requested quietly. "I'd like to discuss a piece of business with you."

Three

"No," KIRA SAID FLATLY. "Why?" she revised, when realizing her father had invited her with his tone, not ordered her.

Nicholas only extended his arm to her. He appeared every inch the influential lord of the realm, waiting patiently for her. The image, Kira admitted, only increased her apprehension of what he had in store for her on this "walk."

Only by looking to his eyes once more did she decide to comply with his request. Again, the sensation overcame her that she looked into a mirror, for how many times had she beheld such an unquenchable hazel fire in her own gaze?

That knowledge encouraged her enough to curl her hand around her father's arm and let him lead her out to the garden.

Though lit only by the light from the mansion, the bushes, trees, and flowers brimmed with misty, peaceful beauty. Kira wished she could enjoy the scene but gave up the fantasy as impossible. She'd be more comfortable walking here with the King of Prussia himself, she speculated as she searched for something, *anything* to say. But her brain only gave up more words laced with sarcasm and bitterness. Useless words.

"It's pretty, isn't it?" Nicholas finally asked, gesturing to the beds of tulips, irises, and other bounties of flowers they passed. He emitted a small chuckle when Kira slanted him a look condemning him for using "pretty" to describe this natural resplendence. "Imagine this multiplied a hundred-fold," he went on. "That's what awaits you in Yorkshire."

Kira halted so fast and spun on him, spray flew off the bottom of her skirts. "Awaits me *where*?"

This time her father didn't chuckle. "I told you I had a piece of business to discuss with you, Kira. Your trip to Yorkshire is involved in that business."

Kira longed to tell him she had no intention of going anywhere but back to the docks, but, she admitted, her father's confidence captured her curiosity. What made the man so sure of her compliance in his little proposition? She awaited the answer to that in glaring silence.

Nicholas didn't make her wait long. "I want one year from you, Kira."

She sent him a perplexed scowl at first. But the next moment, comprehension set in. "You're insane," she blurted.

"No" came the unruffled rebuttal. "I'm serious. You're already here—"

"And that makes everything easier?"

"I . . . need you, Kira."

"And that makes everything *all right*?"

She punctuated with a laugh that sounded musically merry—while her mind reeled in chordless chaos. Ironically, tranquility permeated the air around her. A small stone fountain gurgled contentedly nearby. Fred cooed at a bug crawling across the cobblestones. In the nearby carriage house, a man whistled a happy tune to soft-grunting horses.

Nicholas's hands descended gently to the back of her shoulders.

And Kira almost wept, for instead of yearning to bolt from his touch, she longed to whirl back around and burrow against the strength of her father's tall, strong form.

Until he leaned closer to her and spoke again.

"One year," he offered in a murmur so beguiling, she ruled out comparing him to the *bannik* and steeled herself to battle the devil himself. "One year, Kira . . . I ask for only one year out of your life, in which I shall endeavor to prove how deeply England truly flows in your veins . . . how happy you really can be here."

At those words, Kira jerked away from him, jamming her arms across her chest. "Happy," she echoed. "Happy, as in pregnant with your precious heir, is that it?"

"Kira," he said tightly, "I think you may look at things a little differently—"

"When I'm back on the ship, bound for home."

"Postpone your trip, damn it!"

His eruption startled Kira with the force of a lunge from an unruly tiger. Still, her father recovered his composure half as fast as she, settling easily back into his lordly mien.

"Today is May the eighth, 1844," he stated as if his outburst had been nothing more than a sneeze. "If you are still miserable on May eighth, 1845, I'll see you back to the ship myself, along with enough funds to start not only a new life but a new circus."

At *that*, Kira dropped her arms. And gawked openly at him. Nicholas only blinked with slow, almost lazy, assurance.

Certainly she'd heard his words incorrectly, she supposed, or misinterpreted his meaning.

There was only one way to find out. Make him clarify the point.

"I'll want a full menagerie," she started cautiously. "Lions. Perhaps panthers, too. And Arabian stallions, of course."

"Of course." The hint of a smile teased her father's mouth, and she thought a twinkle passed through his eyes, too. "And chimpanzees, as well." He chuckled as Fred, recognizing at least that word, sauntered over and affectionately turned himself into an accessory on the man's wool-trousered leg.

"New costumes will be necessary."

"Designed in Paris," he filled in.

Kira swallowed against her heart's ecstatic outcry to that. "But I'll still need more than that to compete against Barnum and the Flatfoot shows," she pressed, trying to smooth calmness over her tone. "Perhaps Levi North or Isaac Van Amburgh."

"Ahhh. 'The North Star' trick rider and 'The Lion King' animal trainer. Excellent choices. Why don't you hire both?"

Again Kira gaped at him. Again Nicholas's features barely shifted. The most active part of his expression remained his eyes, which now danced with such vibrant gold light, Kira would have sworn he enjoyed creating this dream as much as she.

That surety bloomed into a smile on her lips. Her father's answering smile warmed her deeper. "Ahhh, Kira," he said with a light laugh, "you ambitious piece of hellfire; you truly *are* my daughter."

As they walked back toward the sitting room door, Kira only smiled wider. But in her soul, words bubbled in jubilant celebration. *Mama,* she exclaimed inwardly, knowing that somewhere, somehow, her words went heeded, *you were right! I have found a destiny far beyond what I ever dreamed, and all it's going to cost me is one year!*

The time would pass before she knew it. And then she would be on her way, free to become that "ambitious piece of hellfire" as even Nicholas could not fathom . . . perhaps as even she could not fathom yet.

As for the little "vacation" she'd have to endure to Yorkshire . . .

Well, Kira reasoned, she could do *anything* for a year.

Even dance with the devil.

Four

FOUR DAYS LATER, Kira berated herself for that moment of reckless optimism. Even a year of dancing with the devil wasn't as heinous as one hour in a well-laced corset.

She groaned as the coach jolted through another hole in the northbound road, giving the corset's steel enforcements permission to dig into the tender flesh of her breasts, back, and waist. Her ordeal wasn't helped by a glare across the compartment at her aunt, who napped against the squab with the dainty oblivion of a cat.

She must force her thoughts elsewhere.

Kira shoved aside the green velvet curtains framing the coach's window and indulged a gaze full of the idyllic land where knights had fought and fairies had played . . . a land of ancient stone bridges and creeks shimmering like satin ribbons; of forests that captivated the eye with a hundred textures and valleys swirling with the fertile earthiness of sunshine on clover. They were all flawless vistas she'd seen only painted on stage backdrops before.

She winced then, as her father's words of yesterday morning echoed in her mind. He'd said them while escorting her to the carriage, after promising he'd be following them to Yorkshire at the conclusion of some lord-type business, in a few days at most. *My England*, he'd murmured to her, with that golden twinkle in his eyes. *Scottney Hall is where you'll begin to discover my England, Kira. Drink it in and savor it.*

She grimaced at remembering her reply to him, grumbling she'd already seen more than she liked of *his* England, thanks to the previous three days' worth of a London shopping marathon. Silently, she'd added doubts about her feelings changing at all—but now, an abashed smile rose to her lips. *All right, Father*, she conceded, *this is an impressive start.*

Her smirk dropped as the carriage bounced into the deepest of the ruts so far. "Hell," she muttered, before at last deciding she'd rather die in comfort than decorous torment.

Kira tossed back her velvet shawl, then set about easing her breasts' agony by manually pushing them together in order to allow soothing air down the sides of her torso. The resulting pleasure induced a blissful sigh to her lips—until an outraged gasp sliced into her reverie.

"Kira!" Aleece shot frantic hands to the window curtains, snapping them shut. "For heaven's blessed sake, *what* are you doing?"

"Breathing." She couldn't help returning her aunt's gape with a mischief-inspired smile. "It's a wonderful sensation, Aunt Aleece. Why don't you try it?"

"Ladies do *not* touch themselves like that, Kira. Please compose yourself at once. We've already passed Harrogate, and neighbors may begin to recognize the carriage."

"Well," she countered, "perhaps we should be friendly in return, hmmmm?"

Her aunt answered that by arching perplexed brows. Kira didn't blame her. Her own brain didn't realize what she meant, until she'd spilled the retort. She was only sure of one fact: Aleece's rebuke had brought on an inability to breathe having nothing to do with her corset. She had to inhale something other than leather oil and the hair pomade coating her curls. *Now.*

Without another moment of hesitation or patience, Kira used the handle of her aunt's umbrella to deliver three thunks to the carriage roof. The vehicle started to slow, but she silently swore at the five minutes it would take for a complete stop, a proper set of the brake, and the stepping box to be brought around. Instead, she swung open the door then used the momentum of that action to swing herself to the ground.

"Kira!" came the expected gasp from inside the carriage. "Kira, by all the heavens, what are you doing *now*!"

A small jolt of satisfied vengeance added a bounce to Kira's step. "Tom," she called instead, addressing their driver as he secured the reins. "Do you and Fred have room for one more traveler up on the box?"

At first, the man's jaw dropped beneath his droopy mustache, as if a ghost had appeared. Kira suspected apparitions *were* more common than women hopping out of his carriage at will. "I—I beg your pardon, m'lady?"

"I'd like to ride awhile with you." Kira added a hopeful smile this time. "If, of course, that's all right."

"It's just dandy with me, Lady Kira, but—"

"Ohhh, no" came the interrupting command from the figure now craning her neck out the window behind them. "*No,* Kira! It is appalling enough you've halted us in the middle of this wilderness, exposed us to all sorts of ruffians and wild creatures as you run around in the lane like some dirty—"

"Lady Aleece." Kira issued each syllable with clipped brusqueness. "I am not proposing to skip along beside the

vehicle but to ride on the driver's box, as I watched countless young ladies do in Hyde Park only two days ago." She
chalked up another small victory while watching her statement weaken the support stakes of her aunt's conviction.
"Are you telling me all of *them* were dirty and improper?"
she finished with sardonic surety.

"All of *them* were not gambling on their father's status
and wealth to make all London magically forget their ille-
gitimacy," Aleece rejoined. "All of them were not working
to create a reputation."

"Or to create a baby, either."

"Oh, dear heavens." Her aunt gasped.

Kira shared a rebel's grin with Tom and Fred. "Of
course," she went on, winking at her comrades, "a girl does
need a stud in order to breed a Thoroughbred. Maybe *that's*
why they were all sitting up front, assessing the available
horseflesh."

"Kira!"

She was about to indulge a full giggle, assured she'd sent
her aunt collapsing against the squab in a full swoon, when
she instead witnessed Aleece swing down from the carriage
in the same manner she'd just utilized. The woman did so
with startling agility, at that.

Even so, Aleece wasted no time stomping back into her
"Empress of Decorum" mien. "Enough is *enough*, young
woman," she decreed. "You've disrupted the travelers on
this thoroughfare—"

"What travelers?" Tom muttered.

"Not to mention the demands of our schedule—"

"What schedule?" Kira asked.

"Just get back in the carriage, Kira! Now!"

Kira didn't move. That included the gaze she leveled
back at her aunt. Her smile slowly became an expression of
determined intent. "I'm afraid I cannot accommodate your

mandate, Aunt Aleece," she stated, fighting the longing to turn the words into a mandate of their own. "Because I'm certain my father would like me to arrive in Yorkshire as a *sane* human being."

The rest of the afternoon passed as if only minutes disappeared with the miles. With the sun on her face, the crisp air filling her nostrils, and Fred planted on her lap, Kira recognized contentedness teasing at her heart for the first time in almost a month. She released a delighted laugh as they proceeded into a glen canopied by pines and carpeted by purple wildflowers. The road narrowed here, becoming more of a winding cart path, but the horses continued with spirited purpose, jangling their harnesses like gypsy tambourines.

"They're as enchanted as I am," Kira commented to Tom on the four magnificent grays in front of them.

The man hitched a smile. "Aye. They're fine animals. Your father is a wise man when it comes to picking horse-flesh." He coughed to fill the thick silence Kira issued as reply. "Of course, they've also been showing off for our guest. They like you, Lady Kira."

She smiled wistfully. "We had twelve horses in the Menagerie's show. I miss them so much sometimes."

Tom merely nodded at that, but in the simple motion, Kira perceived his empathy more clearly than any contrived words.

She did not, however, expect his next gesture. With a nonchalant flick, Tom directed the reins at her. "Why don't you take them for a while?"

Kira didn't waste time voicing her gratitude to the man. She eagerly exchanged Fred for the reins, laughing as she wrapped the leather around her knuckles. She instantly savored the feeling of being connected to such beautiful animals again.

The newness of her spectacular surroundings, coupled with the familiar comfort of leading the horses, lifted her beyond herself, if only for a few exquisite minutes. From that same boundless place in her heart, she heard Tom's startled but encouraging praise of her driving. She replied with a small but wicked smile, knowing the horses heard him, too.

"Let's show him what we're really made of, my friends!" she called. She gave the horses a few inches of rein as interpretation.

The grays responded instantly, as she knew they would. With a bit more of a lead, they began to strain at the harnesses, entreating Kira to let them enjoy the untamed splendor of the forest at an unhindered pace. While appreciating their zeal, Kira held them at a firm limit, especially as the path twisted with sharper and steeper frequency.

"I believe you've gained some new friends, my lady," Tom remarked. "Don't think I've ever seen them behave like this for a woman."

Kira turned to thank him for the compliment with a smile. Only Tom never received that smile. Instead, a wall of brown fur smashed into her face, accompanied by a gleeful primate laugh.

"Fred, no!" she yelled in protest, grabbing at her pet with one hand while securing the reins in the other. Or so she thought. Her pet, while determining it was *his* turn to occupy her attentions, turned the right rein into a tangled decoration around his left leg. She tried to toss the left rein to Tom while she struggled with the rest of the mess—

Just as he leaned over to help her with the tangle, as well.

"Bloody Mary!" Tom shouted. He lunged for the liberated leather strip, nearly hurling himself off the box in the process. With a scream, Kira set Fred aside in order to yank

Tom back up. At the same time, Fred pulled himself free of the right rein. After a quick *fwwwipp*, the strap joined its mate, dragging in the road between the harness and the carriage.

Now the grays were not only free but frightened. Kira's shriek, injected into the enlivened instincts already pumping in the animals' blood, might as well have been a whip to their flanks. They erupted into full gallops with instinctual frenzy.

"What is happening!" came Aleece's panicked wail.

"Get back inside!" Tom yelled back, not taking time to trifle with the requisite niceties—for which, Kira thought, her aunt better be grateful. *If* they got out of this ordeal alive.

But suddenly their wild ride crashed to an end. Around the next curve, the road turned back on itself, forming a cramped S. But the horses, taking advantage of their newfound liberty, decided they preferred a more direct route through the foliage. Before Kira or Tom fathomed what was happening, the animals made the carriage part of the foliage, snagging themselves in low-lying bracken and the carriage body between two pine trees. Everything halted with breath-seizing speed.

Kira confirmed that fact firsthand, the air leaving her in an astounded rush as she was hurled off the driver's box. A mound of damp and dirty leaves broke her tumble. She observed Tom had met the same fate, landing in a leaf pile of his own beside the carriage's other front wheel.

Uncaring whether Aleece heard or not, she uttered an oath on behalf of her throbbing bottom. The remainder of her joints urged her to repeat the epithet, yet at that moment Fred came into view overhead, swinging by one hand from a tree branch and emitting what sounded like a chimp's version of "Hee heeee!"

Unbelievably, Kira gave in to the strange urge to join her pet's carefree humor. As she rose, she looked over to Tom and giggled louder. If she looked half as dazed and bracken-torn as he, then she didn't blame Fred for his mirth. Her amusement only grew when Aleece leaned out of the carriage window, features given over to such wide shock, she was reminded of an orangutan Fred had once introduced to her. She leaned back on one elbow and let the laughter overtake her as her aunt fell back inside the coach with a horrified moan.

She didn't stop until, abruptly, Fred and Tom did. She turned, wondering what in the world had jolted a grown man and a chimpanzee into such captivated silence.

That was when she found out they'd not been mesmerized by a *what* . . . but a *who*.

"My God," she whispered.

The man emerged as if created by the trees themselves, for he was certainly as looming, dark, and solid as any of the pines rising around them. He intensified that surreal image by moving nearer on broad strides, his right hand gripping a rifle that might as well have been a battle ax for all its big black menace. He didn't alter his bold pace once, yet the underlying brush didn't let out one protesting crunch beneath his feet.

As for those feet—Kira's stunned survey of him began there first, with the mighty black boots that extended to the knees of his overworn black breeches. A black waistcoat went unbuttoned over his black shirt, with its collar bared wide to reveal thick black curls across the top of his chest. Thick black curls she couldn't rip her eyes from. Good Lord, Kira moaned inwardly, she had to find the only man in this country who refused to wear an appropriately tied stock!

A man who now gave them all a stare that made her

belly ignite with fire but her knees freeze colder than icicles. As those eyes of his locked upon her, Kira knew the reason why.

His gaze was just as dark and powerful as the rest of him.

She chewed her lips between her teeth. She thought of her musings of four days ago, of how she'd carelessly compared her father to the devil; but now she realized her shrewd but shallow father knew no more about being the devil than Fred did.

The devil was hiding inside a midnight-haired forest demon who appeared out of nowhere and dominated her sight everywhere.

And now, God help her, she didn't even try to look away. She didn't even gasp as he drew his sinfully full lips back across his teeth and demanded in a low snarl, "Who the bloody *hell* is responsible for this?"

Five

DAMIEN SAW THE COLOR drain from the girl's face even here, in the darkness of the forest. He watched her skin change from an entrancing, gold-touched creaminess to a mask of colorless terror.

Terror of him.

Oh, yes; he saw the dread curling its way even through this stranger with the proud stance, the eyes the color of fire itself, the hat skewed to one side of her leaf-covered head, and an African chimp playing in her smudged skirts. Christ, she was a regular little hoyden.

But she was a *beautiful* little hoyden.

Who was she? Where had she come from?

The answer, at least to his latter question, came preceded by a slow squeak of broken carriage axles. Damien turned to see a traveling coach bearing the unmistakable gold and green of the Scottney family crest.

He glared back at the hoyden, who was now joined by Tom Montgomery, Scottney lackey number one.

Nausea joined the rumble of hunger in his stomach.

And suddenly her terror satisfied him a great deal.

He watched in secretly satisfied silence as she inched forward, her jaw working to form words. "We—we did not mean—" she began, but then stopped. At last, she sucked in a deep breath and declared with enunciated boldness, "It was an accident, sir."

For reasons he couldn't fathom, Damien countered her forward move by a fast backstep of his own. Still, the bizarre urge struck him to keep retreating until he could run and dunk himself beneath all one hundred freezing feet of Hardraw Force.

Instead, he recovered enough to rock back on his left heel and form a convincingly menacing retort. "Well," he asserted, "your 'accident' drove my dinner away."

"Then we are greatly sorry, but—"

"I don't need your apology!"

The sudden viciousness of his tone came as a surprise. Clearly the hoyden thought so, too. She yanked her pet closer to her side, like a London mother warning her child away from the rat man.

Perhaps, Damien mused, her instinct was absolutely correct.

He sidled closer to her again, close enough that he smelled the earth and pine needles clumped in her dark-auburn curls. Not a trace of rosewater or lilac spray emanated from her. Bloody hell. He'd never smelled a woman so damn enticing.

"What I *need*," he began then, aspiring for a threatening growl but producing a husky rasp, instead, "is my dinner. Now"—he loomed yet closer to her—"how do you propose I satisfy that need before nightfall?"

For a long moment, her only response came in the form of a pulsing vein in her neck. Damien watched the vessel in nearly vampiric fascination. He leaned so close, his breath now stirred her dirty, beautiful curls.

What the hell *are you doing? What the* hell *are you letting
her do to you?*

He hadn't realized how hungry he really was—in more
ways than the needs of his belly. His mind brimmed with
imaginings of what the hoyden's neck tasted like . . . of
how succulent her lips would be . . . of how delicious
other parts of her would be for a dessert feast . . .

The pulse in her neck halted. Just as Damien's heartbeat
stopped. She jerked her gaze up to his, staring at him with a
blazing intensity, almost as if his secret wonderings had
overflowed from his brain into hers. *God, her eyes.* Damien
felt as if he stared at the sun, knowing he should turn away,
helpless in his unblinking state.

A voice sounded from somewhere then, but it didn't
belong to the hoyden, so he shrugged the interruption
away. But then *she* glanced at the speaker, and he was
forced to listen, as well.

"Mr. Sharpe." Damien recognized Aleece Scottney's intonation without looking. The woman made February
mornings in St. Paul's feel like tropical respites. "Mr.
Sharpe, I will thank you to step away from my niece this
instant, before you find yourself being called out by Lord
Scottney when he arrives within the fortnight."

"Called out?" the hoyden interjected on an incredulous
laugh. "Saints, Aunt Aleece, haven't all of you here in
'civilized' England outlawed things like that?"

The woman drew in a pinched breath. "Sometimes," she
snipped, "honor surpasses laws."

The hoyden laughed louder. "Listen," she stated levelly
to her aunt, though her gaze delivered the same message to
Damien, "if anyone picks up a gun to defend me, it'll be
me."

Damien said nothing to that, knowing no pistols would
be have to be drawn in *this* match. He already conceded

defeat to this woman—and her secret weapon of sheer shock. *Aunt Aleece.* She was Nicholas's *daughter.* And an *American*, at that.

Dear God, how the graves must be churning in the Scottney graveyard. *Nicky, old boy,* he chuckled inwardly, *you've been hiding some impressive skeletons in your fancy fine closet.*

But no skeletons could grip his blood as this amazing little Scottney did as she turned back to him, affixing her gaze on him. Damn that mesmerizing stare of hers.

"Believe what you want to, Mr. Sharpe," she stated then, in her clear yet slightly exotic English. "Though we *are* terribly sorry, and there is nothing we can do to bring back your rabbit—"

"Deer," Damien corrected. "One of the finest in the forest. I'd been watching that doe for days."

His silky tone and intimate, unwavering stare were both designed to show her just how intensely he "watched" something—or someone. In short, he intended to bring back a shade of the color he'd first glimpsed in her cheeks . . . for not so very long ago, he'd gleaned many a maidenly blush for this look.

But the hoyden's complexion barely warmed from the ghostly hue he'd first induced in it. As a matter of fact, the dimunitive creature stood there pale and erect and silent as a specter gracing a headstone.

Hell. He didn't need any more ghosts in his life.

"Deer," she finally blurted in response to him, though forcing the sound past her tight jaw. "Fine. Then I am sorry we made you lose your—doe, but I shall speak to my father tomorrow about making restitution to you, and—"

Before caution halted him, Damien threw his head back and laughed. "You'll make 'restitution' to me, will you?" he returned, still chuckling. "Just like that? Just because you'll ask *dear Papa?*"

Again he surprised himself *and* her with the ferocity of his tone. The hoyden blinked at him, confused, but stated anyway, "I'll—I'll work arrangements out with my father, all right? But it's none of your concern. This mess is my responsibility, and I was taught to clean the messes I make."

"Taught to—" Damien queried. "*Your* responsibility?" He didn't try to hide his baffled tone.

"Yes." She gave an awkward nod, waving aside Tom and his scowling protest. "I am at fault for your mishap, Mr. Sharpe, not Tom."

She issued the declaration almost as if proud of her exploit—at which Damien found himself surprisingly but pleasantly bemused. Folding his arms across his chest, he returned past sardonically smiling lips, "And how do you arrive at such an assertion?"

"Because Tom wasn't driving. I was."

"My word!" Aleece damn near shrieked her reaction, which more than justified Damien's surprised quirk of brows.

"Good stars." The hoyden threw up her hands at them both. "This is England, not China! Even here, I know 'ladies' handle the reins on occasion, if they like."

"No," Damien interceded. "No, no no. Haven't they told you yet? No reins for *Scottney* ladies." He ignored Aleece's glowering response to his sarcasm, instead lowering his tone to finish with a statement delivered at the hoyden. "And even ladies do not pick up *one* rein without knowing what the bloody hell they're doing."

"What the bloody hell they're—" She speared him with a glare most women saved for occasions like insults to their hair or tea gown. "If you must know, sir, I have known 'what the bloody hell' I'm doing with a harnessed team since I was ten!"

Her chimp applauded her manifesto. Damien enjoyed the animal's charm but disdained its owner's indignance. The wench had *not* known what she was doing; otherwise, he wouldn't be assessing her entrapped carriage now. "Then what *did* happen?"

"I told you, we had an accident."

"You mean *you* had an accident."

The glare deepened. "I beg your pardon?"

"You said it yourself. *You* were driving, therefore *you* let the situation get out of control."

"I didn't *let* anything happen. It just—happened. Fred got a little frisky, and—"

"So you were playing with your chimp and forgot about paying attention to the horses."

"Why, you obtuse, obnoxious, son of a—"

"Kira!" Aleece rasped. "For blessed sake!"

"It's all right," Damien intervened with soft but determined purpose. He didn't avert his eyes from Aleece's captivatingly furious niece. "I've taken much worse than this from the Scottneys."

He didn't expect his caustic drawl to deter her ladyship Kira (how had a hoyden gotten the name of a goddess?) in the least. She didn't disappoint him. Her pace didn't falter as she stomped forward, this time leaving her chimpanzee behind, and skewered him with an impressively hard glare.

Yet in the moment before she spoke, a glimmer of something passed through the woman's eyes—a glimmer he hadn't expected and did *not* want. "It wouldn't have been an honor for that deer to die by your hand," she murmured. "I'm glad I helped it escape, in my own way."

"Your own way," Damien echoed, his voice curling out

of him like smoke off a funeral pyre, potent and black. "Yes, that's what you Scottneys are all about, isn't it? Doing things your own way, damn the rest of the world."

With that smoke, he effectively dimmed the surface glimmer in her eyes, but not the flames at the backs of those sienna depths. "You're a sad and lonely man, Mr. Sharpe. And I understand—"

"You understand?" Incredulous anger flared inside his gut, exploding into scalding intensity off his lips. "You understand nothing about me, lady."

"Then maybe you should let me try."

"Maybe you should go to hell."

He expected what happened next. He stumbled back without a fight when an unmistakable male grip curled into the back of his collar, followed by Tom's commanding growl. "I think that's enough, Damien."

"*More* than enough!" Stifling violet perfume heralded Aleece's arrival, ribbons and lace flying from the woman as she sliced her way between him and the hoyden. Gripping her niece's shoulders with possessive fervor, she gave Damien one more dagger of a glance. "Stay—away—from—her," she issued as she did.

Don't worry, came the immediate answer from Damien's mind. *Don't worry your head at all about the matter, dear Aleece.*

But the center of his chest clamored with another message entirely. His heart pounded out a cadence so booming and strong, it momentarily deafened his senses to any other instinct except yearning to haul this wild little American to *his* side, keeping her like this forever.

Keeping her from going to the place where she'd learn not to say things like *I understand*.

In the end, Damien locked his legs and curled two fists

to force that temptation into submission. No matter how different, no matter how bold or beautiful, this woman was still a Scottney—and that meant he would never touch her again.

Suddenly he couldn't sweep a mocking bow to Aleece fast enough. He couldn't jerk a quick enough nod to Tom, letting the driver know he carried no fault against him for doing his job.

As for the hoyden . . .

He couldn't look at her. She wouldn't understand, but he didn't care. He *couldn't* care.

Without another word, Damien spun and paced back into the shadows from which he'd come . . . trying not to think how dark they now seemed, so much darker and blacker, now that he'd felt the fire of the sun once more.

Heavy but rainless clouds settled early over the twilight, churning across the sky. They were a perfect image, Kira concluded, of the twisting murk inside her head. As she trudged from the forest behind Tom and Aunt Aleece, she watched the dark mists gather against the crests of proud hills in the distance and likened the sight to the way in which one of those thoughts mercilessly prodded the summits of her own imagination.

She was besieged by the recurring memory of Damien Sharpe. His ink-of-night eyes. His ground-eating strides. His irony-filled smiles. His exasperatingly fast "wit," if that's what one could call it.

His incredible, tangible loneliness.

She couldn't stop seeing him in every dark-fingered cloud caressing those hills. She couldn't stop wondering about where he'd suddenly bounded from in that clearing, or where he'd stomped off to, wrapped in his personal clouds of alienation and pain.

Pain. Oh, yes, Kira confirmed. If she'd inherited none other of Mama's extrasensory skills, she *had* gleaned the ability to discern the pith of a person's pain—

And Damien Sharpe seemed determined to spend the rest of his days in a mental torture chamber.

"That's *it*," Kira erupted in an irritated mutter. She couldn't stop the questions from bursting on her lips and perceived no reason why she had to, either.

"Aunt Aleece," she called, hastening her step to fall into place beside the much-too-quiet woman. "Aunt Aleece, I—"

"Yes, Kira?" came the surprisingly gentle prompt. "What is it?"

"Aunt Aleece, what happened back there? Who is that man? *What* is that man? Why did you and Tom look at him like he was Bluebeard's ghost?"

The tender mien fell away from her aunt's face as swiftly as it had come. "Kira," she stated past pursed lips, "please; I am not in the habit of hiking the last half mile of this journey."

"But what did he do to you? And why did you look like you were about to call him out yourself?"

"Damien Sharpe is none of our business, Kira!"

Her aunt stopped and spun on her, pure fury dominating her glare. Though Kira knew the ire was directed through her rather than at her, she stood and blinked at Aleece in stunned silence.

"He won't come near you again, Kira," the woman finally finished in a decorously taut murmur. "He won't hurt you. I swear that to you. We shall watch over you here."

With that, the woman turned and continued down the road with military precision. Her posture reminded Kira of

Nelson's statue in Trafalgar Square. Reluctantly she hoisted her own skirts and followed once more, no other questions tempting her lips.

Yet while her mouth remained silent, Kira's mind shouted an odd but unrelenting question:

Who would watch over Damien Sharpe?

Six

$\mathcal{A}$T LEAST THIRTY stones' worth of well-muscled horse shifted uneasily beneath Damien again. The stallion jerked hard at his bridle, tossing its black mane into the biting wind that whipped along the high, rocky bluff at the edge of the forest.

Damien retightened his hold to the reins. "Easy, Dante," he crooned. "Take it easy."

In truth, he hardly faulted the animal for its restlessness. If Dante sensed even a wisp of his master's agitation this morning, it was a wonder the horse restrained itself to these mere fidgetings.

Selecting this place as a spot for this morning's meeting was not the wisest decision he'd ever made. As Damien awaited his associate, his view consisted of a dozen undulating hills spreading out on either side of him, their expanses cast from dull green to duller gray at the will of an ugly old witch sky. Atop the largest of the hills to his left, a half mile in the distance, rose a mansion house of graceful beauty, seemingly formed straight out of the surrounding forest.

His home.

Nestled in the valley to his right was another estate, forming an equally impressive scene—if one was impressed with castles rivaling Balmoral in their large, cold grandeur.

The fortress of the clan that had helped rob him of his home.

Dante began his nervous dance again. Damien's attempt at restraining his mount proved only marginally successful now; in a moment, he knew the reason why. A smudge in the valley to the right swiftly took on a discernible form. A horse and rider approached at a determined gallop.

The cloaked figure and his buff-colored bay mare didn't slow until they had nearly cleared the crest of the bluff. As they breached the rise, Dante released a grumpy snort. The bay had gotten the exercise he'd begged for during the last hour. "Soon," Damien promised him, patting the stallion's neck as he waited for the other rider to wheel around and settle six feet from him.

He exchanged no pleasantries with the man. They both knew the quicker they separated again, the better. One day, Damien swore, he'd be able to meet with James as a friend again, sharing a bracing morning ride, then perhaps a shared nip of brandy from a skin flask before heading to their respective homes.

Home.

The word knelled in his brain, yanking him back to the present faster than cathedral bells used to wake him as a lad sleeping in church. "Thank you for coming on the scant notice," he began without turning his head, instead continuing his steady vigil on the countryside, making sure nobody observed them except grazing sheep in the fields to their left, grazing cattle to their right.

"Phoebus needed a good sprint," the figure replied with

winded casualness. "Besides, I expected you'd want to talk when we received word of Lady Aleece's return."

"Return," Damien repeated. "Then she's back for more than a weekend sojourn."

"I'd say so. A baggage cart arrived a few hours after them with enough crates to clothe China." A grunting chuckle accompanied that. "Overheard Tom Montgomery in the kitchen this morn, saying he was surprised you didn't raid the cart in return for some doe they cost you with the traveling coach mishanter."

Damien released a snort of his own, though no humor laced the sound. "So now I'm a highway thief, too, just because I can't eat?"

"That's about the sum of it" came the sardonic but truthful answer. "Yeah, I'd say that is."

Dante tossed his head once more, the violence of the action directly gleaned from the course of Damien's thoughts. Quickly Damien regained control over both the beast he rode and the beast inside his soul. *Concentrate*, he dictated at himself. *Damn it, concentrate on the details that matter here . . . concentrate on the truth.*

Think about the facts that will get you home again.

The credo had kept him alive the last six months. It had filled him with hope and hate, desire and dauntless determination. Yet this morning as the word *truth* resounded in his mind, a persistent image kept marring his thoughts. He conjured a face of dirt-smudged fairy features, surrounded by a cacophany of auburn curls . . . that damnable hoyden's face!

"She's the reason," Damien stated then, barely restraining the growl from his voice, "isn't she? She's the reason they've broken form at the top of the season and come back like this."

"She who?"

"The American," he snapped. Tamping his tone to a more diplomatic cadence, he repeated, "The American. What's-her-name." As if the damn word hadn't echoed in his head for the better part of an hour after he'd left her yesterday.

"Yeah" came the casual reply. "That would seem the way of it." Yet a subtle shrewdness underlined the man's tone. He no more believed Damien had "misplaced" Kira Scottney's name than he thought the livestock before them would stand up and break out into tavern ditties.

Still, Damien conceded the value of shrouding the eagerness from his voice as thoroughly as possible. "So . . . she *is* American."

"Got off the boat from Boston five days ago," James confirmed. "Looking fairly much like a drowned rat, too, from what I hear."

"She's *no* rat." Damien fired the retort before any reasonable thought could intervene. He knew only that timid rodents and Kira Scottney had no place in the same metaphor with each other.

"Didn't seem so to any of us, either. Tom says she handled those horses like a professional driver, and believe it or not—"

"She's no professional, either." The interjection came with even more potent vehemence.

"But she *is*." At Damien's incredulous glance, the man continued, "That's the crux of it. Seems she grew up in a traveling show, over in the colonies. A circus, to be exact."

"A *circus?*"

"In her blood, I wager. Her mum used to be with a troupe over here. She was their gypsy star seer. You know the kind, shilling gets you a look into some fancy crystal ball; you walk away smelling like bloody incense all day."

Damien's scowl deepened. "How did the woman end up in America?"

"Still hazy on that. Just know that's where she landed, after his lordship got her full in the belly."

Damien allowed a grim chortle through the haze of his own astoundment. "A gypsy fortune-teller." He shook his head. "I didn't know old Nick's tastes ran that exotic."

"Neither did anybody at Scottney Hall, that's for certain. Especially when his lordship didn't marry all these years . . ." A long creak of saddle leather belied James's squirming search for tactful words. "Well, tongues wagged, you know? Word had it his lordship was a bit 'sweet.' "

"Yes," Damien replied without inflection. "I know." He'd heard all the same gossip. But on each occasion, he'd discounted all the rumors. Hearsay could destroy a man more thoroughly than a round of cannon shot to his gut. Damien knew that with more certainty than anybody else in this county. And because of that knowledge, he hadn't heeded a single shocked whisper about Nicholas Scottney's "sweetness"—no matter how hard it had been to do so.

No matter how hard it had been, after the man had believed the worst of *him*.

Put it aside, Sharpe, his head ordered at him again. *Fires of fury will only burn you alive. Think of something else. Think of going home. Think of your goal.*

But to replace those flames, his mind's eye could only summon a bonfire. The conflagration of a bold, bright, gold-flecked gaze, lifted to meet his stare with wonderful American nerve . . . with a stranger's unknowing openness. Looking at him. *Looking at him.* Nobody had looked at him like that in six months, not since the rainy October morning when respectful nods and admiring gazes had turned into judgmental glances and suspicious glares.

His jaw clenched hard several times before he summoned his voice again. "So," he finally ventured, "what *has* caused the mighty Nicholas Scottney to acknowledge his bastard now?"

"Only the bloody angels seem to know" came the apologetic answer. "And they sure as shillings aren't talking."

"That's all right," Damien said. "I've got a few theories brewing already."

"As do we all, my friend. As do we all."

Damien debated what to say next. James had called him "friend," and properly so. His trust in the man was complete. But somehow, sharing his hope about this latest twist of things at Scottney Hall—that the arrival of this American hellion would somehow start the fissures of ruin for the Scottney empire—would negate the wish in the telling.

Right now, it was best to exercise caution. And distance. A great deal of distance. For while Kira Scottney might help him recover the key to his home, she sure as hell would never touch that key herself—nor any other keys to his life. He'd learned his lesson about how the Scottneys twisted the keys they were given. He'd learned that lesson the hard way.

"I'll let you contact me next time," he said to James then. He added in a gritted mutter, "I hope there *is* a next time."

"There will be," the man gruffly reassured. "I'll let you know in the usual manner."

"Right," Damien replied. "I'll look for the Scottney standard flown off the castle's right turret instead of the left."

A grunt of agreement served as confirmation of the plan. "More than likely I'll have news for you soon, with this Yank stirring things up."

"I hope your crystal ball is right, my friend." As he

wound his reins back around his hand, Damien added softly, "And James . . . thank you."

His mate didn't render an answer. The distant gonging from Scottney Hall's bell tower provided ample explanation why. It was six o'clock, time to begin another day, and the bay would be missed in the stables before too long. James, on the other hand, wasn't worth so much. He would easily rejoin the other nameless faces in the army of the Scottney Hall staff. His ears, just as anonymous, would spend the days trying to listen through the stone castle walls for even a scrap of information to help a friend who now lived his days in the depths of a black forest, riding the blurred line of distinction between "outcast" and "outlaw."

That final thought coincided with the sixth knell from the bell tower. Damien's whole body clenched hard around the echoes of the gong. His arms strained at the reins Dante now tested with nearly violent anticipation, and his own blood pumped with the craving to let the animal have his furious release, but he didn't slacken his grip yet. Unseen torture irons kept him shackled to that point atop the hill. Yes, torture was precisely the term to describe what this felt like, watching the sky lighten above the two empires sprawled below, imagining the awakening bustle of both households.

He wondered what ribald jokes were being related in those stables and what spices inundated the kitchens as scones were pulled from hot ovens. He wondered about Henry, the stable boy who'd worked to become a horse exercise expert, and whether the lad had proposed to Elsa from the downstairs housekeeping staff yet. On the other side of the valley, he wondered if Fallon, Scottney Hall's kitchen cat, had given birth to her kittens yet. He wondered what Fallon thought of Kira Scottney's chimp.

Kira Scottney.

Damien encouraged Dante into a full gallop, turning back across the wild, empty moor that was framed on one side by the crescent-curved border of his forest.

He had to drive her out of his head. He had to welcome the bite of wind against his face, open the heat of his thoughts to the air's consuming cold sting. He had to remember how that hoyden's father had helped sentence him to this dark solitude, these days of relentless loneliness.

He had to make Dante run faster.

Seven

KIRA DREAMED ABOUT HIM again.

She was as certain of that fact as the arms and legs she now stretched beneath the sheets and blankets of the pink satin cloud of her bed. She looked to the stormy sky beyond the padded window seat where Fred still dozed, using the shifting shades of pewter and black there to better recall the scenes that had dominated her mind's midnight hours.

In her dreams, he rode a stallion black as the shadows that had formed him, steed and rider moving together as one . . . moving with blatantly sensual grace. Kira wondered if her heart had pummeled her chest as wildly in her slumber as it did now, keeping strangely accurate time to the horse's hooves as they came closer in her mind's eye, closer, until suddenly, he pulled her up on the horse with him . . .

Only then the horse transformed into a bank of clouds. The stallion's mane turned into tendrils of mist, curling around her toes as she began to dance on that cloud with Damien Sharpe. Her fingers curved around the hard, defined planes of his shoulders, and she pulled him closer as she struggled to find the light in his endlessly black eyes.

But then those dark depths sucked *her* in. She was helpless to move or resist, as his presence surrounded her, smelling of earth and trees and clouds. His arms enveloped her, long and powerful and unyielding. And then . . . his face descended toward hers, his mouth slanting but an inch over hers.

"The Lord's own *sake*." Kira bolted to a sitting position. She dragged in several deep but shaking breaths, and she didn't dare look at the uncontrollable tremble of her fingers against the counterpane.

Three days, she castigated herself. She'd been here for three days, confound it, and hadn't successfully purged the man from her imagination yet! As a matter of fact, Aunt Aleece's cryptic comments on the road had only intensified her fascination with the brooding loner in the heart of that murky forest.

What in tarnation was wrong with her?

Because what she felt for Damien Sharpe was *not* fascination.

It was compassion.

Because, oh God, she knew just how frightening loneliness could be.

But he doesn't want your compassion, Kira! He wants nothing to do with you! He made that perfectly clear in the middle of his blasted forest, don't you think? Or didn't you catch the dozen snarls he hurled at you? Or the glares that could have sent a tiger's tail between its legs? Or the way he turned and left the clearing without so much as a backward glance your way?

But her heart whispered in stubborn tenacity: *I wonder what he's doing now.*

She wondered if he was alone while he did whatever he did, or if part of her dream was divination, and a big black horse really did keep him company. She wondered if he still scowled through the task, or if the horse could make him smile, perhaps a little. She wondered if he was warm in his cold forest. If he had something to eat for dinner, even if it wasn't fresh venison.

The only reply to her ruminations came from Scottney Hall's chapel tower clock, ringing long and deep through the morning one time, then twice—

Why couldn't she dismiss him as the beast he'd behaved?

Three, four, and five times—

Why couldn't she convince herself he was an outcast from Scottney Hall, most likely for good reasons?

The questions remained unanswered as the bells knelled twice more. As the sounds died away down the hall's empty corridors, Kira looked again out the window. The mullioned glass turned the estate staff into aquaticlike globs as they moved cheerfully through their early-morning duties, toting baskets of eggs here and wagons of hay there, lighting fires and chopping wood, all smiling and laughing with the useful purpose their day already possessed.

Just as her days were, not so long ago.

A frustrated sigh erupted off her lips. "This is getting you nowhere, lazy bedbug," she muttered, and instantly felt those lips turn upward again. She remembered a few of the many occasions Mama wielded the gentle rebuke on her. If only Mama could see her now, she mused as she threw back the covers and—

"Eeee gawwd!"

Kira collided into a five-foot meadow fairy in maid's clothes. The girl's pert features now burst into an openly astounded gawk. "Ally," she greeted to her personal maid, though not certain she'd ever get used to *having* a personal maid. "Good morning."

"Y-yer . . . awake," the maid stuttered. A stack of

hand towels and handkerchiefs wobbled in her grasp like overbuttered griddle cakes.

"Yes." Kira reached to help steady the pile, but Ally pulled back as if the linens were her personal cache of spun gold. Instead, as the maid bustled her way to the washstand beside the fireplace, Kira prompted, "I was awake at this time yesterday, as well as the day before. I'm used to—"

"Well, stop it."

That prevented Kira from taking her final step out of bed. "Stop it?"

Ally, who'd now traversed halfway back across the room, reeled herself back with a wince. "I beg yer pardon, m'lady," she petitioned in a rapid mutter. "I'm given to impertinence, as Lady Trevor has properly disciplined me for in the past."

"I'll bet she has," Kira replied from clenched teeth. Yet at the confused glance Ally dared up at her, she roused a fast and friendly smile. When the maid's big green eyes widened yet further, she hurried down the mattress and over onto the settee, reaching out a hand to urge the girl to sit with her.

"*I* say you are given to honesty," Kira proclaimed while Ally landed on the cushion with a loud crackle of well-starched petticoats. "And right now, I'll value that honesty more than my right leg."

A few copper-colored ringlets fell loose from the maid's mobcap as she gave Kira a glance blended of something between curiosity and bemusement. "Tom was right. You *are* a unique bird, m'lady."

"And you were in the middle of saying I shouldn't get up when the sun rises, like everyone else."

Ally aimed a matter-of-fact look at her polished work boots. "Well, not like a lady, that's for well certain."

"And ladies are so different from the rest of the world that their days are kept by separate clocks?"

To her startlement, Ally's expression didn't falter by a twitch. "Of course they are. Ladies need extra sleep because they're more delicate than most persons, and in order to maintain the beauty of their skin and the health of their—"

"That's the deepest bucket of swill I've ever heard!"

Ally's jaw succumbed to a speechless gape. Kira flung back an incredulous stare. The maid really couldn't believe the conviction with which she'd issued her words, while she longed to laugh at the absurdity of lying about like a sow being fattened for fair to "maintain her delicate beauty."

That image prompted a tiny giggle to her lips. At first, Ally reacted with an even more shocked stare, but slowly the beginnings of a grin teased her own mouth. When Fred decided he wanted a piece of the fun, too—and demonstrated such by scrambling up the bed and tangling himself in the bedclothes—the two humans broke out into full chortles. In that moment, Kira thought with a smile of contentment, the first threads of a friendship were stitched.

"Well," Ally said then, sighing resignedly, "yer awake and you plan to stay that way. We might as well see to yer toilette and dressing, too." She flitted to her feet and disappeared into the closet to the right of the bed. "Perhaps you'd like to wear this new blue serge today," she called. "It's such a pretty color. Almost violet, I think. You'll look right beautiful fer yer first lessons with Lady Aleece."

Now Kira cursed herself for protesting her maid's counsel about returning to bed. "The lessons." She moaned, falling back against the pillows. "Hell. I'd managed to forget about the lessons." *Thanks to Damien Sharpe's visit to your dreams.*

Her schedule, if she remembered correctly, was to begin

directly after breakfast with lessons in vocabulary, etiquette, posture, and dance. In a curious sort of way, she looked forward to *those* regimens. She anticipated showing her aunt an "education" of travel and diversity was effective as ten years of staring at groomed London lady school lawns. Perhaps, she concluded with a smirk, even more so.

But she dreaded the afternoon's itinerary. Aleece apparently saved the more "important" subjects for then: Appropriate uses and styles of correspondence, household management, and dinner party hostessing were to comprise the afternoon's program.

"Dinner parties," she reiterated aloud, shaking her head while the words felt like a foreign language on her tongue. "Why can't everyone bring their favorite stew and a jug of cider, and let's be done with it?"

"Beg yer pardon, m'lady?" Ally queried from the closet.

"Nothing," Kira answered. "It was nothing, Ally." But as the maid bustled back into the room, she muttered, "Just wondering if God could manage a minor disaster to intercede on my behalf."

Ally didn't hesitate about reacting with an instant smile at that—but her expression swiftly sobered at a sudden din from the carriage court. As she rushed to the window seat, Kira and Fred leapt up to join her.

No catastrophe nearing a flood or foreign invasion filled their sights, though they could hardly discern the difference by the sprinting stable boys, the hand-wringing kitchen maids, and a scowling Tom Montgomery. Kira and Ally watched the man command the mob into the corner of the courtyard opposite Kira's window.

"Good God," Kira muttered, astonished at the militaristic severity of the goings-on. "What are they expecting? The four deadly horsemen?"

The next instant, she answered her own question—with a gasp of shock.

The rider indeed could have been one of the mythical demons she'd just invoked, so completely did his presence dominate the Main Courtyard. His mount was big as Troy's war machine and as black as the night those ancient warriors had fought into.

His black horse. *His black horse.*

Kira swallowed but still couldn't breathe as she watched him masterfully slow the steed, then swing down from the saddle on legs sheathed in a buff-colored fabric appearing much like buckskin. Yes, buckskin, she decided with certainty the next moment; worn to the texture of touchable softness, if the way the fabric moved along his legs was any evidence. And oh, his legs . . . endless thighs rose from his knee-high boots, lean sinew and hard muscle blending in two captivating stretches ending in buttocks with interesting muscles in their own right.

"Dear God," she whispered, meaning to castigate herself with the words, meaning to tear her iniquitous gaze away from those legs—but she couldn't. *It's he,* her senses cried in heart-gripping awareness. Even from the distance at which she beheld him now, she knew. *It's he.*

More astoundingly, it was he as she'd envisioned him in her dream, black eyes gleaming with the intensity of newly mined coal, black hair whipped by a wind as forceful as his stride across the court as he approached Tom. He carried a burlap sack in his hand with surprisingly contrasting gentleness.

"Blazes" came Ally's dark grumble. "Here comes trouble."

Kira's reaction to that stunned the maid *and* her. A giddy laugh burst off her lips as she yanked up the hem of her nightrail and dashed out the door. As she raced down the corkscrew of a stairway, a shrieking Ally on her heels, more laughter bubbled past her lips.

Here comes trouble.

She'd heard that a thousand times before—about *her*.

Eight

SHE GOT TO THE Main Courtyard too late. Even though she took the short route through the kitchens, ignoring the dumbstruck gawks of the staff preparing breakfast there, she raced out into the cobblestoned yard to find only three stable boys assessing Sharpe's stallion with stares mixed of wariness and worship.

"Where'd they go?" she demanded breathlessly of the first youth she came to. But the boy gaped at her without a word. Ally was right. Ladies who left their bedchambers before eight o'clock—in their nightrails, at that—were asking to be gawked at.

"Tom Montgomery and Damien Sharpe," she clarified this time, using the final word as an adjective in order to convey her meaning. She grabbed the lad's shoulder. "Where did they go? Tell me *now*."

"R-right" came the all-too-earnest reply at last. "O' course. They took 'emselves off to the Menagerie, they did." He pointed hastily in the direction of the covered portico leading to the stables, at the far side of the wide courtyard. "Mr. Sharpe, he found—"

"The Menagerie," Kira repeated, impatiently jerking up her hem again. "Fine. Thank you."

But she hadn't proceeded six steps before she skidded to a stunned stop. With an equally impulsive jerk, she spun back toward the three boys, still standing there agape.

"Where did you say they were?" she asked her freckle-cheeked helpmate first.

"The . . . Menagerie, m'lady." The words were given with questioning slowness despite what Kira knew was her most intent stare. "Uh . . . surely ye know the lordship keeps it out next to the stables, so all the beasties can keep each other company, and—"

Kira didn't hear the rest. But she had the information she did need—the information so amazing, she couldn't believe it until she saw it. She spun in the middle of the youth's sentence and sprinted toward that portico with twice her speed as before. And twice her anticipation.

She still didn't imagine she'd receive Christmas over half a year early this morning, or in such a magnificent way.

She located the building with ridiculous ease, considering the way the onion-domed building stood out like a fancy Mongol from the Tudor-accented stable houses. Her heart thudded at the base of her throat as she traversed the winding entrance walk, inlaid with multicolored glass stones, and then stepped across the portal—

To release a gasp of pure astonishment.

The exotic roof, she discovered, was constructed entirely of lightly tinted glass, so that the whole area below received a bath of soothing light, much like the depths of a rain forest. Kira had no doubt, however, that such an impression came easily with the help of the trees, flowers, and vines blooming everywhere around her, thriving with the help of a pleasantly warm mist pervading the air and a glittering creation of a waterfall off to her right.

It was the most lavish production she'd ever seen; an illusion so complex and complete, *she* almost believed she'd somehow stepped through time and had landed somewhere in the West Indies. The occupants of this wonderland chose to presume that, too. Kira quickly took inventory of the room. Along one wall, small brown monkeys, bright green iguanas, and even a trio of white-tailed deer romped through a labyrinth of trees and vines. The opposite side of the enclosure was reserved for the spacious cages of a sleek black panther and a majestically reclining leopard.

Between these two habitats flowed the stream fed by the waterfall, sprouting real waterside plants from its man-made confines, connected at the middle via a vine-entwined footbridge. The stream concluded in a small pond that also served as bathing pool for the occupants of a soaring aviary. That enclosure housed so many beautifully feathered birds, it resembled a kaleidoscope.

Except for the large white cockatoo currently residing on Damien Sharpe's left arm.

Kira's heart thundered as she again stared at the reason she was out here in the first place. Rugged and wind-blown, his dark skin even ruddier from his exposure to the morning winds, he almost fooled her into thinking she was back home, meeting a new performer to the show from one of the wild western territories.

He *almost* fooled her. Wild West men usually weren't in the habit of accessorizing their wardrobe with white cockatoos.

Nor did they usually return her stares with such burning, unblinking attention. As if even the flimsy nightclothes she wore didn't exist . . . and he liked what he saw.

"Dear saints." She gasped. She stumbled through a trio of backward steps, coiling her arms across her chest as she did so. But even her blatant discomfort didn't falter Sharpe's stare by a blink. Surely some Wild West wildcat had taught him to do that—only she doubted a wildcat's quarry had to endure the throbbing race of her heart into her throat like this . . . or the terrifying rush of liquid sensation to secret places between her legs . . .

Kira spun around and cut a straight path for the door this time.

She cursed when she found the portal blocked, until she recognized the hindrance was Ally. Her maid had brought Fred and a mercifully thick satin robe.

After helping Kira into the garment with a few colorful oaths of her own, the maid only took half a breath before seething, "What in the blazing world are ya about? Do ya know what this makes ya look like around here, do ya? A barmy American, that's what. Ya rise at the crack of dawn, then tear out into the morning like a harpy, chasing God only knows what for God only knows what reason, and *now*—"

"I'm sure she had her reasons."

Kira whirled around on the first syllable of his interruption. But in the doing, she tripped over Fred then collided into Ally, nearly toppling the three of them to the pathway in a mortifying heap.

The cause for her bumblings now stood but three feet away, his gaze affixed to her with that same unfaltering attention. His posture emanated primal contemplation, and his proximity affected her in the same thought-robbing way it had when he'd first loomed over her in the forest . . . only the ordeal was worse now. Worse, because unlike three days ago, the man now cloaked his thoughts behind a facade of smooth calm and beautiful masculinity.

"My lady." Damien Sharpe dipped her a slight bow—but

not before flicking a gaze that appeared suspiciously amused. "We meet again. Good morning."

"M'lady Kira." The salutation burst off Tom's lips with decidedly more urgency. "Forgive this intrusion." He finished with a pointed glare in Sharpe's direction. "Mr. Sharpe was just leaving."

Not everyone present was in agreement about that, however. Unprovoked in any way except Tom's assertion, the cockatoo let out a sudden screech that prompted everyone to grimace, even Sharpe. Fred answered the bird with a hearty shriek of his own.

"Bloody Mary," Tom grumbled. "It's like a friggin' jungle in here."

"Imagine that," Sharpe quipped, and Kira giggled. She couldn't help the mirth; no more than she could control the sense that with the brief exchange, she and this Yorkshire-style frontiersman had become sudden allies.

Nor could she deny the strange, sweet admission that she *liked* that alliance.

"Cleo's probably just hungry," Sharpe said to Tom. He raised a gentle finger to the cockatoo's neck. He went on in a murmur, this time to the bird, "It's not easy spending the night in a cold forest, is it, sweeting? No, I didn't think so. But I'm happy you have such pretty feathers, so I was able to see you up in that tree this morning."

Fascinated, Kira watched the bird respond to the man's silken tone. Hesitantly at first but with gaining trust, Cleo basked in Sharpe's adulation like a true member of her gender, "answering" the man with soft trills and seductive stretches. Eventually Cleo scooted her way up to his shoulder, where she gnawed on his ear with affectionate coyness.

Sharpe's reaction to the flirtation didn't fascinate Kira anymore. This time he just plain stunned her.

The man looked at the cockatoo and broke into a smile. A full, white, stop-the-breath-in-her-throat-with-its-beauty smile.

And yet not a glimmer of that smile ever ignited in his eyes.

"It was very kind of you to bring her back," Kira offered then, growing more furious with her voice by the moment. She'd performed for mayors and opera stars and even an Indian chief once, and she'd never had trouble speaking as she did now.

Yet that Indian chief had never caused her to wonder how his fingers would feel against her body. . . .

"Cleo is a fine animal," Sharpe stated then, though Kira heard the words as secondary sound. Her heartbeat now thudded out a deafening cacophony in response to this man's potent nearness . . . to his brilliant, lonely smile.

"Y-yes," she managed to stammer back. "A white cockatoo. My father will be grateful to you for saving her life."

The man's princely smoothness abruptly disappeared. He jolted her now with a harsh, caustic laugh. "Grateful," he repeated, though the word might as well have been scooped from a gutter in Whitehall. "Well, thank you, my lady. I'll hold that knowledge close to my heart."

And your horse will jump over the moon tonight, too, came the rejoinder from her own heart. Deepening her surprise was the confession of how deeply that realization stung, and how little she knew of why she had to feel this pain.

What in tarnation had happened around here before she arrived? What did Damien Sharpe have to do with it, and why did everyone at Scottney Hall treat his gesture of neighborly kindness more like a spy's infiltration from an enemy camp?

And why did *she* yearn to ignore all of them and their mysterious hatred, and thank this man with much more than some silly mumbled words? Perhaps she could give him the meal he'd obviously *not* had last night, judging by the growl from his stomach; or maybe the hair trim he was in need of, as he impatiently raked back his thick, shoulder-length waves.

Or a hug.

God, she wondered when Damien Sharpe had last received a hug.

Tom clearly didn't share her pondering. "That's enough, Sharpe," the man snapped. "The bird isn't a calling card, and you're no welcome caller."

At *that*, Kira refused to sit by in such docile acquiescence. She lunged toward her belligerent servant, until a hand held her back. She followed the arm up to Sharpe's face, now affixed with its mask of pleasant composure once more.

"Thanks for clearing up that confusion for me, Tom," he stated as if the man had given him road directions to London, not a tactless order to the door. "I could have sworn that was my calling card on my shoulder when I left the house this morning."

Again Kira found herself giggling. And Tom's glower worsening. "Why the bloody hell *did* you come?" the man-servant snarled, resentment powering the words more than curiosity. "Why, Damien? You could have sent the bird back with one of our herdsmen or, at the least, left it at the outer wall."

"Tom," Kira interjected. "The Spanish Inquisition ended twenty years ago."

"This isn't just about the bird, is it?" Tom persisted. "Is it, Damien? Why did you come, Damien?"

Fight back! Kira goaded inwardly at Sharpe herself. *Tell the churl to go to hell!*

But Sharpe, with jaw convulsing refexively and eyes glittering trenchantly, merely gazed back at Tom for a long minute. When he did speak again, his guttural murmur reminded Kira of a lad apologizing for recalcitrant behavior.

"You're right, Tom. It's time for me to go."

He didn't care about Cleo's objecting shrieks this time. Nor did he care about the bird's frantic flappings as he coerced her to climb from his arm to Tom's. And he certainly didn't care about the battle Tom now waged to calm the cockatoo.

And again, as Damien Sharpe whirled on one heel and strode swiftly out of the Menagerie, he didn't care about affording Kira even one last parting glance.

"This was a bad idea."

Damien growled the rebuke at himself as he traversed the portico as fast as possible, back to the Main Courtyard and the comfort of Dante's saddle.

No, this was worse than a bad idea. This was an idiotic mistake, and now you'll pay for it during many days to come.

Many days . . . and nights.

Nights in which sleep would elude him because he envisioned *her*.

Her . . . oh, *yes*, the creature who'd appeared in the doorway of that building all hair-tousled and pink-cheeked, as if she'd bolted straight from bed to the heights of the north moors this morning. She'd been more gorgeous than he remembered, this captivating little American, with her hair spilling around her shoulders and over the bodice of her virtuous—yet quite diaphanous—nightrail.

Bloody God, that nightrail. It would be the cause of half a dozen sleepless midnights to come, as he recalled its filmy texture against the dark copper discs encircling her nipples

. . . then hugging the dusky triangle where her belly ended and his fantasies began.

"Christ," he emitted then on a soft, scathing laugh. *What the bloody hell are you contemplating fantasies for, Damien? What makes you think you can afford such a luxury?*

Better than any answer his logic could devise came the tolls from the chapel bell tower. The melodious knells rendered silent all living things within a mile's radius of Scottney Hall. Seven-thirty and all was well, the Scottneys reminded the world.

No, Damien revised to that. The Scottneys *commanded* the world.

He reached Dante and mounted the stallion with brutal speed. The horse immediately stomped on the cobblestones, reflecting Damien's tension back at him more accurately than a mirror. "Yes, boy," he murmured, slanting a grim smile. "I agree with you. Let's get out of this barmy bin."

Morning dew and long-stemmed grass flew beneath Dante's racing hooves over the open hills. The air was bracing and clean, the sky a pristine slate of periwinkle and gray. With a deep breath, Damien gave his stallion another two inches of rein. This was much better, he decided as the ground sped by beneath them. All was as it should be. No shrieking cockatoos. No cackling chimpanzees. No glowering Scottney Hall minions.

No nightrail-clad hoydens.

The most vile of oaths exploded off his lips at the unwelcome image. He gave Dante more rein and more speed. Their furious pace threatened Damien's seat if they came upon any obstacle or interruption, but he only gritted a smile at the possibility. Truth be known, he'd *thank* Dante for throwing him to his arse, for giving him a good jolt in the part of his body he'd been thinking most strongly with this morning. The part that he now forced to listen to his head. And his heart.

The head and heart that now told him Tom was right. He hadn't gone to Scottney Hall because of the bloody bird.

Nine

"*M*'LADY? M'LADY! M'LADY KIRA, for blessed sake, yer out here in nothin' but yer nightrail!"

Kira couldn't discern if Ally's concerned rasp was for her health or her character. At the moment, *she* cared for neither. Her senses still attempted to deny she actually stood here; that a lush paradise rose around her in reality and not her dreams . . . that a dark, wild-maned creature named Damien Sharpe had been reality and not fantasy.

That the effect he had on her was real. And frightening. Especially when his fathomless stare took her in from head to toe, potent as a physical caress, making her ache for things she'd never wanted before . . . heated, carnal things.

Enough! she ordered herself. *Stop it!* But no matter how tightly she jerked the quilted satin folds tighter around her, her breasts still shivered in taut new awareness; a million intense tremors assaulted her body; her imagination still swirled with the rememberance of Damien Sharpe's captivating stare . . . as if he saw every midnight fantasy she'd ever had, and how to make them come true.

For the Lord's own sake! The man did *not* care about her fantasies! He'd been barely civil to Tom, and when he'd left, he'd run as if this sanctuary had been infected with the plague—though its standing as Scottney property surely made it worse in his eyes.

She was also certain he thought of her in the same way. As a hated piece of Scottney property. Something to ruin for the sake of—

What?

What had happened in this beautiful piece of the world, to make people glare at each other with such ugly anger? What kept them doing so? What was so important, that they considered such hatred worth the effort?

And why did she care?

The answer to at least the last query came during the trip back up to her bedroom. It came as her memory filled once more with the man's face as he'd caressed Cleo. He'd smiled that dazzling smile, intensifying his rugged handsomeness, but that happiness never reached his *eyes*. In the depths of his gaze, she'd still looked at an unwanted outsider, a lonely outcast.

And she realized she cared because she'd stood in his boots a hundred times in her life. Perhaps her feet had been clad in moccasins or show slippers instead of big black boots such as his, but her footing had been the same: scared and unsure.

"Hell," she muttered. She crossed the room, sank onto the window seat, and gazed at the silhouette of the forest on the horizon, to where he'd most likely retreated.

"That's about the truth of it" came Ally's breathless interjection. Kira heard the maid rush around the bed, swishing muslin and crinolines as she went. "Hell—yeah, that's the best name for what we're both lookin' at, if I don't get ya dressed now, m'lady. M'lady, *please*; are ya givin' me even half an ear?"

She wanted to oblige Ally. She wished she could let the maid turn her into at least the semblance of a lady, shedding all thoughts of Damien Sharpe as easily as she discarded her nightclothes.

Instead, as Fred climbed up into her lap, she held out a hand to the maid and softly requested, "Ally, come here." As the maid's face corkscrewed in a grimace, she stressed, "Please."

"I'm *not* gonna thank myself for this," Ally muttered as she crossed to the window seat, dragging every stitch of Kira's clothes along with her.

Kira gave a small smile of thanks before making her next request of the maid. "Tell me about him," she asked softly, but firmly. "Ally, tell me about Damien Sharpe."

"I—I don't know a thing about Damien Sharpe."

"Hell's bells you don't. Everyone at Scottney Hall does. It's as quiet around here as if the Pope passed through."

Ally giggled. "Damien Sharpe and the Pope have *nothin'* in common."

Kira quirked up one side of her own mouth. "Tell me something I don't know, please."

That hesitating scowl attacked Ally's face again, though finally she moaned. "Ohhh, I guess yer gonna hear things anyway!" She shoved aside the crinolines to motion Kira closer, as she murmured, "Though Lady Aleece has promised to beat, then discharge anyone heard speakin' of it."

Kira looked deeply into her friend's green eyes and knew the maid didn't jest by one syllable. With that realization, she reached for Ally's hands, gripping them hard. "If Lady Trevor lays a hand on you," she vowed, "I'll beat and then discharge *her*."

Ally gave a quick smile at that, but the look fell far short of the giggle Kira expected. She swallowed hard in reaction. The maid was truly risking her position to have this conversation!

What was she about to learn of Damien Sharpe that Scottney Hall servants were threatened bodily and emotionally about its exposure? More vitally, did she *want* to learn those things now?

Her heart gave her no choice about the answer to that. She had to know what force had carved out the endless chasms in that man's eyes.

"Go ahead, Ally," she prompted. She gave the juncture of their hands a reassuring squeeze.

The maid took in a deep breath of her own then. "I suppose ya want it from the beginnin'." Her nod corresponded with Kira's. "All right, then. At the beginnin', Damien's was as welcome a face around here as they came."

"That doesn't surprise me. He . . . seemed quite familiar with everything this morning."

"Yes, well, he should be. He was over here enough when courtin' Miss Rachelle five years ago."

Kira aimed a scowl at the maid. A *deep* scowl. "Miss *who*?"

"Rachelle." Ally looked up at Kira in amazed scrutiny. "Bloody blazes. They didn't tell ya about Miss Rachelle? Lady Aleece's daughter?"

"Aunt Aleece has a *daughter*?" A daughter. That meant she had a cousin . . . somewhere. That also meant Nicholas had lied to her back in London. *Aleece has no children*, he'd proclaimed with that look she'd actually pitied. *You're the only one*. And yet, the facts still didn't all fit together.

"B-but . . ." she stammered, "how did she . . . Aunt Aleece isn't married—"

"Anymore," Ally filled in with a sage nod. "Three weeks after she married Miles Denhope, he went to inspect one of his mines over in Gunnerside. He never came back out. It was one of the most huge cave-ins anyone remembers there."

Kira gasped. "That poor woman. Three weeks a bride before becoming a widow."

"*And* a mother." The maid leveled a corroborating stare in answer to Kira's stunned gape. "Yes, indeed," she pronounced. "Lady Aleece was already in the family way; only then she had no family. Lord Scottney, the angel, moved her right back in to Scottney Hall. After Rachelle was born, he became a father to her in every way except truly siring her."

While the child who truly had his blood was led to believe he was dead. Whom he treated as dead.

Kira's mind and heart finished the statement in unison, one resonating with fury, the other with sorrow. The emotions were useless to her now, she struggled to reason with herself, but she couldn't stop the sense of loss from pervading her . . . the sense of shock in now knowing Nicholas had *not* spent all these years in lonely seclusion, as she'd believed with such thorough pity back in London. As she'd been *led* to believe back in London.

"Aleece has a *daughter*," she said then, through clenched teeth.

"*Had* a daughter," Ally corrected once more.

Kira's scowl returned. "What do you mean?"

At first, the maid just stared out the window, toward the deep green blobs that were the hills toward Middleham. As she did, a strange sheen came over her gaze, and her lower lip trembled. "Just what I said, m'lady. Aleece *had* a daughter, but no more. No more. God rest sweet Miss Rachelle's soul."

"God rest —she's *dead*?"

Ally slid her eyes shut as ample affirmation. "She was . . . murdered."

"She was *what?*"

"Six months ago," Ally plunged on. "Six months." She shook her head and emitted a desperate, I-can-do-nothing-else laugh. "Feels like six years sometimes, things've changed so much."

"B-but," Kira stammered, her mind clawing through confusion thick as London fog, "but were they sure it was—are they positive she was actually—"

"She was stabbed ten times," came the blunt rebuttal. "Yes, they're positive it was murder."

Kira's breath left her in jagged intervals. Fred picked that moment to demand she join him in a clapping game, but she shooed even her pet away, battling to accept what she'd heard as truth. She'd expected the "Scottney secret" to be some affair more elicit than her father and mother's; maybe the existence of another estranged love child, hidden away someplace like the Caribbean.

Not murder. Dear God, never murder.

Kira thought of Aunt Aleece then—and admitted she had a new understanding of the woman's vacillation between chilly aloofness and icy overbearance. Sweet saints, the devastation her heart must still be enduring. What grief must have flooded everyone here, this collected "family" in this majestic castle, many of them probably lifelong friends with Lady Rachelle. What rage they must all still be battling—

Dear God. What rage *he* must be battling.

"Damien," she blurted then. "Dear God. Damien. Was he still courting Rachelle when this happened?"

"Courtin'?" Ally rejoined, her tone a surge of irony. "He was two years married to her by then."

"Oh. . . ."

She forced out the reply from her suddenly tight throat. "Oh . . ." she finally repeated, "oh, Damien. I can't imagine what he must have endured. What pain he must have—"

Ally's sardonic snort cut her short then—an outburst the maid had obviously tried to hold in check, though could do so no longer. "I'm afraid there aren't too many in Yorkshire who share yer sentiments, m'lady."

"Why?" Kira fired back. "For Lord's sake, why?"

Ally preceded her answer by scooping *Kira's* hands back into *hers*. "M'lady . . . when they found Rachelle's body . . . Damien was standin' right over her."

Kira didn't know how long she took to breathe again. She only knew that when she did, it hurt. It hurt like hell. But not in her lungs. It hurt in her heart.

"What?" she at last heard herself rasp. There was more Ally had to tell her, right? There was another conclusion to reach other than the image her mind gave her in bloodred detail. She was certain of it. She waited, impatiently chewing the insides of her lips, for the maid to go on.

Ally did continue—but the details did *not* form the justifiable explanation Kira sought. "He was covered in her blood," the maid murmured, "though there wasn't a scratch on *him*. And he was just standin' there, as if waitin' for them to come find him."

"Nobody thought *that* a little odd?"

"Apparently not. Constable Wickins said he'd seen things like that happen before . . . the killer goin' into a shock after he committed the deed, or some such rubbish like that."

"But they never convicted him." Kira pounced fiercely on the conviction. "He's free today. They never convicted him."

"They never convicted him," Ally confirmed. "But they might as well should've."

Kira glared. "What do you mean?"

"The trial was very long, very ugly, and very public." Ally leaned her head back against the wall, her expression glazing as her mind re-created those months-ago events. "Damien was one of Yorkshire's most muckity-muck citizens and businessmen, and Rachelle was his perfect wife and hostess."

"I don't suppose she learned at the Lady Aleece School for Wives and Hostesses," Kira grumbled.

"She knew her stuff because she had to put it to use every hour of the day" came the matter-of-fact response.

Kira emitted a disbelieving huff. In response, Ally leaned forward and pressed a finger to the window. "Follow me here fer a moment," she directed. "Ya know that big mess over there is Damien's forest, right? Now, if ya trace a line from that point to the other forest, which ya can see out the east window"—she motioned across the bedroom to a smaller set of panes—"and imagine another border stretching north, nearly to Castle Bolton . . . all of that's Hyperion's Walk. That's the estate Damien owned the day they took him to York in handcuffs."

Kira forced her slack jaw to form replying words. "*All* of it?"

"Every last acre," Ally verified. "Until the trial."

Kira was now positive she didn't want to hear an answer but forced herself to ask, anyway: "What happened?"

"Well, first, the obvious. Wickins and his men never did scrape up enough evidence to convict Damien. But they speculated and implied enough to ruin him. And that they did."

Molten outrage poured through Kira's soul. It nearly burned away her reason, yet she knew she only felt a spark of what Damien Sharpe must have endured in a York County courtroom, when he'd lost first his queen, then his kingdom.

And at last, she began to understand the bottomless chasms of the man's eyes.

She rose from the seat and paced to the east window, taking in the vastness of the lush green horizon, dotted here and there with neat gray farmer's cottages. Plumes of smoke curled from the structures' stone chimneys, disappearing at last on gentle puffs of morning wind.

"He lost it all, didn't he?" she murmured. She heard her voice catch and struggled to tamp the sudden grief she felt.

"He had no choice" was Ally's disarmingly pragmatic answer. "Hyerion's Walk went without its owner for four weeks. When Damien returned, he walked into chaos. The tenants had kept up with their crops only to find out nobody wanted them. They couldn't get credit to cover their losses, either. Damien was no longer trusted, and neither were they."

Kira squeezed her eyes shut and bit hard on the insides of her lips. "What did he do?"

"Joined the bats in his bloody bellfry, if ya ask me" came the anger-tinged reply. Kira tilted a questioning look over her shoulder, an ample encouragment for the maid to continue. "The dolt thought he could make everythin' all right again." She snorted. "He wasted another three months tryin' to do it, too. In the meantime, Hyperion's tenants were well near starvin' to death!"

"What happened after three months?" Kira asked with careful calmness. She truly yearned to shout *What happened, indeed? What happened to Damien's people, that they stopped trusting him, too, Ally? What happened that they tried and convicted him, even when the courts couldn't?*

"He did what he should've to begin with," Ally declared

then. "He put aside his damnable pride and turned the Walk over to somebody who could do something with it."

Kira studied her friend's face as she approached the window seat again. "He sold the estate?" she ventured with a rise of astoundment. Still, the maid's affirming nod came as no surprise. "All of it?" Kira pressed. "To one person?"

"Indeed," Ally proclaimed, her tone resonating with such adoration, visions of the Pope swirled again in Kira's imagination.

"And such a person existed, waiting there in the wings to 'just take the place off his hands'?" she challenged, folding her arms across her chest.

"Rolf Pembroke was very near a saint about it!" the maid proclaimed. "Gawwds, I don't know what they would've done over there without that man. He's an angel; I'm sure of it."

"Rolf Pembroke," Kira repeated, searching her memory to confirm the name. But no bells of familiarity rang in her mind. Neither Aleece nor Nicholas had mentioned this person yet. The occurrence seemed odd, judging by the "Rolf reverence" in Ally's eyes.

"Who is he," she urged the maid, "besides a visiting angel?"

"He grew up with Damien at the Walk," Ally clarified. "Rolf's father was chief steward to Kenrick Sharpe, Damien's father. The boys were close as brothers, maybe closer, even after they grew into hearty lads. They went off to London and sowed their oats together, and it's even rumored they saved each other's lives more'n a few times!"

Kira gave an appropriately impressed nod. She waited for the story to continue, expecting to next hear of Damien and Rolf's adventures as tropical pirates or riverboat gamblers.

"When they at last came back home and set themselves

to serious matters, Damien devoted himself to learnin' the business that had enabled his father to purchase Hyperion's Walk in the first place. He pursued only one thing harder than his dreams of improvin' life at the Walk—Lady Rachelle's hand in marriage. Rolf went to work and knew success himself, buildin' himself a small London shippin' empire.

"The two of them kept seein' each other on holidays and the like, of course, even though Rolf got himself a fine home just over in York, but they never really found the time—"

"Until Rachelle's murder."

Ally confirmed that with an emphatic hand gesture. "Rolf put a new meanin' to the word friendship then, I swear it to ya, m'lady. He was at Damien's side through every minute of that trial, exceptin' the days he saw to everyone at the Walk, of course."

"He walked on water while he did this, too?" Kira interjected, though her solemn tone conveyed she *did* pay credence to Ally's account.

"He might as well have," Ally rejoined. "No matter how he did it, that man went endlessly back and forth, betwixt here and York like a bloody bob toy, but he never ached or moaned about the ordeal even once."

Kira nodded once more, but it took effort to do so with conviction. "It sounds like they were lucky to have him," she murmured. It sounded more like the man was the second Messiah, she mused cynically, and the rest of the world hadn't discovered that fact yet.

What *wasn't* Ally telling her about the man?

"Now ya can understand a bit of the shock everyone felt when Damien first refused to sell to Rolf, especially when Rolf told him he could keep the old hunting lodge and live there for free. God only knows, it was the solution for everybody's quandaries, especially Damien's."

"God only knows," Kira echoed. But within her soul, a doubt persisted that Damien Sharpe had never viewed the "solution" as the miracle everyone else did. Nor would he ever perceive it as such.

Her mind flung out an instant reprimand for that presumption. She no more knew about Damien Sharpe's finances than Ally knew about Rolf Pembroke's water-walking prowess—though the maid, now tittering, had yet to be informed of the fact.

"Betwixt you and I, m'lady," she murmured conspiratorially, "I've sinned on more'n a few occasions, wishin' it was *our* lands that man had cause to take over. The girls from the Walk tell me it's like waitin' on a god with Mr. Pembroke. It's not just that he looks like Adonis, mind ya, because to my thinkin', they make too much of that, but they also say he's even glorious in the mornin', as polite as a prince when he sits to the bloody breakfast table. Can you imagine that!"

Kira was rescued from having to form an answer when her bedroom door suddenly swung open. On the other hand, she thought, she might have indulged in her relief too swiftly. She hadn't yet come to associate Aunt Aleece's presence with salvation of any kind.

"Dear heavens, Kira." The woman harrumphed as she rounded the bed. "You haven't even begun to dress yet."

"M'lady Aleece!" Ally vaulted up from the window seat, clutching Kira's clothes as if shielding her own nakedness. "I was just—we were just startin' to—well, and then there was a disturbance and we were out in the Menagerie, and—"

"I heard all about the disturbance, Ally." The woman's tone matched her high-necked, stiff-starched black-and-white day ensemble. She impatiently jabbed one stray strand of hair behind her right ear, then stabbed glares at both the maid and Kira.

But unlike Ally, Kira didn't lower her gaze one inch for the woman. "Ally's been trying to dress me for the last hour, Aunt Aleece," she stated. "My untidiness is my fault, not hers."

"I am aware of that, as well, Lady Kira." Aleece returned her regard to Ally with a noticeable gentleness. "Please dress her quickly, Ally. We must begin our lessons posthaste. We've much to go over in just two days."

Kira frowned as a foreboding chill seeped to her bones, having nothing to do with the wind shivering the window at her shoulder. "What happens in two days that's so darn special?"

She wouldn't have believed the phenomenon had she not seen it, but before her eyes, Aleece transformed into another person—a person resembling a ten-year-old about to share a delicious secret. Her lips curled upward and her eyes twinkled in mischief.

"Our return to Yorkshire has caused some excitement," she divulged. "And now, that excitement shall be the *right* sort, as well!"

"The right sort?" Kira lifted a baffled brow. There was a *wrong* way to be excited?

"How wonderful, m'lady Aleece!" Ally crooned. "Please do tell how."

Aleece's smile grew ridiculously huge then. Still, she paused like an inexperienced soprano milking a dramatic moment for everything it was worth. "Rolf Pembroke has chosen to personally endorse our presence . . . by agreeing to join us for a formal dinner two nights hence!"

Ally gasped, then shrieked.

Kira swallowed, then swore.

Ten

SHE SWORE MANY MORE times during the next forty-eight hours. The oaths had a number of causes, ranging from Aunt Aleece's insistence on selecting every thread she wore tonight, to being ordered off the main stairwell because it had been meticulously polished, to the realization she'd not get to visit the Menagerie before sunset due to a tableware lesson that ran two hours overtime. When she finally declared to Aleece she'd been walking since the age of one and needed no further help, she escaped upstairs—where Ally endlessly fretted as if the Emperor of China was expected for dinner.

She'd been tempted to swear twice then. But now she was glad she hadn't, for *this* moment deserved it more. Still, she almost laughed her way through the expletives, for their sole cause was sheer amazement.

Standing before the three-sided reflecting glass in her dressing room, she gawked openly, certain the image was some stage trickery wielded at her expense. That respectable Englishwoman couldn't be her. That refined beauty, in the gown of quilted dark-pink satin layered with an over-skirt sculpted of heavy iridescent lace, wasn't *her*. That certainly wasn't her hair, either, coiled and wound around a crown of fresh pink roses that cascaded to her neck along with a multitude of satin ribbons.

"It's beautiful, Ally," she pronounced, gingerly touching the perfect ringlets at her temples. "Thank you."

"Heavens, m'lady"—the maid giggled—"it's just a bit of a coiffure."

"It's *artwork*," Kira insisted. She straightened and again took in her reflection. She would have shaken her head with the impact of her surprise, but by no means would she risk turning Ally's mastery into disarray. "I'll be tarred and feathered," she murmured. "It *is* me, isn't it?"

Ally's contented sigh answered that. "Indeed, m'lady."

"Nothing I ever wore in the show compared to this."

"Ya look beautiful. Like a princess."

"She looks like a *queen*."

Kira swiveled a startled gaze to the doorway on the heels of her maid's similar look. But by the time her sights alighted on the dashing figure standing there, a smile graced her lips. Only Fred, who dallied with a leftover length of ribbon on the floor, missed the unmistakable surge of pride in her father's voice. Nicholas's handsome face was stamped with equal conviction; with genuine feeling this time, not some expression he'd tried to copy from Mama.

"Welcome home, my lord," Kira greeted, stretching out her hand and receiving her father's dutiful kiss on the knuckles. Again she fought the temptation to shake her head in bewilderment. Twenty-four hours ago, during Aunt Aleece's tutelage of this action, she'd felt more clumsy than an elephant trying to balance on a thimble. Now the pose felt born from years of familiarity.

"Was your trip pleasant?" she queried of him then.

"Pleasant enough," Nicholas answered. "But it's good to be here now, with you." He lifted a tentative smile. "I missed you. Did you . . . miss me?"

Kira was tempted to answer him in the negative. She was confused and a little hurt, and she wanted to know more about the cousin who was the closest thing she'd ever have to a sister. She yearned to talk about her feelings with Nicholas, when they could steal a private moment together.

Because of that admission, she answered her father as honestly as she could. "Perhaps," she hedged, smiling. "Yes, perhaps I missed you a little, too."

"Good." Her father's eyes twinkled with even more gold lights as he kissed her hand again. "Good." He took her in from head to toe again. "My." He chuckled. "You clean up well, my lady Kira."

She batted him playfully with her fan. "You're not a peasant yourself, my lord."

As a matter of fact, her father formed one of the most striking sights she'd ever seen. He was flawlessly turned out in his black swallow-tailed dinner jacket with matching breeches and shined ankle boots, with crisp white stock and dinner gloves that gave his ensemble a noble finish.

"Shall we?" Nicholas offered her the crook of his arm as he turned back toward the door.

"Must we?" As she issued the discomfited mutter, she felt an elephant again. She attempted to close her fan in one fluid motion, but instead whacked herself in the face with the contraption's pearl framework.

Doing his best to hide a snicker, Nicholas replied, "Well, no, we absolutely mustn't. You may dine up here if you like. I'm certain Ally will be happy to fetch your plate from the kitchen, as soon as she's helped you change out of your gown into something more—"

"No." The protest spilled off Kira's lips before she realized what she'd actually expressed by it. With a resigned sigh, she inwardly conceded the truth: that the London "couture tortures," as she'd come to call those endless fittings, had been worth every tedious moment. That being the "pretty one" of the party felt nice . . . very nice. And that she wasn't ready to change into "something more comfortable" yet.

With that decision, she hooked her arm to her father's with gritted determination. "Lead on, Lord Scottney. I'm not ready to say good night yet, no matter how torturous this . . . um . . . adventure may be."

"That, my dear," her father murmured as he molded a protective hand atop hers, "was spoken like a true Scottney."

At that, Kira waited for her stomach to begin squirming. Instead, to her shock, her father's words inundated her belly with warmth and lifted her mouth into a smile. Ten days ago she would have denied this moment would ever happen. *Two* days ago she would have denounced it.

But her father had made her smile . . . really smile. No matter how many times he'd made Rachelle do the same thing, it mattered most that he did it for *her* right now. It mattered that he'd lent her a dose of his Lord Scottney–size strength when she needed it the most. For that, she silently deemed him her hero for this evening, no matter what happened with the man waiting downstairs to meet her now.

At *that* thought, her stomach began its acrobatics. As Nicholas and she neared the stairwell, the somersaults increased. *Glide, glide,* she exhorted at herself between measured breaths. *A lady doesn't walk,* she repeated in the same singsong Aleece had used to instruct her, *a lady glides . . . glide, glide!*

That litany almost became *slide, slide* as they reached the stairwell in all its polished glory. The moment Kira stepped onto the wood with her slippers, they provided as much stability as Mama's tea leaves on a pool of oil. But her father was in full hero form this evening; Nicholas prevented her from taking a full tumble by securing an ironlike grip around her waist.

"Well," he declared as he did, chuckling heartily to give her a moment to compose herself, "here she is at last, everyone."

"Wonderful!" someone answered from the foot of the stairs in a honey-sweet croon. Kira blinked in astonishment. Did that exclamation come from the mouth of the same woman who'd drilled her like a military cadet for the last two days?

Surely enough, as Aleece shooshed her way up a few steps, the dulcet tone accompanied her in fine form. "My dear!" She beckoned to Kira with both hands outstretched. "You look absolutely lovely!"

"Thank you," Kira returned, though the second syllable lilted with uncertainty. Should she curtsy now? Salute? "You're a pretty choice tomato tonight, too, Aunt Aleece," she finally said, and smiled to show how much she meant it. Her aunt was a radiant sight this evening, in a royal-blue gown ornamented with glittering violet trims.

Aleece flinched, clearly telling Kira "choice tomato" wasn't the best "choice" of words for the situation. Yet a smile again took center stage on her face, and she let out a thin giggle. "Oh, Kira," she effused, "how I am enchanted with the amusing things you say!"

"It's not difficult to see why."

The smooth baritone words caused an expectant silence across the entire foyer. Kira blatantly understood why. Though the Emperor of China indeed didn't stand waiting in the gaudy, gilt-framed doorway of the Grand Hall, she discerned there'd be no difference between the monarch and this man other than appearance. Standing regal and tall yet comfortable and confident, here was a person who knew exactly what effect his chiseled features and golden blond hair had on a room. Many liked to say a person like him had "presence." If that were so, then "presence" oozed from him like wax drippings down a sleek golden candle.

Which isn't a horrid attribute, came a voice from inside. *Barnum has presence. Isaac Van Amburgh has presence. Tarnation, even Queen Victoria has it.*

Give him the benefit of a doubt, Kira.

"Mr. Pembroke, I assume," she murmured, pleased with the decorous cadence of her tone. Not bad, for someone wrestling through her first hour in fifteen pounds of satin and lace.

"My lady Kira," he responded, "you assume correctly."

As he took her hand and leaned over it, she couldn't help feeling that she once more touched one of Sheena's snakes, with its scales so smooth . . . and cold. The sensation continued as Rolf Pembroke gazed at her and stated, "It would be my honor and pleasure to escort you into our meal." He directed his next comment at her father. "Cook announced the pheasant's readiness just moments before you two came down, Nicholas."

"Splendid," Nicholas returned, all joviality and camaraderie as he offered his arm to Aleece. "Splendid, Rolf. Lead on!"

And so she was passed off from her hero of the evening to the man who called her father by his first name yet called *her* nothing at all. Instead, Pembroke chose to send her unspoken and utterly bizarre messages throughout the evening. During the oxtail soup and salmon mousse, Kira attempted a cordial smile at the man, who sat opposite her—

he returned the courtesy by giving her stares she could only describe as smoldering and silly. She changed her tactic during the dressed lobsters and orange-potato pudding, giving him coolly neutral glances. He did things with his food that caused more of it to end up on his plate than in his mouth. Silly *and* wasteful.

By the time the raspberry champagne sorbets were brought out, marking this ordeal as only halfway done, the man found creative ways to bring his *utensils* into his show. Kira had to admit she found it fascinating that he could lick pink goo off a spoon with so many angles of his tongue, especially when the only encouragement she supplied was a disgusted grimace.

She never imagined she'd find the explanation for his antics merely by glancing to her right. Aunt Aleece, seated next to her, was the epitome of a woman in the throes of enthralled infatuation. The woman's enraptured stare provided ample kindling for Rolf's overconfident display, stirring a strange pity for him in Kira's gut. The man really didn't know that tongue acrobatics on silverware weren't interesting *or* sexy.

As a matter of fact, she began searching her memory for what Aunt Aleece told her about the discreet way to stifle a yawn, when her father saved her yet again. As the creamed asparagus and Cornish game hens emerged from the kitchen, he broke the pervading silence at the table by turning to her with a warm smile. "So, my lady Kira," he stated with a touch of obvious pleasure, "I understand you've already found the Scottney Menagerie."

Kira smiled. Perhaps this meal would have an interesting turn, after all. "It's beautiful," she replied. "It's more than beautiful, really. How long have you had it? Did you design it, my lord?"

Nicholas let out a hearty chuckle. "You flatter me, Kira."

He pressed a humble hand to the center of his chest. "I'm afraid I cannot lay claim to your praise. I commissioned an architect named Charles Barry to create my flight of fancy. He's got quite a future ahead of him, with that eye for extra flair and detail; wouldn't you say so, Rolf?"

Rolf appeared to contemplate that subject for a long moment—though in truth, Kira knew the man fought to divert his focus away from the erotic possibilities of asparagus spears slathered with white cream sauce. "He's done fine work for me at the Walk," he finally said with sophisticated smile firmly back in place. "As a matter of fact, the renovations to the ballroom are almost complete." He encompassed Kira and Aleece with his gaze then, as well. "I insist you all come for a visit to see them."

"Mr. Pembroke, you are *too* kind," Aleece gushed. "We'd *love* to pay you a visit!"

"And . . . what about you, Lady Kira?" Rolf queried while slowly circling his fork tines in the white sauce. "Would *you* love to come pay me a visit?"

Kira lifted only her gaze at Rolf. A brief connection with his unflinching brandy eyes confirmed the man had less questioned her than challenged her, trying to ensnare her now by tempting her with control instead of sex. She dawdled with her own fork in order to stall her reply, trying to decide on thinly veiled contempt or a show of outright sarcasm. Tarnation, how she wished the table weren't the width of the Mississippi. A swift kick to the man's shin would resolve everything.

On the other hand, an enthusiastic assault from a chimpanzee could do the trick equally well. Kira eagerly welcomed her pet into her lap, voicing approval at how he'd dressed himself up for the occasion in the ribbon remnants from her bedroom floor. He grinned and clapped before turning curious eyes to the food in front of him—and eventually, curious fingers, too.

To his credit, Rolf Pembroke reacted to the arrival of their new dinner guest with arched brows, but little else. "An African chimp?" he asked, not surprised by Kira's affirming gape. "A healthy animal," he commented. "You take excellent care of him."

Kira opened her mouth to voice a sincere thanks, but Aleece's huff filled the pause, instead. "But she shouldn't be rendering that care at the *dinner* table," the woman voiced from clenched teeth.

"*Au contraire, Mademoiselle Aleece.*" Rolf grinned at the blush he induced in Aleece's cheeks. "At many Paris dinner parties over the last several years, I've seen seats especially held for the family chimp or pedigreed dog. It's quite à la mode now."

Aleece reacted, of course, as if the man had imparted the secrets of the Sphinx. But Kira took the moment to contemplate what he'd said.

"That sounds like a good bunch of traveling," she commented. Rolf merely shrugged in feigned humility. That was when she pressed him: "Tell me, did Damien Sharpe ever go with you to Paris, or did you two just go carousing and wenching in London together?"

Aleece's fork clanged onto her plate. Nicholas took a gulp of wine. But Kira didn't veer her stare away from Rolf. For a reason she couldn't explain, every nuance of the man's reaction mattered to her.

The problem was, his answer had no nuances. No surreptitiously averted glance or uncomfortable mouth twisting. Not even another shrug. Nothing except a flirt's smile and a charmer's chuckle.

"My lady, your directness is more invigorating than India spices." He added with a look of hooded intent, "And just as delicious, too."

"Well," Aunt Aleece piped up. "On that note, I think it's time to adjourn for dessert in the library."

A windy chill pervaded Scottney Hall despite the promise of warmer weather the day had rendered, so the large fire below the library's mahogany mantel was a welcome sight. Kira found herself actually smiling as she let Fred lead her to the dessert tray. The sweets were positioned atop a sideboard that, like most of the room's furniture, was fashioned in mahogany, adding to the room's comfortable ambiance.

She smiled as she perused the platter full of colorful confections. Perhaps, she admitted, this party wasn't the horrid trial she'd expected it to be. As a matter of fact, she thought while taking a bite of a strawberry filled with syrupy ambrosia, the only way this moment could be more perfect was if she enjoyed it in her billowy nightrail, curled before the fire with an absorbing book.

And if Rolf Pembroke had finally decided to go home, as well.

She tried not to flinch as the man appeared at her side, sliding a hand around her elbow. "I'd like to thank you, Lady Kira," he said, bringing on mental pictures of the Eden garden's serpent slithering toward poor Eve.

"What, pray tell, would that be for?" she quipped in a light parody of his accent.

To his credit, Rolf accepted the jest in its intended spirit. Though when he replied, he did so with a serious gaze. "For a delightful evening," he stated. "I can't remember when I've been this enchanted . . . truly."

"Of course," she returned flatly. "Truly."

She gazed longingly at a chocolate mound with nuts and pink sugar bits. But as she reached for the dessert, Rolf caught her hand. He brought her fingers to his lips. His mouth was smooth—and cold. "Kira," he whispered, slanting a cautious look toward the fireplace to make certain Nicholas and Aleece couldn't hear, "please say you'll come and visit me. We'll have so much fun . . . I promise."

Kira yanked both her hand and her self to a safe distance from the man. Without thinking, she wiped the fingers he'd kissed along her skirt. They felt dirtied. Actually, *all* of her felt that way now.

The sensation was weird and disconcerting, and Kira was glad when Fred sensed her agitation enough to abandon a cream puff of his own to come hold her hand again. Her pet chittered loudly at her, his way of voicing his concern. The sound sliced distinctly through the air, needing no interpretation.

"For God's sake," Rolf sputtered. "My lady, I did not mean to—"

"I know you didn't," Kira stated with a diplomacy she forced to sound sincere. "But now I think it's time you said good night, Mr. Pembroke."

Rolf muttered something beneath his breath before curling a grip around Fred's wrist. "*I* think it's time we speak without flying fur in our faces!" he hissed.

At that, before Kira could think or move, she watched him hurl Fred against a divan six feet away. The soft cushions were the only impediment stopping her pet from crashing into a curio cabinet filled with a deadly cavalcade of china and glass.

Her shriek sliced across the room, a prelude to an interminable pause in which only the pops of the fire dared challenge her taut glare. Perhaps those sparks took the risk because they realized they had furious brethren flaring in the core of Kira's soul.

"Mr. Pembroke," she at last pronounced. The words

emerged thick and black as slow-burning coals. "I think it's time I said good night."

Aunt Aleece rushed forward. "She—she doesn't mean that!"

"The hell I don't."

"Kira!" came the mortified rasp. "Mr. Pembroke, she—she merely needs some air . . ."

"I've had enough air tonight, thank you," Kira interjected, still arrowing her stare at Rolf. "Yes, more than enough empty substance to last me awhile. Now if you'll excuse me—"

"Kira!" The woman frantically followed her and Fred down the carpeted hall. "Kira, you are insulting Rolf"—she flustered her way through an embarrassed pause before correcting herself—"*Mr. Pembroke* beyond the decencies of—of—decency!"

Kira fixed her aunt with a sardonic half smile. "Then that makes us even."

It was then that they both noticed Nicholas had emerged into the hall, too, and played witness to their exchange. Kira held her breath in apprehension of her father's reaction.

She didn't have to wait long. Yet just as swiftly, she learned she'd worried in vain. Her father strode forward and smiled gently down at her. He leaned and kissed her on the cheek with equal intent.

"I'm sorry to hear you're not feeling well, my dear," he followed. As he pulled away, their gazes met in mutual understanding. He'd sanctioned her escape. He *supported* her, even if he didn't agree with the tactics she'd taken.

"Thank you, my lord," Kira murmured softly . . . and again, knew Nicholas comprehended the multiple meanings of the words. She finished with a smile that came from the deepest well in her heart.

She stepped away from Nicholas, then wasted no more time in departing the room. Once out in the massive foyer, she dashed directly for the nearest set of stairs.

As she slipped into the welcoming white softness of her nightgown, she heard Rolf's coach rumble out of the courtyard and into the night. The ensuing silence wrapped around her as comfortingly as the nightrail. Kira released a sigh of contented relief. The evening was finally *over*.

The sound didn't put a nick in Ally's piqued bewilderment. If anything, the maid jerked harder on the counterpane as she pulled it to the foot of the bed, then accordioned it atop the velvet settee there. "Glad to see him leavin', are ya?" she snipped as she did.

"Yes," Kira answered. "Thank you for your concern, Ally." She smiled wider.

"Concern," the maid repeated in an incredulous mutter. She tossed the bedclothes aside and spun to where Kira now curled up in the window seat. "*Concern* is *right*!" she exclaimed, the force of her ire eclipsing her caution about any "reprimands" from Aleece. "Beggin' yer pardon, m'lady, but are ya outta yer blazin' mind?"

Strangely, Kira's smile dropped as she responded to that. "I'm beginning to think I'm the only one around here who's *kept* their mind."

"Ya practically gave Rolf Pembroke the cut direct!"

She nodded somberly. "You're right. He didn't deserve that."

"Bloody straight he didn't."

"He deserved to have his privates kicked in."

"Ohhhhh!" Ally threw up the pillow she'd been carefully plumping. "By all the saints and—"

"You weren't there, Ally," she persisted. "You have no idea how he treated Fred—"

"And perhaps the little stinker needed it?"

"—or the way he looked when he did it."

"I'll wager he looked divine."

"He looked like an animal."

"A *divine* animal."

"A *rutting* animal," Kira spat. "He was so berserk to get his hand up my skirts, he treated Fred like a couch cushion that merely got in his way."

"A couch—" The maid tossed up her hands. "Do ya expect me to believe that?" When Kira rendered no answer, knowing she could call the spirits of all twelve apostles to help her and still end up with Ally's skeptical stare, the maid stalked to the door leading to her quarters. "I'm goin' to bed, m'lady, where I'll pray God brings some water to thin out that oatmeal in yer head. Good night!"

"Good night, Ally."

The words spilled out on a chuckle. Kira couldn't help it. The same way she couldn't help shaking her head in wonder about the maid's adoration of a man more reptile than human. Yet still, she reminded herself, a reptile who had slithered his way into the respects of all Yorkshire and a good chunk of London.

The realization made her feel more a confused foreigner than the day she'd stepped off the ship from Boston. She scowled as she wrapped her arms around herself, despite the warm comfort of the room. Thoughts of Rolf Pembroke induced a gut-deep yearning to protect herself . . . and scrub herself. She still couldn't forget how filthy he'd made her feel at the sideboard, staring at her like one of the desserts themselves. No, worse. He looked at her like a stack of the riches that had purchased those sugared morsels.

She never felt filthy when she thought about Damien Sharpe.

So many sensations inundated her when she summoned those hewn, hard features to mind, but not a single one made her yearn to scour herself raw. If anything, the man instead stripped her mind clean of all trivialities; his presence burned away all else from her soul except the awarenesses reborn at his command.

No, he didn't make her feel dirty.

He made her feel desired.

And God help her, Kira conceded, she desired him, too.

She desired him right now. She desired to go to him, finding him in the forest where not even starlight penetrated the darkness, and hold him against the confusion and pain that assailed him.

And then she'd kiss him. Oh yes, she'd kiss him, sweetly and softly, taking her time so that she also took some of that pain from him, so that he could finally sleep. He'd slumber with his face pressed atop the place where her heart beat, his body pressed to hers . . .

"By the saints and sinners!"

Immediately she banished those heated images out of her mind. "What in the confounded world are you thinking?" she berated herself. "That you'll just gallop into Damien Sharpe's domain and be welcomed with champagne and roses?"

She slumped against the wall as she uttered the last of that. She did so because her head, followed by the sinking stone of her heart, wasted no time in issuing an answer to the query.

"Damien Sharpe doesn't care whether you live or die, Kira," she told herself in a tremoring whisper. "The sooner you remember that, the better."

Eleven

*S*HE DOESN'T CARE *if you live or die, Damien. The sooner you get that through your head, the better.*

The trouble was, Damien ruminated, he wasn't thinking with a proper head at the moment. In this hour of the night when even the owls slumbered, he lay wide awake, staring at the beasts carved into the beams high above his head— and he saw a different creature entirely. He saw not leaping stags and growling bears but a nymph with eyes enticing as candied almonds, lips succulent as glazed strawberries, and a body smooth as fresh-whipped cream, so ready to be appreciated, savored . . . impassioned.

And he remembered how good fresh cream tasted on the tip of his tongue.

And his erection for Kira Scottney grew harder.

With a snarl, he lunged out of bed, landing to the bare wood floor with two violent thunks. As he did, he glared at the sheets one more time. Tonight marked the first time he'd ever bounded so eagerly from them. He loved this bed; he'd loved every foot of its massive mattress and carved oak frame even while paying a king's fortune to have the craftsman hand-assemble it here, upstairs in what used to be the Hyperion's Walk hunting lodge.

The craftsman had called him ten kinds of a lunatic for spending so much on a piece of furniture he'd only see on twice-yearly hunting expeditions. Damien had just grinned, feeling right about the decision though unaware there'd ever be a time he'd call these walls home. When he could call nothing else home.

That thought compounded the fire of his arousal with a conflagration of frustration. He stomped from the loft and down the lodge's wide stone steps, willingly letting the inferno engulf him. Hell, he even welcomed it. This blaze burned through his soul's emotion and fear, clearing the only necessary path for his life now—the path leading to complete vindication of his name and his honor.

His lips curled in grim satisfaction as he entered the crescent of amber light emanating from the arched, ten-foot-high fireplace. As he pulled a tarnished brass candlestick from a side table and used the waning embers of the fire to ignite the wick, the fury settled around him like a comfortable winter cloak. *This* feeling was right, he affirmed. This was the only way he could think clearly about that morning six months ago and the weeks that had preceded it.

This was the only way he could afford to think.

A baritone bark suddenly broke the silence. Another woof followed, replete with enthusiasm only a canine brain could garner at this hour.

"Ham," Damien called to the small mountain of black fur curled in a faded wingback chair to his right. "Come here, you clod-wit." His undertone was gruff but affectionate as the labrador cheerfully complied, rewarded by a dozen vigorous scratches behind his ears.

Clearly in hopes of garnering some more rewards, Hamlet trotted along as Damien approached a chopping block that had once supported the fresh trophies of the day's hunting or fishing. Now the large wood slab was strewn with police reports, pages filled with personal notations, and maps displaying all of Yorkshire in every conceivable context. Damien leaned over the documents while Hamlet propped both front paws up to the counter next to him.

"Looks like a hurricane hit, eh?" he muttered. Ham emitted a sympathizing whimper.

Damien braced his elbows on the block and laid his head in his hands. Yes, it was a hurricane, he confessed. But *nothing* would be tossed. For something, anything, perhaps *all* the paper on this table would turn a lock in a baffling riddle he had every intention of deciphering.

For everything on the table contained some detail about Rachelle's last month on Earth.

Yes, came the voice from that pit between his heart and his gut, like the colorless core where a candle's flame burned most intensely. *Yes, fill your mind with nothing else but what's on this table. You will not let any person detract you from this again, let alone a woman.*

Let alone a Scottney woman. Especially not a Scottney woman.

He mustn't remember how that woman looked in the filtered day glow of the Scottney Menagerie, clad in little else *but* that beautiful light. He mustn't remember that lilt of softness in her voice, as if she understood the depths of his pain. And he must *not* welcome her to the realms of his dreams, where she helped him forget that pain in sweet, exquisite ways . . .

"Damn it."

He spun away from the chopping block and drove his fist against the wall. Damn it, he had to forget!

He had to forget . . . by remembering.

He had to remember how her family—the family who'd called themselves *his* family, too—had turned away from him. How their doors had slammed on him. How their hate had ruined him.

He had to remember how he was going to make them reopen those doors somehow, someday. And the first step to accomplishing that might lie somewhere on this table. Somewhere in this chaos, a diamond of irrefutable logic was waiting to be found—to help *him* find the bastard who had really murdered Rachelle.

Damien leaned lower over the chopping block. He didn't look up again until the lamp's light was joined by mist-tinted morning beams.

"Kira. *Kira!*"

Kira jerked her head up but didn't pull her sights away from the groomed dirt in front of the Scottney Hall stables. From the third-floor window, she had a full view of the ring where the trainers worked out a new arrival to her father's prized collection of fine horseflesh.

The stallion was magnificent, she admitted—but her attention centered on the man holding the opposite end of the lunge rein. He strode on long, powerfully defined legs, matching the horse's grace move for move, his actions flowing with a hypnotizing, primitive poeticism.

His actions looking so strangely, unforgettably familiar.

She stared harder at the trainer, but a broad-brimmed hat obscured most of his bearded face. Mentally she noted his attire—buff shirt and breeches; open black leather vest—so she could seek him out later and commend his mastery of the horse.

"Young lady" came Aunt Aleece's pinched prompt, "are you ready to—"

"Aunt Aleece," she swiftly interjected. She wasn't "ready" to concentrate on much of anything on this gloriously crisp spring day, and perhaps she could distract her aunt into playing the recalcitrant along with her. "Do you know, perchance, who that man is?"

She held back her smile of triumph as Aleece rose and crossed the sitting room's Aubusson carpet. She'd wagered that her primly voiced question would at least warrant a cooperative glance out the window from her aunt.

"He's one of James's new men in the stables," the woman supplied with another pinched sniff. "Nicholas needs more help, since he's insisting on purchasing *more* Thoroughbreds." Aleece's tone descended to the same complaining drone she used when lamenting about Nicholas's cigars. "I think his name is . . . errmmm . . . George, or something."

With that, the woman swished back into the room. "*Now* are you ready to continue, young lady?"

Kira's teeth ground against each other. She'd been cooperative about these lessons for two weeks now, and today, she decided, was simply not a day for "continuing" anything at all. Today was meant for taking new chances, even if they were with her pinch-faced aunt.

Perhaps especially if they were.

Kira slammed a satin ribbon bookmark into her forebodingly thick copy of *The Mirror of the Graces* and dared an impudent grin up at the woman across the carpet. "I don't wish to read any more," she declared, rising with a dramatic swish of her own skirts. Before Aleece could sputter a word of protest, she yanked her aunt to her feet. "Let's practice more dancing."

Dancing, she'd ruled last week, was her favorite subject. She even tolerated the lectures about proper fan etiquette and seemly ballroom chat topics in order to get to the good part of the lessons: executing the fascinating steps of the reels, the cotillions, and, her favorite, the sweeping beauty of the waltz.

She grabbed her aunt's hands as she lunged into those steps now, orchestrating with a humming version of the tune usually played for them by Marcel, the multitalented downstairs butler. "Come on, Aunt!" she coaxed. "One, two, three; one, two, three!"

"You are one, two, three days behind on your *reading*." Aleece yanked away. "And there shall be no dancing until we've come current with it. *Sit*," she charged—but abruptly interrupted herself with a dismayed gasp. "Oh, Kira, look what you've done. The corner of this page is going to be permanently creased!"

"May God strike me dead," Kira muttered while dropping back into her chair. Creasing a book page. Why, certainly that was even worse than the faux pas outlined in the volume in her lap. The book dared to broach "the peculiarities of dressing" and "the importance of temperance," but there was no mention anywhere of what happened when one creased a book page. Yes, she was assuredly going to burn in hell for this. She only hoped waltzing was allowed in hell.

"We shall begin at chapter two," the woman prompted, arching expectant brows across the top of her own book. "Ready?"

With a resigned sigh, Kira opened her book. But then she closed the cover again. In the moment it took for her aunt to discern she wasn't planning on cooperating, she looked at the woman . . . truly looked at her. She looked and she suddenly saw not Aleece's aversion to having fun but her *fear* of indulging herself. As the woman raised a frustrated glower to Kira, the furrows in her face no longer belonged to a stern shrew but to a grieving mother.

A *mother*.

"Kira, how are we *ever* to get through all of this, if you won't—"

"Aunt Aleece," she interrupted, softly but determinedly. "Tell me about Rachelle."

For the first time since she'd stepped foot on Scottney property, including those first days in London, she witnessed her aunt's composure falter on a tightwire of emotion other than anger. "Who—who told you about Rachelle?" Aleece fumbled with her book, trying to hide the trembling of her hands.

"It doesn't matter. Tell me about her . . . please? What was she like? Am I anything like her?"

"Stop!" the woman hissed. But her tone faltered and became a desperate plea of its own. "Oh, Kira . . . *stop*."

"My lady Kira!"

The appearance of Amy, the downstairs maid, granted Aleece her request by default. Kira didn't invite the maid in to the room as she usually would, but rose and met the servant in the doorway with a friendly smile.

"Amy," she greeted, "I'm afraid Aunt Aleece isn't available at the moment. She's a bit under the weather. I think I'll take her up to her room."

"But . . . your father has sent me for *you*, my lady."

At that, Aleece's skirts rustled to life. "For Kira?" The woman's voice was suddenly sharp as always. Kira wanted to be surprised at the woman's "recovery" but wasn't.

Despite that, Amy continued to address Kira. "He'd like to see you in the main sitting room," she stated. "He said he'd like to see you now."

"*Now?*" her aunt exclaimed again, thoroughly beating Kira's claim on the words.

Amy dared a small but clearly affronted sniff. "I believe I

heard him correctly, Lady Aleece. You can check my hearing against Mr. Pembroke's. He was standing there, too."

"Mr. Pembroke's!" The woman's "health" had definitely returned. Aleece converged on the doorway with anticipation, her smile breaking into rosy cheeks. "Well, well! I suppose you're right, Kira. Today is no day to study at all."

Kira, on the other hand, speared the maid with an anxious huff as her aunt disappeared down the hall. "Rolf Pembroke is here? Now?"

Amy slammed hands to her curvaceous hips. "I must be speaking another language today."

How Kira wished that were true, so she could simply plead she hadn't understood Amy. She even wished she could stay here with Aleece now, ingesting the ins and outs of deportment and modesty, instead of trudging downstairs wondering what on God's green earth Rolf Pembroke wanted with her now.

The trapezes of the man's mind were pitched all backward. Her dismissal of him at the dinner party had only spurred him to a flurry of visits over the past fourteen days. Sometimes he arrived with elaborate excuses; at other times he showed up merely because he "happened to be in the vicinity" and was interested in everyone's welfare.

Everyone's welfare. Kira snorted as she remembered the words. Then let him explain why he never asked about Father or Aleece, and seemed to endure the latter only because somebody had to serve as "proper" chaperone to his calls.

Smoothing the apple-green skirt of her afternoon gown as silently as possible, Kira slipped into the main sitting room through the side door while Rolf and her father finished a hearty laugh, apparently about something a now-preening Aleece had said.

"Kira!"

She stopped reluctantly behind a three-sided Turkish couch. "Good afternoon, my lord," she greeted her father with a halfhearted wave. Dropping her hand and her tone, she added glumly, "Hello, Rolf."

The three of them simply stared at her then. Kira raised a hand to her hair, wondering what odd item her curls had managed to ensnare *this* time, but her search gleaned nothing. She looked back at them—

And endured a queer twist in the pit of her stomach. All three of the faces on the opposite side of the room wore expressions filled with too much mystery. A mystery she wasn't sure she wanted to solve.

"Perhaps we should all sit down," Nicholas stated coolly. Why did his tone remind her of a judge about to issue a life sentence to a prisoner?

Rolf and Aleece murmured their immediate agreements to the suggestion, but Kira instead walked toward the windows. "I'll stand, thank you," she returned, her heartbeat thudding in her throat.

"Well," Aleece chimed then. "We're all here, aren't we?"

"Indeed," Rolf murmured.

Kira tried to tamp down an impatient sigh.

"Mr. Pembroke, has my uncouth brother offered you a libation yet? Cook's cinnamon tea is the finest in all the county, I'm certain of it."

"Thank you, Lady Aleece, no," Rolf responded. "I'm confident Lord Scottney has a plethora of duties to attend before the day is out. There shall be many other occasions when we can linger over refreshments."

"You are so right, Mr. Pembroke."

Kira snapped a questioning stare back upon them. *He is?* her senses railed. *Many other occasions for lingering?* What was the man talking about? Her upset stomach wasn't an encouraging answer, either.

"Yes," her father murmured then. "Pembroke is correct. The sooner we finish this, the better."

Kira's heart thundered in her ears. He sounded like a judge about to sentence a prisoner to death; a Pilate anxious to be done with the ordeal of his duties as quickly as possible. Her gaze caught Nicholas's for one moment. Yes, she saw in his eyes, this was an ordeal for him.

"Kira . . . Mr. Pembroke has come today to express his growing affection for you. He has asked my permission to court you, and I have agreed."

The words shouldn't have surprised her. Yet she sucked in a fast breath as invisible bonds squeezed her lungs. She spun back toward the window, attempting to force words past her constricting throat. Syllables stampeded in her head, a herd of sounds as wild and frustrated as the stallion fighting against its tethers outside. Straining against that stranger in the broad-rimmed hat, in the breeches so snug around his powerful legs . . .

Inexplicably, that memory tightened the restraints around her chest, causing her reflexive recoil as her father approached her.

"Kira," he said through clenched teeth, "blast it, give this a *try*. Rolf is an upstanding citizen. He's a good man."

She laughed in helpless confusion. She trusted Rolf as far as *Fred* could throw the man, but this was her father asking this concession of her. Her father, who had made innumerable efforts over the last two weeks to be with her, to know her. This was her father, who had promised her the fulfillment of her dreams in just another eleven months.

"What do I have to do," she ventured cautiously, "for this 'courting' thing?"

She veered a glance at Nicholas. His gaze warmed like

the brandy he sipped during their fireside chats. "That's the beauty of it," he told her. "*Rolf* must do all the work. He'll call on you in much the same way he has been; however, now you'll receive extra gifts, such as flowers and baubles and trinkets of his admiration."

"Trinkets." Heaven only knew what "trinkets" Rolf would deem as appropriate symbols of his "affection." She looked to the man for an answer, only to behold an unnerving glint at the back of his gaze.

As fast as possible, Kira jerked her sights away from the man. "It just seems much ado about nothing," she muttered.

"Well, it's what Rolf must do" came her father's chuckling answer, "if he wants to win you as his bride."

Immediately his laughter stopped. Aleece glared at him. Rolf stared at *her*. Kira swept unblinking eyes to all three of them.

"Is *that* it?" she finally rasped, though her words felt separate and disjointed in her throat. "Is that it, then? Rolf's 'affections' . . . his 'tokens of admiration' . . . it's all still the means to the end, isn't it? To get your heir planted in my belly."

"Kira," Nicholas grated, "*no*. That's—"

"Were you planning to *tell* me about this marriage, Father? Or were you just going to drag me to the church, hoping I wouldn't notice Ally had dressed me in a wedding gown that morning, then ask me if I minded doing a 'little favor' for you, like marrying a lascivious boor?"

"Kira!" Aleece exploded.

"Kira, for God's sake," Rolf said with a snarl. "Think about the advantages of the alliance. Your bloodlines will never even be *whispered* about in London if we post the banns by Christmas. After that, with Scottney Hall and Hyperion's Walk united as one—"

"Stop it!" She yanked up her skirts until her knees had enough room to move—to run. "Just stop it, all of you!"

Now she really couldn't breathe. She had to get out of here; out of this place with its unrelenting stone walls and its people pressing her harder against those walls, trying to flatten her into something she wasn't. *Somebody* she wasn't.

Somehow she found herself in the hall once more, then the front foyer, the vestibule, and finally the front drive. Still, she didn't stop running. She ran faster, toward the vibrancy of the gardens, then the wide freedom of the valley beyond that. She ran until pain and instinct pushed her toward the thick embrace of a dark, green forest.

Twelve

HOURS PASSED, BUT she didn't care. As the forest bathed her in shimmering depths of emerald shade, the heat of her rage was also gradually soothed, like a slow swallow of Mama's comfrey and hyssop cough tea. Kira breathed in great breaths of the woodsy air, verdant with the scents of moss and grass, of pines and willows.

Oh, to live here with these contented creatures, she yearned, ripping away her shawl and rolling up her sleeves, reveling in the crisp breeze upon her arms. Traveling farther, she came upon a moss-banked stream, its shallow pools emptying over smooth rocks, performing a dance of its own for an appreciative squirrel audience.

Eagerly approaching the water, yet finding her crinoline too cumbersome to handle, Kira hurriedly shucked that, too. She didn't even bother with the buttons on her day shoes, opting to pry them off with opposing toes, peeling down stockings at the same time. With a laugh of soft delight, she at last tugged up her hem and waded into the cool eddies.

The water gurgled around her shins as she smiled up into

the leaf-filtered sunbeams. Songbirds began to accompany the stream's orchestra, and she quickly decided she'd not heard more beautiful music in her life.

Soon a contented tune formed in her own throat, an aimless melody that flowed over her lips in happy, hummed notes. She swayed a little to the cadence of her melody, surrendering herself to this perfect moment. A minute, perhaps two, passed without a thought entering her head of dressing peculiarities, proper fan etiquette, or becoming Rolf Pembroke's wife.

Especially not becoming Rolf Pembroke's wife.

A rustling along the stream's bank jerked her attention back to the present. She pulled her head upright and her eyes open in time to watch the last member of the squirrel family dash away up a tree, bushy tail swishing as the adorable creature went.

She smiled and was about to let the expression bubble into a chuckle but an awed gasp instead left her lips. A pair of perfect almond eyes blinked tentatively at her. Dappled sunlight fell across those hypnotic eyes, along with the alert ears, the elegant neck and the graceful body, all covered with fur that defined the creature itself: sleek, soft, and tawny.

Why, hello, she greeted the doe through her gaze instead of her lips. *Are you thirsty, pretty one? Would you like some water?*

The doe, like the shy maid she was, dipped her head and pretended to sniff a patch of daisies while assessing the status of the trespasser in her stream. *Friend or foe?* her stance asked in the language of the wild.

It's all right, Kira assured. *I'm friend, pretty one. I'll share the water if you will.*

The doe came two steps closer.

Just before an equal number of gun shots blasted through the clearing.

A flock of bluebirds burst into the sky as if their sheltering oak was an exploding inkwell. The squirrels squealed in terror, and the doe, thank God, accompanied them on a panicked retreat into the thick foliage.

Kira waited until she could no longer hear the creatures' escaping skitterings. Then she didn't let another second of hesitation pass. She spun, splashed out of the stream, and marched furiously up the bank. Ignoring the twigs and rocks biting into her soles, she stomped straight toward the wild-haired, black-eyed beast now emerging into the clearing.

She tried not to notice how much more foreboding he seemed, now that the strong, straight edge of his shoulder supported a rifle and not a cockatoo. The feat wasn't easy. She supposed that's why she stopped a full six feet from him and issued her accusation from there.

"What in tarnation do you think you're about! Are your eyes open? For that matter, has your *brain* busted open?"

At first glance, Damien Sharpe appeared calm enough to be merely posing for one of those gentleman-in-the-forest parlor portraits. But then Kira looked into his eyes. His stare glittered with coal-black malice; his antipathy toward her had clearly reached new levels since the first time they'd confronted each other in this dark wood.

Still, his reply was a low, almost cordial, murmur. "Well spoken, my lady," he stated. "Though I am chagrined; you stole most of the questions I would have posed to *you*."

"*You* would have—" She momentarily forgot her trepidation, incredulity sparking her to a burst of laughter instead. "I see," she drawled. "Your dinner again, I take it?"

Something changed in his eyes before he replied to that. Despite the utter blackness there, preventing someone from discerning shadow from light, his gaze gleamed with a sharper edge. A *much* sharper edge.

"*Yes*, damn it," he at last bit out. "And this time, princess, I'm not taking promises of pleadings to Papa as recompense."

She should have bitten her lip. And her tongue. Instead, she flung back at him, "Good, because I wasn't about to offer such."

"Then what *are* you prepared to offer?"

Kira's senses came up with no reply to that except the throbbing din of blood through her veins and the alarmed beating of her heart against her ribs. For as Damien Sharpe issued that all-too-quiet demand, he stepped slowly forward, the edges in his eyes now looking like moonlight on the blades of a hundred daggers.

The kind of daggers that could cut a woman's heart out as it still beat in her chest.

Damien knew exactly what state of mind he'd manipulated her into. He watched the pulse throbbing wildly at the base of her neck; he heard her take frantic backward steps. He imagined her ladyship Kira would leap at a tap from her own shadow at the moment—which was his precise intent since coming upon the clearing and seeing her all but ask his doe to a few rounds of whist.

But now, her dread sickened him as much as any thought he'd had of deer hunting in the last two weeks. It was true; venison had come to be as appealing to him as castor oil. When he'd come upon the clearing just now, he'd been searching for rabbits.

Instead, he'd found a hellion looking more adorable than she had a right to. Ah God, he'd raged, what was she doing in his stream like that, with her hair half toppled from its pins, her skirts so soggy, they molded sexily to her bottom, and her face, *her face*, kissed with dappled sunlight and the sublime beauty of her soft-humming smile. *What*, damn her, was she doing?

His brain answered with inexplicable jealousy and anger. He was jealous of the happiness she found in the simple act of wading in a stream. Angry because she chose to express it in *his* domain, which he deemed to keep decidedly *un*happy for the time being, thank you.

"So . . . what about it, my lady?" he growled at her then. "What *is* going to be the apologetic sacrifice to the forest beast this time?"

He pinned her in place with his stare as he closed the three steps of space between them. Without looking down, he wrapped a fold of damp skirt around his fist, then pulled. "An offering of virginal flesh, perhaps?" he murmured huskily.

A sharp breath escaped her lips, and he watched a tiny bead of perspiration form at the corner of her mouth. Damien clenched his jaw, hoping she interpreted it as a sign of his growing ire, not his growing arousal. Holy God, how could a woman make him so hard and so incensed at once?

To his grudging respect, she still didn't falter her gaze from his. "I don't think you comprehend me, Mr. Sharpe. *I* am not the individual who owes penance in this instance."

For a moment, her words hovered in his brain like a seagull above a wave, waiting for the right moment to dive in. When understanding came, it threw his head back on a bellow of laughter. "Penance?" he echoed, trying not to chuckle his way through the syllables. "I owe *you* penance, for doing what I see fit with the resources on my land?"

Her reaction began with those ever-present embers in her eyes, which now exploded into fury through her body.

With a sharp snap of her wrist, she reclaimed her clothing from his hold. "Was that creature a resource, Mr. Sharpe, or a pawn of revenge?"

Damien didn't know whether to continue laughing or spear her with the blackest of glares. Finally, he decided simply to let her see the full extent of his bafflement. "What?"

She slammed her hands to the curve of her hips. The action did *not* help his effort to forget she stood there clothed in nearly nothing, so close to him and so far from anyone else.

"This may come as the jolt of the season to everyone around here," she pronounced, "but that doe doesn't belong to anyone or anything other tham its Creator. It's on loan to you, *mate,* along with all the other creatures here. By the disrespect you give that agreement, it doesn't amaze me that you go hungry half the time!"

Even the thought of an appropriate reaction eluded him now. "Agreement?" he finally uttered.

She fired him a glare. "You really think this is all yours for the taking, don't you? You don't think you'll be held accountable for what you've done with the richness of this land, for the indifference you show to the spirits of the creatures who belong to it?"

"The spirits of the creatures . . ." Damien opted for a glare of his own now. "Lady, what the hell are you about?"

She huffed as if he were missing the very nose on his face. But her reply came on a compassion-filled tone. "Just because animals can't talk about their souls doesn't mean they don't have them. And those souls are represented in the heavens by certain saints, the same way ours are. When you dishonor an animal's soul by killing it without honor or thanks, you're also offending its guardian saint." She took half a step forward, into a beam of light that illuminated her growing smile. "In retaliation, that saint may send certain events to foul up your plans . . . or even certain people."

He stared even harder at her. "Let me get this straight—now you're telling me you're a messenger from heaven?"

Her head tilted at that; a pixie's response of genuine surprise. "I don't know," she murmured. "It's a nice idea, I suppose."

Damien began his retreat from her with half a dozen slow but steady backsteps. Yes, he affirmed, the retreat. He had to get away from this woman, from this . . . *creature* with the dark beauty of her face and the blazing spectrum of her spirit, who'd invaded his stream like a half-wild forest nymph and now threatened to penetrate the thicket of his soul with equal damage.

"My lady Kira," he finally said into the air that had thickened through an uncomfortable silence, "I think it's time you wandered your wet little arse home."

He flung the profanity with calculated intention, expecting either a shocked huff or an affronted withdrawal. Kira Scottney's aggravated sigh was *not* on the list of options. "*Please* stop calling me that," she said while she was at it. Damien blinked in shock as she concluded the whole thing by dropping onto a boulder with graceful guilelessness, again just like a sprite who'd lived there for centuries.

"Wh-what?" he at last stammered.

"That 'Lady Kira' balderdash," she answered, pulling a knee up beneath her chin. "I don't think I'll get used to that." A slight crease formed in her brow. "I'm not sure I want to."

"Of course you do," he rebutted. "A lady of the House of Scottney . . . it's every girl's dream; surely they've schooled you about that so far."

"*Don't* mention schooling, either." She emitted an

I-may-be-sick groan. "How to smile. How to nod. How to walk. How to talk. By the saints, I *know* how to talk. It's madness, all of it!"

Damien dipped his head, battling to repress a chuckle. It spilled out, anyway. Odd . . . from all the boulders of derision he'd heaped in his soul over the last six months, he couldn't find a single chunk of the stuff to hack off now. "I don't believe you mean all that," he goaded gently instead. "Scottney Hall isn't Newgate Prison, after all."

"It's not home, either."

Her retort came swiftly, almost angrily. Yet as Damien looked on, yet another emotion assaulted her features.

Pain.

It wasn't just a twitch of physical discomfort or a wistful breeze of longing. Sheer agony inundated her gaze like a February downpour: a consuming wash of grief, of lost love, of lost life. Of a home she longed for in more than words, because that home no longer existed.

Ah, God. He knew exactly how she felt.

The recognition froze Damien there, and they stared at each other—for much too long. And still, he didn't run. He didn't command *her* to run.

He wanted to know more about her.

He found his way to a fallen log near her boulder. As he lowered himself to the rough wood, he took in the sight of her again: damp and small and beautiful, even in the sorrow that so clearly enveloped her.

"Tell me about home," he asked of her at last, drawing in a breath as conclusion. When was the last time he'd spoken to anyone so gently? He truly couldn't remember.

At first, her answer consisted of a solitary tear down her cheek. "The answer doesn't matter," she snapped, swiping the droplet into her impossibly tangled hair. But then, she erupted into an irony-filled laugh. "It's not as if that wagon wasn't about to fall apart, anyway. The fire just accomplished the job quicker."

"The fire," he repeated, his tone questioning but empathizing. That she'd lived in a wagon was strangely effortless to accept; a vision easily bloomed of her in satin gypsy garb, her hair bound with a tasseled scarf. But the image was torture to maintain when picturing her standing in the charred remains of a once-colorful wagon, alone and homeless.

"Fires are a fact of life in the circus," she explained, her gaze directed down the streambank with a faraway sadness. "Unfortunately, with a little help from a panicked crowd and a strong wind, they can be a killer, too."

"I'm sorry," Damien murmured, and meant it.

Her sigh conveyed the obligatory thanks—and somehow, Damien sensed, they both knew it was enough. Another minute of silence passed before she spoke again. "I just wish I'd been able to get Mama's things out. Her embroidered shawl, her silver amulets, her books of herbs and potions . . . her treasures, she called them. She'd brought them with her from the old country."

Curiosity sparked his query this time. "The old country?"

"Russia," she supplied. "Mama left when she was only fourteen, but she remained true to the Orthodox saints and the spirits of nature her whole life."

"The saints *and* the spirits?" He quirked a genuine scowl. "A paradox of a woman, was she?"

"To the people of your world, yes. But the Creator Mama taught *me* about is not so small."

To his amazement once more, Damien felt himself reacting to her unconventional talk with a concurring nod. He conceded the startling rightness of her words. The startling rightness of *her*.

The revelation shot a bullet of alarm through his chest—though his brain barely registered the impact. Still, he rose to his feet. He moved to stand directly in front of her.

He said nothing as she rose, as well. Her head reached the level where his heart beat out a rhythm surely filling the clearing with its deafening cadence. Perhaps not the whole clearing, Damien rectified, but he knew *she* heard the cacophony. He knew because she turned her face up to him, and it was adorned by a soft, knowing smile. A soft, soul-inundating smile.

"You are the oddest woman I have ever met," he said in a growl as retaliation to that smile—to the barrage of warning bullets now slamming into his senses. That's why he wondered where the hand came from, looking terrifyingly like *his*, that raised to the corner of her smudged, beautiful, captivating lips.

Funny . . . that hand even felt like his, as she turned her head and breathed across the suddenly trembling fingers. Hell. Bloody *hell*. She *was* a forest fairy, he ruled, and now he was caught in her spell. And the hex felt wonderful.

Until she issued her whispered reply to his statement. "And you, Mr. Sharpe, are the first outlaw I've ever met."

He jerked his hand away. *You had it coming,* his brain bellowed. *You had it coming even before you snarled at her, yet you dawdled here with her, trying to believe otherwise. You fool!* His heart pounded with the chill of a hibernating grizzly's, a beast forced into darkness until spring's salvation.

His mistake was in confusing this hoyden for spring.

"Wh-what's wrong?" Her voice faltered with confusion and hurt. She was good, this little performer from the colonies. He almost believed she felt those emotions.

He glared directly at her as he leveled a demand of his

own in return. "Where did you hear that?" he asked her in a lethally soft murmur.

"Where did I hear what?"

"You *know* what. You don't call a man an outlaw without bloody good reason, princess. You know, don't you? You know all of it." He began to advance upon her but stopped short as comprehension struck. "Ally." He sneered. "I should have known. The little prattle-hen. Ally's your maid, isn't she?"

Her downcast gaze told him the answer to that. But as Damien spun on his heel, spitting an oath, she pulled him back by the elbow and met his glare with a stare brimming with her own resolve.

"I commanded her to tell me," she pleaded on behalf of the maid. "So if you're going to gnash your jaws at anyone, gnash them *this* way, all right?"

Damien ran his regard down the rigid line of her arm, coming at last to the white-knuckled fist still clamped around his elbow. From beneath hooded lids, he asked, "Why?"

She rendered her reply with surpising softness. "I wanted to know why you were so . . . why you were hurting so much."

He pulled away from her slowly, numbed by the force of shock. He didn't need this, he raged inwardly. He didn't want it! He didn't need her pity, so thinly disguised as "concern." He didn't need the exhilaration of her touch, the warmth of her gaze, and most of all, the beauty of her vulnerability . . . her trust in him. He *didn't* need any of this.

He *couldn't* need this.

"My pain is none of your bloody business," he retorted then, forcing himself to pace a few steps.

"Perhaps I'd like to make it my business."

"Perhaps you aren't invited."

"Perhaps I don't care."

"Then you're a bigger fool than I thought, because you're wasting your time."

"Damn it!" she erupted at last. "No wonder nobody cares about you anymore. You won't let them!"

Damien dropped his head and stiffened his shoulders. She was right, he conceded. She was so bloody right, he sucked in a hard breath from the force of the realization. She was the first human being he'd been within three feet of in the last half year, and holy God, just the wisps of her warmth and life had felt magnificent. Too damn magnificent.

"Go home, *Lady Scottney*," he willed himself to drawl. "Go back to your papa's castle, and don't trespass in my forest again." But though weariness had laced his words, he underlined his meaning by scooping up his rifle like a highlander grabbing for his claymore.

Then, without so much as a parting glance, he turned and left her.

That's better, he told himself, escaping down a path back into the thicker trees, where night dripped darkness already. His blood began to cool. It would return to its usual safe frigidity, as soon as she got out of here.

As far as her repeating the mistake . . . Damien didn't give the thought more than a passing shrug. After Ally and her cohorts pumped her with a few more tales of "Damien, the Forest Beast," Lady Kira would not come venturing within a mile of this wood.

So she was truly out of his life now.

He felt much better about things already.

He only wondered why his soul didn't seem to hear that declaration, as well.

Thirteen

MEN, KIRA RESOLVED, had "evolved" backward. As Fred eagerly greeted her in the garden, she was even more certain of it. Her pet's tender kisses were the most civilized behavior she'd received from a male today.

"You snuck away from Ally again," she murmured to the chimp, failing at her mildly accusing tone. Fred himself was fractionally to blame, playing with her hair and making her giggle from the ensuing tickles.

"Oh, Fred"—she finally sighed—"perhaps you *are* the only man around here who doesn't belong in a cave."

The chimp echoed her wistful tone with a soft whimper before resting his head back against her shoulder. "Why don't we run away and join the circus?" she asked. Again, as if understanding not only her tone but her words, Fred flashed a toothy grin.

But her mind rendered another reply. *And why don't you jump over the sun and the moon while you're at it, Kira? Attempting that would be easier than convincing yourself to leave . . . breaking your promise to your father . . . and abandoning the dream he's now placed within your reach.*

You've got another eleven months to spend with this tribe of lunatics, Kira. Get used to it now.

"Get *used* to it?" she muttered while trudging up the stone garden steps, onto the south verandah. Get used to batting her lashes in time to her fan; to pretending hemlines and bodice styles actually meant something to her? Get used to having no choice about her clothing, her books, the time she spent and whom she spent it with?

She began to wonder if she could pull this act off. She hadn't even gone inside yet, and she already yearned to run for the depths of a dark emerald forest once more.

A forest she'd been banned from, as of an hour ago.

She dropped onto a stone bench as the memory of Damien Sharpe's dismissal assaulted her again. Her mind's eye watched his retreating back, his anger-tautened muscles visible even through his buff-colored shirt, his equally furious stomps. The stomps of a bitter, frightened man.

A blind man.

He was the worst kind of a blind man at that, she concluded, because his infirmity had nothing to do with his eyes. The man had sealed shut his *heart*. He had shut himself so thoroughly in that darkness, he mistook an extended hand of friendship as an attacking sword of enmity. He treated words of kindness as if they were chunks of diseased meat: sniffing them, grimacing at them, then dismissing them as vehemently as he could.

Tears assaulted her eyes, but she forced them back by flinging her head up. Then, determinedly setting her jaw, she softly spat one sentence.

"Go to hell, Damien Sharpe."

She dropped her head. The oath didn't carry half its intended strength. All too swiftly, she identified the reason why.

Even if Damien went to hell, she'd willingly accompany him.

Yes, she'd offer her hand to him again without hesitation, showing him he was not alone; showing him she understood the pain of being prejudged and cast out. She'd show him she wasn't afraid of him—she was only afraid of *her* reaction to him. She was terrified of what her body did whenever she even looked at the man, standing on his impossibly powerful legs, glaring with his impossibly fathomless eyes. Even now the heat puddled in her belly then brimmed over into her limbs, thick and hot and consuming . . . and dangerous.

They're positive it was murder, m'lady. She was stabbed ten times. He was covered in her blood. But there wasn't a scratch on him . . .

"Kira!"

Her aunt's summons broke into her dark thoughts, making this the first occasion she welcomed the woman's intrusion. Kira rose from the bench, gratefully leaving behind all broodings of blood, knives, and murder trials. She plastered a reasonably serene expression on her face as the woman approached like an impending thunderstorm.

"God's sweet mercy." Aleece gasped once she drew near enough to discern Kira's Cleopatra smile and Cinderella tatters. In horror, she assessed Kira from disheveled head to bare toes. "Your—your shoes," she stammered. "Your stockings . . . your crinolines; for the love of heaven, Kira, how did you manage to ruin your *crinolines?*"

"Good afternoon to you, too, Aunt." Kira added a courtly nod to her sardonic tone. "I am quite fine, thank you for your concern. No lasting damage, as far as I can tell. And how do *you* fare?"

"It's evening, not afternoon, young lady. Tea was served well over an hour ago. Now we shall clearly have to delay dinner because of you, though I am sorely tempted to simply send a tray to your room, instead."

While Kira concentrated on cloaking her joy at *that* prospect, the woman harrumphed on. "You have so disappointed your father and me, and now this. Oh, *what* unearthly beasts did you find to take you to hell and back?"

Though she admitted the news of her father's disappointment made her cringe in a strange way, Kira's lips quirked at her aunt's unwitting accuracy. What kind of beast, indeed, she ruminated . . . and what kind of hell. *I'd like to know those answers myself, Aunt Aleece,* her heart added with sad wistfulness. *But I never shall. Nobody shall.*

The admission sank deeper into her soul, finally lodging itself at the bottom like an anchor stuck in a drift of mud. She reacted by jerking a furious shrug. *If you want to keep on wallowing in a pond of your anger and resentment, you'll do it alone, Damien Sharpe,* she silently proclaimed. *I said I'd go to hell with you, but I refuse to live there!*

". . . sometimes I wonder if you even like living here!"

The uncanny similarity of Aleece's words and the voice of her thoughts pulled Kira back to the confrontation at hand. "I . . . enjoy quite a few aspects of living here," she replied swiftly in her defense, though she hoped Aleece wouldn't ask for supporting details. She doubted the woman had ever noticed the balustrades of the north wing were the perfect height and width for her tightwire practice, nor would her aunt appreciate the value of having a chambermaid who didn't mind colorful cursings in the morning.

"Well, you choose to show your enjoyment in utterly obtuse ways." A cluck shot off the woman's tongue. "Surely, Kira, even you were not raised to think debacles like this afternoon are acceptable. Regardless of what you think of the man, Rolf Pembroke is still a neighbor. He didn't deserve—"

"You're right." The words spilled off Kira's lips before she acknowledged their presence in her mind.

Aleece blinked hard at her. Finally she forced her mouth around some stammering syllables. "I-I'm—"

"You're right, Aunt Aleece," she repeated, even nodding an affirmation. "Rolf may be a bit of an arrogant bird, but he didn't deserve to be screeched at by a harpy dodo, either." She attempted a congenial smile. That still didn't make her next statement easier to articulate. "Perhaps . . . we can see about making it up to him in a special way."

Amazement grappled with vindication for possession of Aleece's features. Yet the moment the woman reclaimed her composure and prepared to issue an appropriately gloating response, her face tautened into silence once more.

Kira turned to see the reason why. She looked up as her father wrapped a hand around her shoulder, his eyes sparkling with bronze shards of delight and his mouth curved with a mysterious sort of pleasure.

A pleasure, Kira admitted, she *liked* bringing to his face. The smile warmed even the color of his skin, luring her to burrow closer to him as the first of the night winds snuck around the west tower's parapets and sent a chilled shiver through her.

"You heard?" she asked him then, though merely as a formality. Her father's answer read as plainly across his face as a child's alphabet letters.

His smile, however, suddenly sobered. Nicolas pulled back and fixed her with an equally serious stare. "Kira, your offer is generous—as well as unnecessary. A letter of apology by your hand will be a fair enough token to Rolf. You needn't propose doing more."

"I know. But I want to. Rolf has been a good neighbor to

you, and everyone thinks so well of him. He . . . should have proper recompense."

She battled to add her heart's conviction to her mouth's words. But the effort didn't work. To this minute, the only "recompense" she wished she'd given the self-sure churl was her palm print across his jaw.

Confound it! she argued with herself. *Not everyone in Yorkshire can be wrong about the man! There's something you're missing about Rolf Pembroke. Something you're just not seeing.*

Why did those words only tighten the mangle that squeezed her heart? Why did they not summon Rolf's smooth, handsome, safe features, but *Damien's?* Why did her memory linger on eyes shrouded in shadow, jaw set in hatred, full lips hidden beneath a slash of compressed bitterness? Why did they make her think if she only looked long enough and doggedly enough, she'd find the man behind that forest monster . . . the innocence beyond the accusations?

Why did they make her gaze to that forest now, as if she could begin the miracle from where she stood? And *what* in the world made her believe she'd be successful? She had wrested barely a smile from the man when sitting but three feet from him.

Kira bit hard on the inside of her cheek and forced her soul to accept the ruthless conclusion of her mind. Damien Sharpe didn't *want* anyone to know his truths. Damien Sharpe didn't *want* to smile with anything other than cynicism or live in a world other than his dismal forest.

Damien Sharpe wanted her to leave him alone.

"Fine," she retorted softly to that. "Fine, Mr. Sharpe. If that's the way you want it, that's the way it shall be. I only hope you're perfectly miserable with your decision."

Helping divert her attention further was her father's reassuring touch, both of his hands alighting on the backs of her shoulders as he said, "I'm sorry, daughter; your aunt was distracting me. What were you saying?"

With a smile filled with more gratitude than Nicholas would probably ever know of, Kira pulled on one of his hands, bringing his arm back around her in a comforting embrace. "Nothing, my lord. Nothing at all."

She felt her father smile. "Rolf and I are scheduled for a ride tomorrow morning. Would that be too soon to deliver your invitation to him?"

Suppressing a wince, Kira replied, "No, my lord. As a matter of fact, it won't be soon enough."

Fourteen

SHE SHOULD HAVE tried this cooperation routine a long time ago. Kira could have slapped herself for not thinking of it sooner, but she tossed away the urge along with her hairpins as she chose to enjoy the dramatic cloudscapes and bracing wind that greeted she and Fred on their free afternoon together.

While he hadn't told her so directly, the "time gift" was Father's way of saying thanks for her agreement, however halfheartedly rendered, to give Rolf another chance. The man's cheerful departure from the breakfast table gave him away this morning, though he'd allowed Aunt Aleece the pleasure of telling her about the reprieve in his stead.

"Pleasure," Kira surmised, probably wasn't the word the woman herself would select to describe the task. Perhaps her aunt's pinch-nosed delivery came from the discomfort Kira had sensed as they'd discussed gown selections for the upcoming visit to Hyperion's Walk. It seemed that since Rolf's disastrous dinner visit, Aunt Aleece got flustered as a loose tent tie at any mention of the man or his estate.

Kira motioned permission to Fred to trot on ahead of

her. This time was too precious to waste considering anything but the invigoration of being part of this land. After Aleece had released her from the last of the morning lessons, she hadn't even had the patience to wait for Ally to change her into simpler clothes. She'd grabbed a light velvet afternoon cloak then sprinted out through the herb garden, her volumnous skirts swishing every which way as she went.

Now those layers of poplin and crinoline swirled more wildly than a mop wielded by a blind woman. Kira only grinned every time they did, reveling in the powerful wind sweeping her along without direction or manners. Above her, the clouds waltzed across the sky; at her feet, fragrant grass brushed her ankles. The verdant stuff flowed on endlessly, the way Mama's hair used to cascade along her pillow. Just as she did when she used to run her fingers through those silken strands, Kira began to hum a little tune, letting the wind compose the soft melody just as it guided her feet . . .

Oh, Mama, her heart cried as her lips sang, *Mama, I miss you.*

A loud snap of underbrush to her left startled her. Kira jerked her sights in that direction, to discover the wind had steered her and Fred to quite an interesting locale. A flower-strewn meadow was lined on two sides by towering, dark pines.

The pines of the forest Damien Sharpe had banished her from.

And right now, from the edge of that forest, a prettily spotted doe stared at them in unmoving vigilance. Only the tips of the animal's ears twitched, showing the doe's piqued assessment of them. The animal appeared to issue its own rendition of the proclamation snarled at her yesterday.

Get out. Get away from here, and don't come back!

Though the command stung nearly as sharply as it had the first time, Kira grudgingly respected it. Slowly she began to step back.

Fred, however, did not receive the same message.

Kira realized that fact as her pet, instead of following her, cracked a friendly grin at the doe. "Fred!" she whispered as loudly as she dared. "No!"

Fred answered her edict with a mutinous grimace. He turned that into a series of affectionate grunts as he decided to greet his new playmate in a more effusive manner. In horror, Kira watched her pet throw open his arms to the doe and run toward the animal with affable abandon.

"Fred!" The predicament called for a full shout this time. "No, confound it! *Stay!*"

But like a dog who recognized the let's-give-you-a-bath tone of its master, her pet intensified his rebellious flight. The doe bolted. Fred shrieked excitedly and ran faster. As the pair sprinted into the densest section of the woods, Fred's cackles were punctuated by smashing underbrush and the whipperings of birds taking frantic flight at their approach.

"Fred! Fred, blast it, get your sorry rump back here now!" *At which point, I'll kick it all the way back to Scottney Hall.*

Suddenly her anger froze into fear. A barb of realization struck: If she wasn't wanted in the forest, her hell-raiser of a chimpanzee certainly wasn't, either. She couldn't bear contemplating what Damien Sharpe would do if he came across Fred frolicking after *his* doe, through *his* forest.

Two seconds of pondering the possibilities were all the influence she needed to make a decision. Hoisting her skirts to her knees, Kira lurched into a full run down the path her pet had forged. Sharpe's ultimatum could burn in Hades.

And if he so much as touched a strand of Fred's fur,

much more than the man's words would burn in Hades, too.

"You should be darn grateful I'm not pining for a chimpan-zee fur coat."

She snarled the words nearly thirty minutes later, past a scowl so peeved, it hurt. Dripping in sweat, pine needles, and mud clots, Kira had finally burst into an open space in the forest, only to trip over a tangle of underbrush. Though the clearing was drenched in shadow, enough thin shafts of light broke through to illuminate her pet hunkered on a fallen log, as if merely waiting for her to catch up during their leisurely afternoon stroll. The doe, of course, was no-where to be seen.

"Are you happy with yourself?" She huffed while push-ing up onto her elbows, then her knees. "I'm filthy, Freder-ick, and we'll soon add *late* to that, too, if we don't find our way out of here."

She emphasized the last of that with a disparging glance around the clearing, which appeared to be just that: a small hollow carved out of the pith of this forest, almost like a secret wizard's cave formed in the depths of a vast moun-tain. There was no discernible way in to the clearing and no simple way out. The walls of dense, dark foliage rising all around her might as well have been boundaries of stone.

If stone walls also had numerous pairs of little yellow eyes.

Stifling an unsettled gasp, Kira scooted closer to Fred. So he was only a four-foot-high simian who preferred snug-gling instead of fighting, but he was better than the mysteri-ous creatures that possessed those scuffling paws and gnashing teeth, coming louder from the impenetrable murk.

A shiver sluiced down her spine. Her mind did *not* help matters, echoing loudly with Sheena's voice now, dipped to the low cadence the gypsy woman used when all fires had been banked and midnight reigned over the circus camp. *"Holes to hell,"* she'd chant, baubles jingling from her shawl while twirling her arms in dramatic reenactment for Kira. *"They're all around us, Kira. You must watch for them carefully, but especially in the forest. That was where I nearly fell into the Dark Realm myself . . . in the midst of a forest darker than the night. . . ."*

"Stop!" Kira dictated to the memory—as well as her thundering heart. "Fred, put that stick down. We're getting out of here *now*."

She held her hand out to her pet as she determinedly shoved up from the ground.

She went nowhere.

A hand slammed her back down to the ground. A hand dark and stiff and corroded with wet earth—as if it had just emerged from the pit of hell itself.

Fifteen

SHE SCREAMED. LOUDLY. But then she continued to scream and Damien almost relented his hold, wondering if he'd hurt her.

What the hell do you care if she's hurt or not? came the savage bellow from his senses, joining the tortured ringing in his ears. *The reckless fool deserves whatever penalty she has coming. She's violated you—again!*

That thought detonated the outrage in his gut into a ferocious sound on his lips. He punctuated the roar by hauling the hoyden to her feet, then spinning her around to face him.

Her scream gave way to a stunned gawk. But the bronze defiance in her eyes didn't wane by a spark—an observation Damien should have allotted more importance. *Much* more. At least if he'd wanted to elude the sudden whip of her palm across his jaw.

"What the—"

He managed to sputter the two words before her physical backlash exploded to verbal form. "You conniving, sneaking, skulking"—she paused, breathing hard, mouth working to find the right word—"bully!" she finally blurted. "For God's sake, you scared the living ghost out of me! Probably the dead ghost, too."

The last line, muttered as half an attempt at humor, rendered the opposite effect on Damien's temper. He shook her hard, no longer caring how she interpreted his burning glare or harsh breaths.

"Do you think this is a game?" he asked her in a growl. "This *isn't* a game, damn it. Papa's riches can't rescue you here, you little fool!"

Her chin jerked up and her eyes glistened even brighter—but at least now, shards of fear began to show amid the brazen gold audacity of before. The sight pumped him full of such exhilarated satisfaction, it panicked him.

He wrenched away his hand—and wished she would step back with equal vehemence. But no, damn her, her ladyship Kira had to stand there rubbing her shoulder as if he'd truly hurt her arm. She stared at him as if he'd truly offended her heart.

She didn't stop her torment at that, either. "You really think I came traipsing back here on purpose, don't you?" she murmured with wounded softness.

He locked his teeth and returned on a taut sneer, "The court does find the evidence overwhelmingly convincing."

"Well, the evidence is wrong!" She threw one arm up in furious emphasis, leaves and mud clumps flying as she did. "I trespassed again only because I was retrieving Fred—because he went on a tear after *your* stupid doe, and—"

"Fred," he interrupted, incredulity carving new furrows into his forehead. "Fred . . . your *chimpanzee*? Are you telling me you violated my express request in order to—"

"That wasn't a request. It was a royal decree."

"Stop digressing from the subject."

"That *is* the subject. Your ridiculous edict *is* the subject, and the fact that you think I 'violated' it, for whatever small-minded reason you've concocted." She slammed both hands to dirt-smudged hips. "Let me make you aware of something, Mr. Sharpe. I don't give a fig about your decree, or whatever it is you're hiding because of it. I *do* care about my pet, who has more compassion in his toenails than you have in your entire body."

She concluded by striking a pose of smug vindication. But Damien had been called a compassionless bastard, and much worse, before. He attached his attention instead on the accusation she rendered before that.

"Whatever it is I'm hiding," he reiterated. "Is that what you think, lady? Is that what *they* think, up at that goddamn castle of yours?" The words came from lower and lower in his throat yet shot seething pain higher and higher into his head. "They think I'm *hiding* something?"

The hoyden didn't say anything. But she didn't have to. No matter what she told him, Damien observed her answer in the frantic rubbing of her lips, in the hasty diversion of her gaze from his face to his boots.

"They—they don't tell me much of anything around that place," she finally blurted, and Damien conceded a grudging respect for her protection of the servants who'd clearly become her friends, as well.

"But you listen," he asserted softly. "You listen well, don't you, princess?"

"No. *No.* Stop—stop staring at me like that. I don't know anything!"

He cocked a casual shrug. "I believe you. You don't know anything. But . . ." He took a step toward her with *un*casual precision, making sure she heard every last crunch of every last leaf beneath his boot, "you've formed some opinions, haven't you?"

"I told you, I haven't 'formed' anything. Look, I'd just

like to take myself and my chimpanzee out of here, all right? Come on, Fred." A nervous huff spilled off her lips. "Fred, *come!*"

She sidestepped him to motion more urgently to her pet. Against his better judgment, Damien made the steps with her. He wasn't done with her yet, he decided belligerently. He wasn't done with this insolent Scottney who had walked herself into the lion's den he'd clearly warned her away from. *His* den. Meaning he had the right to bare his teeth at her.

Teeth he'd wanted to sink into the Scottneys for six long, damned months.

"The possibilities *are* endless, wouldn't you say, princess?" he drawled with all-too-feigned gallantry. "After all, I live here alone, without a soul to bother me or police me. But you didn't know that, did you?"

"No," she retorted, lying as clearly as she stood there. She frantically darted her gaze, looking for her chimp.

"No matter. You have, after all, been warned of my need for privacy in a firsthand manner." A stroke of sardonicism inspired the sensual purr of his next words. "Perhaps you've even wondered what I've done about the people who didn't respect that need."

He didn't expect her, of all women, to swoon at that. But nor did he anticipate her to erupt in such explicit anger, as her chimp reappeared and she snapped a commanding finger to put the queen herself to shame. "Fred, get over here. We're leaving Mr. Sharpe and his forest of delusions. *Now.*"

But Fred, it seemed, had other plans, for which Damien suddenly found himself glad. The moment she began to stomp toward the chimp, who had decided a fallen log needed investigating before they departed, Damien caught her around the waist. He used the momentum of her determined stride to swing her around and pin her against a broad oak tree.

"What on—" came her spitting, seething reaction. "Let me go!"

Damien retaliated with a slow, feral smile. "I don't think so. No, not yet. Not until we discuss just who has the delusions around here."

A snarl erupted from her throat. Damien's smile spread wider. God, this felt good, so damn good to have the upper hand over a Scottney once more. The exultation coursed through his veins, leading him to press his advantage— literally. He leaned his whole body into the purpose of holding her against that tree, halting only when his face loomed but inches over hers.

"You—damnable—barbarian," she bit out then.

"Well," he murmured back, "at least we're in agreement about something."

"What the hell does *that* mean?"

"Because that's just what I am, my lady. A damnable, dangerous barbarian"—he leaned and smiled against her temple then—"who's now got you trapped in my lair."

"Let me go."

He almost heeded her demand—because suddenly, his own senses screamed for that separation. Damien swallowed against a terrifying mix of frustration and stimulation . . . dear God, and stimulation. The rush of sensation was intense and primal, battle triumph now heated with sexual awakening, the yearning to bolt away from her yet the craving to thoroughly conquer her.

His vacillation made him more vulnerable by the minute. He had to launch another offensive on this cunning, beautiful opponent. *Now*.

"The Indians of your Great Plains are private people, too, aren't they?" Before his lips finished the query, they curved in a predatory smile. He lifted his hand to her hair as he delivered the final stroke of the assault. "They scalp their violators, don't they?"

"Mr. Sharpe, I asked you to—"

"And the ancient Celts . . ." he went on with ruthless ease, working his fingers to her nape. "Their invaders were drawn and quartered. Interesting, don't you think?"

"Let me *go*."

"But the conversation is getting so interesting, princess." His voice descended into a husky sibilance, for while he spoke to her of violence, he moved against her in suggestion of just the opposite, of creating life. "I'd like to know *your* thoughts on this matter."

"Let me *go*!"

This time Damien complied with her. At the same time, she shoved desperately against him. The result was a thrust of her hand forceful enough to catch him soundly on the jaw, jarring what little perspective he maintained on the situation, while still propelling her free from him and the tree. She stumbled back, legs working to regain her balance, but instead, she transformed her skirts from a wrinkled mess into a hopeless tangle.

Too late, he wrestled to catch her. And too late, he saw the twined tree roots jutting through the soil behind her—

Waiting to snag her foot.

Waiting for her to fall hard against them.

Breath held, Damien awaited her ensuing oath—for once she shrieked at him with that, he could start his own swearing at her stupidity. And damn it, would he give her an earful. The little idiot. The meddling, intrusive little idiot!

The little idiot who now also remained ominously quiet. Much too quiet.

And still lay heaped on the ground, much too motion-less.

"Christ. Ah, *Christ*."

Kira's brow furrowed of its own accord in response to the rasped words, emitted somewhere to her right and sounding like they came from Sharpe himself. But obviously, her ears had been as damaged by the fall as her now-throbbing ankle. Damien did *not* say those words. Too much urgency seized the tone. Too much concern turned the last syllable more into a broken breath. Too much fevered swiftness marked the leaf rustlings and dirt churnings that followed, bringing the oath-maker to her side before she took two more breaths.

Kira wondered who that person was. Damien Sharpe would race to rob a grave before he raced to be by *her* side.

Yet when she opened her eyes, he filled her vision. His own eyes, still endlessly black as the depths of this forest, bore into hers without blinking. His hand, big and rough, engulfed hers, but she didn't remember him taking hold of it in the first place.

She wondered if she'd taken a harder fall than she thought, and she was imagining all this. Yes, that had to be the explanation, she thought with satisfaction. She was dreaming, and he really wasn't here, kneeling next to her, staring at her as if she actually mattered to him—

"What the bloody *hell* did you think you were doing!"

That was more like it.

Oh yes, Kira confirmed, she'd definitely been hallucinating. The man followed his snarl with a glare so intense, she almost laughed at the distorted absurdity of his features.

"Good heavens," she blurted. "You'd better be careful,

Mr. Sharpe. Fred may confuse you with one of his cousins and decide to follow you home."

She decided to giggle at the quip, after all. Sharpe did *not* share her mirth. His lips screwing into an agitated grimace, he instead shot to his feet, pulling her up like a rag doll as he did.

That was when she attempted to step down on her left foot, and found she couldn't. Her options in the next instant were clear: Cling to Sharpe for balance, or tumble to the rocks and tree roots again. Despite the bruises on her thighs and the pain now shooting up from her ankle, Kira almost opted for the latter.

The instant after that, Sharpe helped render the decision. He clasped one hand firmly around her waist, while the other steadied her balance at the most logical point of contact—the top of her hip.

Kira went utterly still the moment he touched her there. Just the sight of the man's hand on her body—*there* on her body—brought a strangely weak yet wonderful feeling to her limbs. The sensation was a more intense version of what she'd experienced the first moment he'd loomed over her . . . an awareness of her smallness next to him, her womanliness next to him. Yes, this feeling was just the way he'd affected her then, only today she endured thousands of torturous, marvelous tremors because of it.

If only the man himself would notice those quiverings, too. "Damn it to hell," he muttered while jerking aside her skirt and giving her ankle a closer inspection. The problem was, he examined her leg with all the dispassion he'd give the forecannon of a lame horse. A lame, *ugly* horse.

"You're swelling like a soufflé," he said with a growl.

"Then make it apple," she sallied. "Ow! Confound it!" She swatted viciously at his shoulders as well as the hand he prodded against her tender injury. "What are you do-ing?"

As he rose, his features revealed nothing of the answer to that. His brows still slanted low over the gaze he kept directed at her foot; his mouth remained a hard-set slash against his firm-angled jaw. "It doesn't feel broken, but it's one devil of a sprain."

"Thank you, Doc," she drawled. "I wouldn't have been able to figure out the answer on my own."

He grumbled something else; an unintelligible curse of some sort, Kira guessed, though not prompted by or di-rected at her. "Hang on," he directed suddenly, and before she could question what he meant, she found herself swung off her feet, supported in his arms. Without another word, he set off through the trees down a path it seemed he alone discerned. Kira had barely two moments to call back over his massive shoulder to Fred, who followed them in obedi-ent silence.

Kira ruled her pet's behavior as a wise cue. She shut her mouth and kept it shut. She dared not speak out now, when she could see this man's beard stubble more clearly than she could fathom his state of mind.

The silence of her lips intensified the barrage of ques-tions in her head. Where was he taking her? And what was his purpose once they got there? When would he let her leave? Or would he let her leave at all?

Dear saints help her. She'd gotten herself into a world of trouble this time.

She just wondered why that realization didn't make her heart slam in terror against her ribs or her stomach churn with terrified nausea.

As a matter of fact, Kira conceded, she felt quite secure, ensconced in Sharpe's sturdy embrace and broad chest. From where her forehead nearly touched his jaw, she could smell the forest on his skin, the leather of the vest he wore against a simple lawn shirt, the damp hair against his nape. Male smells. Working smells. Everyday smells to her at one time, when she'd join the Menagerie crew for their midday breaks.

And yet . . . the essence was different now. It was different in this wild, ancient wood; it was different on the body of this large, commanding man.

This man, she suddenly comprehended, whom she trusted.

A smile exploded on her lips. *That* was the clarification to her confusion! She *trusted* Damien Sharpe. Yes!

No.

Her instinct issued the mandate—and would not let itself be ignored. *No! He's been hiding in this forest for a reason. They found him standing over the dead body of his wife! They took him to court and put him on trial for that. If not for the lack of evidence, he'd be in prison right now, not carting you off to God knows where.*

Never in her wildest imaginings did she think her expectations would be so wrong. But never did she realize Sharpe had such an incredible destination in mind. Not ever would she have dreamed he'd step forth from the trees onto a plane of flat, moss-covered rock, then stop because even he had to take in a breath at the grandeur of the scene before them.

The rock ledge jutted out over a swath of green grass as thick as a bolt of new velvet, only much more luxurious. Edging that miniature meadow were the entwined roots of several trees, which Kira took cautious note of before raising her sights to their boughs, leafy and abundant, spilling over the iridescent layers of a dancing stream. The stream was fed by a pool more stunning than any decorative reservoir she'd seen in London, its satinlike waters swirling in patterns dictated by a silver wand of a waterfall.

Kira took in the scene with equal parts of awe and joy. It had been a long time since her heart had halted from the force of sheer beauty. But it had been longer since her heart felt as if it had come home.

The impressions grew stronger as Sharpe made his way down a narrow dirt path to their right. Fred romped ahead and had nearly finished his exploration of the grass patch by the time they arrived. Kira smiled at her pet's antics and issued a soft "Go ahead" at the chimp's questioning glance. Fred took the words and literally ran with them, scrambling up the trunk of one of the waterside trees, happy grunts indicating his progress into the boughs. A truly contented smile bloomed on her own lips, as well.

Until Sharpe set her down.

Kira winced once more as he bent to settle her on a boulder near the water, but lost an inch of his footing on some moss and ended up plopping her on the rock, instead. Her ankle bumped against the stone in the process.

"Sorry," he emitted on his own wince. "Hell. I'm sorry."

"Oh," Kira quipped in return, her smile returning, "you should be flogged at the least."

Sharpe didn't react to that, instead returning his cobalt gaze back to her leg. "There's no other way to do this," he stated then with a similar dose of efficient coldness. "I shall try to have a lighter hand this time."

Before Kira could query what he was about, he cupped her ankle with one hand while gingerly unhooking her boot buttons with the other. After he slid the shoe off, he turned his attention to her stocking . . . after, of course, he moved his hands up to her knee with as much gentlemanly decorum as possible.

But nothing inside Kira felt decorous during those moments. Nothing at all. His fingers barely touched her skin, yet those unintended grazings were the exact cause of her involuntary tinglings, racing their way up her leg . . . and collecting in the private depths between her legs. Before she could contain it, a shuddering breath escaped her in response, releasing a rush of heat across her face, as well.

"I'm *sorry*," Sharpe roughly answered her exhalation. "There's no way to divert some of the pain."

Kira suppressed the urge to let out more demented laughter. Instead, she said on another wobbling breath, "You're not hurting me."

If she'd told him the waters had turned to wine, his hands wouldn't have halted against her flesh with such sudden stiffness. The gaze he raised back to her wouldn't be permeated with half the unblinking intensity he focused on her now. And he'd be breathing, Kira affirmed, not as statue-still as he was now, making it maddeningly easy to fill her own gaze with his hewn, bold features and his untamed waves of black, black hair.

Breathing . . . yes, perhaps *she'd* be breathing now, too.

Perhaps that was why the sound of her own voice sent her stomach into a somersault of surprise. "I can see why you're such a monster about protecting this place." She even managed to circle an admiring gaze around the verdant borders of the glen. "It's beautiful here."

She was too late with the second half of her comment. Or perhaps the praise wouldn't have made a difference in the words she received as reply to the former. "I'm a monster for many reasons."

If not for his guttural delivery, the man might as well have been affirming he was a chimney sweep. For one instant, the contradiction jerked Kira's sights back to him with the swiftness caused only by unguarded shock.

But only for an instant. Kira hadn't made it to her eighteenth birthday without learning to keep her head when a beast challenged her with the unexpected. So what if *this* brute had hands that felt wondrous as they laved water over her ankle . . . and a torso she easily imagined touching, now that a breeze tugged his shirt away from his body, allowing her glimpses of his dark-haired chest . . .

"Sharpe," she heard herself say, dragging out the name's beginning, turning its end more into a puff of air than a note of punctuation.

"Hmmm?" came his answering murmur, equally soft . . . as gentle as the continuing ministrations of his fingers. The man was turning her attempt at composure into a hopeless fiasco. Between his fingers and his voice, he easily coaxed words from her. Unbelievable, unconscionable words.

Yet out those words came, uncaring of what he'd think of her or do to her for so baldly hurling them at him. "Did you . . . kill her?"

A pulse beat in his temple once. Only once. "No."

"Did you . . . love her?"

This time, the pulse beat twice. "No. I didn't."

He'd barely moved his lips or raised his voice, but Kira heard the answer clearly as a choir. She swayed slightly with her answering shock to it. But this blow was much more deep and disturbing than the other jolts he'd dealt her already. For what reeled her senses this time hadn't been his admission—

But her heart's rush of joy as he made it.

By Satan and all his hounds, what was this hoyden doing to him now?

The demand whirled through Damien's brain like a tempest of leaves in a March wind—much like the gust that invaded the glen then, bringing a chaos of tree castoffs in its wake. Pine needles, acorns, and dried foliage husks sprinkled the air behind Kira Scottney's head . . . behind the eyes that seared his soul with every whimsical, wonderful glance. And behind her lips, too—those lips spouting such egregious questions, he should hurl her into the stream like the slick little carp she was.

Instead, he *answered* her damnable queries. Good Christ, he'd answered her *honestly.*

Oh, Nicky, came the inward snarl, mingling effortlessly with his frantic confusion. *You've trained this one well. She's taking careful notes for you somewhere behind that entrancing almond gaze, and I don't give a bloody damn. I don't give a damn about anything except how right she looks on this rock, next to me now . . . about how good her skin feels beneath my fingers . . . about how good it feels to touch anybody again.*

God . . . God, when was the last time he'd just talked to a woman like this? When was the last time someone had just let him be a gentleman?

When was the last time someone believed he *could* be?

A sensation assaulted his lungs then, slicing his breath in half. The sensation was so foreign, it took him half a minute to recognize the intruder and another half a minute to repress his responding laughter to it.

He was nervous.

The revelation returned his heartbeat to him but didn't prevent an awkward gulp from thudding down his throat as prelude to his next clumsy mumble. "How—how does it feel now?" He gently prodded her foot.

"Fine" came Kira's quick answer—sounding as if her nerves danced at the mercy of the same fiddler as his.

Certainly enough, Damien kicked a glance up at her

face, to see she already fixed *him* with a stare so open, so unschooled, he saw clear through to the thoughts inciting it. And he detected not a trace of terror in those thoughts. She was afraid, yes, but not terrified. He also noticed that the anxious sheen sparked brighter each time his fingers trailed along her foot. When he lingered an extra moment during one caress, a consuming shiver also claimed her.

He almost stopped then. He should have stopped then. But the triumphant tremors that claimed his own senses attacked his self-control with equal greed. Good Christ, he couldn't remember when he had last induced a woman to shivers with his touch. Long before conceding to the logic that had guided his pursuit of Rachelle. Long before any of the entanglements full of skillful sex with practiced partners who shivered during appropriate cresendoes in their play-acts of love.

But when *this* woman trembled for him—this unmannered, unpretentious, and thoroughly unpredictable woman . . .

It made him wonder what would happen if he lingered again.

So halfway down the bridge of her foot, he slowed his fingers once more.

Kira Scottney didn't bite her lip.

She was too busy releasing an unsteady sigh.

The sound impacted Damien like an intoxicating summer wind. He didn't have to wonder at the breeze's influence on his body. He had but to watch this woman's eyes blink slowly, drugging him with their hooded, dark brandy pools . . . the eyes that gave him the courage to press not only his fingers but his whole hand around her foot.

Kira sucked in another ragged breath. Still, her gasp was so intense that he slackened his hold until only the tips of his fingers still touched her. "Am I . . . hurting you again?" True concern underlined his query.

"N-no."

Only as she issued the reply did he realize how deeply he'd hoped for it and how heady the affirmation would be at hearing it. Ah God, this was insanity, thinking he could play the tender suitor again; thinking Kira Scottney would be his willing leading lady; thinking her suddenly bashful murmur and averted eyes meant his nearness made her senses career in confusion, too.

Yes, he was courting madness. Because he was courting nothing. A reckless dervish. A chimpanzee's mother. The side-slip spawn of the man who had led the cause to ruin his life. A dream. Not even a very comfortable dream, at that.

Nonetheless, he didn't want to wake up yet.

"Then am I . . . tickling you?" He heard the humor sneaking into his tone this time but managed to prevent his lips from surrendering to it.

Flickerings of a smile played at her own lips. "No." She drew the word out as she tilted her head back. "No, it feels . . . nice."

It was Damien's turn to fumble for breath. He returned the pads of his fingers to her skin. "Nice?"

"Mmmm-hmmm."

Another breeze rippled the branches overhead. Another current of awareness crackled between them. Leaves rained down. His heartbeat thundered louder. In the distance of his brain, alarmed screams sounded.

Listen to them, some desperate voice implored him. *Listen to them before it's too late!*

"Do you . . . want me to stop?" he asked her in the barest of murmurs.

Her first reaction came with miniature explosions in her

eyes: hot gold sparks screaming at him *no!* But her lips moved a moment later, stammering "Y-yes. Yes, I think . . . thank you; I think perhaps you'd better."

Damien lowered his gaze and nodded hesitant agreement. He shifted his hand to cup the heel of her foot again, taking care to slide his fingers as gently as possible along the way.

In direct contrast to the ruthless spray of water she kicked into his chest with her opposite foot.

"What the bloody—" he choked, gaping at her smug expression.

Not a trace of surprise tinged the hoyden's features, however. Nor remorse. As a matter of fact, she stated with the peace of a damnable angel, "*That* tickled."

Damien stared at her. Hard.

She gazed back. Innocently.

"That tickled," he finally repeated. He finished with an expectant upturn of brows.

"Yes."

"And do you do this to everyone who tickles you?" His pitch contained equal parts amusement and sarcasm. It was an accurate embodiment of the sensations doing battle in his brain.

"Not everyone," she qualified while diverting her gaze to study the length of the waterfall. "Only grouches who need to have their scowls rearranged a bit."

So blithely did she issue the imputation that Damien didn't immediately recognize it as such. Then a rankled growl rumbled up his throat. "Who the devil are you calling—"

Another wet blast cut him short, though she didn't even veer her gaze to hit her mark this time. "You're scowling again."

Damien truly found himself wishing Nicholas had been

a good little libertine and sired a male bastard. He couldn't give this wench her true come-uppance, even if she used that talented foot on his face. There was simply no way to gain vengeance upon the self-sure little Scottney yet retain the few tatters of decency to *his* name.

No way except one.

Not hesitating another second, Damien scooped a hand into the stream, gathering enough water to properly douse her ladyship's all-too-tranquil face.

Her stunned outcry filled him with more satisfaction than he expected. But he hadn't expected the gleaming droplets on her eyelashes to make her appear even more a dew-kissed wood sprite, nor the flecks of fire in those eyes to spark with such unfettered defiance. Such mesmerizing defiance.

Such mischievous glee.

He detected the ensuing upturn to her lips a moment too late—the moment she used to turn her own hand into a substitute paddle and jab a thick spray of water across everything from his waist down.

But Damien hardly felt the soaked chill in his legs. Not when he had the music of her ensuing giggle to distract him—and to warm him. Oh yes, to warm him as he hadn't been warmed in so many years . . . from the inside out.

The effect on his body was instant and exhilarating. He felt like bellowing into the trees. He felt like *climbing* into the trees, swinging from the branches with her impudent chimp.

Instead, he forced himself to arch one brow and slowly pronounce, "You've declared war, madam."

The woman next to him angled up her own dark-auburn brow. "Perhaps I have."

Before she was finished, Damien bent again to the water. But Kira Scottney, he rapidly discovered, was capable of maintaining an angel's countenance while devising a devil's scheme. She waited until he reached his lowest point over the water before sweeping another small squall into his chest and face.

He waited for rage to flood him with equal alacrity. The wrath never ignited. Another kind of heat formed behind the curling ends of his lips—the same inner warmth she'd introduced him to moments ago, only this time, dear Christ, the heat remained.

This time, dear Christ, the heat grew. It swelled into a magnificent tidal wave that cascaded down his body and flooded him as he sent a massive retaliating splash. The action instigated the start of a water skirmish that, had the great painter Joseph Turner been witness to, would have been immortalized on canvas to preserve its glory. It seemed an impossible phenomenon, but it was true: The more this woman soaked him with her kicks and splashes, the higher she stoked the flames rampaging his senses and his mind.

She made him smile with her tempest of giggles. She made him start with her unabashed baring of knees as she yanked up her skirts to better attack him. She made him think—really think—in order to counter the astute strategy she utilized to soak him completely.

Then, in one flash of a precious moment, she made him forget.

She made him forget who he was. Who *she* was.

In that moment, Damien laughed for the first time in six months.

Sixteen

THE MAN'S SMILES didn't near the brilliance of his laugh. Kira's own laughter halted in her throat as she sat and watched the beauty of his mirth illuminate this shadowed glen to the radiance of a sun-dappled meadow.

A meadow that darkened again all too rapidly.

As spontaneous as his laughter had come, it was eclipsed by a stare of hard anger. He directed the look at her but somehow, she knew, Sharpe intended it more toward himself. As if he'd again broken some law applicable only to the kingdom of his soul.

Kira dropped her own gaze then as a sudden downpour of hopelessness inundated her. The feeling chilled her, and she trembled from the illogical but inescapable grief.

Just yesterday she'd raved at this man about trusting someone—if not her, then *someone*. Her anger had been ignited by the assumption he simply wouldn't do that.

Now she realized he *couldn't* do that. Dear God . . . this man had lost more than his lands and his honor six months ago.

So much more.

"I—I think I should go now." She tried to steady the rasp of her voice while sliding slowly from the boulder. "My ankle feels much better, and—"

"And you're shivering like an icicle in a morning wind." Sharpe cut her off in a tone sounding more command than observation. He swung around her, halting her path with his firm-footed stance. "You look like one, too," he appended, curving one finger beneath her chin, raising her gaze back to him.

The sight of his face, now realigned into its usual veneer of untouchable composure, deepened the chill of her sadness and the intensity of her shiverings. To *that*, the man responded with one cluck of his tongue, then a softly drawled, "Princess . . . you're a real mess."

"Thanks," Kira snapped, yanking her chin away with equal pique. "I'll be sure to invite you to my show when I'm looking for a son of a bitch to help generate bad reviews." She ignored the confused frown she generated on his face to shout into the trees, "Fred! Fred, get down now. It's time to—"

But as if the man in front of her had dominion over the heavens, as well, an ominous rumble of thunder doused the rest of her words. Looking up higher, Kira beheld bundles of dark-gray clouds, the promise of a deluge evident in their rolling girths.

"That's it, princess," Sharpe murmured matter-of-factly. "It's going to dump like Noah's flood any second now, and you've got the beginnings of a cold at best. I'll not have Papa Nicky blaming me for pneumonia, as well."

Before she could form half a question about what the tarnation he was getting at, she found herself hoisted off her feet once more and pressed again to the man's chest. At that moment his prediction came to pass. Fat raindrops plopped around them with increasingly steady fervor.

Sharpe moved forward with confident strides, crossing the water about ten yards downstream, where a row of slick stones formed a natural bridge of sorts.

At the other side, it occurred to Kira that she should protest their progress until he informed her where he was headed. In the next moment, she confessed she didn't care. Whatever destination Sharpe had in mind, she knew she would be safe there.

Again she confessed the strange but sure conviction that she trusted this man.

Sharpe himself confirmed her belief wasn't so wide off the mark when he abruptly halted, even though the rain shower threatened to become a full downpour any moment. To Kira's questioning glance, he explained, "Just making sure Fred gets across in one piece, too."

"Thank you," she replied softly. The words were shillings representing a fortune's worth of gratitude. That was why she repeated more boldly, lifting her hand to his face this time, "Damien . . . thank you."

Though Fred now rolled delightedly in the mud at his feet, the man didn't move on. "You're welcome," he murmured back, responding to her gaze as well as her words, his black eyes emanating an intense message from their depths.

A message telling her he was just as grateful as she was.

Dear God, Kira thought, absorbing the impact of that look into the depths of her heart, *has it been so long since somebody last touched you, Damien Sharpe?*

Sharpe's reaction saddened but didn't surprise her. He flinched back from her hand as if it had become a branding iron proclaiming her contemplation. He turned and now raced the rain through the trees, proceeding on a path only he seemed to know, for Kira couldn't discern any visible trail herself. She merely identified that the blanket of trees got thicker, the depths of the forest got colder, and the rain fell increasingly harder.

Between one blink of her eyes and the next, the lodge seemed to appear. But perhaps the dwelling had been visible for a while and she hadn't recognized it as such. Its angled roof and dark-wood construction had been so clearly designed to complement, rather than stand out from, its lush natural surroundings that it looked like a diminutive cousin of the pines closing in on the dozen stones serving as a front walk.

But as some wise biblical author had said, *Look not on the outward appearance.* Nothing "diminutive" existed about the beauty of the room the man carried her into. Its high ceilings rose over a room populated by six overstuffed sofas, ten equally comfortable chairs, and two sturdy tables, all arranged with artful abandon around a massive stone fireplace that was surely built with the intention of roasting an elephant. If the elephant escaped, it could easily run to hiding places up the broad staircase flanking the wall opposite the fireplace, its banister designed more for function than decoration.

"What-wh—" Kira stammered, interrupting herself to take in the fascinating smaller details of the room: the bookcase full of well-used tomes, the spirits cart stocked with mismatched bottles, the patchwork of rugs across the floor that gave way to an enticing bed of furs in front of the fireplace. "*Where* are we?" she at last revised to her query, turning around on the sofa Sharpe had settled her on.

"Home," he answered with same pragmatic economy he employed to scoop up a sheaf of loose papers on one of the tables. He hastily stuffed them into a wooden box filled with the same. "Or at least what I call such these days."

"It looks as if half of Yorkshire helped decorate it."

"They did, I suppose." In any other conversation, the

statement would have been delivered with a chuckle. Sharpe sounded more like he revealed military secrets under torture. "My father built the place after he returned from his battles in France. He called it the Hunting Lodge, though it was more his excuse to invite thirty friends out for a weekend of rustic cooking, home-stilled spirits, and all the cigars they could puff away before my mum detected the smoke haze on the horizon."

"And all of this is the collected result of those weekends."

"Right."

"A bit too rustic for Rolf's tastes, I suppose."

"Right," he repeated, though Kira didn't miss the way he issued it this time: from a thoroughly clamped jaw.

Through the next moment, she just watched him. She took in the defined angles of his profile, now cast into shades of gold and black by the flames he stirred to life. She looked at the shadows of memory, both pleasant and awful, fall upon the depths of his eyes . . . she recognized the battle for self-control as he inhaled a long, uneven breath. A droplet of rain fell from his hair and trailed down the bridge of his nose.

The yearning to hold him rose in her heart and radiated through her whole being.

She knew how he felt. Saints, did she know how he felt.

"So," she began again, pulling in a deep breath of her own and praying for its calming effect through the tumult of her limbs, "I take it you continued your father's tradition."

She reaped the tiniest of smiles on the man's full lips. "Of course."

Another moment passed. Kira couldn't drag her stare away from his lips. Curved in that mysterious expression, the sight of the man's mouth had a maddening effect on her senses. A racing yet weakening effect at the same time.

An effect that brought a giddy smile to her face, too.

As that feeling blossomed fully inside, she felt the barriers to her innermost feelings fading in its radiance. "I love it here," she confessed without hesitation.

Sharpe's humorless laugh cut through the air. "That's heartening to know, princess," he followed with an equally sardonic slant.

Kira didn't let either of the actions hinder the mischievous smirk she tilted then. "So do you have any cigars around now?"

Sharpe shot her only a cursory glance in return—until he observed how serious she really was about the suggestion. His smile grew into a full grin, and Kira triumphed at the laugh she just about coaxed from him, too—

But he yanked the laugh back at the last moment. Instead, he crossed to a closet built into the underside of the stairway. "I have *this*," he told her, producing a maroon satin smoking jacket that had to be one of the most luxurious garments Kira had ever beheld. "It shall benefit you infinitely more than a cigar."

"I'm not going to argue with that," she replied in awe as he handed her the ornate garment.

"Well. There really is a first time for everything."

"Hmmm?" Already anticipating the decadent pleasure of the robe's warmth, she only faintly heeded his remark.

"Nothing." The hint of a laugh again snuck into his tone. "I've got to fetch more firewood. While I'm gone, get out of your wet things and put it on."

"Aye aye, Captain." She gave him a zealous flourish of a salute and a wide beam of a smile.

Sharpe didn't salute back. But he did smile once more, before disappearing out into the rain. He took no lamp with him. But if he wielded the full power of that smile, Kira mused, it stood to reason he didn't need another light source.

That thought kept her own lips fixed in an upward bend throughout the shucking of her cloak and fan-front bodice. Yet as she worked at the back hooks of her skirt, she gave in to a long sigh of bewilderment.

How was it possible for one man to possess such a spectrum of personality?

Ally had called Sharpe trouble. Tom glared at him like Satan incarnate. The rest of Yorkshire County knew him as wife killer, acquittal or not. The man himself hardly helped to negate the images. He was unbending and impenetrable, a secret with legs, an uncharted territory who posted the same sign on his soul that he did on his forest: NO TRESPASSERS ALLOWED.

And yet . . . Kira had never seen anyone calm a skittish cockatoo with such instinctual gentleness.

Nobody she'd ever known had stopped in the middle of an encroaching rainstorm to check on the safety of her chimpanzee.

And *nobody* had warmed her whole body by dipping her ankle in an icy stream. Or glided his fingers up her leg with such deliberating grace. . . .

Touching her as a man touched a woman.

Kira's arms slackened to her sides as she remembered those moments next to the stream. She remembered the thunder of the waterfall in her ears . . . the thunder of her blood in her veins . . . the thunder of awakening sensation in parts of her body she'd never imagined.

Thunder crashed suddenly over the forest.

She jolted out of her reverie with a stunned gasp. No, she thought, the clouds had descended to earth and collided *in* the forest, so thoroughly did the booms fill the air for a very long moment.

But then the thunder came accompanied by a damp, cool wind.

And she realized the storm sounded so loud because the door of the lodge had been opened again. She realized a figure now dominated that portal, large and rugged and dark against the wet emerald world beyond. And silent. He stood there so tense and silent, and just stared at her . . .

That was when the last realization struck her—like a stampeding *herd* of elephants.

She stood there before Damien Sharpe with a smoking robe clasped in her hands and nothing but her drawers and corset clinging to her damp body.

Damien felt rain droplets fall from his hair and trickle down his back, but he couldn't shake his stare, let alone his whole head. The weight of the ten logs began to burn the muscles of his upper arms and shoulders, but he gripped the wood like an armful of diamonds . . . or a makeshift battle shield.

God, yes, he decided, a battle shield; for war *was* what he waged here—an agonizing war between the sight before him and what his body wanted him to do about it. Between the half-nude nearness of Kira Scottney and his instant craving to turn that proximity into intimacy.

Between his craving to satisfy his first surge of desire in well over a year . . .

And the look on her face that said she'd let him.

Seventeen

"I'M—SORRY," HE BLURTED at last, and clenched his jaw against a surge of fury at the damnable, beautiful chit for making him stammer like an untouched whelp. "I should have knocked—"

"Hogwash," she cut him off. She followed by shrugging as if she'd donned a kitchen apron to protect her gown instead of a smoking jacket to shield her nakedness. "It *is* your home, and I was dallying instead of dressing."

Damien's eyebrows bunched together as he considered that. Were all American women as frustratingly logical in the midst of being so tempting?

After a minute of rumination, the answer became no clearer, and was now eclipsed by the growing aches in his arms. Deferring to the call of instinct, he no longer hesitated about proceeding to the fireplace to deposit the logs in the wood box.

The intuition, he admitted, hadn't been so difficult to obey. The ease with which *she'd* slipped back into propriety, as if her state of undress had been more natural than iniquitous, once more made him a man in control of his urges.

At least as controlled as he could be when standing alone with a wood nymph sheathed in his smoking jacket and not much else.

"So . . ." he ventured, congratulating himself on the steady stretch of his hands toward the flames, "is dilly-dallying a regular habit for you, Lady Kira?"

"My mama preferred to call it daydreaming." She chuckled softly.

"Ah." He drew the syllable out. "And . . . what were you dreaming of just now?"

To his startlement, the question threw a rain cloud over her sunny expression. "Nothing," she muttered. "Nothing of great importance."

Her reaction fell far short of satisfying his curiosity—an intrigue he could explain no more clearly than the source of his next persisting question. "Were you dreaming about your show?"

She fired him a stunned stare. "How did you know about that?"

"Directly from the source." Though threads of sarcasm laced his tone and small smile, Damien attempted to share his mirth with her rather than fling it at her. "Or don't you remember? I think your exact words were, 'I'll be sure to invite you to my show when I'm looking for a son of a bitch to help generate bad reviews.'"

At that, her mouth pursed in mortification. "I did say that, didn't I?"

"Rather well."

She gave him an adorable version of an apologetic smile. "My mouth doesn't always mind my head, Mr. Sharpe."

"Thank God," Damien returned. Her answering chuckle rewarded his benevolence with a warmth that inundated his chest. After a moment of easy silence, he offered, "I'll be bold enough to conjecture your tongue is connected more closely to your *heart*, Lady Kira."

Now she slanted him a twinkling glance. "I suppose it is."

"And is that where your heart lies? With this 'show'?"

Solemnity straightened her posture again, but this time the stance was born of pride, not apprehension. "Yes," she answered him after a lengthy pause. Then with gathering conviction: "*Yes*. It—it's not that I don't think your country is beautiful, because it *is*—"

"Yes," he interjected with quiet conviction, "it is."

"—but I've got members of a family in *my* country. Now my father has given me a way to gather them and keep them together again. In exchange for a year of my life here, Father will give me the backing to form the most prestigious circus in the world. We'll not just rival the best, we'll *be* the best."

For a small explosion of a moment, her enthusiasm became a living force in the room, sparking excitement even in Damien's gut before she aimed her happy gaze back toward the flames dancing in the fireplace. "Most important," she finished in a satisfied murmur, "we'll be together again."

She barely took a breath after that, so deeply did she plunge into the haven of her dreams. It came as little wonder that she didn't notice Damien indulging in a long stare of her before he spoke again.

"Together again," he reiterated. "Just as you all were before, eh?"

"Yes," she answered, a smile growing on her lips. "Yes. Exactly as we were."

"And you'll be happy then?"

"I'll be very happy then."

So emphatically did she issue the rejoinder, Damien almost felt reprimanded rather than reaffirmed. That was when astonishment struck him—and a surge of anger. The woman truly couldn't be so daft. No, despite all the antics he'd seen Kira Scottney instigate, not once had he thought her a halfwit. She couldn't sincerely believe if she surrounded herself once more with the facades of her old life, those false fronts would transform from canvas, paint, and nails into happiness, joy, and satisfaction.

She was dreaming. Dreaming dangerously. The past *was* one of those scenery flats, burned down to its foundations. The past could *not* be reconstructed again.

Nobody knew that better than him.

Damien clenched his jaw as the fury raged hotter inside him, as it always did when he forced himself to eye the bitter truth of his fate head on. But he managed to gain control again within a handful of deep breaths, telling himself he might as well turn her ladyship back out into the forest if he was only going to sit here and smolder at her.

No, that wouldn't do at all. He had to say something to her. He had to save her from the silliness of her fantasies.

Just as he wished someone would have saved him from his.

"So," he said. Just that. *Superb*, came the inward jeer, as he shifted on his feet and admitted to the strange sensation of . . . nervousness. *Simply, bloody superb. You've saved her now, Sir Lancelot.*

If only she wasn't so close. And so damnably unaware of how lovely the crimson of the robe looked against the cream of her skin.

"So," she repeated, not helping his dilemma by slanting a look at him full of the same curiosity in her tone . . . only infinitely more entrancing. The depths of her eyes pulled in the hues of the firelight and were filled with more golden magic than he thought possible in a woman who wasn't some artist's fabrication.

For a moment, Damien gave his senses permission to swim in those deep, dark-gold depths; to experience their radiance inside of himself as well as outside. Then he released an amazed laugh, for the moment at last presented him with *words*.

"So," he began again, bracing an elbow to the mantel with at least a measure of renewed confidence. "Absolutely nothing can persuade you to stay in Yorkshire?"

"No," she replied, though a slight breath wobbled the word. "No. Nothing."

"And . . . nobody, either, I suppose."

"Nobody, either."

He would have dismissed the hesitation in her voice to the bumblings of his own senses—had he not witnessed the vacillation in her gaze at that moment. Oh yes, he verified, she vacillated, all right; just as her sights urgently swerved around him now, searching for an object, *any* object, to free her from the heavy haze of awareness settling between them. The air grew more potent by the moment . . . more heated by the moment.

Nobody can persuade me to stay here.

Then why, princess, do you quiver as I step nearer to you? Why do you frantically nibble the insides of your lips, making your mouth so irresistable? Why do your eyes flutter shut, as if expecting me to say something, to do something . . .

"Perhaps," he heard himself say, the sound emanating from his gut more than the lips hovering a breath over hers, "that's for the best."

"Y-yes . . . for the . . ."

She said no more. Damien robbed the remaining sound off her lips with the passionate downsweep of his own.

She tasted like rain and wind, like wetness and wildness,

her mouth a more delicious maelstrom than he ever imagined or dreamed. And yes, he *had* dreamed of this moment, he confessed now without compunction as he kissed her deeper still. Because now he knew how minuscule his fantasies had been compared to the reality of having this woman in his arms, against his body.

At last, he reluctantly pulled away and gazed into her face. He raised an exploring hand to her cheek as he took in the lights now glimmering in her gaze, almost painful in their intensity; as he explored the damp smoothness of her skin; as he watched her release a ragged sigh when his fingers traveled over a vein in her neck, pulsing out the evidence of what her own body experienced in this unbelievable moment. This moment, he now saw, she'd been dreaming about, too . . . perhaps, like him, since those first sleepless hours after she'd careened into his world.

Damien curled a bewildered smile at that thought. Officially, an "accident" had been responsible for forcing her life's path across his. Yet now the incident didn't seem an accident at all.

It felt right. So right. As right as she felt, so warm and soft and smooth beneath his touch. Damien wanted to feel more of her.

He slid his fingers beneath the collar of the robe, yearning to shove the damn thing away completely, wanting to unwrap her. Hell, simply *wanting* her in a way he never remembered wanting a woman.

His own breath came raggedly now, terror fusing with need in his veins, rendering him motionless. He hadn't been this awkward even when tumbling his first countess behind a strategic Vauxhall hedgerow! But then, Charisse hadn't been an intrepid, inquisitive little American without a pretentious bone in her body or a status-seeking fiber in her fingernails. Charisse hadn't been able to madden him with one quip of her tongue, then enflame him with one glance full of her fearless spirit.

Who could press closer to him, just as Kira did now, and not appear at all calculating or coy about the action. On the contrary, his little hoyden only brought to life the fulfillment of his deeper fantasies as she let out a soft cry born out of an instinct she didn't understand yet. An instinct he yearned to teach her about.

An instinct now flooding *his* body with undeniable demand. With hard demand.

On a groan of exquisite agony, Damien sealed his lips over hers once more. He curled his hands around her shoulders, wordlessly approving her advance, silently showing her his growing need. Kira responded with an explosion of passion, echoing his moan from a place so deep within her, she trembled. Every inch of their bodies now touched, her damp warmth driving the last of the chill from his skin, her fervor setting a blaze to life in parts of himself he'd thought forever blackened and dead.

"God," Damien grated as that conflagration raged hotter. "Ah, *God*."

Her concurrence with that came as another head-to-toe cry, as she slid her mouth up to his again. She began to move against him with unconscious sensuality, fitting herself around his hardness with a need woven into the very blood and sinew that made her a woman. With every writhing stroke, she stirred his primal hungers into a frenzy he imagined a starved man endured when a king's feast was suddenly his for the taking. His hands raked down her back and cupped her bottom, fitting her more snugly against him. Damien's senses began to burn with one obsession: tasting more of her, having more of her, letting more of her inside his bleak and lonely soul.

And being inside her, too.

Another epithet left his lips at that thought. Madness, he concluded; surely this was what madness felt like, this feeling of being so aware of his body, yet not part of his body at all. This feeling of knowing who he was, yet knowing that person only in terms of dates and figures. That Damien was a distant stranger who couldn't be engulfed by this fire, breathing in the heat of this woman, shuddering from the texture of her skin as he pulled her down with him to the furs at their feet.

When they lay there together, he at last peeled the satin jacket away from the silken beauty of her body. "Ohhh . . ." She sighed, repeating the syllable as he suckled the hollow of her throat, nipping his way up the damp column of her neck, rocking against her as his erection throbbed more painfully against the scant fabric barriers between them. He quivered violently—yet upon feeling a corresponding shiver claim her own frame, he nearly stopped.

You've got to douse the blaze, now, *idiot!* he forced his brain to bellow at his body. *She's frightened and shaking, and you're half a minute away from adding "rapist" to your reputation around here!*

But then she whispered his name. Breathlessly. Imploringly.

She slid her hands from his back to his buttocks. Urgently. Unthinkingly.

She repeated his name again. Directly into his ear. And this time added one word that incinerated his endeavor at self-suppression in a bonfire of pure desire.

"Please," she rasped. "Damien, *please.*"

He was lost. Lost to that fevered flood she made of his blood, racing hot and uncontrolled through him; lost to the amazed realization that she didn't shake in fear but in passion. Then he was lost to the ecstatic comprehension that came after that. Kira trusted him. She *wanted* him to take her; here, now; with the same drenching intensity as the storm pummeling the world around them. Crashing together with the magic of lightning and the force of thunder.

Crashing.

Something was crashing outside. Loudly.

A dog's frantic barks interspersed with the sound. *His* dog's barks.

"What the bloody—"

Damien had a chance to discern the door didn't burst open by itself. Two wet-furred forms took credit for figuring out how to flip up the portal's simple bar closure, then celebrating their achievement by erupting into the room with all the cackling, barking glee of ancient savages. Only these invaders rendered twice the damage.

"Good Christ!" he bellowed as the forms bounded over an arm of the sofa, refurbishing the thing in fresh mud puddle before discovering where their *real* conquests lay. Down to the floor they bounded, still chasing each other as they attempted to greet him and Kira with as much slobber as possible.

"Hamlet!" he shouted, to no effect. The Labrador got in three hearty licks to his face then moved on to the greater challenge of bestowing the same to the chimp, who insisted the two of them play a rowdy version of peek-a-boo first— using Kira as their peeking shield. Damien wished he could admit shock as a reaction upon witnessing the woman not only oblige them the game but join the pair of mud balls in their sport. In truth, the surprise would have come if she'd done anything else.

Even so, in under a minute he found himself working to hold back his own grin at viewing the three of them tussling in undomesticated abandon, cooings and pantings and giggles blending into a din that filled the room. The heat took just another thirty seconds to permeate his chest, as well. The sensation spread so swiftly across his heart, Damien lifted a hand to the area, pressing it in confused irritation.

Hell. If any region of his body deserved to be buggered about this sudden change of the afternoon's plans, it lay farther south than his chest. What the blazes was *this* attack, that it rendered him struggling for air as if a humid tropical storm surrounded them, not a chilled front from the Cheviots?

So immersed in contemplating that conundrum, Damien almost missed the moment Kira's indulgent giggles turned into whole laughs. She did so as Ham made another enthusiastic lunge for the chimp, but crossed his front paws too fast and ended up sprawled in her lap, instead. Deciding to make the best of his predicament, the Labrador gave his new friend an affectionate swipe of muddied paw, then apologized by licking the dirt away. Kira's answering laughter instantly ignited her whole face.

Damien's comprehension instantly clamped around his whole brain. Hard.

He didn't just want this woman with his body.

He hungered for her with his soul.

God, yes; it wasn't just her skin he still tasted in his mouth, but her vitality he still savored in his blood; the joy she took in life because she lived for something other than vengeance. Because she was driven to create and to build, not demean and destroy.

He'd once strived for those goals, too. They were the ideals Father had imbued him with. *I've begun the dream, Damien, and now I pass it to you. I pass this land to you, and all the pride I take in it. I know you dream the dream now, too, and I know you'll honor it. I know you'll honor me.*

But Damien hadn't honored Kenrick Sharpe.

He'd killed him.

Perhaps he hadn't squeezed a trigger or wielded a dagger, but Father's heart hadn't known the difference. After he'd walked free of the York County courtroom, Damien might as well have taken a rifle and loaded it with bullets called scandal, shame, distrust, and eventually, dishonor.

Bullets that Nicholas Scottney and his barristers had helped produce.

Damien jerked backward. Yet his eyes never left the woman who still sat and played so innocently with Fred and Ham. This woman, he now realized, he shouldn't have even invited into his home, let alone his soul.

Or, bloody blazes, considered taking with his body.

For an instant, he let his gaze fall to the mud tracks across the sofa again—and silently promised Ham a place of honor on the bed for the next month. His dog had been the only one to save him from his own reckless stupidity.

Moments after that recognition slammed its full force into him, Damien made a second vow: Ham would not be called on to rescue his sorry arse again.

The mission to honor that pledge began now—no matter how inviting Kira's twinkling gaze was as she looked up to him once more. "Damien Sharpe," she said, the hint of a laugh tinting her voice, "you're not turning into a moping gargoyle again, are you?" She gave a teasing huff. "Come here, gargoyle. I think your handsome friend wishes a proper introduction."

So much for nominating Ham for knighthood. *Dog*, Damien decided, would serve fine to describe the traitor who now reveled in the woman's scratches behind his right ear. At the same time, the chimp enjoyed some gentle rufflings at his nape. The three of them formed a portrait of a perfectly cozy, if perfectly bizarre, little family.

The fire of conflict sucked the air from his lungs once

more. He was *not* a family man, Damien told himself. He hadn't been for six months. He could never be, as long as Rachelle's killer walked this earth beneath a guise of innocence while he trudged it beneath a stigma of guilt. Especially when *her* family had the best cause to believe—and enforce—that stigma.

"No," he said to her at last, glad of the fact he hadn't even made an effort to sound so dead and cold. "No, I don't think that's wise, my lady."

"My lady," she repeated in the kind of murmur a person used before they got ill. Yet she didn't surprise him when she yanked her chin aloft the next moment. "My name is *Kira*, sir, and I'll thank you to call me that unless I really *am* your lady."

Damien gave no comeback to that. In her own idiosyncratic way, the woman had a rational point.

"I'll also thank you to tell me what the blazing tarnation is wrong, Damien."

He said nothing to that. Pivoting to her clothes, which she'd draped between two chairs, he briskly scooped up the pieces of soiled but warmed fabric.

"It's late," he finally muttered, thrusting the garments at her. The sooner she was covered with them again and out of his life, the better. "Yes," he repeated, making it a demand this time, "late. You should be going. Now."

She didn't agree with him. As a matter of fact, had they been opposing lords in Parliament, she would have forced the entire chamber to keep hours until midnight due to her silent protest to his assertion.

She didn't speak until, almost an hour later, Damien carried her across the crest of the high knoll overlooking Scottney Hall. He stood just steps from where he and James had wondered about her mere weeks ago. He looked to the spot where he'd pondered her boldness, her recklessness, her quirkiness . . .

And he inwardly groaned. That day seemed a minute ago yet, at the same time, a lifetime ago.

Because now he knew. Now he knew exactly what kind of a diamond a man held when he stirred this woman to desire. A radiant, fiery treasure of a diamond.

For a splinter of a moment, Damien retightened his hold around Kira. And fought like hell against the urge to whirl back around, return to the lodge, and hoard his jewel forever. *His* jewel, damn it. The prize *he'd* unearthed beneath the recalcitrant hoyden.

A journey he never should have begun in the first place.

That thought effectively helped him bring this hike to an end. He crouched to set Kira down as gently as possible but needn't have bothered with the courtesy. As soon as she was able, she shoved against him and tumbled out of his arms like a cat frantically escaping a trip to the bath. She landed hard on the mushy ground—and her left leg.

"Damn it," Damien growled. The exclamation was inflected with more savagery because he really meant it for himself. Nevertheless, he then fired, "Have a care for what you're doing!"

Kira flung away the arm he proffered. "Do *you* 'have a care,' Mr. Sharpe?"

Touché, he yearned to chuckle darkly. *I deserved that, hoyden.*

And yes, damn you, I do care. No matter how hard I tried to fight you off and order you away, you made me really care again.

And that's why I'm doing this. That's why I'm doing this now . . . before I bruise much more than your ankle and your ego.

"I shouldn't accompany you further," he muttered. "And it looks as if the clouds are clearing off. Can you make it from here?"

"Would you care if I couldn't?"

When he gave her nothing but silence as reply, she raised her gaze to his face, using that one unguarded moment to make certain he beheld the intensity of the pain in her eyes. Damien's senses raged at the confines of his skeleton, but he forced himself to meet her look. Perhaps, he hoped, for a shard of a second she'd peer through the facade of his stare and glimpse once more the man she'd reignited in the lodge.

If she did see anything, Kira didn't let her observation show now. Instead, she bade her chimp to her side with a stiff snap of fingers, then turned from him.

"Don't waste another of your precious thoughts on me, Mr. Sharpe. I've vaulted off speeding horses on worse sprains than this," she informed him with cold calm.

As she took her pet's paw and began limping away, Damien willed his jaw to open, even forced air up from his lungs—only to find his brain a mutinous participant in the endeavor for words, any right words, to say to her.

It's better this way.

He didn't know what part of him produced that announcement, but he knew his gut recognized it as truth, however bitter the dose. At best, Kira was pure danger to his control, with her arrows of adorable Russian tirades, uninhibited readiness to laugh, and intoxicating passions. At worst, she was the gust that would start the hurricane once more, whipping the winds of Yorkshire gossip into a tormenting tempest. And this time he was certain Nicholas Scottney wouldn't rest until the tatters of his honor had become dust in the wind.

Yes, it was all better this way. Better that he had found

the strength to turn her away with his cad's mask firmly in place rather than with tender explanations and agonizing kisses. Better that she abhorred him for that charade.

It was better, Damien commanded himself, that she didn't look back at him once as she neared her home, even though *he* watched *her* until she became an imperceptible dot against Scottney Hall's back garden wall.

Odd, he thought then. If his whole body wasn't clenched so tightly, he might just chuckle at the scene: the grandeur of the Scottney empire swallowing even the identity of its heir apparent.

Though he was certain the effect was only temporary. Once Kira Scottney bestowed a person with her cocky little smile, she climbed under their skin to stay. The first moment she tossed that mane of auburn curls and cracked that impudent grin, her prey was forced not only to acknowledge her identity but to be smitten by it.

As for the man who experienced the sweetness of her kiss . . .

There would be no forgetting her at all. Even if that kiss had been a mistake. A very bad, very dangerous mistake.

Eighteen

A MISTAKE.

He'd considered her a mistake.

The surety of the conclusion blurred Kira's vision as she hobbled toward the garden's back gate, though she swiped angrily at her face several times with the hand she didn't use to pull a weary Fred along. Still, the stinging drops insisted on assaulting her eyes then welling over and sliding down her cold cheeks. And every time one of those tears declared its triumph over her self-control, the tormenting thought came again, too:

A mistake.

Damien might as well have gone ahead and stated it with his lips as well as his eyes. Oh God, his eyes! Why the blazes had she believed it possible to stir embers of warmth or light in those piths of black ice? Why had she even taken the time to look for such? What the devil had she thought she'd find, other than a churl who truly fooled her for the devil, with his taut forehead, clenched jaw, set mouth, and *those damn eyes*. They'd been agonizingly clear in their message, though their depths remained the color of one of the abandoned Swaledale lead mines.

My lady Kira, touching you was a huge mistake. And kissing you . . . well, I must have been out of my mind.

She slammed the gate shut with a hard *whoosh*. Nothing like pain and fury to lend a body some strength when they needed it, she mused grimly. She rushed past the rain-kissed peonies, daisies, and even her beloved pansies without a second glance. Neither did she give half an ear to the rise of twilight wind through the willows, along with the night birds' awakening harmonies. It was an after-storm symphony she'd normally give one arm to savor, but tonight she'd never hear it past the stinging throb dominating her head and the thrumming ache resounding in her soul.

She sought out a place of unfettered solitude and dark aloneness, some forgotten nook or closet in the castle's labyrinth where her ankle and her heart could scream in pain together without anyone telling her to sit properly while she fell apart inside. She didn't want to dab her tears daintily as she battled to forget Damien's hands trailing the water over her foot at the stream . . . then those same hands running up her leg, so gently, so gracefully . . . and, dear God, those hands later on, gliding on her body in front of his fire, holding her like she was more precious than silk and her body more miraculous than fire.

Making her feel like fire, too. Stirring flames within her that had been but unsure smolders until today . . . the flames celebrating her womanhood in passionate splendor.

The flames he'd extinguished with such violence, she'd almost laughed at the "ruse" he played on her. But that look into his eyes had given her the truth, leaving her to sweep up the charred remains of her heart in confused silence.

Just as she'd had to do two months ago. Two months ago, when she'd stood kicking at the dead, burned rubble that had, but twelve hours prior, been the glory of the Webber's Magnificent Menagerie and Circus. Two months ago, when she'd entombed a part of herself with Mama and Sheena and the others, when she'd promised her heart it would never have to know such a pit of betrayed pain again.

To hell with her precious promise now, she seethed. The devil himself had stolen it. For who else but the devil could be responsible for this heartache that made her ankle's injury feel little more than a bothersome throb? Who else could have made her forget herself so completely today, made her treasure the amazing magic of life again . . .

Made her *feel* again.

"Damn you," she rasped, stumbling harder and faster down the path. "Damn you back to the abyss you came from, Damien Sharpe!"

"Kira."

The voice reverberated across the garden at her with such ominous portent, she wondered whether her profanity had indeed summoned a member of the Underworld. But upon identifying the voice up on the verandah, she swallowed a laugh at her presumption. She doubted her three-times-a-week-to-chapel aunt would ever come within shouting distance of hell's gates.

"Good evening, Aunt Aleece." She was proud of the pleasant-enough tone she managed to feign.

"Kira, you are late."

"I am also tired." She took a deep breath, praying to heaven now herself for an extra resource of patience. "So if you'll please excuse me—"

"You are also filthy. *Again*. Where are your gloves? And your hat? And all your hairpins?"

Another urge to laugh mingled with bitter tears as she

contemplated simply blurting the truth to that. *If you must know, I was playing in a stream with Damien Sharpe. Then the rain came, so he carried me to his home and I took off my clothes and draped them in front of his fire. And then . . .*

Then he confused me more than all of you combined.

"I've got the hairpins in my pocket," she stated past a throat constricting once again. "Aunt Aleece, I am going to bed."

"I hardly see why. It looks as if you've just come from there." A grimacing sniff contorted the woman's face. "And lying there with swine, I'd wager, as well."

"Lying with swine." Now she did let out an exhausted laugh. Her mind's eye didn't help, using the words as permission to broadside her with visions of Damien's legs intertwining with hers, sleek and muscular and powerful, as he'd lowered her to his rug in the dancing firelight.

Lying with swine. For once, Aunt Aleece, you have a perfect selection of words to describe a situation.

"Fred decided he wished to go on an adventure," she continued instead, working at calm constraint. "In retrieving him, I discovered some new parts of the countryside."

The wan smile she used to emphasize the humor, not to mention the sarcasm itself, received only a tighter pinch of her aunt's features. "Well," Aleece finally stated, "we attempted to hold dinner for you, but your rudeness met its limit at thirty minutes."

"I understand." She also understood her aunt's "we" as a paraphrase for "your father." At Aleece's table, delaying dinner for Victoria herself might require a decree from Parliament.

"Cook prepared a lovely meal." The woman was determined to wring every drop of reprimand from the reservoir she'd obviously gathered, even if that meant disguising the censure in "casual" conversation. "Honeyed game hens and herb pie."

"Yes," Kira agreed absently, concentrating more on masking a pained wince as she ascended the steps. "It sounds lovely."

"It was, though the best was assuredly saved for last. Cinnamon-baked apples. Your favorite, I believe?"

"That sounds delightful, as well." She finished the response at the same time she concluded the grueling climb, rewarding herself with a heavy sigh. She occupied herself with ordering the throbbing in her ankle to let her breathe again. When it did and she opened her eyes, she grew aware of the odd silence now permeating the verandah . . . the silence, she realized, because not another quip emanated from her aunt.

She glanced at Aleece—to see the woman had indeed abandoned her twitting disposition in favor of a halfway puzzled look. Perhaps that was because the other portion of her expression looked like . . . compassion.

"You really *are* exhausted," Aleece murmured, prefacing a deeper softening to her features. Kira nodded a reply slowed by fascination. For the first time, she beheld the Aleece whom Rachelle must have known as Mother . . . the Aleece who felt something other than grief and anger, who cared for something other than her brother's cold castle. Right now, Kira admitted, it felt nice to be that something.

"I'll go speak with Cook," the woman said then, an edge returning to her tone as "Lady Aleece" once more stepped. "A tray can be warmed and sent to your room. While you're waiting, I'll have Ally prepare a bath." She angled a knowing glance toward Kira's hem. "And I'll take a look at that ankle personally."

It took several seconds for the relief to flood Kira, succeeded by a wash of gratitude. That single look might as well have served as symbolism for a padlock, for in volunteering to tend the injury herself, Aleece also declared her intention to keep the results of Kira's afternoon shenanigans "just between us girls." Nobody at Scottney Hall would know what a mess the American had made of herself today. Not that Kira cared much what anyone here thought; in a year, everyone from Ally to the courtyard chickens would be only fond memories, anyway. The *meaning* of Aleece's goodwill was what mattered the most.

"Thank you," she replied then, truly meaning the words. "Thank you, Aunt Aleece. I—" She stopped and sighed in resignation, conceding she'd have to *show* her appreciation to Aleece in some way.

"I know," the woman filled in, her eyes showing a flicker of a smile as she brushed tangled curls off Kira's forehead. "I know. Get going now. This wind isn't helping you avoid a chill, and you've got quite a full day ahead of you tomorrow."

Kira obliged, but not without a baffled frown. A full day? Whatever did Aleece mean? She'd assumed today's afternoon reprieve was a special occasion, and that they'd be back to lessons again after breakfast tom—

"Oh, no."

The words might as well have been oaths, so vehemently did she emit them as she stopped halfway up the servants' stairwell. Aleece would *not* have her back at lessons tomorrow morning, came the scathing reminder. Her aunt would be hand-selecting the gown she'd wear to suffer an afternoon in the clutches of Rolf Pembroke's "hospitality."

"Damnation!" Kira felt at least a degree better as the true curse left her lips. But not "better" enough. She drummed a fist against the stone wall and wondered if the queasy sensation in her belly and the acidic burn in her throat could be forged into a true bout of something, *anything* to render her bed-bound for the next few days.

No, she concluded, that was no good. After those few days, she'd still have to face the ordeal, only it would be worse, because she'd have spent all that time in dreading anticipation of her fate at the hands of a smooth-as-oil letch.

Not to mention the rough-as-stone devil she'd rather be spending that time with.

Another oath escaped her lips as that realization, and the memories it surged anew, attacked her senses. Again, she inwardly wished Damien Sharpe to hell for all eternity. Wishing him there for making her feel what nobody had before—certainly none of the boys from whom she'd endured selfish gropes before; definitely none of the men she'd known, mostly the Webber's crew, for all of *them* had been too consumed with protecting her like a daughter or sister to notice she'd grown fully into a woman.

A woman awakened today by a forest demon with midnight in his eyes and starfire in his touch.

A woman cast aside by that demon like nothing better than yesterday's ashes.

And yet, even now, a woman whose body warmed all over from the memories of his caresses . . . whose nipples hardened, whose throat convulsed, whose legs threatened to fold beneath her because of the sweet heat pooling between them.

A fool.

A fool who needed to cast Damien Sharpe out of her mind now.

For once Kira's heart completely agreed with her brain. She compelled her body to obey, as well, straightening her spine and ascending the rest of the stairs with a new attack of energy. Yes, she resolved, she'd banish Damien from her thoughts just as he'd evicted her from his damnable forest. Swiftly. Efficiently. Heartlessly.

What better way to start accomplishing it than by seeing Rolf Pembroke? Who, after all, would remind her more that men were conscienceless beasts in thin disguises?

It would be a boring, banal, absolutely perfect day.

She had never made such a wrong presupposition in her life.

Her heart didn't hesitate in concurring with her mind's conclusion this time, because it was so irrevocably true. *Oh yes, Kira,* that heart now admonished, *you were wrong. So wrong, wrong, wrong!*

The inner litany intensified as the Scottney carriage cleared the arched gateway bidding them welcome to Hyperion's Walk and rumbled down the extensive crushed-shell drive. *Hyperion's Walk.* She had never paused to think about the reason for the estate's name, but during their journey, she observed the truth beyond the poetic title—in vivid, glorious detail. Surely the father of the sun himself had deemed this valley would bear his name; what other explanation existed for the caress of golden light upon every tree, flower, and shrub they passed?

And what trees and flowers! Kira marveled with more amazement at each new vista they encountered. Around the first bend, lush evergreens cradled a rabbit family's meadow. Around the next, a butterfly corps de ballet pirouetted along a wall overgrown with clover and thistles. Farther up the road, ancient oaks climbed to the sky in tangled grandeur, rising from a bounty of bluebells, dandelions, and wild pink tulips. The banquet of beauty went on for at least a mile, but she devoured each new course with enraptured anticipation.

Hyperion's Walk, she repeated in her mind, but her senses gave the name new and exhilarated meaning. Everywhere she gazed, nature and splendor bloomed boldly and honestly.

Everywhere she gazed, she saw Damien.

Kira winced. Why hadn't she realized? Why had she thought just because this place no longer called the man its leader, it would no longer bear the evidence of his administration? Why had she assumed Hyperion's Walk would look more like—

The manicured grounds they entered now.

Like a bank of fog giving way to a blast of sunshine, the wilderness suddenly deferred to an expanse of precisely cut grass bracketed by pristine stone walls. The carriage wheels clattered on symmetric tile stones as Tom steered them toward a soaring but somehow inviting structure. The Tudor-inspired gables and windows imparted the feeling of arriving not at a castle or hall but a home.

If only the master of the mansion really wasn't at home.

Surely enough, however, there stood Pembroke himself before the front steps, a portrait of suave grace even in his casual afternoon attire of loose stock, brocade waistcoat, and jacketless white shirt. Nicholas stood next to him, having ridden ahead of the carriage during their journey from Scottney Hall. Kira didn't understand why her nerves calmed when seeing her father, but she was grateful for the sensation, whatever its source.

All too soon, the coach stopped. Tom swung open the door, yet Rolf superseded the servant when it came time to help her down the stepping box.

As the man took her hand, Kira wondered if the day would ever come when she'd not think of a python when coming into contact with him. She doubted it, especially if he planned on continuing to wear his hair as he did now, forced into fashionable waves with half a jar's worth of styling fixative. Kira managed to bite back the dozen gibes that instantly rose to mind at the expense of the fancy coiffure.

"There's no explaining some people's taste," she muttered to her father, who offered his arm to escort her behind the still-chattering Aleece and the patiently nodding Rolf.

"Or the whims of fashion," Nicholas replied, also speaking beneath his breath.

"I guess the world needs a few remaining mysteries." She couldn't help a tiny giggle as punctuation then but was validated by the crinkles deepening around her father's eyes, as well.

She was taken by surprise, however, when the next moment, he slanted that expression at *her*. And this time, Kira noticed, he really *looked*, not just glanced. "You have, however, seemed to have unraveled that mystery today," he told her as they emerged from the porte cochere into the sunlight flooding an expansive back lawn. With a proud smile, Nicholas explained, "You are the loveliest of visions, Kira."

A blush suffused her cheeks. Though Aleece had, as usual, selected an ensemble for her to wear today, Kira had defiantly ordered that pink confection—which had reminded her of a puff pastry even when they'd purchased it back in London—back into the depths of the closet. Instead, she'd chosen this simpler dress, fashioned of peach-colored muslin and trimmed in copper velvet piping, with a faux copper rose connecting the ivory lace fichu along the V-shaped neckline.

Running a hand along that lace now, she murmured in a

teasing imitation of a beguiled London debutante, "Why, thank you, my lord. You speak the prettiest flattery."

"I thought that was *my* job."

Her spirit swiftly deflated at Rolf's voice—the voice belonging to the lips now brushing gracefully over her knuckles. Funny, Kira thought sarcastically as she watched, she didn't think snakes possessed lips.

On the other hand, Rolf seemed intent on proving her wrong, curving his mouth into a smile displaying those lips to what some women would term "sensual perfection." Kira preferred the words "lascivious" and "leering."

If the man himself discerned that turn of her thoughts, he didn't betray that knowledge beyond his steady smile. Just like Eve's beguiling serpent, Kira added to her musings with an upturned brow.

"My lady," Rolf bade, dipping another cultivated bow. "Welcome to Hyperion's Walk." As he rose, he swept a hand toward the stretch of lawn before them, its trimmed perfection interrupted only by a collection of white lawn furniture islands in the center. "My home is your home."

Thank God Aleece decided that declaration worth a bout of enchanted laughter. For while her aunt reattached herself to Rolf's arm and once more tittered away about Rolf's charm and wit, Kira had a moment to swallow against the instant, instinctual acid that had twisted through her belly at Rolf's little innuendo. *My home is your home*.

"My arse," she spat, narrowing eyes at the glare of sunshine on the snake's brocade-covered back.

Her father's soft *tsk* resounded in her ear then. "He's just being nice," Nicholas whispered. "You could try to do the same."

Kira dropped her sights to the grass, which she scuffed contritely. The remorse deepened as Nicholas wrapped an arm around her shoulder, reminding her once more of the hundred ways *he'd* been trying to make *her* happier since he'd arrived. "You're right," she admitted softly, and compelled herself to offer a sincere smile up at him. "I can't really get mad at a clod who has no idea he's a clod."

"*Kira.*" A heavy huff helped dispense the chastisement. "Rolf may be a touch cocky—"

"He's a clod."

"But a clod with a beautiful home . . . yes?"

Kira obliged him on at least that prompt. Circling her gaze around the area, she imbibed the breathtaking view of the peaks protecting Reeth, Fremington, and Grinton beyond, their heights adorned in mosaics of gleaming snow. The mountains descended into foothills that became the valley occupied by a good portion of this estate, its air redolent with fresh-cut grass, sprouting acorns, and the savory tang of the luncheon Rolf's kitchen staff now prepared al fresco.

"Yes," she finally, though reluctantly, concurred. "It *is* wonderful here."

An approving sound resonated from Nicholas's throat. "I knew you'd think so."

Despite her staunchest efforts, however, she exhaled her next breath on a suddenly melancholy sigh. "It must have been horribly hard for Damien Sharpe to give it up."

One moment passed, then two, before the horror at last struck—the horror, Kira realized, that her thoughts had once more overrun her tongue, this time in a disastrous way. Her father jerked his hand away from her, curling it into a tense fist. His profile tightened into harsh angles. She opened her mouth, attempting an apology, but the proper words eluded her like forgotten dance steps in the middle of an opening show.

"Kira." Nicholas's low inflection told her he understood

her dilemma, but he was speaking to save him, not her, from it. "Rolf Pembroke may be a clod, but he's not a murderer."

"*Accused* murderer." Hell, if her composure was surrendering the reins to raw emotion this afternoon, defiant anger might as well have a turn at the driver's box. "He was accused, Father, never convicted."

"I don't care if the Archbishop of Canterbury gave him pardon. I won't tolerate that bastard's name spoken in my presence, Kira. Please remember that, beginning now."

Those were the last words between them for the next grueling hour, for just then, Rolf called them over for lunch. Aunt Aleece fawned over the gelatin mold, fashioned for the occasion in a lime and lemon version of the Scottney family crest; she went on to praise the grilled salmon, spiced potatoes, corn salad, goose pâté, and fresh dark bread as if she'd not eaten in over a week. Rolf responded to her patter with drollery that increased with each glass of wine he emptied. Kira tolerated the whole situation by stealing more looks at the mountains and imagining herself ensconced in some cool glade there.

But when the man picked up an extra fish fillet and made it "swim" its way toward Aleece like a shark, Kira knew even the mountains would provide no further patience. She rose to her feet in one emphatic motion. "Air," she explained, ignoring Aleece's reprimanding glance at favoring an exit that didn't take six hours. "I need air. Lots of it. Now."

She already had a perfect route in mind, and set herself on that course with no wasted steps. The untamed foliage through which they'd first driven lay close now, beckoning like a mischievous best friend, and Kira fought the temptation to bunch her dress up to her knees and break into a run for the wilderness. She was certain her abrupt exit from lunch had already earned her a lecture come tomorrow, so she moderated her pace to a steady stride. When her feet finally left the spongy grass and crunched on pine needles, she indulged in a relieved smile.

"I promise I come bearing no talking fish."

Her smile plummeted as she came to a halt. "Mr. Pembroke," she replied to the bearer of that verbal olive branch, "I would like to be alone right now. Besides, my aunt was taking a real liking to your talking fish." *And your vintage wine.*

She could practically hear the ropes and pulleys in his brain whizzing, trying to weigh her remark as compliment or insult. In the end, coming to no conclusion, he simply changed the subject. "And you've 'taken a real liking' to Hyperion's Walk, haven't you?"

Kira laughed softly as she took several paces from him. She had to give the man credit for one thing: his uncanny ability to identify his prey's most tender spot. "It *is* beautiful here," she confessed.

"Ahhhh," the man said, now leaning against a pine tree. "Methinks I have found the good lady out."

Unbelievably, Kira found herself chuckling again, though as she pressed her back to a tree about eight feet away, her voice dropped to a wistful murmur. "It reminds me of Virginia, back home." With the words came the all-too-clear images in her mind, of the resplendent mountains and valleys she'd traveled and loved so well. Of course, her imagination was aided by the breathtaking beauty surrounding her: the lush trees, the brilliant flowers, the crisp wind, the vast sky.

"Just wait until you see what I've got planned for all this, Kira."

She shot a fast, perplexed stare across the clearing. "What?" she blurted, enduring a shiver so sudden and strange, she wondered if the tree at her back had been replaced by an uprooted glacier. "What do you mean, what you've got 'planned'?"

"For the development of the land, of course." Rolf's well-tutored baritone still modulated his voice, but his body now resembled an eager tiger, beginning to pace back and forth, biding his time until his ferocity could be vented. "Damien, in all his rustic charm, was also a stubborn savage, if you'll forgive my vernacular. He saw some kind of wild poeticism to all this. He'd get rather wild himself defending it to me when I suggested that a reflecting pond and sculpture garden—"

"A *what?*" A wild indignation fired Kira's own blood as she pushed from her tree. Forgive his vernacular? She had a feeling that on the list of things she'd have to forgive him for today, his language would be last on the list.

"Surely Aleece took you to a garden or two before you left London," the man continued, practically chastising her. "Well, think of the grandeur of such a place, aided by these mountains and a collection of the finest sculptured works, commissioned from the most renowned artisans of the world today. The reflecting pool will be fashioned of Italian marble, of course—"

"Brought here on an army of imported pack mules, as well?"

"Of course not," Rolf rebuked, again thinking her intensity reflected her true interest, not astonishment. "It shall all be brought in by train."

"Train," she repeated. "You mean, to the station in York, and then—"

"No. I mean brought by train *here*."

"Oh, God." She groaned. "That's what I thought you meant." Frantically she peered around, overcome by a bizarre urgency to gather all these woods into her arms, load them into the carriage, and take them back to Scottney Hall with her like protected treasures from a shopping spree. "B-but—" she stammered, "but how—"

"A few pounds go a long way toward building friendships in London government, Kira." The dog before her rocked back on his heels, actually proud of his corruption. "My friends have been all too happy to necessitate the grants and permits for a private rail line from York to Hyperion's Walk. The first spike on the line will be driven before summer."

She couldn't repress a stunned grimace any longer. "I don't believe it."

"I don't, either." Rolf chuckled. But the sound quickly turned into another sound, a growl reminding her of a tiger once more, only now in a state of delicious conquest. A sound making her want to throw up.

"The best part about this is that I'm *making* money on the whole project. Half a dozen buyers have already committed to shipments of the lumber from these trees. A small mill will have to be built, of course. We'll position it right next to the switchback on the line."

"A small mill," Kira echoed, the words tasting like sour milk in her mouth. "Next to the switchback."

"Precisely."

No, she thought, *not* precisely. Not at all. Something still wasn't right. Something still didn't work correctly into Rolf's grand plan.

On a surge of glaring realization, she recognized what that something was.

"What about your tenants, Mr. Pembroke?" she asked him then, her voice no longer hesitant, her stance straightening and stiffening. "What about the people in your employ, who have so loyally served you? What about the land they've farmed and the animals they've raised for generations? The last time I checked, sheep couldn't graze on switchbacks."

"And the last time *I* checked, time didn't stand still for anyone." He didn't attempt to confront her eye to eye. Instead, looking out to some point on the distant horizon, he finished, "People will simply be taught new skills, Kira. They'll have to change as Hyperion's Walk changes."

"And what if some people are too old to fell trees or cut lumber? What if they're not *people* at all? What are you going to do with the creatures who have found refuge in these woods—the wildlife that depends on you for its sanctuary?"

He dropped his head then, emitting a huff sounding strangely like the beginnings of a . . . laugh. "That's really not my concern."

At that, Kira's lips formed a dozen of the most vicious oaths she knew. But she ended up shredding each curse between her grinding teeth. The effort would be wasted on any man who possessed half Rolf's callousness.

Instead, now feeling like a provoked wildcat herself, she whirled from the ass, hoping the leaves and pine needles she scattered also rained a coat of dust on his preciously shined boots. She continued in the direction she'd set before, even though her steps were now savage stomps. Lord, what an earful she'd have for Ally tonight! She wouldn't cease, she decided, until every girlish illusion the maid harbored for the bastard was annihilated like the forest *he* planned on razing for the sake of some marble statues.

In the great name of "civilization."

The civilization in which she'd yearned to prove herself an accepted member.

Revulsion roared through Kira, clawing free on an anguished cry. She fled faster, until her legs threatened to tangle in her petticoats and topple her to the ground. As if she'd care. Let the dirt cake on her precious satin dress. Let the pinecones tangle in her hair. At least she'd be part of something *real*.

But her skirts never got the chance to trip her. After rounding a thick copse of trees, she was halted by another impediment altogether.

She took in the sight of a good-size building. The structure had been created then maintained in beautiful detail, she surmised from the elegantly carved eaves and the masterful detail to the stained glass windows. Those panes all depicted different kinds of flowers—at least the ones that weren't broken or boarded shut. The paint accenting the carved mountain scene in the door now peeled and flaked from the wood, and a strip of curved windows down the center of the roof was also in need of extensive repair.

And yet a definite pathway cut across the dust of the broad stone serving as a front stoop, indicating this place was still used for some purpose. "An abandoned hothouse," she muttered. "The perfect venue for pulling wings off butterflies, eh, Mr. Pembroke?"

She was answered by a low, tormented moan. A sound that gripped her belly with dread and her heart with anguish.

Because a human hadn't produced it.

Kira cocked her head to one side, physically enacting the baffled keeling of her thoughts. The mewl came again, confirming to her its source: from inside the building.

"What in the world?" she whispered, and trembled anxiously. The last time her whole body had been gripped by such trepidation was the moment during that last show with Webber's in which she'd smelled acrid smoke.

She shook her head to release the terrible memory. Though her vision cleared, the weight of apprehension remained in her stomach, heavy as a cannon ball.

The creature's outcry came once more.

As it did, distress transcended Kira's fear, inexorably dragging her forward. As she moved across the stone and reached for the door handle, she even chastised herself for her ominous portentions. *Tarnation, Kira. A trapped kitten in a hothouse is not a tent full of perishing animals.*

But then her mind could form no more words. For that matter, neither could her lips. The shock overwhelming her heart nearly rendered it impossible to *breathe*.

She'd found a baby cat, all right. A baby *wild*cat. It was a scruffy little tiger cub she'd guess at six months old, give or take a few weeks, romped around an area dictated by a cage no bigger than ten feet square—or at least the poor thing attempted to. While swatting at a brown bug scuttling through the hay, the little one had no understanding that the chain secured to its back leg wouldn't allow it more than a six-foot radius of movement. With each lunge it took at the bug, the chain went taut and the iron dug into the cub's flesh. The cub's exclamations of frustration and pain gnashed clear to the depths of Kira's soul.

She wrenched her gaze away from the tiger and assessed the rest of the enclosure and its tenants. *Tenants?* her heart spat. *Prisoners* was the more accurate designation, though she was certain some penitentiaries would show these creatures greater compassion. More of those brown bugs boldly zipped across her path as she passed cages containing a large and lethargic bear (held by *four* leg shackles), a llama with chewed-off sections of wool, several nasty-eyed mongooses, and an ape that returned her stare with weary regard.

She nearly threw up her lunch when coming to the enclosure next to the ape's. Lying there on the dirty hay were three African chimpanzees. Two of them picked hordes of fleas from each other's fur. The third looked asleep.

No, Kira thought as she pressed a quivering hand to her lips, the third looked dead.

This morning she'd reluctantly left Fred behind, not wanting to wrest him from enjoying a tart-making session with his bevy of admirers from the Scottney Hall kitchen staff. Now she realized that coincidence as heaven's intervention.

For now she also fathomed how much hell could make itself known on earth, too.

"So here's where you've gotten off to."

Kira spun around, less surprised by the voice than by the relaxed ease of its tone. Her stomach turned again while watching Rolf stroll up the aisle to her, one hand in a pocket, the other swinging casually at his side. He reeked of the same attitude Aunt Aleece had adopted during their sojourns through Picadilly Square in London, when they'd pass the begging waifs and cripples like so much mud beneath their heels.

"So it seems," she replied, still struggling back oceans of bile. Her expression, more a grimace than a smile, wasn't lost on him this time. She saw that much in the twitches of his own eyes, before he flashed her a false plastering of a smile.

"Forgive me if I say I'm not surprised," he stated smoothly. "Somehow I knew you'd sniff this place out."

"It's a miracle *everyone* hasn't." Kira sucked in her lips and clamped them between her teeth in order to stay the sting behind her eyes—a burn caused not only by anguish but the practically visible stench of animal sweat and feces.

"Well, that's the beauty of selecting this site in which to keep our acquisitions." Once more he rocked lazily back on his heels. "It's downwind from the main buildings; far enough away so the noises don't keep the household awake at night, but close enough that—"

"Acquisitions." It had taken Kira half a minute to wrangle her voice up her throat again, but now that was back, she used it with vehement force. "Acquisitions? Is that your name for these creatures?"

"That's what they are, Kira." Rolf's tone began at condescending and worsened from there. "Do you think I've got hunters and agents scouring the globe because I enjoy having smelly, snorting, dangerous beasts lurking about my home?"

"They're *not* beasts. They're living creatures, damn you, with minds and souls and—"

"They're profit-making commodities." He severed her off with a quiet but lethal tone. "You may not like that truth, Kira, but you won't change it. Look out your own *boudoir* window. Haven't you noticed your papa is one of my best clients?"

She coiled her fists to keep them from lurching for the man's neck. "You have no right to even whisper about my father's compound," she retorted from tight teeth. "My father has invested thought and care into the treatment of his animals. My father—"

"Is an eccentric, like many others of his kind during these colorful times we live in. And as long as those eccentrics find it de rigueur to have a llama or a bear to show off during dinner parties, these animals are money in my pocket. The orders are placed and I fill them, that's all."

"My, my, my." Kira batted her eyes in mocking punctuation of each exclamation. "Mr. Pembroke, I had no idea. So you're the Great White Hunter now, too, in addition to the Princely Patron of Artists. Indeed, what a man you are!"

"And what a flippant, disrespectful girl *you* are." The man's nostrils flared and his lips twitched, as he battled to repress his ire like no more than a scandalous burp or sneeze. "I have fully explained my position in this matter, my lady. Ergo, your hostility is wrongly placed."

"My hostility," Kira seethed, "lies right where it should be. When was the last time these cages were swept and scrubbed? And the hay changed?"

An eye twitch joined the spasms of Rolf's lips. "I have an experienced staff on hand for the maintenance of the acquisitions and their needs. I'm certain my men know—"

"Do they know one of those chimps is close to dying? Think of how many pounds *that* will cost, Mr. Pembroke. And these creatures are exotic animals, not convicted murderers. You have them in iron shackles like—"

"Only the dangerous ones." Rolf raised a righteous finger.

"The dangerous ones—like a four-month-old tiger cub? Don't bother to tell me he'll grow into something more fierce, because you've assured he won't see his first birthday, anyhow. Whatever you're feeding him won't equal the nutrition and attention he should be receiving from his mother."

She faltered then, trying not to sob. Still, she expected no other reaction than the response she received: a taut crease across Rolf's forehead, his fingers raising to pinch the bridge of his nose. "Kira, I think you're overreacting a bit."

"And *I* think," she swiftly returned, "you just may be a bigger bastard than I imagined."

The insult hardly expressed her rage, but instinct ordered her to escape from here before she acted on her true impulses. She spun and raced out the door, eager to be as far away from this monster as possible, as swiftly as possible.

Until, just as she stumbled off the stone step, the monster's lethally soft voice cut into her senses. "*Tsk, tsk.* Such nasty words to hurl at me, your ladyship, when I was about to propose a mutually satisfying solution to our little problem."

Our little problem. Rolf's purposeful selection of words, in addition to his actor-perfect delivery, should have spurred Kira to a more frantic escape. Instead, she halted and turned, cocking her hands expectantly on hips. "Well"—she sneered—"I've got to hear *this*."

With both hands still ensconced in his pockets, Rolf strolled off the step and curled a sickeningly urbane smile. "The answer is terribly simple," he stated. "*You* should be in charge of this place, Kira. And . . . you can be."

Her brows slammed low over her eyes. He was right about the first assertion, of course. But there was a trapdoor to the second, she was certain of it. "What are you talking about?"

Rolf's smile kicked up by a fraction of an inch. A fraction that carried a mile of meaning. "You can do anything you want with any part of these grounds . . . as soon as you've become Mrs. Pembroke."

Nineteen

"I'LL MARRY A LIZARD first."

The words, however harshly she ground them out, had not been Kira's first choice of reaction to this bastard's combination of proposal and insult. Her first inclination had been to break out in laughter, until she realized Rolf was utterly serious.

Still, as the briefest of dignified scowls rushed across Rolf's face, she wondered if the man comprehended he'd just experienced defeat at a marriage proposal, not a horse auction. Yet when he spoke again, his intonation bespoke his all-too-clear understanding of the situation.

"My lady Kira, I must caution you against speaking in such haste. I *do* possess your father's sanction in this endeavor."

"Then my father can go swim in the same swamp you crawled out of." The retort was colored with the bitterness of betrayal. All the "understanding" and "respect" she thought Nicholas had been showing her . . . lies, all of it! Fighting her soul's screams of pain at that realization, she rushed on, "Furthermore, I don't care if St. Peter himself arrives with your precious 'sanctions.' The answer would still be *no*."

The pain radiated to her belly as Rolf merely *tsked* at her again, a placid smile playing at his lips. "You're making this much harder than it has to be, my dear."

"No, Rolf. *You're* making this harder." She cocked an incredulous glare at him. "Are you really so daft? I am not fond of you, Mr. Pembroke. I don't even *like* you."

A surprised glance flashed at her. "What does that have to do with anything?"

At that, Kira did laugh. As she expected, Rolf didn't. The absurdity of this whole scene suddenly struck her. How many times had she dreamed, as all girls did, of the moment a man would ask her to marry him? Her fantasies had included bowers of roses and stacks of candles, and were usually accompanied by the nighttime sounds of Chico's soulful violin. Even her most creative variations of the scene had never included a fetid stand-in for a barn and a putrid excuse for a suitor.

"Good-bye, Mr. Pembroke," she murmured, lifting her skirts. "I think we're finished."

"I suppose we are" came the alarmingly easy agreement, even for Rolf. "For now."

Once more Kira stopped. She pivoted a taut glare back at Rolf, not saying a word. Indeed, he appeared the cobra who'd just mesmerized a mouse into submission.

"I assume your father has told you about the Hyperion's Walk May Day Ball next week," he stated.

"He mentioned it." Kira doled out her response with quiet caution, her hands remaining posed to grab up her skirt again.

"It's quite a grand tradition." Again seemingly guileless as a boy bragging about his marble collection, he grinned, giving Kira a glimpse of the façade that had won the man devotees like Ally. "The London season gets to be a bit wearisome by now, and the ball affords many an ideal opportunity to get away. We always have quite a crush, but this year the affair should be extra well attended, as it marks the grand opening of the Pavilion Ballroom, my pet project for the last four months."

"That's . . . er, nice." What was the man up to?

"More than nice, I'd say. I'm sure you saw it when arriving. The new building with the golden shingles . . . it's been patterned on the grandest palaces of Persia and India."

"I'm certain you'll have a very nice time, then."

"Yes. I should, at that—especially as I am looking forward to having your father, your aunt, and yourself as honored names on my guest list."

Kira slanted the man a confused grimace. Surely he now fathomed she didn't care to be on his *market* list.

She instead decided to call the sneaky serpent out from beneath his own grass. "Rolf," she fired, "what the *tarnation* are you about with this?"

"Not a thing, my lady" was the maddeningly calm answer. "Not a thing. I look forward to receiving you next week, that's all. I bid you adieu until then."

He turned and disappeared with more stealth than he'd used in his approach. Kira didn't follow, choosing to plop herself on a nearby rock and reassess what had just transpired. She concentrated particularly on Rolf's behavior after he called her back for the second time. Why had he halted her once more just to throw in a mention of his ball? Why had he babbled on about the whole thing, only to capitulate and depart so easily?

Rolf Pembroke didn't make anything that easy.

And somehow, Kira now knew, the man was preparing

to make the May Day Ball his pièce de résistance of difficulty.

Several hours later she was finally able to dismiss that foreboding premonition—though the feat required two hours of walking the Scottney gardens with Fred. As late-afternoon shadows made their way around the Main Hall ramparts, she found herself soaking up the beauty of the lovingly tended wildflowers, liking the way the grounds staff let this section of the garden be defined by simple dirt paths with stone borders.

There were certainly no marble reflecting pools. Nor was there an ounce of commissioned statuary.

The flowers weren't complaining, and neither was she.

"I had a feeling I'd find you out here, Lady Kira."

The greeting made its way down the path on undertones of friendly levity. The problem was, Kira didn't care to be on "friendly" terms—or *any* kind of terms, for that matter—with the voice's source.

She nevertheless replied with perfunctory deference, "My lord Scottney."

Her father's boots made soft but steady thuds on the walkway. "How are you?" he queried in a similar cadence.

At first, she responded by turning her sights to the mountains rising in the distance. The setting sun made the peaks appear dipped in a huge vat of Cook's honey apple glaze. "It's a lovely evening, isn't it?" she finally murmured, almost to herself—and purposely so.

She started in surprise then. Unconsciously she'd just utilized one of Aunt Aleece's silly "etiquette tactics." But before she could properly condemn herself, her father gave her a bigger shock: proof that the maneuvering worked.

"Bloody hell, Kira," Nicholas pronounced. "You're going

to unpack your goods right here and now, no matter what they are, or we'll stand here all night until you do!"

For a fraction of a second, a handful of flippant quips sprang to mind. She might even have used one of them, if this was yesterday. If a few hours ago, her "England Experience" hadn't been enhanced by a royal-size dose of disillusionment.

But this was today. Today her father commanded honesty, not frivolity. And today she was ideally prepared to give that to him.

So, she looked at her father and "unpacked her goods" by emulating his angry clarity. "Is it true you gave Rolf Pembroke consent to propose marriage to me?"

Within the next instant, she observed why her father was so highly desired as a business partner. Not a muscle on his face gave away his answer.

"So," Nicholas at last stated, "he did speak with you."

"Because he *did* have your permission."

"Yes. I gave him my approval . . . in broad generalities."

"In broad general—" She cut herself short with a burst of sheer exasperation and rising anger. "What the hell is that supposed to mean?"

"It means that Rolf asked my views on the matter, Kira," her father replied with that same remorseless calm, "and I gladly shared those views, which are certainly no secret to you. A union between our families would be a highly advantageous match."

"Advantageous!" The outcry came on a frantic laugh. "I can't stand the wretch!"

Equally insane was her father's insistence on continuing his placating gentleness. "Compatibility in a marriage is a blessing that comes with time."

"And *you're* the authority on the subject?" This time

true hilarity inspired her harsh laugh. "I think you've got your contracts crossed, my lord. A marriage bed isn't the House of Commons."

"And *I* think you should give the matter a second consideration."

"Then maybe you should also think about going to—"

"Damn it, Kira!" He clutched both her shoulders as he continued, nearly beseeching her. "You're not a mindless gull. You've traveled; seen the colonies and the territories, too. You've seen enough and experienced enough to know the world runs right over those who get in its way."

Reluctantly Kira nodded. She couldn't dispute a word of his statement. Her father closed his eyes while releasing a relieved sigh.

"All right," he went on, "then all I'm asking is that you place all of that on the scales of your consideration, as well." He brushed some stray curls off her cheek. "Kira . . . my beautiful Kira," he murmured. "Rolf can give you a happy, easy life. You'll never have to work hard again. And you'll see the entire world—"

"Without my circus."

She should have taken her father's replying silence as clear enough confirmation of that. But she wanted explanation. She wanted to know what made Nicholas think she'd simply abandon her dream—the aspiration that had kept her from boarding the next train for London over the last month—or if he'd ever really recognized her goal at all.

"Kira," he said softly at last, "everybody must grow up at some time."

"So that *is* the way of it," she rasped. "You really did think you'd convince me to—" She jerked back from him. "You thought my circus some silly girlish whim, didn't you?"

"Bloody *hell*. It *is* a girlish whim! Damn it all, Kira, you're a woman now—"

"Yes, I am." She emphasized that by marching directly to him again; by securing the same obstinate stance as his, her toes two inches in front of his. "Yes, I *am*, Father. Look at me, and see that. Look at the dreams I cherish in my heart. *Look* at them, damn you, instead of throwing some of your worthless words at them!"

"Wait a minute." At last he did snap his head up, and his eyes burned with the intensity of the sun's last rays upon the horizon. "Our agreement is binding," he said with a snarl. "My word is *not* worthless."

"Neither are my dreams," Kira reciprocated. "So if you thought all it would take to turn my head from them was a handsome face and a mountain of money, then you have much to learn about your daughter, my lord."

At that, it was her father who stepped back then turned away. But he didn't relinquish an inch of his stone-hard stance, his shoulders straighter than the parapets of the castle he faced. "I'm sorry to hear that, Kira," he murmured in an equally rigid tone.

"So am I, my lord. So am I."

"Damn!"

If he'd been able to glean a pound for each time he'd gritted the word in the last five minutes, Damien surmised he'd have a small fortune puddled at his feet—the feet now losing their hold in the slick mud as he waged a losing battle with a stable latch that refused to slide shut.

The entire structure, though a tenth of the size of the Walk's stone-walled stable, needed to be razed and rebuilt. Not that it had been assembled right in the first place, if Damien remembered the occasion correctly. In honor of his sixteenth birthday—and ergo, the first time Father had included him in on a weekend jaunt to the lodge—twenty of Yorkshire's most upstanding gentlemen were also invited to help usher in his manhood. Of course, the lot of them did so with enough brandy and vodka to float the back teeth of an army.

Sometime shortly after two in the morning, Father had proposed they add to the festivities with a groundbreaking ceremony for the lodge's new stable. The trouble was, nobody wanted to stop at simply breaking ground. The bigger trouble was, everybody had their own ideas about the ideal design of a good stable. The foundations were laid for what Damien beheld—and battled—now.

He'd let the whole lot of them have at it again, if they stood here now.

If only he were sixteen again. Hell, if only he were twenty-seven again. One year ago . . . was that too much to wish for? Yes; he needed but one year from time's relentless clock, so that he could stand here with these memories and only have to reply to them, *I miss you, Father* instead of *I'm sorry, Father. God, I'm so sorry I've let it come to this!*

A horrifying sting surged behind his eyes. Damien battled it by throwing himself against the bar with a sound between a snarl and a sob. The bar didn't slide an inch. His feet, however, made up for that. In an instant, the slick ground gave up its tenuous support. He went down into the muck with a swift *thwop*.

The first thought to penetrate the equally thick yet infinitely darker mire of his senses was the conclusion that mud tasted as nasty as it looked. Hamlet, however, differed with that inclination. As Damien finished grimacing and began spitting, the Labrador halted him with an attack of wet licks.

"Christ's sake, Ham," he snarled. "You're shoving this swill up my nose. Bugger *off*!"

Ham forced him to emphasize the command with a vigorous shove; behavior he immediately hated himself for, since it usually resulted in a good three-hour sulk on his pet's part. But in astonishment, Damien watched the dog not only acquiesce to his rebuke but accept it. Ham fell back into the sludge and rolled over three times before bounding back to his paws, ready for more, grinning like an idiot.

The beast's antics had Damien wishing for the sulk, instead. He didn't feel right about Ham's abnormality. He sure as bloody hell didn't trust it.

The next moment he knew why. And wished he didn't.

Hamlet barked ecstatically at the chimpanzee who bounded from the trees. After some affectionate tussling, the pair took off for points unknown on the other side of the stable—but not before they managed to spray more mud Damien's way.

He felt Kira's gaze upon him as he attempted to backhand some of the slime off his face.

In shock, he noticed his hand trembled at the effort. The tremors corresponded to the sudden, painful thudding in the center of his chest.

Her voice, more rich and vibrant than he remembered, did not help his torture. "Can I . . . give you a hand?"

Worst of all, her intent resonated with sincerity. Damien squeezed shut his eyes, gritted his teeth, and told his mind to command his body she really wasn't here. She was merely the one-hundredth mirage he'd created of her in the last two days, since touching her in the first place, and regretting he ever had.

"What are you doing here?" he finally replied in a lethally low murmur. He steeled his gaze on the hopelessly askew stable latch. He commanded himself to hold the position until Michaelmas, if it took her that long to leave.

"Well . . ." Her feet nervously scuffled some leaves. "I have to admit, I asked myself the same question a dozen times while walking here."

"Sounds like you should listen to your instinct."

"This . . . isn't easy for me, you know."

"You think it's a stroll in the garden for me?"

"At least I'm trying to be civil."

"And *I'm* trying to tell you the effort is wasted here."

She expelled a long sigh. Damien didn't trust the sound at all. It was too pretty, too carefree . . . too calculated.

"Well," she at last said, "if you want it *that* way, Mr. Gargoyle—"

"Don't."

"Don't what?" He could only imagine her wide, innocent, adorable stare. "Don't call me that!" he exploded, advancing on her with a savage glare. "I'm not a building fixture! I have a name, damn it. I have a *name.*"

He didn't expect her to understand. Christ, of anyone he had to go and unwittingly bare his soul to, he wouldn't have picked her. Not after her last visit. Not after the way he'd ended it.

But her reply stunned him with its solemn consideration. "I know you have a name," she stated softly. "It's Damien Sharpe. Damien Sharpe, the master of Hyperion's Walk."

So much for self-commands. Damien's inner arsenal hadn't girded itself for the impact of those words, for the strength she gave him because of them. Nor had he prepared to show her his gratitude for that gift and have to confront the sight of her. She wore no fancy walking gown or multiple layers of crinolines today; instead, her Napoleonic-style jacket and matching dark-blue skirt helped promote the captivating complexity of her features: alert eyes, imp's nose, slightly lopsided lips parted on a half smile with the same alluring irregularity.

Despite all that, he might have still been able to look upon her with a platonic eye—

If he observed her hat on her head, instead of swinging by its ribbons from her right hand. If the hair that was supposed to be piled beneath the bonnet didn't fall around her face and shoulders in a curly cacophony that somehow still looked exquisite enough for the court at Versailles itself. Luxurious enough for his caressing hands.

God help him.

Damien cleared his throat. "What the hell's blazes are you getting at?" he demanded.

"Precisely what I said." Kira neither rose to nor shrunk from his surliness. She didn't need to. She stood there absolutely assured of the honesty with which she stated her facts.

"We visited at Hyperion's Walk yesterday," she at last went on in explanation. Damien visibly stiffened; she mercifully averted her gaze—though the next moment, he saw that mercy might have been for her sake as much as his. "It was beautiful, Damien," she confessed with a soft sheen in her eyes. "Everywhere I looked, and everything I saw . . ." Unbelievably, a bashful laugh stumbled across her lips. "I thought about you a great deal."

He coughed again. To her mind, she'd merely expressed a fact, forthright and frank, but he didn't think he'd feel more warmly satisfied if Victoria marched up and conferred him a knighthood. He hadn't felt this way in a very long time. "Which is why you're here?" he managed to grate.

"Which is exactly why I'm here." Her smile broadened.

"Because you visited Hyperion's Walk, and you thought about me?"

She gave him an agitated huff. "They were more than thoughts, all right?" Then, before he could anticipate it, she tromped right through the mud to grab up his hands into hers. "Damien, *you're* the rightful master of that land! You understand its magic, its beauty—"

"And its tenants understand that I'm a murderer." The word never failed to burn bitter bile up his throat. "Or did you forget that crumb of information, princess?"

"I didn't overlook anything." Her grip only tightened fevently on him. "Especially the fact that *I* don't think you're a murderer."

He should have broken the contact then. Good Christ, he should have gotten away while he still could. Every syllable from her mouth was a potential lie sanctioned by the Scottneys—hell, perhaps even scripted by Nicky himself.

But at the moment, he didn't care if it *was* a script. At the moment, Damien felt only the pressure of her hands in his . . . he felt another human being, unafraid to touch him. He watched the steady fire of her gaze . . . another human being, unafraid to look at him. Ah God, how he wanted to believe her!

The subject of his deliberations prevented them from becoming broodings by a few seconds. Kira returned her hands to her hips and angled a look at him replete with efficient cheer once more. "So," she piped, "*now* do you want to hear my offer?"

It took him ten seconds to concentrate on her words, not the lucky pine needle lodged in her hair. "Your offer?" he repeated hazily, but suddenly straightened. "Your *offer?*" He punched the word out this time.

"Yes." She rocked up on her toes, her face suddenly animated with mischief. "An offer that will yield advantageous results to us both."

He arched a brow at her. "Do you realize you're talking like your father?" It was the truth, but only partly so. On *her* lips, words like "advantageous" became bright opportunities. Sexy opportunities.

Ironically, she now snapped him a glare filled with anything but brightness or fun. "My father can go freeze on the iceberg that spawned him."

Well. If Nicky was thinking of submitting this script for London production, Damien pledged his place in the queue for a ticket now. "I think I may be interested in this, after all."

"Good." She smiled again, though the look was fleeting. Quickly she firmed her features and straightened her stance, almost giving Damien the impression she wished to look like . . . Aleece.

Finally she pronounced, "I have been forced into a dilemma, Mr. Sharpe. And I'd like you to help me . . . contend with it."

At that, his own instinct began to send him signals. The trouble was, the feelings felt more like warnings. "And if I do?" he queried. "What's the 'advantageous opportunity' for me?"

The imp who'd proposed merry mischief in the last minute suddenly turned toward him like a pouting wood fairy caught under glass. "I suppose I should just come out with it."

"What a unique idea."

His sarcasm was muffled by her despondent sigh. "I've been ordered to attend the Hyperion's Walk May Day Ball next week."

He found it no effort to maintain his blank stare. Finally he challenged, "*This* is why you've wished Nick Scottney to Antarctica?" When her scowling silence provided ample enough answer, he at last found himself surrendering to a bemused chuckle. "Pray forgive my impudence, your lady-ship, but perhaps you haven't been informed that invita-tions to the Hyperion's soirée are considered an honor second only to offers from Victoria herself. You are about to live the fantasy of half London's ladies . . ."

But the words faded on his lips as he looked to Kira. She didn't know about what London fantasized about, nor did she care. But hell, how he wished he didn't see that. For in doing so, he separated the two parts of her yet further: She became more "Kira" and less "Scottney." She became more the woman he'd kissed to life two days ago, not the daugh-ter of the man from whom he most desired exoneration— and through it, his vindication, as well.

In a phrase, she just became much more dangerous to him.

"I have indeed been informed of just how 'lucky' I am," she answered him irritably then. "The point is, I feel as lucky as a jailbird about to swing from Deadman's Tree. But mighty Lord Scottney has issued me an ultimatum about the whole thing."

"No Kira at the ball, no Kira in the ring of her own circus," Damien supplied, discernment dawning.

She rejoined with a sullen frown, "Give the man a prize."

Damien said nothing to that. It wasn't that he didn't understand—only heaven knew how explicitly he *did* know what frustrated helplessness felt like—it was simply that he hadn't received all the facts, either. She was an American and a hoyden, yes, but she was also a woman, and no woman usually compared the opportunity to dress in satins and dance on marble to the dread of facing a hangman's noose.

What pages of this proposal was she leaving out?

"Damien," she cut into his thoughts at that moment,

soft and yet cautious, as if knowing precisely what course his deliberations had proceeded. "Damien . . . I can't do this by myself."

He leveled a long, hard, accusatory stare at her. "You are *not* suggesting what I think you're suggesting."

She retaliated with a long, hard, pleading gaze of her own. "Damien," she murmured, her voice more melodic than he ever remembered, "please. I—I know you aren't particularly fond of me, but in this case, that doesn't have to matter."

He couldn't contain an acerbic laugh. "It doesn't, now? Princess, I've been cut out of society for six months, not six years. Mountains erode faster than the mores of the Mayfair crowd."

"But I really need an escort for this ordeal, and you really need to get back inside Hyperion's Walk."

His incredulity about the second assertion instantly overshadowed his curiosity about the first. "I've got to know how you arrived at this idea."

She actually rolled her eyes at that. "The scene of the crime," she answered impatiently. "That's the best place to go for the most telling clues, right? Well, until now, you haven't had the opportunity for access to that—at least not honorably so. Now I'm giving you the chance to have it. Who knows? Perhaps you'll find the key piece of evidence for your case."

"My case?" He floundered in astoundment. "What the bloody hell are you talking about?"

In contrast, an assured smile again spread across Kira's lips. "You're working on proving your innocence in Rachelle's murder. Don't gawk in such surprise; I've suspected for a week, and I've known for certain for the last two days." She actually winked at him then. "When you first brought me here during the storm, you put away those papers on the table like you were harboring Queen Victoria's corset size."

Damien shifted away from her. "Maybe that's what I *was* harboring."

"Right. And maybe you really don't want to reclaim your name, your honor, and your home. Maybe you just want to mope in this forest forever and watch Rolf turn Hyperion's grounds into a bunch of reflecting pools and statue gardens and—"

He spun back toward her. "Into *what?*"

Kira met his vehemence with a preparatory stance. "*Now* do you understand why this can be advantageous to us both?"

Damien halted his advance an arm's reach from her. He selected the distance on purpose, since he didn't know which yearning took priority: kissing her or strangling her.

Damn it, he let his senses rail. Damn it all, the worse thing was, he *did* understand what she meant. He knew that this woman had just issued him more than an invitation to a ball. The offer even went beyond the golden opportunity of searching out clues in the morning room he hadn't seen since they'd dragged him from it six months ago—in chains.

This offer surpassed all that. This offer represented the chance to let his tenants see him at home again. They'd all be there, too, on this most special of nights at Hyperion's Walk. His people would see him in frock coat and white gloves, not in a courtroom defendant's box, not in a prisoner's shackles.

They'd all see him at *home.* Where he belonged.

Or would they see that at all?

He cursed viciously at himself for the doubts that pelted him like a hive of enfuried bees. God, was Kira right? Was he really perfectly happy "moping about" in a forest where he was called nothing, rather than confronting a society where he was called murderer? Was he going to sacrifice the prize of his honor on the pyre of his pride?

But damn it, pride was all he had left.

He glared that conviction at the woman with the pine needles in her hair and the determination in her face as she approached him once more. In her outstretched fingers was a pristine white envelope. The missive was sealed with a tormentingly familiar wax crest: the Greek-style sun, Hyperion, shining down on a scene of pastoral perfection.

As she took his fingers and curled them around the invitation, a message emanated from her eyes, too. *Please come, Damien. I know it'll hurt, and I know it'll be hard . . . but I'll be there, too. I'll be there to help you.*

I'll be there waiting for you.

Then her gaze fell silent. And she let her lips do the rest of her speaking, though no words passed between them.

Softly yet deliberately, she leaned up and pressed a kiss to the corner of his left jaw.

Long after she pulled away, summoned her chimp, then departed, Damien remained standing there. He felt the cold mud caking on his skin; he watched the afternoon shadows lengthen into twilight. He still didn't move. For inside he fought tremors of heat that wouldn't stop radiating down his limbs. He fought the way this insolent American had somehow tunneled her way to his soul and brought along the blinding light of her spirit. He fought the way she had touched him merely by believing in him.

Ah, God . . . by believing in him!

He fought all the things that realization made him feel. He shuddered in terror at this bonfire of sensation, erupting against the icy midnight he'd wandered for so long. The exhilaration, the anticipation, the uncertainty, the fear, the desperation . . . the hope. *The hope.*

All represented by a square of vellum, clutched in his hand.

"Damn," he rasped at that muddy missive now.

She was offering him so much.

She was asking him for so much.

Twenty

WHAT DID IT FEEL like to be on the verge of suffocation?

Over the last six weeks, Kira thought she was well familiar with the answer to that. Not a day went by when at least one memory didn't assault her with ruthless force, taking her back to that night when flames had roared to the heavens and animals had screamed in fear; when she'd battled frantically to save all her beloved beasts yet had come far short of her purpose. Her throat had closed as the smoke closed in around her—

But at least smoke allowed a body to *move*. Smoke was also finicky, favoring places to hoard itself, grimacing in black disgust at those who chose not to play in its domain, but never daring more retaliation than that.

Not like rosewater perfume.

Rosewater perfume, Kira decided, was the undiscriminating spinster of the scent clan. The poor thing clung to everything and everyone in hopes of sticking *somewhere* and, instead, gave new meaning to the word *suffocation*.

Rolf's glorious Pavilion Ballroom nearly floated on a

cloud of the flowery aroma, as the stuff wafted with increasing potency from the dewy shoulders and necks of "London's most influential *dames de société*," as Aunt Aleece had glowingly phrased it two hours ago. *Two hours,* Kira groaned inwardly, the words blending perfectly with the throb of her rose-scented headache. Somehow, 120 minutes sounded much more appropriate. A torturous term to match a torturous ordeal.

The worse realization was: It wasn't over yet. One hundred twenty *more* minutes stretched between here and midnight—a persecution, Kira suspected, of which she'd feel every agonizing second, if all those minutes had to be spent like this one.

She was alone, she was discouraged, and she was trapped.

She stood pinned between Miss Marietta Traybrow of Hightower Grange and Lady Lucille, future Baroness of Fitzwater (of *those* Fitzwaters, Aleece had also pointed out), both young women of ages near hers, donned in gowns similar to the ensemble she wore. Respectively, they preened in off-the-shoulder coral-pink taffeta and dark-blue silk brocade, both their bodices then tapering to tight-corseted waists. Crinolines—unbearable layers of them—then took over, creating skirts that rivaled the bells of Notre Dame for gaudy size.

Yes, from her coiffed head to her silk–slipper-covered feet, Kira looked like she'd grown up behind the walls of some fashionable London address down the street from these two.

She might as well have been positioned between a pair of exotic flamingoes.

The scary realization was, the comparison was quite accurate. Marietta and Lucille wrested their necks in all kinds of contortions as they perused the crowd, at the same time flouncing their skirts and spreading their fans—displaying their "feathers" to best advantage. Their antics would be entertaining, Kira mused, if she didn't realize *she* served the purpose of being their "advantage."

"Now, Kira," Lucille said then, "*may* I call you Kira? Well, of course; we're going to be such good friends; how silly of me! Kira, you simply must tell us all about yourself. We're fairly bursting to know about you."

"Oh, yes!" Marietta echoed, punctuating with a scrunch of her elfin nose. "We're bursting! Bursting!"

Kira, personally engrossed in wondering how the girl had managed not to permanently affix her face in that expression, didn't respond. Lucille obviously interpreted the silence as permission to sidle as close as their skirts would allow and slide a gloved hand to her shoulder.

"You're quite the mystery lady, you know," she murmured. "All we've heard in Town is that you're from the colonies and that you brought an adorable monkey with you."

"A monkey!" Marietta chimed. "Adorable! Adorable!"

"A *chimpanzee*." Kira pointedly stepped away from her new "friend's" hold. "He's *not* a monkey. I'm also afraid you've received other erroneous information, Lady Lucille. I'm from America, not 'the colonies.'"

"Well, of course" was the indulgent answer. The hand realighted on her elbow. "Now you must tell us where you had this gown made. It's exquisite, Kira; really."

"Oh yes, really! Exquisite! Exquisite!"

Another inner groan reverberated twice as loud as the first. No, Kira affirmed then, perhaps she truly didn't know the meaning of suffocation; at least not the slow, steady, wrap-its-claws-around-you-even-in-a-crowded-ballroom kind. She yielded to the dread that she was about to find out.

Especially because no new arrivals to the ball had been announced in the last twenty minutes.

No long-legged figure dominated the Pavilion's silk-draped main portal, appearing a dark and exotic foreign prince himself. No black waves of hair cascaded about a face of ruggedly arresting features, no eyes raked every corner of the room, their fathomless depths possessing more than enough room to accommodate whatever information he gleaned.

Nobody remotely different from the peacocks in this palace who called themselves men.

No Damien.

He truly didn't want anything to do with her, then.

The realization struck her solidly enough to sway her on her feet. Not that Lucille and Marietta noticed, the two now immersed in a discussion of gowns that would make a war council appear a tea party. She fixed her gaze to an elevated candelabra against the opposite wall and forced herself to swallow back tears while a headache grew along with her heartache.

The man was clear as Venetian glass to you, Kira, a voice resounded inside. *You were a dalliance to him, and nothing more. He'll never see you as anything beyond the bizarre little appendage of the family that accused him of murder.*

She struggled to assure herself this was all for the best, anyway. In ten more months, she'd almost be done with this cold island full of cold people. She'd be preparing for her journey back home, and she certainly wouldn't need to be worrying about forest beasts with the gentleness of rain in their touch and the power of thunder in their kisses . . .

"Kira! Kira, aren't you coming along?" Lucille prompted. "This is the most delightful part of the evening!"

"Delightful!" Marietta crooned. "Oh, indeed; delightful!"

Kira surprised herself by managing a wan smile. Dare she entertain curiosity about what these two considered "delightful"?

It didn't appear she'd have a choice about the answer to that, anyway. Her new companions hooked an elbow through each of hers and pulled her toward the expansive dance floor, its shiny black marble fashioned into an onion shape. The fast swishings of their skirts joined with the rising hum of excitement through the room. The twelve-member orchestra had ceased playing, and only one figure now occupied the dance floor: an impeccably attired, casually smiling Rolf.

At the sight of him, Kira unhooked herself from Lucille and Marietta and shifted backward. She'd managed to avoid contact with her host beyond a brief nicety per hour and had no intention of changing that status now, no matter how incredulous the gape Lucille spun and wielded on her.

"Kira! Have you mice in your attic?"

"No," she countered tersely, her gaze still watchful of the dance floor. "Just a rat. A very large one."

"This is no time for teasing, love. Come on; this is when the fun begins!"

She couldn't help the sardonic angle with which she raised one eyebrow. "The fun?"

"Indeed!" Marietta collaborated.

"You see," Lucille responded with gentle patience to Kira's deeper puzzlement, "it's the midpoint of the ball." Her eyes sparkled with excitement as she swept her fan toward the dance floor. "Now is when we get to leave those silly cotillions and quadrilles behind and begin the waltzing."

"The waltzing!" Marietta clapped her gloved hands.

"The *waltzing*?" Immediately Kira's interest piqued. "There's going to be waltzing?"

Lucille's black sausage curls bobbed on either side of her nodding head. "And could there be anything more romantic than waltzing with that man?"

"That man?" Kira's frown returned. "What man? Where?"

"There, silly! Right in front of you. That man . . . Rolf Pembroke."

"Ooooo, yes," Marietta chimed. "That *man*."

Kira didn't know what expression to select then, having narrowed her choices to a grimace of either nausea or dread. "What do you mean?" she managed in a discomfited mutter.

"As host of the ball, Rolf gets to dance the first waltz of the evening." Thank heaven Lucille was a walking encyclopedia about all this pomp. "Normally he'd select his wife, but we all know *that* isn't possible!" She shared a giggle with Marietta that stretched to lengths Kira didn't even wish to understand. "Anyway," the girl at last continued, "he shall select a partner for this first dance, then that lucky bird gets to be his partner for every third dance for the remainder of the evening. Oh, what a divine, *divine* dream!"

"Simply divine." Marietta sighed.

Kira closed her eyes and shook her head. Many words entered her mind at contemplating the fate of spinning around a flat marble onion with a self-important ass. *Divine* wasn't one of those words. *Punishment* was, perhaps. *Impossible* came closer to the mark.

That last thought gave her the fortitude to open her eyes. She could have used an infusion of common sense, instead.

God, no, Kira raged as she looked out across the dance

floor, to where Rolf's stare awaited with the smoothness—and coldness—of latent lamp oil. Oil, that unblinking gaze told her, he intended to ignite in a waltz with her. *No,* she prayed desperately. *Please God, no.*

"No!" Lucille suddenly gasped.

"No!" Marietta swiftly seconded.

It took an instant to fathom the pair couldn't possibly be commiserating with her unspoken thoughts. Another instant brought the awareness that Lucille and Marietta weren't the only ones in the room voicing such sentiments.

A presence had entered the room, Kira realized. A presence imposing enough, commanding enough, and dramatic enough to freeze this throng of hundreds right in their patent-booted, dance-slippered feet.

In that half moment of shimmering comprehension, she smiled.

For in that moment, she knew he was here.

Twenty-One

"I CAN'T BELIEVE HE'S HERE," Lucille muttered with a disdainful sniff. Marietta, too shocked even to echo her friend's words, made up for her muteness by sniffing longer and louder than her friend.

"Damien Sharpe" came a concurring whisper from behind them. "I never thought I'd see him in *this* ballroom again."

"What a positively delicious surprise," someone responded. "And just think, we were about to leave."

"I don't think anyone's going anywhere now."

"True, darling, true."

"He's a savage," Lucille hissed. "Just *look* at him. His ensemble is medieval, it's so old. Did he think this was a costume ball? And his hair—ecchh! He's fooling nobody with that pomade."

"Nobody!" Marietta agreed with swift vehemence.

"How did he get in?" Lucille sniffed. "Who invited him?"

"I did."

Immediately after issuing her declaration, Kira concluded her ordeal of the last two hours had been worth every minute, after all. She even would have endured the torment with a smile if she'd been told she'd have the satisfaction of watching horror blanket Lucille's face, as the priss realized she no longer appeared best girlfriends with "the mystery woman of London" but "the scandal maker of Yorkshire."

The moment had its ideal conclusion when she turned her back before Lucille recovered enough to do so first. She left a round of titillated murmurs in her wake. At that, Kira curled her lips in a sublime smile. It was well past time a few ripples livened up Rolf's little pond.

Ripples, she conjectured, that were going to spread much wider within the next minute.

"Mr. Sharpe," she said softly, arriving at Damien's side after traversing the neat path the crowd had cleared for her.

But while the journey had been easy, the going from here presented a complication. Damien's attire, though not truly fulfilling Lucille's "medieval" depiction, was still a good ten to fifteen years beyond the modes of the men surrounding them. And that, she ruled, made him the most captivating sight in the room. His cream-colored stock was wrapped tightly around his neck, a perfect aid to show off the bold angle of his clean-shaven jaw. A regal blue, tight-buttoned jacket molded to the strong lines of his torso, and matching breeches fitted snugly around the defined muscles of his legs, until black Hessian boots took over from the bottom of his knees. With his hair pomaded and pulled back into a black-ribboned queue, he looked like a gentleman pirate from one of Sheena's fantasy tales, or perhaps a rogue prince from one of Mama's equally romantic stories.

He looked more beautiful than she'd ever fantasized.

How was she going to form coherent sentences with him looking like that?

Again, choices were pulled from her control; she forced composure to return to her nerves as Rolf appeared before them, flared nostrils and blazing gaze contradicting his otherwise cool mien. "Damien," he ground out. "What the devil—"

"Good evening to you, too, my lady," Damien cut him off, selecting that moment to respond to her greeting. Kira grinned, enjoying herself thoroughly as he took his time kissing her hand.

"My, my, my," she managed to quip as he did. "Don't you clean up nicely."

"I believe you purloined *my* line, princess," he murmured back, finishing with a fast wink that didn't help the butterflies dancing in her belly.

At last, he rose and turned back to Rolf. The black velvet of his eyes hardened to iron during the coldly decorous moves. "Mr. Pembroke," he said with tight decorum.

"Sharpe." *That* low growl came from the space next to Rolf's left shoulder, now occupied by a glowering Nicholas and a gaping Aleece. "Get your hands off my daughter," Nicholas commanded.

Indignation surged Kira forward, where she curled an arm beneath Damien's elbow. "My hands were on *him* first." Surprise flooded her at the calm of her tone, though she knew she owed Damien thanks for the feat. Her strength was merely a loan of his amazing serenity.

"Move away from him, Kira," Aleece intoned. "He's dangerous."

The advantage clearly mounting in his favor, Rolf curled a confident smile. "Don't despair, Aleece. He's about to leave."

The man held his features in that expression of sickening self-assurance. The crowd held its collective breath. Kira held her stance next to Damien, who didn't move except to slide a mud-smudged envelope from his jacket, place it on a silver tray he borrowed from a nearby waiter, and hold the offering out with smoothness that made a pulse in Rolf's forehead leap in irked envy.

"Even if he's an invited guest?" Damien queried quietly then.

Two veins jumped at Rolf's temples now. He snatched the tray and glared at the envelope as if he'd just been presented with a platter of raw animal entrails. Still, when he lifted his sights again, one of his beloved statues couldn't manage a more impressively regal façade.

"Where did you get this?" he inquired in a tone that didn't require an answer, providing one already in its accusing inflection.

Kira felt Damien's frame clench in reaction—though she knew he prepared more to hold her back, not himself. He didn't take the precaution in vain. Every muscle in her body yearned to lunge at the letch who'd once called himself Damien's friend but now stood here linking his "mate" to insinuations of murder and thievery.

She swallowed deeply and fought to borrow another dose of composure from the one occupant in the room who shouldn't have any. Yet a glance at Damien's steady profile proved he had self-control to spare.

A soft laugh echoed inside her heart. He'd welcomed her to Yorkshire with a demon's snarl, yet now he helped her deceive all Yorkshire with a pirate's smirk. The man was out either to show her the way to the asylum, or to show her he'd at last separated the identity of her first name from the stigma of her last.

She was willing to take a chance on the latter, Kira decided. As proof of that pledge, she looked up again at the glaring trio opposite her and Damien, yet refused to surrender to the enticement of marching forward, grabbing the invitation off the platter, and informing them *she* was the traitor behind this imbroglio. No, this time she would play the game as Damien would . . . and have twice the fun.

"Mr. Pembroke," she pronounced then, stepping forward with a graceful sweep of her fan and an elegant swish of skirts, "I believe you were about to begin the waltzing." Without waiting for an answer, she spun back toward Damien. "How fortuitously timed your arrival is this evening, Mr. Sharpe. We were about to begin the waltzes—my favorites."

She bit the inside of her cheek to avoid giggling at Aleece's horrified gasp. Rolf wasn't the only sneak around here who could imply things with his tone. The expectant emphasis on her final two words was not only understood but appreciated by the man who now met her gaze with eyes twinkling like a night sky full of stars.

"Shall we, my lady?" Damien asked then, proffering his arm. His tone resonated with a secondary meaning all his own . . . a meaning that spurred Kira's smile higher.

Because that meaning was meant for her ears alone. Her heart alone.

Because that meaning vibrated with the warmth of how proud he was to have her on his arm.

Because that meaning couldn't possibly equal how happy she was to be there.

"Mr. Sharpe," she declared with the full force of that joy, "I *knew* there was a good reason I invited you."

A loud crumpling of skirts denoted Aunt Aleece's scandalized sag against Nicholas. The woman didn't grieve in solitude, though. A cloud of shocked gasps and whispers formed over the room, thickest around the dance floor, where Damien and she took their beginning pose then waited for Rolf and his own partner to do the same. The orchestra conductor, seeing that the master of Hyperion's

Walk had returned to the dance floor, would begin the musical strains to set them all in spinning motion.

But while they waited, something happened.

The music began, anyway. It was a thick, exotic kind of melody, seemingly written to be played in this similarly appointed room. Perfect for waltzing.

Confused, Kira looked at Damien. But his stare was fixed on the conductor, who in turn gave him an I-know-what-I'm-doing glance—and an encouraging nod.

"Damien?" she queried. "What's going on?"

As prelude to his response, he actually let out a soft laugh. "It's my favorite waltzing music," he told her, clearly moved by the lush strains flowing around them.

"But why is he—"

Sheer emotion made her interrupt herself. She lifted her gaze to the perimeter of the room, beyond the murk of rosewater perfume and appalled whispers, to where another contingent of people had gathered to watch the stunning goings-on.

The household servants of Hyperion's Walk.

And right now they stood there as a united whole for one purpose: to confirm their agreement to the message just sent by the conductor to all of London's and Yorkshire's elite.

Listen, that message said. *Listen and look. The master of Hyperion's Walk has returned to his dance floor.*

"Damien? Damien, are you in here?"

Damien took his time about answering the fervid whisper. Finally having escaped to the darkness of the Walk's drawing room, he was enjoying his first reprieve of the last hour, a blessed few minutes of escape from the emotional bombardment that hadn't relented since he'd stepped foot into the Pavilion sixty minutes ago.

Sixty minutes, he ruminated, that felt sixty years. Awkwardness and anger, exhilaration and indignation, pride and humility; *what the hell is a homecoming without them all?* his heart and mind had gleefully proclaimed to his nerves and his gut.

Then there were all the sensations he'd endured when *she'd* approached.

"Damien?" came her voice again, moving closer through the back vestibule, then down the hall. "Now where in the world do you think he got off to, Fred?"

They were the same sensations making themselves known now, merely with her nearing presence. The bittersweet catch of his heartbeat. The anticipating tugs at the corners of his lips. The complete interruption of his anger, his bitterness, his—

The complete interruption of everything in his world. Just the way she'd done things since the beginning.

"Dam—"

"I'm here," he called, finishing by giving in to that smile. He may have just taken advantage of his only chance to interrupt *her*.

All too quickly, however, he set his jaw again. He needed to regain his control, no matter how fiercely some *un*controllable body parts fought him at the task.

Especially when she walked around looking like that.

She was illuminated only by flickering light from the torches lining the garden paths outside, but Kira turned him into an unblinking imbecile as swiftly as she had beneath the full chandeliers of the ballroom. She'd chosen to clothe herself in the colors of the forest, the deep-green velvet of her bodice and skirt accented by gold and copper "leaves" fashioned out of gold-threaded silk, then bunched into strategic arrangements on her waist, between her breasts, in her coiffure.

God, to turn his fingers into fabric leaves. Damien rendered the appeal to heaven more ardently than he had back in the ballroom. Back when he'd held her again, then guided her body across the dance floor . . . and as he had, remembered what it was like to guide her body in other ways. Remembered what it was like to watch her passion for life become passion for *him*.

"Fred got conveniently 'hungry,' " she told him with a light laugh as she and the chimp entered the room. They came to stand in front of where he sat in a high-backed Queen Anne chair, which faced the windows overlooking the lawn separating the main Hyperion's Walk buildings from the Pavilion. Chuckling again, she said to her pet, "As if you're not always hungry, eh?"

Fred cooed contentedly as she ruffled his fur, shameless primate sounds gurgling up his throat. *A raised cup to your health, mate*, Damien nonetheless expressed to the animal. *If her hands were all over me, I'd be babbling incoherently, too.*

Hell. He didn't even want to think about the implications of her touch when at the moment, being the object of her dark copper stare presented an excruciating enough challenge to the distance they maintained. Still, he managed to quip with convincing informality, "Do you take that beast *everywhere*?"

She smiled, obviously used to the query. "If he's so inclined."

Her answer, surprisingly, was just what he expected. Damien gave in to his own smile as he returned, "Becomes a good stand-in when your dancing partner disappears into the night, eh?"

"More like a perfect excuse to get out of the ballroom when Ally needs a break." She emitted a small laugh, though the sound seemed forced and awkward. "Even chimp nannies need a few minutes away from their charges."

Damien tried to help her by releasing a chuckle of his own. But it also sounded staged, and became the prologue to a long, gawky silence between them. He knew she suddenly shared the same awareness as he. They weren't on a dance floor anymore, with a thousand eyes watching their every movement.

"I—er—" Kira at last stammered. "I—um—just wanted to make sure you're all right."

"I'm all right," he returned so swiftly, he doubted Mother would believe him—if she were here. Bloody *hell*, he seethed, not for the first time this evening, *she should be here*. Honora Sharpe should be sitting in this nook with him, contemplating the silliness of the couples outside as they sneaked away for their trysts in the gardens, chuckling gently as she needlepointed another of the pillows still scattered across so many sofas and chairs around here.

Except for one chair in the room across the hall. The chair that had cradled the pillow Rolf threw into the fire that fateful morning, thinking fast when Damien hadn't been able to think at all.

The pillow with Rachelle's blood all over it.

The cracklings of fast-moving crinolines shattered the stillness in the room. Damien looked up to watch Kira walk along the large fireplace, her fingers skimming the equally lengthy mantel as she went.

Without turning, she posed the question he'd been expecting from her—in the hesitant rasp he'd expected it in. "So . . . is this the room where—"

"No." He cut her off swiftly, closing his eyes against a surge of remembered horror. "I didn't find Rachelle in here. It was the Morning Room, across the hall."

"Have you . . . been in there yet?"

Damien couched his chin in the L he formed with his thumb and forefinger. "Yes."

She hurried back across the room, animatedly studying him as she did. When she got to his side, she dropped down so that she clutched one of the chair's padded arms with one hand and his forearm with the other. "Did you find anything?" Intense interest underlined each of her words.

He waited through one beat of time, simply drinking in the lovely life of this woman's face . . . wishing they sat here in the dark talking about anything, dear God, *anything* else besides evidence and clues and murdered bodies.

Giving in to that impulse for just a moment, he grinned and murmured conspiratorially, "Won't your father and Aleece be sending out the Royal Guard for you soon?"

"Not if they think I'll bring Fred back with me, too." She barely paused for a breath before persisting "What did you find?"

"Nothing."

A long moment of silence stretched between them again.

"I'm sorry, Damien," Kira said at last, her voice moving into his consciousness with the gentleness of one of her silk leaves. Her hand rose from his forearm to his jaw, pressing tenderly there.

In response, he cocked her a brief but weary smile. "Not as sorry as I am, princess." Galileo he wasn't, but he knew that even if he could clarify the anomaly this moment, the clue would very likely link to little concrete evidence—the only kind of evidence a magistrate accepted.

He gave her hand a quick squeeze before rising and crossing to the window, where he looked out on a sky in which the moon danced its own cotillion with regal clouds.

His land. *His* land, he repeated inwardly. Land as much

a part of him as the heart beating in his chest, as the Sharpe blood flowing in his veins, as the legs he now braced against the window seat's edge. *It's still mine, Father. It's still mine, Mother. It's all still mine, though I may never stand here again . . . though this may be the time I truly tell you both good-bye.*

"My mother . . . loved to sit at this window," he heard himself murmur then as he raised a hand to the glass pane. "For hours sometimes."

"I can see why" came the woman's voice behind him, a musical and comforting sound. "I'll bet the sunrise looks beautiful on the gardens."

"I . . . miss her."

"I know."

In that black moment, in that dark room, he dropped his head as he dropped his voice . . . as he let his spirit plummet, too. One last warrior of Hope marched valiantly into his psyche, and Damien snarled at the foe while brandishing a broadsword of fury. *I'm tired*, his soul bellowed. *Can't you see I'm tired? This is useless and I'm tired and I'm giving up. I'm giving up.*

But just as Despair snapped open its jaws and bade him welcome into its blackness, an amazing force intervened. A pair of arms caught him, tenderly wrapping around him from behind, saving him from his fall.

Those arms belonged to the gypsy princess who now held him even tighter, imparting to him not only the warmth of her body but the strength of her voice. "I would have liked to have known your mother," Kira said softly. "Many people spoke kindly of her earlier this evening."

That statement produced a conflicting reaction from his gut. Pleasure filled him at hearing Mother was remembered as a saint. But wrath stepped onto the scene upon remembering those same people still called him Satan.

"The May Day Ball tradition was begun by her, you know."

"No." Pleasant surprise resounded in her voice. "I didn't know." Sardonicism, however, quickly took over her tone. "But lucky me; I got invited by Rolf Pembroke. The man only has enough time for *necessary* information between talking about himself, himself, and himself."

She started snickering at her crack, but Damien used that moment to turn around in her embrace. He slipped his arms around her waist as he did. Her giggles faded swiftly as he let her behold the solemn intent of his stare.

"I was invited by the most beautiful woman in the ballroom tonight," he told her in a whisper worthy of the midnight fast approaching them. "And now I'd like to properly thank her for that."

Her breath caught, Damien noticed—just as his did. She swallowed deeply as he urged her closer, and his attention descended to the hollow of her throat, where a deep-golden topaz hung from a green velvet choker. Ah God, he didn't think it possible, but she surpassed his fantasies of how lovely she'd be in his arms, in this dress, tremoring in sensual awakening . . .

As that thought ignited red-hot flames through his mind, Damien dropped his lips to that creamy dip in her neck, shuddering when Kira not only gasped in reaction but fervently grabbed the back of his head.

"Yes," she beseeched him. "Yes, Damien, please don't stop this time. . . ." He answered by cresting the curve of her chin and greedily eyeing the open fullness of her lips . . .

"M'lady! Oh my heavens, Lady Kira, you've got to stop *now*!"

They opened their eyes together, dazed at first, as if yanked out of a shared dream. Their stares widened in shock as they recognized the urgent cry had indeed emanated from a real person: Kira's maid, the never-at-a-loss-for-many-words Ally.

This time, however, Damien had an ominous suspicion he'd be thanking Ally for her loquaciousness in a few short minutes.

"My heavens," the servant fretted again. "M'lady, we've got to set ye aright, and we've got to do it fast!"

"For God's sake, Ally, *breathe*," Kira rejoined, walking to the maid but pulling Damien along by an unrelenting handclasp. "Unless I'm about to be sold into white slavery or Fred's about to be offered as a May Day Ball midnight snack, I don't understand why you're about to swoon."

She even laughed then, concentrating so much effort on calming her maid that Damien was certain she didn't discern the opposite effect had been accomplished. Ally's eyebrows sprang skyward in alarm while suddenly, amazingly, the blush blanched clear off her cheeks.

When the maid spoke again, she addressed Kira in a cautious but calculated tone. "M'lady, I only know that both yer father and Rolf Pembroke are demanding ye be found and brought back to the Pavilion. They say they've got an announcement to make, and they're commanding yer presence for it."

The Pavilion Ballroom was accessible only by traversing one hundred feet of vine-covered walkway between the Carriage Courtyard and the Pavilion's foyer. But even after traveling that walkway through the chilled night, Kira didn't truly shiver until she arrived at the ballroom's entrance. She was bustled a dozen steps inside, while the stodgy footmen had blocked Damien's way with a militaristic crossing of their pennant standards.

By then it was too late. A series of strange hands attached to bodies with strangers' faces pulled her to the dance floor again—where she was thrust face to face with Rolf again.

An all-too-relaxed, all-too-confident Rolf.

She decimated the insides of her lips as she offered a frantic prayer to whatever saint was minding the store upstairs tonight. *I want the other Rolf back,* she implored. The Rolf who'd been so thoroughly incensed an hour ago that he'd retreated to a seating alcove with Nicholas and Aleece and began licking his wounds with a vodka-soaked tongue. Kira hadn't given him another thought after watching Lucille make her way to the alcove, instead joyfully surrendering herself to Damien's lead in the next ten dances.

It didn't look like he was going to let her ignore him now.

The alcohol had extracted its price on his face with savage thoroughness, turning the "Pembroke charm" into pathetic ugliness. From his bloodshot gaze to the ruddy flush of his cheeks, Rolf had aged ten years in the last sixty minutes. And then there was the grin. That insolent, disturbing grin.

"Your ladyship," he proclaimed, hoisting a glass aloft as two smiling strangers urged her out on the dance floor. "Thank you ever so much for joining me!"

The caustic bite to the words couldn't be ignored any more than the flute of champagne he clumsily thrust into her face. A similar flute teetered in his own hand, though half its contents had been depleted.

Kira gritted her teeth and forced herself to lean closer to Rolf. If he listened to her now, perhaps he'd thank her tomorrow. Perhaps he'd even agree to stop bothering her altogether.

"Rolf," she uttered, "you're drunk as a French Quarter cat. You don't know what the tarnation you're saying, or—"

"I know exactly what I'm saying!" he shouted, snatching her around the waist and shoving his leering features so close, her stomach turned from the smell of his breath. Vodka, champagne, and cod with egg sauce. By the saints, where was a gallon of rosewater perfume when she needed it?

"Rolf—" she attempted again.

"I know exactly what I'm saying, and I'd like all of our friends to hear it, as well, Kira darling! Does everyone have their champagne now? Good!"

As a buzz of expectancy sizzled through the crowd, a thudding of dread grew louder in Kira's chest. She glanced behind her right shoulder to selfishly soak up a strengthening look from Damien, but at the edge of the dance floor now, she saw only her father in his normal lordly stance and her aunt in an *ab*normally emotional state. Neither one of them met her gaze. Nicholas scanned the crowd, and Aleece's eyes followed every step Rolf took. The woman's expression tightened to tearful intensity when he spoke again.

"My friends! My thanks to you for joining us for the ball this year. Hyperion's Walk has undergone quite a few changes in the last months, and I've been proud and elated to hear so many of you approve of them."

The man paused to let the reacting murmurs, as well as some spatterings of applause, fade down. He coordinated his next words with a grand motion of his arms. "I am also pleased to say we shall soon break ground on more renovations. I invite you all to return for personal tours, of course."

A slightly louder hum of murmurs voiced approval at that, and Rolf craftily let the tide of energy bolster his continuance. "But despite all of this, Hyperion's Walk is missing one important addition," he stated with calculated mystery. "And I have gathered you all here to announce the plans to rectify that."

He turned to Kira then, his gaze as carefully orchestrated as the swill preceding it. She nevertheless forced her eyes to meet that stare, even as her whole being resonated with agonized thunder because of it.

For dear God, she knew exactly what that stare meant.

Because she knew exactly what his next words would be.

"Lords and ladies, friends and family, I am pleased to announce to you my betrothal to Kira, Lady Scottney, of Scottney Hall!"

Twenty-Two

*A*PPLAUSE EXPLODED THROUGH the room. Horror exploded in Kira's senses. She shook with the force of the shock, her eyes riveted to the amber bubbles in the liquid that fizzed and popped in a flute held by quavering, cold fingers.

This isn't happening, her brain screamed, and the sound reverberated to the depths of her heart. *This isn't happening! How can this be happening?! How can this bastard, no matter how drunk he is, possibly think I'll consent to marry him after—*

She snapped her head up as a second firestorm burst through her faculties—a firestorm ignited by heart-searing comprehension.

Rolf thinks I'll consent because that sanction has already been given to him.

Her epiphany concluded with the appearance of the very monster who was its subject. Nicholas strolled up as if right on cue, acknowledging the well-wishing shouts from the crowd as he held out both arms toward her, his face the epitome of paternal affection. *Isn't it wonderful?* she could practically hear the matrons coo and croon. *Nicholas has welcomed his poor bastard daughter back into the Scottney fold and now has secured for her the hand of Rolf Pembroke! Such a lucky girl, loved by two such splendid men!*

"Don't touch me," she ordered the older member of that "splendid" pair. "You, neither," she spat at Rolf as he approached, too. "Especially not you!"

She wouldn't have thought it possible, but Rolf's face deepened by another shade as he lunged for her, instead. His eyes burned to demonic intensity above his flaring nostrils and snarling lips. Yet he was the most pathetic sight she'd ever seen, Kira decided. His rage was born of nothing but fear.

Fortunately, her father rushed forward and threw a restraining arm in front of the moron. Though the crimson hue of Rolf's face didn't lighten, he nevertheless halted as if a burning bush had appeared in front of him.

"Your frustration is acknowledged, Pembroke," Nicholas asserted lowly. "But I think this is a situation best left to me."

Kira fired a sardonic chuckle at that. "Yes, Rolf. Leave the *situation* to him." She narrowed her glare at her father. "Because the *situation* is about to inform him what a lying, betraying flesh peddler he really is."

"Kira! Dear God!"

"Stay out of this, Aunt Aleece."

"She's right, Aleece; stay away," Nicholas pronounced in a tone emananting from deep in his gut. "It's time I speak with my daughter directly about things like lies and betrayals."

Kira blinked for a moment, battling the sting of tears at the accusation underlying his voice. "Then you're not denying you're behind this," she said in a rasp. Some part of her still prayed for it not to be true. She still prayed the nobleman's calm of her father's face would break by just a wrenched eyebrow or a quirk of lips.

Instead, he moved those lips just enough to level "Are you denying you invited Damien Sharpe tonight, without my knowledge or consent?"

"Did you care about *my* knowledge or consent when blackmailing me to come in the first place?" When Nicholas didn't look as if he even contemplated an answer to that, she pressed on. "So you're telling me yes. You're telling me you gave Rolf your blessing to make that announcement to half of Yorkshire."

"I did what I had to, Kira—to save you from yourself."

"To save me—" She laughed, pure incredulity sparking the outburst. "To save me from *what?*"

"You heard him." Apparently the burning bush had waned, for Rolf stomped back over. "To save you from yourself—and the damn enthrallment Sharpe was casting over you!"

"The what?" she repeated. "For God's sake, Rolf; that's—"

"That's the truth." He issued the words with more solemnity than a priest. The disparity of that analogy with his Satanic appearance forced Kira to bite back a renewed giggle. "I'm sorry," he went on, "but you need to know. You have only to look as far as Rachelle Sharpe's grave to behold the depraved killer beneath the man's flirtations."

"That 'depraved killer' was your best friend," she charged with swift amazement. "Your best friend. Nobody ever proved he was a depraved anything, yet you stand here flinging accusations about him like facts, and—"

"And attempting to save your life in the process!" The gritted vehemence of his retort came with the bruising grip of his hand around her arm, so that Kira spilled half her champagne down the front of her skirt. At last, her father's face furrowed in concern, but Kira lifted her other hand to Nicholas in a reassuring motion.

"Don't do me any favors," she ordered at Rolf as she wrenched free from him and stepped back. "And don't *ever* try anything like that stunt again."

At that, she spun toward the door. She was definitely done with this ball.

But she'd only cleared two and a half steps before a hand clamped around her elbow and yanked her back around with less care given a rag doll. Though Kira had half expected such retaliation, the savagery with which Rolf delivered it drove a new arrow of shock through her.

"You will *not* turn your back on me!" he ordered her in a feral shriek. The crowd suddenly fell silent as a Quaker congregation. "And damn it, we *shall* be married!"

A hundred enfuried reactions barraged Kira's mind. But in the end, she broke the room's stillness with a single action. She discharged the remainder of her champagne into Rolf's face.

The crowd gasped, but she effectively shut them up, too, getting rid of the empty flute by breezily tossing it onto the marble floor. Just before she sent the shards flying farther with a spinning swipe of her skirts, she muttered with fully intended disdain, "I think it's time you cool off, Mr. Pembroke."

The woman was either the most bold and brilliant creature Damien had ever known or the most reckless and dangerous nutcake running free in Yorkshire.

Either way, every instinct in his body told him her flight from the Pavilion wasn't the nonchalant show she wanted everyone to believe. She shouldn't go running out in to the night unsupervised, even if the guardianship was taken on by the only guest at the ball who'd witnessed her horn-locking with Rolf from the ballroom's foyer.

Then again, he pondered, who else was better for the task? He certainly had nothing better to do. Returning to the scene of Rachelle's murder had convinced him even more it *wasn't* the scene of Rachelle's murder.

Despite the explosion of scandalized conversation, matched in urgency only by the strain of craning necks across the ballroom, he found it easy to slip out of the foyer unobserved. He almost chuckled as he did so. For once he didn't harbor a shred of envy toward Rolf for usurping him—not when the title was "Man Most Likely to Be Gossiped About for the Next Three Weeks." Therefore, his erstwhile mate was now the sudden object of everyone's attention.

Fate dealt him a fortunate hand once more, as he located a certain hoyden relieving her maid of chimp nanny duty for the evening. Kira grabbed Fred's paw and led him on a determined pace down the path leading to the hot-house. In order to beat her there, Damien cut through the unoccupied pantry then used his boyhood "secret path" through the trees.

He didn't have long to wait. On incensed strides, she broke into the clearing in front of the building where Mother had once tended the prized Hyperion's Walk orchids and hothouse roses. Kira looked at the hothouse and her face crunched into a grieved frown, as if she shared Damien's own consertation about the decrepitude now creeping around the walls and roof.

"The idiot!" she spat then. "He's an idiot worm, Fred, and I should have kicked in his kneecaps when I first had the chance!" Fuming, she paced the clearing. "Now that I think about it, I should have kicked in much more. Perhaps those balls that have a constant royal audience with his brain. No, that wouldn't hurt him so much. To *hurt* him, I'd have to start with his face. . . ."

She continued the tirade, adding profanities Damien hadn't heard for a year. It had been about that long, he estimated, since his last visit to the Whetted Wick ale house on the Thames.

Yet the venting did let him indulge a moment's satisfaction. His instinct back in the ballroom was a bull's-eye hit. The well-heeled disdain she'd given Rolf was a mere hair on the harpy of wrath she truly yearned to unleash on the man.

Damien found himself wondering just how far Rolf's trespasses extended. Beyond a mere marriage proposal, he would wager, even if it *had* been delivered more in the manner of announcing a cock fight. His senses sharpened with a protective edge. What the *hell* had Rolf done to hurt her so?

The question burned so intensely for an answer that he almost gave up his hiding place in order to ask her. But Damien had taken just a step from behind the two pines that provided his camouflage when she lifted her face into the moonlight, releasing a cry to the heavens clamped in pure, aching anguish. She clearly intended this moment for no eyes but those of the angels, though her face conveyed her doubt even in their attentions.

Christ, he wanted to hold her. To tell her he knew exactly how she felt. On the other hand, he mused, maybe she wasn't thinking of heaven at all. The oath she spat next invoked just the opposite realm, as she spun for the hot-house's door with such impassioned deliberation, she nearly tripped herself.

Another string of curses followed, this time in Russian. If that didn't drop Damien's mouth agape, the next moment took care of properly inducing such shock. He watched as Kira hiked every layer of overskirting all the way to her waist, so that nothing covered her legs except her drawers, her dancing slippers, and half a dozen crinolines.

Within the next half a minute, the crinolines were sent the way of the dirt clods in the path.

A dry gulp slammed down his throat as she reveled in a brief moment of freedom from the undergarments she obviously dreaded. A brief moment in which her adorable, silk-clad bottom was guilelessly exposed to his stare . . . the bottom encased in *his* robe last week . . . the body he could have had beneath him, around him, offered so freely to him . . .

Damien gripped a pine branch to battle the arousal that rose fast and hard beneath his breeches, the worst of the hundreds this American had already induced in him. But he had to tamp the damn thing if he wished to move at all within the next minute—the precise deadline Kira unknowingly gave him, as she proceeded into the hothouse with a determined shove at the door.

She had definitely *not* ventured out here on an arbitrary whim, he concluded. Something—or someone—awaited her inside that building, and Damien had to command his body to move *now* if he wanted to fill in that mystery.

Swallowing a groan of discomfort, he edged closer to the hothouse's entrance. As he moved nearer, his heart sank a notch. The damage to the structure was worse from this proximity. And the stench was more atrocious than that. Holy God, the *stench*.

What the bloody hell was going on here?

His answer began with a desperate sob, emanating from inside. Damien rushed up to the stepping stone before the entrance, but paused there, torn between invading her privacy and yearning to help the source of that cry.

He pushed in the door by a fraction.

And endured the shocking shattering of his senses.

She only needed the proper attire—furs and leathers instead of velvet and satin—to appear every inch the jungle princess gathering with her denizens. From the hopeful lights in the eyes of the exotic creatures beholding her, it seemed this tiny kingdom had found their own sovereign to adore, as well. Of course, those were the eyes of the animals that raised their heads. Some of the beasts tried, he noticed, but they gave up the effort with weak swiftness.

But while he noticed the creatures' feebleness, Kira breathed in their agony—and choked on it. She sobbed on it. While it surprised him little that Rolf had taken an abandoned hothouse and turned it into an *en vogue* profit producer, Kira's hands curled into fists as if a desecration had been dealt to the whole universe.

Hell, how he wanted to go to her.

She stopped when a beseeching mewl sliced the air, louder than the other creatures' grunts and snorts. Damien had to prod the door open a few inches more to watch where she went in responding to the sound, but the door's squeak went unnoticed beneath the frantic *swoosh* of her skirts—and an instant later, by the filthiest curse he'd heard from her yet.

He watched her fall to her knees beside a scraggly tiger cub, who cried again and attempted to climb into her lap. The cat succeeded, but only after tripping twice over its back leg chains.

"Oh, God," she rasped. Her hand quivered as it gently stroked the cub's head. "Oh . . . God."

Under his breath, Damien emitted a curse of his own then. The naked anguish in her voice and the pure grief riding her shoulders would liquefy the heart of Satan himself.

She shouldn't have to suffer that misery alone.

After half a dozen steps he was beside her then kneeling next to her, wrapping her in the brace of his thighs, enfolding her in his arms. Such a tragic irony, he ruminated, that in this world her sadness should result in his strength, but that increased his resolve to pour that strength back out in the security of his embrace, in the kiss he pressed to her temple.

"He's a monster," she said in a rasp, voice shaking with tears and rage. She didn't clarify to whom she referred. Nor did she have to.

She gave further evidence to support her claim, however. *Horrifying* evidence. Leaning deeper into him so he could see the tiger more fully, she gently turned the cub over onto his back. The action exposed a belly infested with dirt and fleas and back leg wounds saturated with blood and pus. The wounds were the exact width of leg chains.

"You're right," Damien told her in a voice now as taut as hers. Silently he thanked God for Rolf's absence at this moment. If the bastard was present, perhaps he'd give the courts real reason to call him a murderer. Cruelty like this broke the bounds of wanting to turn a fashionable profit.

Cruelty like this broke the bounds of the man he'd once called friend.

"The rest are just as bad," she continued, a bitter hardness suddenly fortifying her voice. "None of them has been fed or watered in days. There was another chimp in here before. Now I think he's . . . oh God, he's—" A soft but gritted sob sucked away the rest of the sentence.

"*Damn* him!" she burst then, and her shoulders convulsed when the tiger batted her chin, offering comfort in its innocent animal way. "He says he has a whole crew hired. He says they're trained and experienced. Well, where the damn hell are they?"

"Kira," he murmured, though hardly knowing why. He definitely didn't know what came next. "Princess—"

"Stop it!" She gathered the cub to her breast and wrenched from him. "Don't placate me, Damien! Don't try to calm me or soothe me or tell me it's all right. I'm not calm, and I don't wish to be!"

"And I'm not the enemy." Though he stared at her as he issued the soft words, he stole fast glances at the bear, who restlessly paced his enclosure now. Like a dutiful centurion, the creature felt his queen's agitation and prepared to defend her from the black-furred creature who apparently agitated her.

"I know you're not," Kira answered, breaking his heart yet again with her face, torn between giving in to hopeless defeat or hopeless wrath. "The enemy is that—that barbarian and his friends, hiding behind their sickening waistcoats and top hats and fans and feathers . . ." She sighed and shook her head as the tiger spied an interesting dust ball to roll over and play with. "They aren't rolling around in filthy hay tonight," she muttered. "They aren't fighting leg chains, or trying to sleep on empty bellies. They have plenty to eat, don't they, up there in their fancy ball—"

While a door seemed to slam on her words, a window opened upon her face. Damien, on his way to help her up, stopped in the captivation of watching her brows suddenly jump, her eyes suddenly sparkle and her mouth pop open in amazed delight.

He only wondered why that look made *his* pulse skip a beat in trepidation. "Kira . . ." he said again, though this time he tinted the word with warning, not consolation.

"They have plenty to eat in the ballroom," she repeated,

fixing him with a disconcertingly intent stare. "They have plenty to eat in the ballroom!"

Despite his continuing flounderings through befuddlement, her impish grin was impossible to ignore. Past his own quirking lips, he decided to take a try at hitting her mark of meaning. "So . . . you're proposing we bring them platters from the buffet?"

His pulse omitted *two* beats as she popped to her feet, the imp's grin growing into a mischief's smile. She held off her answer to him until she opened the cupboard Mother had used for gardening tool storage. After a moment of tentative searching, she pulled out not pruning shears but a ring of jailer's keys. Swinging the thing from her finger so it jingled with dementedly melodic triumph, she then looked at him with waggling eyebrows and dancing eyes.

"I'm proposing we bring *them* to the buffet."

A laugh bubbled up Kira's throat as Damien gaped like she'd just proposed they steal the queen's jewels. She'd anticipated the response, but its actual occurrence surpassed her expectations. Heavens, the man's handsomeness became devastating when she stunned him beyond words.

But words he eventually did find . . . sort of. "Bring them—you want to—of all the—Kira!"

By the time he finished his stammerings, however, she'd already successfully found the key to the chimpanzees' cage. The creatures cackled their enthusiastic thanks then milled around her legs as she freed the mongeese, the llamas, and the tiger cub. She scooped up the little thing, who still had a hard time walking with his impaired back legs, and took him over to the man who stood looking thoroughly dazed and wonderfully adorable.

"You'll have to carry Rico," she said, gingerly handing

the cub over. "He won't be able to make it all the way. I'll tear some of the table linens up for bandages when we get there," she finished with a sly wink.

"Rico?" Damien queried, fumbling with the cub like a father holding his newborn for the first time.

Kira shrugged and smiled. "An old friend who was also a fighter," she explained. "Now take him and the others outside while I let this big guy go. I think he's been trained from birth by humans, but he's also hungry. As soon as everyone's outside, their noses will take over."

Her words proved to be prediction before she'd even finished them. What she didn't foresee was the depth of joy *she'd* feel in the next fifteen minutes, returning up the path at an ever-increasing pace behind creatures who hurried to eat again . . . to live again. She smiled at the bear's suddenly alert eyes and twitching nose; she laughed aloud while watching Fred take his two new chimp friends into care, chattering at them about the wonders awaiting ahead. The mongeese, of course, had disappeared, but she'd assumed that. After a few hours of necessary shut-eye they'd be more happy with kitchen rats than pâté molds.

What made this elation complete, however, came with another unexpected advent: Damien's own laughter. She joined him when she looked to see him give Rico one last affectionate pat, as the cub settled itself more comfortably atop the bear's upper back.

Damien lowered his hand and curled it into her own. As he added a smile to the gesture, leaning close to do so, it suddenly hurt Kira to breathe—though she hardly could blame her lungs. How could they concern themselves with breathing when a feeling broke out inside her with more force than a tumbler bursting through a fire ring? How would she feel *anything* again, after this intensity of sensation that had her wishing the universe would stop so she could right her mind? Just for a moment, she begged.

No . . . just for an eternity. An eternity she'd gladly spend by this man's side.

An eternity that was shattered by a scream from inside the Pavilion Ballroom. Then another. Then hundreds more.

To her shock, Damien reacted with a devilish jump of eyebrows and a gleaming flash of a grin. "Come on," he urged, running around the last curve in the path, still grasping her hand. Willingly, Kira followed.

Five minutes later she conceded serious regrets about doing so.

In order even to enter the building, they combated a throng of epic proportions. They struggled through a mania of rosewater perfume, hysterical keenings, and drunken panic, both she and Damien mercifully unnoticed in the chaos.

But despite the mass exodus, they came upon a large contingent of the crowd still inside the ballroom. Men comprised the majority of the group, most of them armed with chairs, rapiers, or, in the case of one bold orchestra member, a violin bow. The women clustered in a fretful throng behind their warriors, shrieking at appropriately dramatic moments—though as Kira evaluated the scene, she wondered what definition everyone used for "dramatic" tonight. Most of the screams erupted when any of the animals so much as made a move. In truth, the creatures were so occupied with chomping down the remainder of the dinner buffet, they had no time or inclination to remember what danger or mischief were.

That was, until Rico decided the gourmet goodies were just as much fun as they were delicious.

"Rico!" Kira called as the tiger cub ran and slid his way

into the orange truffle being enjoyed by the llama. "Rico, no!"

But the little beast compounded the stunt by swatting paw-size gobs of the dessert into the llama's snout. The llama brayed and stomped in protest, but Rico merely rolled across the plate, as if following his own recipe for a new confection, Tiger Cub à l'Orange. He glanced at the women, who naturally followed the llama's complaint with an outbreak of high-pitched hysteria. The cub cocked his head in what looked like utter perplexity.

"Rico!" she called but again voiced the plea too late. Her command was stifled by an outburst of sound from the men in the room, as well. Kira threw an irritated glance at whatever had gotten *them* so riled.

The glance abruptly became a stare of surprise. And alarm.

Rico still lolled about in the orange and chocolate mush, with no idea of the events he'd just dominoed into happening. The llama, in its stomping frustration, had managed to hit a perfect mark in the form of the bear's front flank. The result was one irked bear. The animal stated its indignation in a bawl heard from one end of the room to the next.

The trouble was, the beast decided to issue the declaration from the vantage point of his back haunches. Raising his front paws toward heaven and repeating his chorus with a mouth of impressive white teeth, the animal became a fiercely daunting sight even to Kira.

That was the moment the ape elected not to be upstaged. The big primate lumbered over from the dance floor and cut loose with a primal bellow of its own, beating solidly on its chest in punctuation.

Pandemonium fell far short of an apt depiction for the bedlam that ensued. Everyone in the ballroom crashed and trampled each other in their bids for escape from the "rabid" creatures gone amok before them. The intensity of the mêlée was escalated by the bellows outside, as the throng there dealt with the skittering reappearance of the mongeese.

Kira lunged for the buffet and snatched Rico into her arms just before the ape and the bear decided a tandum effort would benefit them more. The creatures peered around the room with docile enough expressions, but when they thundered together back toward the food, ravenous intent defined each of their heavy steps. The crowd still struggling out the door reacted with a collective shriek that contradicted their dwindling population.

She was no longer part of a spectacle, Kira realized then, but a disaster. Screams and wails filled the air; confusion and fear thickened the brew.

"Come on!" she heard someone order, and Damien's face loomed into view. She responded with an odd laugh; he still looked pristine and collected enough to join her in a few quadrilles, while hair feathers, tie pins, fans, and canes rained from the throng racing past them.

Yet she and Rico found themselves part of that horde the next instant, with or without her permission. Kira had no idea if she was pushed forward by Damien or pulled by the throng's frenzy, but she clung to an equally frantic tiger cub through what felt like interminable minutes. Fear dominated minds and bodies, turning everyone into a mass of unthinking instinct with only their own survival at concern.

At last, she gulped in reasonably fresh air again. She found herself out on the lawn, an anonymous face in the crowd who wandered and embraced with each other as if they'd just survived a tornado. If a newcomer took in the scene now, he might think so, too. Chairs, linens, and broken china looked like a gale force had hurled them across the lawn.

Hurriedly, Kira rounded up a pair of the chimps and secured a tattered curtain tie around the llama's neck. As she observed the mongeese finally scampering their way toward the kitchens, she finally let out a breath of relief.

She never inhaled that breath back in. Her senses went rigid as a jolt of horrifying dread seized her whole body.

She'd been so busy verifying the welfare of the other animals, she'd forgotten to assure Fred's presence at her side.

He wasn't there.

"Fred," she cried. Then in a shout she tried, and failed, to keep from breaking in panic. "Fred!"

He didn't answer. He didn't come.

The last time she'd seen him, he was plopped down on the Pavilion's dance floor next to his new ape friend, happily attacking a bowl of fruit.

She stared now through the chaos, down the foyer at the tangle of destroyed debris the dance floor had become.

And she screamed.

Twenty-Three

DAMIEN HAD PUSHED KIRA and the tiger into the frenzied exodus from the ballroom but deferred his own departure to help the dowager Countess Raincroft, who had tangled herself between her walking cane and her crinolines. Realizing the woman's escape from the structure just might be hindered by a rampaging ape if she wasn't assisted, he'd extricated her despite the hostile glare he'd gotten for the effort.

After handing Raincroft over to her sister, who speared an even more affronted look his way, he instantly sought out Kira. He'd just confirm she was safely clear of the Pavilion, he told himself, then he'd cut back to the stables for Dante and leave with no further delay. At least no further delay like saying some sort of official farewell to her. After their interrupted passion in the drawing room, combined with the exhilaration of working together against Rolf's maltreatment of her beloved animals, he didn't possess even a drop of "official" feeling toward Kira Scottney.

Everything he felt for her now was very *un*official. And indecent. Heatedly, excruciatingly indecent.

Bloody hell. He needed to douse himself in some ice water. Lots of it. Soon. He just needed to locate her in this chaos of humanity, assure himself she'd gotten out of the Pavilion in one piece, then be on his way home, with a required detour by way of the stream and the waterfall. Their currents would be wonderfully frigid at this time of night, he mused gratefully.

If he could only find where the *devil* that hoyden had gotten off to.

His dilemma was resolved the next instant. He knew exactly where to find Kira as soon as her horrified scream rent the air.

Barreling over or through the idiots who chose to get in his way, Damien sprinted to her side as if he'd departed the Pavilion with his shoes on fire. He grabbed her hands and peered into her eyes and, for the first time since meeting her, saw not an ember of defiance in those dark amber depths—only the glitter of raw fear.

"Princess, what is it?"

She emitted her explanation in a distraught rush. "Fred—it's Fred—no, it's not Fred, because I can't—because he's not—Damien, he's not—"

"Ssshhhh," he soothed, stroking her cheek. "*Think*, Kira. Where do you remember seeing him last?"

Her face contorted harder as she drew in breath for her reply to that—a reply stolen from her during that faltered moment. The thief wielded a dagger of sharp laughter as his weapon.

"Lost our little monkey, did we?" Rolf jeered at them, approaching with redness in his eyes that had been forced too quickly from drunken frustration to sober outrage.

Kira turned then and took a shockingly polite step toward Rolf. She even bowed her head slightly in respect. Damien swallowed, moved by the mettle it took her to simply do that, yet half surprised she didn't fall at the man's feet, too. She was ready to relinquish even the precious possession of her pride if it would bring her pet back.

"Rolf," she pleaded from gritted teeth, "please . . . have you seen him?"

"Not since he and his pals helped you destroy my home" came the merciless snarl. "Not since I watched him infest my fruit with his filthy fleas."

"Rolf!" Damien told his best-not-to-intervene resolution to go to hell. "For Christ's sake, did you see the chimp or not?"

They were interrupted by an ominous crash from inside the Pavilion. Ensuing shouts announced the bear and the ape had been subdued again, though the pair clearly hadn't surrendered without taking casualties with them: a central support beam of the ballroom, plus a chunk of the ceiling surrounding it. And still, the beasts refused to capitulate peacefully. The din of splintering wood, shattering glass, and shouting men continued to punctuate the night.

"Dear God." Kira gasped. "He's still in there; I know it. Fred! *Fred!*"

With the same swift panic, she abandoned her humble position toward Rolf, but Damien wished she'd remained where she was in favor of where she now lunged. He arrested her from breaking into a full run at the Pavilion only by grabbing her by both shoulders, grunting greatly in the effort.

"Let me go, damn it!" She sobbed, beating at his chest. "You don't understand! We've got to do something!"

"Looks like your brat's done it already," the man behind them taunted. "Went back for more from the buffet one too many times. Perhaps he should have had a little snack before coming tonight."

Damien didn't bother wasting even a glare on the bastard, but he wondered if Rolf realized how lucky he was that a chimp needed rescuing more than he needed his face turned inside out. Yes, right now his rage had to support him in the effort of ordering Kira—and her voluminous skirts and satin dancing shoes—not to dare a step more through this miniature disaster zone. He did so just before wheeling around himself, and sprinting toward the ballroom's glass-strewn foyer.

Insanity, he castigated himself while barreling onto the dance floor, directly into the bear's rampaging path—where a terrified chimpanzee had also managed to get trapped. *This is insanity, Sharpe! Are you insane? You're risking your life for a hoyden who's not playing with balanced dice herself. No, you're risking your life for something more ridiculous than that. For a reckless chimpanzee who—*

A chimpanzee who now locked his arms around Damien's knee and clung with the tenacity of a five-year-old welcoming his father home.

"Hello there, mate," he greeted Fred, trying to ignore the leap of strange joy in his chest in favor of his brain's more assuring instinct: to get out of this predicament as fast as they could.

"You're one lucky bounder, Fred," he muttered while scooping up the trembling animal. "Let's hope your star of destiny follows us now."

Fortune indeed chose to look upon them with benevolence; the men secured the bear's tethers at the moment the beast lunged within inches of the dance floor. But Damien didn't break his concentration or stride until his feet hit the night-dampened lawn again. As they did, a huge rush of air left his lungs.

Fred's burst of excited cackling prompted him to set down the animal and raise his sights toward Kira. He expected to smile at her tear-filled face and her outstretched arms, ready to wrap around her pet once more.

But he couldn't see her face. And her arms—well, they were stretched out, though an embrace appeared the furthest purpose she deemed for them as Rolf grabbed her by the wrists and shook her, shouting something savagely. As Damien ran nearer, he discerned the contents of the man's diatribe.

"You're *sorry?*" Rolf seethed at her. "You're *sorry*, are you, Kira? Well, why don't I believe that? Why don't I believe you're not an ant's piss sorry about any of this?"

"Rolf" came her strained plea. "Rolf, you're hurting me—let me go!"

He only answered her with a laughing bark. "You're not sorry, Kira. I'*ll* give you a reason to be sorry!"

Kira watched as Rolf's upraised hand blocked out the moon. She winced, bracing herself for the blow into which the man would drive all his seething wrath.

Yet at the moment she expected the painful imprint of his palm across her cheek, her world went careening again. She was grabbed and spun around, then thrust behind a stone pillar that erupted out of the lawn from God-knew-where.

Only then the pillar let out a vicious snarl. And she realized the pillar wasn't a pillar at all.

She opened her eyes to confront Damien's taut, braced spine, bracketed by one arm ending in a coiled fist and another arm ending in an outspread hand. That hand conveyed one message to her: *Step back and stay back.*

"The lady said she was sorry, Rolf," he growled. "Which is more than what I've heard from you since humiliating her with your sotted antics."

Rolf's retorting laugh sounded unreal, a bit demented. "Humiliating her?" he drawled, though his tone swiftly hardened into a bitter bite. "Funny, Damien. Most of that ballroom thought I was doing the chit an honor. You remember 'honor,' don't you, mate? That little commodity that dictates one doesn't murder his wife?"

"The same little commodity that dictates a man believe in his best friend?" Damien countered. "Is that the one you're talking about?"

Kira peeked around Damien far enough to view half of Rolf's face. Half was enough. The man glared at them both with feral threat. "You're not welcome here anymore, Damien," he stated. "Stay away."

Surprisingly, Damien yielded an acquiescing nod to that. But that was before he responded, "I don't think Lady Kira wishes you sniffing around her borders anymore either." He borrowed Rolf's exact emphasis to add, *"Stay away."*

Another string of strangely light chuckles trickled from Rolf's smirking lips. "Well, well. So that's the way of it." He sneered. "Going to take down another Scottney bird, are you, Dame? Though I don't blame you for wanting to put other things down her throat before you slash it."

Damien issued no retort to that. Instead, without a word of preamble, he drove his fist hard into Rolf's jaw.

Semiconsciousness struck Rolf before he hit the ground. Even so, with a groan, he battled to push up onto his elbows. Damien vanquished his effort by pressing one boot between his ribs. "I think that settles our accounts for the evening, Mr. Pembroke," he said with bizarre calm, "so I'll say good night. Smashing party, by the way. The best yet."

The soft, drawling sarcasm with which he concluded was a contradiction to the brusque force of his turn back to Kira. He secured a hand around her elbow, but neither of them moved. For in that moment, their gazes intertwined, and Kira found herself seared to the spot more assuredly than if a flame from one of the chandeliers inside had burrowed beneath the grass and melted the soles of her shoes. But in truth, she knew, the fire came from inside her . . . just as it came from inside Damien, too.

She knew that because in the depths of his black, black eyes, she suddenly beheld two pure, blue-shadowed flames.

She held her breath as that beautiful midnight light grew brighter, showing her just how much of this man's soul had been torn open tonight . . . showing her how deeply he'd excavated that soul in order to confront Rolf.

Then with a self-conscious blink, the flames were extinguished. Damien's features returned to their hard-hewn fury. But as he slid his hand down to hook his fingers through hers, his voice came incongruously soft . . . and intimate.

"You're coming with me," he said, pulling her toward the stables. *"Now."*

Twenty-Four

*N*OW. KIRA THANKED HIM for that word as she let its simple beauty dictate her mind for the next minutes . . . or perhaps they were hours, she didn't know. All that mattered was *now*.

The swiftness of *now* was exhilarating, as Damien thanked a groomsman who had his massive stallion at the ready, then swung her and Fred into the saddle ahead of him. The darkness of *now* was welcome, as they left Hyperion's Walk and the night wrapped around them, cloaking them as they galloped into the forest.

But most of all, the man of *now* was perfect, with his warm breath upon her neck, his powerful torso at her back, his commanding hand upon the reins. In the vortex of Damien's hold, she felt the strength she needed to trust, at last; to surrender, at last . . . to release the agonized clench her body had become since stepping onto the dance floor and facing Rolf's drunken leer. She entrusted her weight against him just as she entrusted the night shadows with her streams of releasing tears.

Now, she decided, was a wonderful place to be.

She didn't know where Damien was guiding them, but when they at last halted, she wasn't surprised when she heard no other sound but the sough of wind through pines and Hamlet's gentle whimper of greeting. Damien didn't answer his pet, his silence thick with the same tangible tension that had defined his mien since they'd left Hyperion's Walk.

Without a word, he dismounted with economical grace, but didn't help her and Fred down until he guided the stallion to the barn and turned up the lamp. The lamp's dim glow nonetheless highlighted the strain across his features: the jaw that hadn't relaxed since he'd spun and gone for Fred, the deep lines of weariness around his eyes, the all-over coating of dust, now smudged in several places.

As she gazed at him, Kira pulled in her lips and bit them hard, struggling against another surge of tears. He'd never formed a more beautiful sight to her eyes.

Fred and Hamlet romped away somewhere outside, chattering and panting enthusiastically at each other. Giving their departure barely a glance, Damien led the stallion to his stall, secured the reins, and removed the saddle. All the while, Kira didn't wrest her gaze from him. She *couldn't*. When he finished slinging the saddle over the stall wall, she knew he realized that, too. He stood with both arms braced on either side of the saddle, his stare affixed to the leather as if his death sentence was emblazoned in it.

Kira didn't begrudge him the ominous intuition. Not if his blood thrummed the way hers did—so deafening, her ears hurt because of it. Not if he heard each of her heartbeats the way she suddenly heard his . . . aware of each breath he took, too . . . sentient of every move he made.

Wondering if he thought of all the insane events that had conspired to bring them together this night, and if he questioned Fate and its extraordinary hand: *Why?*

Wondering if the only answer his heart rendered made him shake with desire and need . . .

And love.

She gasped audibly as the revelation rang through her senses with astounding truth. *The saints help me,* those senses cried out. *Help me, I've fallen in love with this man. I've fallen in love with his depthless gaze and his surly scowl; with his hands on my ankle and his face in my dreams. I love his majestic forest and his doting dog; I love the boy who speaks of his mother and the hero who faced a furious bear to rescue my pet.*

I love him as the woman I've become because of him.

She now battled the tears in vain. Kira blinked to clear her vision, but before she had the chance to wipe the salty tracks off her cheeks, Damien looked back up. Straight at her.

Her heart pounded once. Twice. Before she watched him shove away from the wall and march out of the stall. Straight toward her.

Not another sound left her lips as instinctively, eagerly, she opened her arms to him. She received the crush of his body as she surrendered to the domination of his kiss, reveling in the heat of him, the power of him, the hardness of him. In turn, she gave back her own passion, her own heat, her own need.

Oh God, she thought, more tears welling to her eyes, that's exactly what this sensation was . . . a raw, blinding need not only to feel her love for this man but to *show* him. It was the name for the yearning that had encouraged her to wrap her arms around him in the drawing room, that had given her succoring words for his grief and welcoming words for his kisses.

It was the name for the force she let enflame her now.

She sobbed with the strength of that force as Damien

parted the folds of her mouth. His tongue swept against hers with a hungry ferocity; his hands raked her body with fevered intensity. He was everywhere: around her, against her; pulsing with hard strength and with a yearning finally allowed to flare into desire.

And still, she wanted more. More, as she delved her own tongue into the hot recesses of his mouth. More, as she licked his lips, savoring their taste of sweat and midnight and man. More, as she let her hands explore him, too, seeking the places she had lain awake dreaming of on so many nights: the curve where his neck met his shoulder, the muscled vale down the center of his back, the dusky circles surrounding his male nipples.

"*God*," he murmured as she touched him there, tautening the nubs to erect attention. "Oh God, yes, Kira . . . my Kira."

At that, her lips released a smile of trembling joy. "Say it again," she commanded as that bliss shimmered its way to the tips of her toes and fingertips. "Say it again."

She felt Damien's smile before it reached his face, erupting from a rumble of laughter deep in his throat. "As many times as you want, my Kira," he whispered. "*My Kira.*"

Then his lips were on hers again, and with a whimper of enkindled desire, she opened to him as she never had before. She opened to him because in that moment, with the final urgent and hoarse utterance of those words, she knew Damien comprehended what overjoyed her so much about them, too.

Rolf Pembroke and his arrogance and his violence had no jurisdiction over her anymore, nor could Father or Aunt Aleece threaten so, either. *My Kira.* From now on, her skin would know the imprint of one man's touch, her body would know the feel of one man's possession . . . just as her heart, for the last four weeks, had known the sweet ecstasy and fear of dreaming for one man's loving.

If she in fact dreamed now, she sent a prayer to God to never end this night. She never wanted to wake up from the magic of the masterful hands that entwined their fingers as they descended into the hay, bodies pressing, heartbeats merging into one.

"Damien." She gasped as his lips descended against the sensitive corner where her jaw met her neck, causing the night to explode into even more intense beauty. "Oh, Damien . . . we're not going to stop this time, are we?"

She felt him swallow deeply. And his body tighten perceptibly. "No, princess," he answered huskily. "No, we're not going to stop."

"Thank God!"

Damien's reacting chortle spread warmth through her heart, as his corresponding kiss sent heat through her body. The effect on Kira's senses reminded her of how she'd felt once before a summer dust storm in Kansas: restless, breathless, and full of wild, inexplicable animal impulses.

She moaned from the potency of those instincts now . . . from the undeniable need to act on them. Damien answered with a similar sound, though his emerged as more a masculine growl. She knew that because she felt the vibrations of the sound as he dipped his mouth to her bodice and pushed aside the velvet there. She cried out his name once more, this time in aching ecstasy, as he freed her other nipple in the same way.

"Heavens." Yes, that's certainly what this was, she thought as her whole body arched against Damien, giving him fuller access to the peaks he suckled and enlivened. She finished the word with a sigh of profound elation, as she felt him reach beneath her and loosen her corset.

They kissed deeply again, and while they did, she made

short work of dislodging his queue, restoring his hair to the tangled black waves she knew and loved. But removing just his hair ribbon wasn't enough, Kira swiftly decided. Not nearly enough.

Now she wanted to see his nipples, too.

No . . . she wanted to see all of him.

Perhaps, she concluded, the best way to show him that was to let him see all of *her*.

A deliciously powerful tingling took over her belly as she gently scooted back from him and rose to her feet. Though Damien frowned his protest at first, a fine sheen of arousal quickly formed again over his features as she unfastened the half-dozen hooks securing her bodice. When her skirts, chemise, and drawers also puddled at her feet, a dark and mysterious force transformed his face into a vision that halted Kira's breath.

She waited through a tormenting stillness. He said nothing. Damien only emitted a half-strangled sound that followed a deep swallow.

Tears threatened to brim over in her eyes. Perhaps Aunt Aleece had been right all this time, she thought. Perhaps a man did appreciate a coy coquette instead of a forthright gypsy. Or perhaps her body didn't please him. Her skin wasn't ethereally translucent, as so many of the women she'd seen tonight, and her limbs weren't soft and rounded, but lean and defined by years of tumbling, riding, and performing. She was an American wildflower, not an English rose. And now, oh God, he was remembering he preferred roses!

But then Damien stood.

Before he reached his feet, he'd torn his shirt away from his torso. But Kira barely had a moment to behold the muscled magnificence of the sight before he tugged and tossed aside both his boots, then started to rip at the buttons of his breeches.

Her breath eluded her completely as he freed his erection.

In contrast to her silence, Damien unleashed a moan sounding strangely of relief and pain at once. The sound escaped him again as he took his hard length into one hand.

"Look, Kira," he said to her then, low and rough. "Look what you do to me . . . what you've been doing to me since the day you crashed your gorgeous arse in my forest."

"Damien," she whispered, smiling, and the tears at last did break free—only this time, in happiness.

"Come here," he entreated, now raising both arms to her. "Come here, darling, and feel what you do to me. Come here and touch me."

She joyously obliged him. They collided in an ecstastic explosion of an embrace, pressing and writhing, igniting and enflaming, conquering and consuming. A beautiful, primal need began to pulse in Kira's blood as she reveled in the feel of this man's nakedness against her; as she savored his sculpted chest, his ridged stomach, his swollen desire. She moaned as heat throbbed between her own thighs in response to his arousal; she delighted in the similar sound from Damien's throat when she slid herself tighter against him, wanting to feel more of him. Wanting . . . *wanting*.

"Damien," she pleaded, trying to express that scorching need, but finding her voice an abysmal intercessor for the exquisite sensation. "Oh, Damien, I—"

"I know," he assured, and somehow, she knew he did.

He repeated the words while he pulled her down into the hay again, making them an increasingly urgent litany against the skin where his mouth roamed: first along her neck and shoulder, then over the rise of her breast, down the plain of her stomach, teasing against the line of her hip bone, at last dipping to softly lick the inside of her thigh. The excruciating gentleness of his action sent a vibration of trembling pleasure throughout her body.

His mouth . . . dear sweet saints, what this man could do to her with his mouth! Kira gasped with the sweet torment he induced, hardly believing she felt this erotic, this ecstatic. For eighteen years, she'd been trained to consider her body an instrument, only a prop for a show, year after year. Nobody, not even Sheena, had told her about *this*. Nobody had told her the mere flick of a man's tongue could transform her body into a magical ribbon of sensation. Nobody had told her she could transform into a burst of fire, bold and bright, aroused and alive and ready to—

"Damien!" she cried out, suddenly not knowing what she was ready for at all—but certain it had something to do with the press of his mouth to the most intimate part of her being. "Oh . . ." she rasped raggedly as he parted her feminine folds and kissed the tender nub he unveiled.

"Kira," he answered, murmuring the word against her, bringing her tears anew as he cherished the most womanly part of her. "You taste so damn good, darling."

He proved it to her the next moment. As tears seeped down her cheeks, Damien slid up her body and joined his mouth to hers once more. He brought sweet warmth and delicious tanginess with him, delivered with the passionate sweep of his tongue and the masterful sucklings of his lips. Kira mewled from deep in her throat as she buried her hands in his hair and took him in yet deeper, craving the ambrosia of him like a starving woman.

When they broke apart, their heavy breaths mingled together while their slick bodies writhed together. His heartbeat thundered between her breasts like a plummeting anvil; she clutched the quivering tension of his shoulders with a mixture of awe and desire. He was ready, more than ready to take her; he valiantly fought the building forces in his body that pounded and throbbed and ached for release. He was waiting for her, she realized, and the knowledge of that filled her heart with joy anew—for now she comprehended the enormity of such a feat.

For now she battled the same clamoring forces in her own body.

The confession, even made inwardly, exploded the dam on a new flood of the maddening pressure. It crashed over her and through her, resulting in a head-to-toe quiver she seriously doubted had an end. It also toppled any restraints she had left. Direct proof of that came from the hand she descended down Damien's side, around his hip . . . then around his beautiful erection.

"God!" He groaned, his own tremor joining with hers. "My God, Kira, what—"

"You invited me to feel you. Don't you remember?"

He surrendered a tight sound that attempted to be a laugh. "Yes; vaguely. Oh, princess, your fingers . . ."

"Are they all right? Is—is this all right with you?"

Now he *did* laugh. "Oh yes, Kira. Oh . . . *yes*."

He kissed her to emphasize his point, sliding his tongue against hers to correspond with the same motion of his erection between her fingers. Soon, however, they both breathed too fast and intensely for that, the heat and tension and friction exploding like a thousand colliding stars, igniting even the midnight heavens in sweet fire.

"And . . . how *do* I feel, darling?" he managed to ask her shakily, while his body rocked against hers ever faster, ever harder.

Kira wondered how he got the words out. All she achieved was a half-strangled "Dayyy . . ." before reason succumbed to instinct and she rendered her answer by way of movement, instead.

Sliding hesitantly at first, but with increasing surety, she opened her legs for him.

Damien fit perfectly into the wet, warm valley she created for him. The essence of him pulsed against the entrance of her, hardness stroking impatiently against softness, man aching to become one with woman. He breathed passionate nonsensities against her ear. Yet still he tarried, his body awash in the sweating strain of holding back. Why was he holding back?

"Damien," she pleaded as an unnameable maelstrom swirled hotter through her body. She writhed unthinkingly beneath him, seeking surcease from the tempest, while at the same time, craving more of the storm. Oh, sweet saints, *yes,* she wanted—

"More," she implored aloud. "Damien . . . *please.*"

"I know, darling" came his strained-to-the-limits grate. "I know what you want, but—"

"Damien!"

"But I don't want to—"

"*Damien!*"

She arched as he plunged. She moaned as he groaned. Her outcry swiftly became a wondrous gasp, though, as she soared into heaven, her body convulsing in pleasure around his erection. Sheena had told her there would be pain and Kira supposed somehow there was, but her senses barely acknowledged the physical consequences of what she'd done, at least not now. Not through her haze of such exploding bliss, such sublime completion, such sheer fulfillment.

Damien gave her even deeper pleasure as he moved inside her with increasingly urgent abandon, his breath coming with faster frequency, his face awash in mindless, reckless passion. "Kira," he murmured with an undertone of apology, gripping her hips, "Kira, it's been so long for me . . . and you feel so good. . . ."

"Don't stop," she begged. Her hands roamed up and down his flexing, thrusting body. He was a magnificent creature, as sculpted and sinewy as the most graceful panther, as powerful and strong as the most commanding lion. She reveled in his untamed domination of her body, telling him so in the intense feline sounds vibrating up her throat and singing from her lips. Faster she urged him on; faster and hotter until—

"Kira!"

His body shuddered as he drove into her with a final, beautiful motion. His head fell back; his chest gleamed with sweat. And again Kira's tears came, as she watched him and moved with him through the gentle rockings that evened his heartbeat and cooled his skin.

And she loved him.

In this sweet, wonderful *now*, she loved him.

And in this sweet, wonderful *now*, she told herself that would have to be enough. For it was perhaps all she'd ever have.

Tomorrow—and the uncertain reality it would bring— would come soon enough.

Tomorrow lay just a few minutes away.

Damien accepted that fact with grim reluctance as he watched the sky laboring to shed its stars in favor of a lavender and peach dawn. Tomorrow would officially begin when sun threads wove their way past the pines and fell into scattered stitches along the foot of the bed in which Kira and he lay. The bed he never thought he'd share with anyone but Hamlet.

But this woman felt right here. Very right.

And at the moment, he refused to acknowledge the danger of thinking that. He only wanted this moment . . . and then he'd allow tomorrow to come.

He slowly turned to his side and propped his head on a bent elbow. After gathering her up in a blanket and bringing her up here from the stable last night, he'd let the darkness woo him into an exhausted sleep. So he indulged himself a long, lingering stare of her beauty now—though "beauty," he mused, was hardly the sufficient term for the sight that filled his gaze.

Even in slumber, Kira Scottney was more a firebrand the angels decided to turn into a woman. Her hair spread across the pillow like curling smoke tendrils from a gypsy incense burner . . . bayberry scented, he decided, observing the mahogany tints in the strand he fingered. Centered in that cacophony of dark curls was the flame of her face, her brows set in expressive dashes even now, her lips slightly parted and promising lush warmth, her skin the color of candle glow on ivory roses. God yes, her skin. . . .

Merely recalling how the golden silk of that skin extended to her toenails—and the manner in which he'd discovered that fact—was enough to make his groin jump to life with arousal again. *You're not making things easier on yourself*, he commanded while watching the knuckles of his free hand brush a savoring trail around the curve of her shoulder, down her arm, to the slender hand resting against the counterpane. He swallowed, berating himself for starting the action, for he wished to finish it by moving his hand beneath that cover, then embracing the soft mound waiting there. He imagined how her nipple would feel as it tautened to life beneath his touch; he clenched his teeth against allowing the fantasy to continue further.

Until the woman beside him brought that fantasy to life.

With her eyes still closed but her lips curving into a smile, Kira guided his hand to the very curve of flesh for which he'd been yearning. Their breaths caught together as his hand closed over her breast, awakening its dusky bud to attention. The rest of her body came alive with swift succession, and she writhed her way next to him with impatient abandon.

The texture of her skin and the feel of her body were all the prompting he needed for what he did next. Sliding his mouth to hers, he explored the sweet heat of her like a child discovering the deliciousness of his first candied apple, only with one important exception. Candied apples didn't emit such sexy mewls while being ravished.

When they pulled apart, many minutes later, he still kept her burrowed close to him. "Good morning," he murmured, brushing another kiss to her forehead.

She didn't respond in kind—not a surprising occurrence, since he was beginning to expect anything but the expected from this woman—though the furrows that formed beneath her lips were definitely not on his roster of anticipations. Kira explained the frown by way of a soft protest. "No. Make it go away. Make it night again."

She needed to expound no further. The night had been their reprieve, their black forest of time where names meant nothing and passion ruled everything. The morning razed that forest and built manicured gardens in its place, gardens filled with stone formations that called themselves people.

People like the man who'd once been closer to him than anyone else in the world.

Squeezing his eyes against the sickening remembrance of the confrontation with Rolf, Damien succumbed to a grimace of his own. "Ah, princess," he whispered, "I wish I *could* make it go away. I wish I could make many things go away."

This time it was she who shifted to bestow a soft kiss against his forehead. "I know you do," she returned, and he opened his eyes to the intent glow of her sienna stare. "I know what you wish for every time I look into your eyes."

His reaction to that took him by greater surprise than her first frown. The fear jolted up from his gut like a geyser, pummeling the backs of his eyes and slamming them shut again. "Really, now?" He concealed his uneasiness behind a gruff chuckle. "I'm just a bloody open book, is that it?"

"Only to those who wish to read." Her voice was smooth with the same steady warmth of her gaze, only heating *his* agitation higher. "I read it in every stare you took of the drawing room last night," she went on, anyway. "I read it in the way you spoke toward those servants, who weren't just servants but friends. You love Hyperion's Walk like a part of your soul."

"Yes," he answered, swallowing tightly. "I do."

She lay down against his chest again, and he instantly acknowledged how perfectly she fit there, in the place atop his heart—though with her next words, she did manage to stop the beat of that heart altogether.

"Your mother would have been so proud of you last night, Damien. And your father."

The ache in his chest erupted into a dark laugh off his lips. "Well, that shows how much of my book you have yet to read, my lady."

She tensed at his deliberate use of her formal title, but he assured her the barb of his bitterness was aimed elsewhere by running a caressing hand over her head and down her back. He just wondered if she knew his target was the very heart beneath her ear. Of course not, he debated. Until this moment, *he* hadn't had the courage to admit

what his soul now bellowed at him in resounding fury . . .
he hadn't had the courage that Kira Scottney now gave to
him.

He hadn't had the courage to concede that his hatred
wasn't reserved for the Scottneys alone.

The realization exploded inside him as if a dozen Pavil-
ions had been built there then put to flames at once. He
breathed in and out once, putting his body through rigorous
torture as he did so, though barely throwing a drop of water
on the blaze igniting him deeper.

The only way to cool the torment, he realized, was to get
help doing it.

Bloody hell.

"Damien? What is it?"

Both questions came gently, almost politely, verbal ver-
sions of help given generously. Still, he took only harsh
breaths in answer. Damn. *Damn.* So intent had he been on
remembering the morning he'd found Rachelle that he'd
almost been able to forget about the years before that . . .
almost.

Now he knew he'd forgotten them only in mind and
body. Souls never let a man forget.

With that conclusion closing in on his mind more fervently than the approaching dawn, he took a deep breath
and surrendered an answer to her at last.

"Your father and your aunt have good reasons to believe
I killed Rachelle."

It came out all wrong, of course. He instantly felt like
going after the words with a grappling hook, but instead
spent the energy preparing for Kira's terrified flight from the
bed.

To his shock, she only glanced up at him, her face
scrunched in a piqued frown. "What the tarnation does *that*
mean?"

Damien almost replied by bellowing out a laugh. She might as well be stomping her way up a streambank at him again, raving about frightening squirrels and crushing flowers. She had no idea he'd once crushed much worse.

That thought swiftly sobered his laugh. "It means I haven't always been this charming and debonair, darling."

"Stop cutting up."

"The hell I'm cutting up." He apologized for his irritated growl by running a gentle hand over her mussed curls. "Kira . . ." Christ, this wasn't easy. "Kira, you didn't know me ten years ago."

"I didn't know you ten months ago. What does that have to do with anything?"

He stared at her again, unsuccessful in restraining another soft smile. There was much he'd learned from this woman with gypsy in her blood and America in her spirit. So much about trusting the moment at hand, not the specters of the past. So much about visiting that past, but not living in it.

Ah God, what all of Yorkshire could learn from her. But they hadn't yet, and that's why he compelled himself to go on.

"I wasn't what you call a dutiful son." He let out a self-deprecating grunt. "Hell, I wasn't what you call a dutiful anything. I suppose I had too much time on my hands and too much money in my pockets. The crux of the whole thing was, my father even encouraged my rebellion at first; I used to hear him calming Mother, telling her I was going through the 'rites of manhood' and other babble such as that. But his casual attitude only made me angrier, and by the time I was sixteen, he and I were strangers. My 'happiness' lay in whoring and gambling with all the wrong kinds of friends, in all the wrong kinds of places."

A strange shadow fell over her gaze then, as she looked

at a place on his chin with deep concentration. "Was Rolf one of those friends?"

"Yes." He answered her honestly—but also knew the honesty wasn't complete until he expounded further. "But he was also the friend who pulled me off the bricks of a London alley after a gang of cutpurses had beat me, robbed me, and left me there for dead."

At that, she jerked up her head. Her expression widened into an incredulous gape. "He saved your life?"

He nodded. "In more ways than one, I think."

She shot him a brusque huff. "Let me get used to the one first, please."

Damien retaliated by playfully swatting her shoulder. "Easy, princess; the pea in your mattress is beginning to take its toll." He settled his fingers more intimately against her skin, caressing the irresistible curve between her collar bone and neck. "And believe it or not, Rolf wasn't always such a monkey's ass."

She arched a skeptical brow. "You were saying . . . about the cutpurses?"

"Yes," he replied, "the cutpurses who almost killed me."

She winced. "I'm so sorry that you had to go through that."

"I'm not," he returned—and meant it with every muscle and bone of his being. He traveled his grasp to her arm as he looked to the ceiling, the memories now too numerous to battle . . . memories of those exhilarating, terrifying days in which more than his body had fought to live wholly again. "I'm not," he stressed again, "because that attack not only brought me back to Hyperion's Walk for my recovery but brought me back to reality itself."

"What happened?" Her prompt was gentle, as if she saw the shadows of his thoughts, if not their source.

He pulled in a deep breath before answering. "I looked

into my father's eyes for the first time in three years, that's what happened. And what I saw there made me wish as if those thugs had killed me."

"Damien!" Shock and concern formed triple underlines beneath her blurt. The tone brought all his own feelings of that day back like a ship full of shame and remorse unloaded onto the rickety dock of his soul.

"He was so . . . saddened by me," he heard himself mutter, though the sound was muffled by the interminable stacks of those shipping crates. "I kept wishing he'd just explode, just find some rage and swing a good fist at me. But I'd hurt him much deeper than that." He finished in a fading mutter "Much deeper."

"What did you do then?" She caressed his chest gently.

"First, I gained my strength back as rapidly as I could." He filled a pause with a fast snort of mirth. "I think Father was of the impression I was craving a swift return to my London hedonism. Instead, one day I marched myself into his office and demanded he begin to teach me about my responsibilities, about the land and the tenants I'd inherit from him one day. I also told him it was my intention to start courting Rachelle Scottney, with the goal of marrying her and expediting the creation of his grandchildren.

"While he smiled and poured celebratory brandy for us both, I silently gave him one more promise. I vowed I would never be the cause of such sadness in his eyes again."

He stopped there, on a long and difficult swallow. He squeezed shut his eyes, struggling to hold back the rush of his thoughts, but they inevitably surged toward that day— *ah God, that day*—when his life had been doused in a pool of bright red blood . . .

"Oh, Damien . . ." came her whisper through that nightmare haze. "But you did see that sorrow in his eyes again, didn't you?"

He felt himself nod. He raised his hand to the bridge of his nose and clamped two fingers there with the force of a vice, yearning for the pain between his eyes to eclipse the sting behind them.

Still, he forced himself to speak. He ordered himself to finish the story, so he could lock it away again and get this torture the hell over with.

"The trial sucked away his spirit," he said gruffly. "And the scandal sucked away his life." His breath escaped him on a shaking sigh. "The afternoon after I was released from prison, a letter arrived from one of his biggest buyers, stating they'd decided to purchase their wool elsewhere that season. In the middle of that night, we were awakened by Mother's scream. He'd had a seizure of some sort. He never woke up from it. She died . . . shortly after him. I think it was because her heart simply broke."

An odd sense of relief filled him as he emitted the last syllable—at least as much as he could define relief, when the woman against him dampened his chest with her tear-spiked lashes. "It must have been so difficult for you," she rasped.

He didn't respond for a long moment. When he did, the hardness of his tone came as a shock yet a reassurance. "I didn't stop to think about that. I couldn't. I had an estate to run and a murder to solve."

He felt Kira raise her hand to his shoulder blade, wordlessly telling him she knew he had more to say. But what would that "more" be? Ally had no doubt supplied her with every detail of his financial ruin, which only left behind one subject: a killing, and what he'd found out about it. The theory he hadn't disclosed to anyone.

The theory he shouldn't divulge to her, of all people.

But at that moment, she moved by a slight inch, and he

felt her shoulder beneath his hand . . . her heartbeat against his ribs . . . her tears drying on his skin . . .

And he once more remembered the tears she'd cried last night. He remembered how she'd trusted him with those tears; how she'd trusted him with *herself*.

And for a moment, he told his mind to go sit at the edge of the dock, while he trusted her with his own heart.

"Believe it or not," he began then, very quietly, "there's a funny side to all of this."

A pause preceded her reply, a long enough space for the formation of her perplexed moue. "And how have you determined *that?*"

Damien meted out another pause before answering. "Because if all the information I've gathered already is even half correct, then the key to discovering Rachelle's real killer doesn't lie at Hyperion's Walk . . . it's at Scottney Hall."

Twenty-Five

"SCOTTNEY HALL?"

Kira pushed up sharply as the words spilled from her mouth. The syllables sounded foreign and unattached, as if she referred to the Tower of Pisa or the Globe Theatre, not the place she'd called home for nearly the last month.

"Why-wh—" she at last stammered, unable to form something more coherent through the muck of her confusion. "How in the tarnation . . ."

"I wish I had those complete answers for you, princess," Damien replied, and she watched a cloud of frustration settle over his own features. "I only know that right now, it's the only explanation that makes sense." He finished with low conviction, "A great deal of sense."

His words and tone were filled with certitude, but as he spoke, he kept his gaze fixed on the painted designs in the ceiling beams. His eyes glittered with the apprehension not only of revealing what he had so far but of wondering if he could or should continue.

Kira's heart swelled as she looked at him, and she knew she had the ability to fill in the answer to that for him. She did so by pressing her hand to the side of his face, urging him to gaze once more at her. When he did, she smiled softly in encouragement. "Go on," she requested with her lips. *It's all right,* she told him with her eyes.

Damien didn't say anything as he took her hand, then fitted his lips into the center of her palm. For a long moment he remained like that, his eyes closed, as if drawing in her strength directly through that contact with her hand. Kira watched him through every precious second of that time, wordlessly heartening him to take all he wanted and needed . . . for in seeing his renewed strength, she gained precious sustenance, too.

Without preamble, he began speaking. "The night Rachelle was murdered, I was summoned out of dinner by a message from Scottney Hall. My presence was requested at once. Naturally, I complied."

Kira's brows lifted in curiosity. "Did my father send it?"

"No. Your father was in London. The request came through the stables. During my courtship with Rachelle, I'd gotten to know the lads there well. There was a beautiful bay mare I'd been keeping my eye on, especially when I heard she had a foal on the way. I'd made some offers to Nicholas, was even considering giving the foal to Rachelle as a surprise. In any case, the boys knew I'd enjoy being present for the birth."

"And that was the reason for the message?" At his confirming nod, she gave him an opposing move, shaking her head. "So . . . shouldn't that have supplied you with a locked-up alibi for the night? If all those people saw you at the Scottney Hall stables—"

"I never showed up at the Scottney Hall stables."

In the ink-dark depths of his gaze, she saw he was telling the truth—but she also saw he explored her stare in return.

He searched for a safe harbor, Kira surmised, where he could continue telling her the truth.

"Damien," she murmured, pressing her palm again to his stubbled jaw. She wished she could touch him deeper, in the soul that had lived so long in spurned solitude, it had to be retaught how to trust. *Damien, I wish I could take away all that pain for you.*

Instead, she could only tilt a small smile and say with gentle sarcasm, "You certainly know how to make things interesting, don't you?"

He compensated her effort with a genuine, if sardonic, laugh. "I received a hearty share of help that particular evening. Just as I'd crossed over onto Scottney land, I was stopped at the Two Rivers' Bridge."

Kira nodded at that, albeit with a puzzled frown. She knew the location, had marveled at its beauty during her first footbound entrance onto Scottney Hall lands. A heavy wood bridge spanned twin rivers plus the fifty feet of wetlands created between them. For that reason, the area possessed a wild, remote ambience—an odd selection, she ruminated, for any kind of a security stop.

Her expression must have disclosed her thoughts well, for Damien explained then, "The crew was checking the bridge itself, not travelers on the road." But then he qualified, "Or so these fellows told me. To this day, I have no idea who they were or what they were doing 'repairing' a bridge in the dark of a winter's night, but at that time, their Scottney liveries seemed enough. I obliged with their detour instructions without another question. Hell, who was I to argue with representatives of the uncle-in-law who was about to practically give me a prize foal?"

Kira nodded again. The reasoning made sunlight-clear sense to her. She didn't, however, understand where the account went from there. "So you're saying that the detour wasn't a detour at all?"

Damien's reply first came in the form of a trenchant grunt. "Let's put it this way"—he sneered—"by the time I realized I'd been directed to the middle of nowhere, then found my way back home through the sheer luck of a clear night sky, it was well past midnight. The whole house was asleep."

Kira voiced the obvious following to that. "Including Rachelle."

"Of course. So I thought."

"So you thought?" she rejoined. "You didn't *know*?"

Surprisingly, Damien glanced at her and chuckled then. He gave her upper arm an indulgent squeeze. "My little hoyden, we do things a fraction differently in England than you do in circus camps. Rachelle's bedroom had an adjoining door to mine, of course, but I would never think of barging in on her in the middle of the—"

"Her bedroom!" Kira exclaimed. She jerked from his hold as she examined his eyes for the gleam of a jest. "Adjoined to yours? You mean you two were married, but you had completely separate—"

"Everything," he filled in, and she indeed saw that no teasing mirth sparkled in his gaze, only the haze of an unusual but apathetic sort of loneliness. "We had separate everything. Separate lives."

He attempted to make that addition into nothing more than a casual quip by accenting it with a fast shrug. But the disparity rang as false as Aunt Aleece hiking up her skirts for an Irish jig . . . and Damien could do nothing about the truth, stalking through its own lonely dance in the shadows of his eyes. A loneliness, Kira now suspected, with beginnings long before the scandal that merely gave it physical form.

Almost a month ago she'd stood before a window, looking out on a forest, wondering how a man could so easily seclude himself from the world. Now she realized that man had already been doing it for years.

She stared at that man now and ordered away the heavy, hot sting behind her eyes. The tears were not hers to shed. Instead, she poured her compassion into her voice, asking him "When . . . did you finally find her?"

"In the morning," Damien answered after a tense, tight-muscled delay. "I'd dressed quickly, because Rolf and I were scheduled for an early morning ride." Another pause was created by a quirk of a smile, his memory clearly turning up an unexpected image. "We never worried about being pretty when we rode, Rolf and I."

She mirrored his smile for a moment. "I imagine you looked every inch the incorrigible rogue."

"I did." As he issued that, the corners of his mouth fell again, a dark and quiet tone curling back around his voice.

"She . . . wasn't in her room when I entered," he at last continued. "But even that occurrence wasn't so extraordinary. I wagered she'd just fallen asleep in the library, where she ended up many evenings. I went down, but she wasn't there, either." His next words came from even deeper in his throat, as his body tensed tighter. "That was when I went to the Drawing Room . . . then the Morning Room."

The last of that fell raggedly from his lips. With the splints of tension he kept secured around his limbs, he begged her not to ask for any more, either.

The request was fine with Kira. More than fine. She remembered the next events of the story in gruesome detail from Ally's accounting of that day, details that now made her face grimace, her heart ache, and her arms wrap closer around this man who had been forced to live the nightmare. She laid her head back against his chest and eventually, slowly, she listened to his heartbeat thump at a more regular rhythm—though she yearned to help render the same effect to his body. But his returning embrace was wooden at best; his limbs remained captive to an unseen apprehension . . . as if now the person he entreated silence from was *himself*.

If indeed the battle he waged was an inner conflict, then one party claimed a startling victory. For the "last tidbit" of information he now surrendered sent Kira's own senses leaping from startlement to astoundment.

"I knew bloody well I wasn't supposed to go near her, let alone touch her. But do you know what made me do both those things, Kira? It was the knife—the knife that monster used to first cut out her throat so she wouldn't scream, and then—"

As his voice faltered, Kira pressed a gentle hand to his chest, telling him her imagination could fill out the rest of *that* thought. "I'll *never* forget that knife," he went on. "I'll never forget how I wanted to drive it through somebody's heart myself, seeing her blood all over it. . . .

"Seeing her own family's crest carved into its ivory handle."

There was more to say. There was nothing left to say. The incongruity formed a tangled wad in Damien's throat just as all the remembered horror and confusion twisted together in his gut, forcing him into a silence he both welcomed and dreaded.

A thick lull fell, filled with nothing but the twittering birds outside and his thudding heart inside . . . as he waited and watched for this woman's reaction to the fact he'd just dragged her family into a mire called murder and scandal.

"It . . . was a dagger from Scottney Hall?" As he expected, her voice quavered with a quiet, unsure disbelief. Next to him, her body tightened and her breathing went shallow.

"Yes," Damien replied, trying to level his tone as neutrally as possible.

"You're sure?"

He fought the urge to bellow his response. Nicholas, just like any other bored nobleman on holiday in Yorkshire, had loved spending many an evening demonstrating the might of his lineage by way of the accumulated "treasures" that had once taken God knew how many lives. The Scottney arsenal was as plentiful as it was gaudy, both factors working to the favor of Damien's memory.

But she didn't need to know all *that* about dear Papa. It was important only for her to hear the conviction behind his tightly growled "I held the thing in my hand. Yes, I'm sure."

She fell into deep contemplation of that for a moment, during which time Damien watched her features. She appeared to be merely figuring a tricky sum, a mien he didn't accept for a moment—

Until she issued her next question in a tone so even, it indeed might qualify as mathematical. "Well, what happened to it?"

Damien raised both brows, then hunkered them low into a profound scowl. He'd been searching for her reaction on a separate path, expecting her bewilderment and outrage, and eventually, her escape back to her papa. Instead, *she* ambushed *his* course, turning his mind into a hostage of the most unlikely thief: hope.

Dear God. Could it be she was really willing to believe

he didn't kill Rachelle? Could it be she really wanted to know all this so she could help him?

The mere consideration of the miracle opened the flood-gates of his soul, releasing a torrent of conflicting forces and emotions. He wanted to entrust her with the rest of the story but also yearned simply to bolt from the bed himself and risk her frustration over her censure—the same censure he'd experienced in that courtroom months ago, when the magistrate had ordered him hauled away for "unruly conduct" rather than letting him tell the rest of his story. Before anyone could hear his truth.

"I don't know," he said then, the crest of that flood sweeping the words from taut agitation into snarled stress. "I don't know what happened to the damn knife, that's the pissing irony of everything." He stopped and concentrated on taking in a breath. "I remember holding the thing in my hand, then Rolf came in, and . . . everything becomes a blur in my mind then. I didn't know they'd never recovered the knife until the next day, when Rolf came to see me in prison."

The flood seeped its way into the marrow of his bones then, making him shiver from the inside out. He'd shivered the same way in that grimy cell, in that gray world interrupted only by the brief flicker of Rolf's visit that day—and the news his mate had brought of the mysteriously vanished murder weapon.

Just as he had done then, Damien emitted a dark grunt of a laugh. "The loss, believe it or not, turned out to be my salvation. Without the knife, they couldn't convict me."

Kira's reply came after another thoughtful pause. "But without the knife," she stated at last, "you couldn't prove your innocence, either."

"Right on target, princess. Just as I said; it's a—"

"Pissing irony." She supplied the finish for him with

three times the vehemence he'd planned on throwing into the words. Her reaction was strangely but potently adorable, leading Damien to cough back a laugh threatening to erupt from the depths of his belly.

But swiftly, another reaction seeped its way into him like warm honey. That golden nectar was Kira's heart . . . the heart she offered him so freely, so fervently, that he could no more resist her than a gift of delicious sweetness.

Just like the sweetness of the kiss she lowered to his lips now.

Damien not only accepted her with a pleasureful groan but drew her mouth tighter against his, steadily sucking her in, gently playing with her tongue and lips in a dance of moist nips and caresses. At last she pulled away from him yet he didn't let her go very far—though now he admitted the instinct of his body, not the counsel of his mind, as the instigating culprit.

He looked into her eyes and swallowed at seeing the earnest, urgent force of her heart there, staring unblinkingly back at him. "Damien," she whispered, "you took a great risk in telling me this."

He drew her words in for a long moment before answering. "Yes." It seemed too short a word to adequately convey his gratitude . . . his thanks to her for seeing that he'd given her not just information but his trust—and with it, a vital piece of his soul.

"I'll keep it all safe for you, Damien."

A tender smile came to life on his lips. With one finger, he stroked her cheek. "I know you will, princess."

"Do you know why?"

"Why, princess?"

"Because I love you."

His smile dropped.

Not a muscle in Kira's own body tensed, not even after

the interminable silence that was clearly the only answer he'd be able to give her declaration right now. Perhaps the only answer he'd ever be able to give.

You took a great risk in telling me this. Ah, God. The woman didn't level such words lightly. When Kira Scottney talked of taking risks, she didn't speak as a casual observer on the pastime. She committed to her emotions as completely as she embraced life itself, whether the experience be the joy of wading in a cool forest stream, the anguish of petting an abused tiger cub, or the unsurety of professing her love for a man who had nothing to offer except an isolated hunting lodge, a slobbering Labrador, and a soul full of grief.

She deserved more. And yet he bluntly admitted that if he stood on the Pavilion lawn once more with the choice to take her or leave her, he'd not change last night's actions by a step. A life as Mrs. Rolf Pembroke was *not* the "more" she had due. Just thinking of her standing before an altar with that bastard spurred his pulse again with furious speed.

He diffused part of the rage by releasing a rough cough. He funneled the other part into the clipped statement he gave as he threw back the counterpane. "We'd best be hying our naked arses out of here, my lady. They'll have the Scottney hounds out after you soon."

But before he'd finished the sentence, he shoved the blankets back into place and pulled her close again. "I want to keep you here all day, damn it."

She eagerly burrowed herself back against him. "And all night?"

"Yes"—he chuckled indulgently—"and all night." But the mirth fast gave way to a heavy sigh. "But I can't."

"Well, of course you can't." She punctuated that by pushing up from him with the same ardor she'd thrown into her cuddling, not realizing she sorely tested his concentration by letting one pert-nippled breast fall loose from its blanketed confines. "We both have work to do."

If her actions jerked him down one unexpected path, her statement hauled him down another with twice the speed. "Work?" Damien heard himself echo through the upheaval of his thoughts. "What are you—what do you mean, work?"

"Finding evidence of who really killed Rachelle," she said as if reminding him the sky was blue. She gave the bedclothes a brisk snap of her own. "And the sooner we get going, the—"

Damien jerked short her retreat with one hand, deftly ensnaring her wrist. "Hold on, wild thing." He lowered his tone to convey his seriousness. "There's nothing *we* are getting to, all right? I'm going to get you home, then I expect you to—"

"What?" Kira fired, for once giving him a reaction for which he'd more than steeled himself. "What exactly do you expect me to do, Damien? Go back to my embroidery lessons and my gown fittings and my Latin readings, and pretend I don't hear anything or see anything that may exonerate the man I love?"

When he only glared tautly at her, an incensed breath hissed from between her teeth. "That's exactly what you expected me to do, wasn't it?" she said, her voice quivering. "You were going to shut me out again, weren't you?"

"*No.*" He emphasized the protest by hauling her fingers to his lips and crushing them there. "For God's sake, Kira, that's not it."

"That's precisely *it*. That's precisely what you mean, if you've trusted me enough this far, telling me a murderer may sleep beneath the same roof I do, but forbidding me to do anything about it!"

"I'm not—"

"*Then* you tell me the evidence to prove your innocence may lie beneath a cushion I sit on or a desk drawer I open, but you command me to be a mindless figurine, instead, as if—"

She released a harsh sigh instead of completing the vituperation. As he watched her features wage a losing battle with maddened frustration, Damien's gut cramped painfully. His mind detonated in bellowing rage.

Why? Why can't everything be different? Why can't I simply return this woman's declaration of love, then spend the rest of my life proving it to her, instead of having to prove I didn't commit a murder? Why can't I hold her here, safe in my arms, instead of letting her go . . . possibly into the path of the bastard who really drove that knife into Rachelle?

"I don't understand," she went on at last. "I don't understand. Damien, I can really help you this time!"

"No," he returned evenly, "you can't."

"I can be your eyes—"

"No."

"I can be your ears—"

"No," he persisted, "you can't."

"Why?" She pushed at him hard, the American hoyden version of a tavern drunk itching to start a brawl. "*Why?*"

Unbelievably, Damien cocked a small smile at her then. "Because it's too dangerous, that's why." He gently ran his finger down her arm. "Because you're too valuable to me."

"That's a sorry excuse and you know it," she rebutted. "Damien, you need some help!"

"I don't need help."

"You need someone to be watching for things at Scottney Hall!"

"I *have* someone watching for things at Scottney Hall, thank y—"

The word died in the middle of his throat. Tensely he

watched the transforming hues of reaction across Kira's face. Her blank confusion suddenly exploded into a comprehending stare.

"You have someone," she reiterated softly. "You have . . . *you*, don't you?" An excited giggle skittered off her lips. "Dear God! You're the mysterious one from the stables . . . the trainer with the wonderful legs! Everyone's said there was something familiar about you, but they've never come close to guessing *this*!"

Damien returned an enigmatic smile. "Why should they?"

"Exactly," she concurred. "Why should they? It's the obvious beneath their noses." She turned and plopped a fast kiss on his lips. "Damien, you're brilliant!"

"Well, I . . . ." He shrugged, beset by a strange attack of bashfulness. Yet as he looked to her again, he forgot to feel even that. He forgot the fact he'd just surrendered the secret known only by one other person in the world: James, his friend from the Scottney stables who'd not only risked everything to give him his job as "George" but who routinely repeated that risk to bring him information at times when it wasn't safe for "George" to be "at work."

He forgot all of that . . . and saw only the resplendent beauty of the nude woman before him.

"So," he asked with a carefully neutral expression and a distinctly jealous tone, "you think George has wonderful legs?"

Clearly not fooled by him for a moment, she nodded zealously. "The most wonderful legs I've ever seen, I think," she replied with exaggerated coyness.

"Really, now?" He accompanied the words with a purposeful swing of one leg from beneath the covers, extending it in front of her, then flexing. He qualified his intention for the action as completely noble, of course. By making her forget her mission to help him, he'd assure her safety a degree further—perhaps the degree that would matter.

Yes, he commended himself, that was certainly the most honorable of incentives. His motion had nothing to do with the appreciative surprise he sparked in the captivating shards of her eyes, nor the ascending admiration of her brows, nor the audible gasp she let slip as she was now face to knee, as it were, with one of the very limbs for which she'd just been swooning.

"George . . . is a very nicely formed man," she murmured after a long, swallowing pause. "I wouldn't know firsthand, of course. . . ."

"Of course." Damien held his tone at the texture of Oriental silk . . . and held his leg tight and close to her.

Too close.

The realization blared through his senses like a warning siren. But it was too little, too late. Too little because the moment she lowered her hand to his thigh, flames of awakening licked the length of his leg. Too late because those flames also leapt into the juncture between his legs, powering a reaction there. A reaction he could no more cover than he could control. A reaction Kira didn't miss.

A shrewd confidence curled its way up one side of her mouth. Damien battled to school his own features into suave sensuality—an impossible feat. In the space of a few seconds, his hoyden had switched the tracks of this journey entirely. Now he was the hapless locomotive, at the mercy of *her* guiding levers, and he had no idea where their destination lie.

The sensation was alarming. And exhilarating.

"Oh, yes," she said then, caressing the outside edge of his leg, "I've heard George is an exceptionally fine man."

"But . . . ?" Damien hedged, supplying the word implied by her tone but not uttered by her lips.

"But he doesn't have the sense to ask for help when he needs it." That she issued as she brought her hand back up to his hip, while pinning his other leg with the naked weight of her own thighs. "Can you imagine that? Can you imagine he actually has to be trapped and tormented before he'll admit he can't do it all by himself?"

Damien raggedly inhaled air through his teeth. When he exhaled, he vowed, a litany of oaths would ride past his lips, too, all bound for one conniving, calculating, irresistible hoyden-woman.

But the curses didn't sound like such. Instead, he stuttered, "T-torment? Wh-what do you mean?"

"Mmmmm," she replied blithely, lips moving against his neck, hand trailing closer to where the force of his body pulsed in increasing readiness, "you know, the usual torment; the kind where pressure is mercilessly applied until appropriate surrender is given."

"P-pressure?" He rasped the query, dreading for her to show him her answer, praying for her to show him.

Kira showed him.

He hissed again as her hand slid up each inch of his arousal. She emulated the stroke he'd given himself last night before making love to her, closing her fingers around his turgid head and squeezing gently.

Damien groaned.

Just before she did it again.

"Kira . . ."

"Hmmm?"

"*Kira* . . ." Her touch torched his whole body, astounding in how freely she gave it, exciting in how innocently she administered it. He was certain she had no idea where her fingers would foray next, and that made the experience thrice as thrilling and precious for him.

"Yes," he heard himself rasp, hoping she heard the depth

of his pleasure through the sparsity of his tone. "Yes, darling . . . touch that. Touch *those*. . . ." *God, what you do to me, Kira.* "Touch me . . . hold me."

She pressed a finger to the moistened tip of his erection as she slipped her tongue slowly back between his, shyly at first, but intensifying the kiss when Damien stimulated her with a welcoming moan. A shudder claimed him, moving through her, too, as he slid a hand around one sphere of her bottom and squeezed appreciatively. He heard her breath catch and felt her heart pound, and he clenched back the surging explosion in his groin in preparation to turn the tables on his little minx—to roll her over and enter her in a thundering rush, knowing his completion inside her sweet, hot—

In the moment he took to indulge that fantasy, the crafty hoyden reminded him just who was in control here. His eyes sprang open to behold her creamy beauty straddled atop him . . . and wrapped around him. An aroused half smile tilted the edges of her mouth just before she glided the folds of her femininity around his erection.

They gasped together.

And still, the woman summoned the presence of mind to form coherent words to him. "So, Mr. Sharpe," she murmured, "do you now admit that a number of life's circumstances require the efforts of a cohesive ensemble, working together for a common goal?"

At first, Damien could only moan in response. Christ above! Of all the women on the face of this earth, Fate had sent one crashing into his life who spouted not pillow talk on the brink of her climax but half the bloody dictionary. Someone like her could have only happened to someone like him.

And damn, was he grateful.

"Y-yes," he finally managed to reply, albeit after four

heavy swallows. "Y-yes, all right, princess. We'll find the bloody killer together!"

The endeavor was worth it. She showed him her gratitude by crushing her mouth to his again, now vanquishing him with the delicious assault of her lips, tongue, and teeth. Greater satisfaction came as she broke away on an impassioned gasp, as Damien clasped her hips and began to drive their bodies against each other at a fevered rhythm.

She looked at him then, conveying the love she'd confessed in a manner more potent than any words she could ever speak. Damien couldn't even blink in return. He couldn't *think*. Looking away was an option long cast into the realm of impossibility.

He could only grit his teeth and subject himself to the torturous splendor of this woman's gaze, of this woman's body, of this woman's love as she lifted a joyous smile at him and repeated in out-of-breath intensity, "Together . . . oh, *yes*."

"Yes," Damien echoed her, as the conflagration in her gaze licked its way up the length of his arousal. *"Yes."* He was so hard. So hot. So ready to burst simply from the feel of her skin and the caress of her eyes. He tightened his grip and pumped her faster against him. She was going to make him come with the sheer force of her gaze!

"Together," Kira whispered again. "Say it again, Damien."

"To . . . gether . . ."

"Again!"

But his lips couldn't summon the word. His ecstasy-filled groan filled the air, instead, and for a moment, the birds fell silent outside and the wind stilled in the trees.

For a moment, the world stopped, and he knew the bliss of simply being alive again.

Of simply hoping again.

Twenty-Six

TOGETHER.

Kira had never realized the word could have so many wondrous shadings, so many brilliant meanings, but during the next ten weeks, she discovered them all. She created a few new definitions for the list, as well.

Every one of those definitions came accompanied by the precious memory that had inspired it. The memory of the man to whom she'd completely, deliriously given her heart.

Now knowing it was Damien beneath the hat and beard of the mysterious "George" from the stables, her afternoons were no longer filled with just Latin conjugations and needlepoint sessions, but the elation of watching his body at work, striving to move as one with an animal . . . anticipating the moments when the sun would set and he'd move as one with *her*.

Sometimes she simply knew it would be impossible to wait. She'd find a "headache" or some other ailment to wrest her away from the hawklike guard Aunt Aleece now maintained over her and beg for the relief of some fresh air for an hour. She'd make her way across the central courtyard with the excuse of wishing a visit with Rico and his mates, whom Father had agreed to take on in the Scottney Menagerie until Rolf erected some refurbishments to his own animal compound—such as a door with security enhancements, she'd been pointedly informed.

Knowing Aleece would accompany her no further than the covered portico leading to Scottney's animal care area, she'd quickly skirt around the Menagerie and make her way to the back of the stables. Damien would come to her there, in some dark corner of the extensive complex, where they used care to refrain from words or cries, giving in to their passions instead.

The words would come later, after the world tucked itself once more under darkness and lights were slowly dimmed through Scottney Hall. Using the sea captain's eyeglass Damien had given her, Kira sought out one bright light, beaming solitary against the black trees on the horizon. At that, she knew he'd come for her.

She and Fred would swiftly tiptoe downstairs then, following the secret route through the kitchen gardens Damien had mapped out for her. Even Father didn't know about the chink in the wall hidden by the assorted vines there—so his nighttime security force didn't, either. Hidden from view to anyone in the towers by the wall's height, she'd safely make her way to the foot bridge across the creek's narrow bend, knowing that soon, *together* would be a moonlit, star-bright reality once more.

Together. Many times it meant merely lying in his arms through the night . . . awakening to see him by her side; witnessing the transformation of his features as sleep enfolded him; giggling at his disgruntled scowl when Fred and Hamlet decided they wished to "join the party," as well.

Together. As the nights warmed with summer's caress, it also meant midnight adventures such as she'd never known: a journey north to Ilton Temple, where William Danby had constructed his charmingly accurate reproduction of Stonehenge; a night spent in exploration of Aysgarth Falls, turned into a collection of silver streamers by the moon; another trip to Swinnergill Kirk, during which her grinning rake of a lover showed off his knowledge of the secret cave beneath the waterfall there—as well as the interesting uses one could glean from such a place . . .

But her favorite sojourn was their visit to Linton Village. The little town, in existence since the days when Norman invaders had tromped these lands, still seemed "alive" despite the fact that its occupants had banked fires and climbed into bed hours ago. As she and Damien crossed an ancient packhorse bridge then a dew-kissed green, it took no effort for Kira to hear old folk songs in the breeze through the trees; she saw children playing on the lawn in medieval dresses and doublets. When they traveled farther and stopped at the village's thirteenth-century chapel, she saw those children growing up, falling in love, and coming here to have their love blessed before God and Eternity.

That's when the best part of the trip had occurred. As they'd entered the chapel hand in hand, she'd glanced at Damien's profile—and in that instant knew he saw those lovers of centuries past, as well. Yet then he'd returned her gaze . . . and she realized he envisioned much more than just what history had given them.

She realized he wanted to be part of that history, as well. He wanted to be part of it with her.

They'd walked wordlessly to the altar together, moonbeams and confessional candles lighting their way. The pew had creaked as they'd lowered before the crucifix, then pressed their foreheads to each other's and bowed their heads. She didn't know how much time had passed then, nor had she cared; she only remembered feeling as close to

Damien as if they were back at the lodge and his body was intimately fused with hers . . . perhaps closer.

When he brought her head up again by coaxing her face upward with a soft kiss, she gazed back at him through a haze of tears welling straight from the fulfilled space of her heart. That haze thickened with the next syllables he uttered to her past a tender, intent smile.

"Together," he'd said to her.

Her new meanings for the word had burst to life with that comprehension. Indeed, her new meanings for the *world* had sparkled into existence. Now the days weren't so frightening to face, and the nights were a starlit synonym for heaven. *Today* was now just as perfect a place to be as *tomorrow* and *forever*.

She found even Aunt Aleece easier to bear—though she attributed part of that miracle to the fact that the woman spoke to her only during their continued lessons, maintaining a stony silence everywhere in Scottney Hall but the sitting room. In that domain, Kira was subjected to "education" often sounding more like accusation, but she found herself reacting even then with a mixture of bemusement and pity. Aleece clearly felt it her duty to mete out the punishment Rolf himself had refused to enact against Kira. The man had opted to set the Yorkshire-to-London gossip trail ablaze with news of his benevolence in releasing her from all responsibility for the happenings at the May Day Ball, instead blaming the incident on "dangerous" beasts given over to a ravenous rampage.

The missive they'd received from Hyperion's Walk contained many more paragraphs than that, but that's where Kira deemed her stomach had reached its fill of condescension disguised as generosity. She certainly had no right to cast stones at the man now, but was she the only one on this giant island who recognized Rolf had reaped his own bounty of benefits from "the incident," now elevated from a forgettable gala to a historical event, thanks to the beasts *he'd* caused to be ravenous to begin with?

The answer was too perplexing to contemplate—much like the puzzle her father had become since that night. Turning her attention to Nicholas as Aleece read the last half of Rolf's letter, she observed nothing new about the man's profile. He'd become more "Lord Scottney" than when she'd first met him, his countenance cordial but formal, his demeanor courteous but stiff.

In short, he'd begun to treat her like his bookkeeper.

Kira actually found herself grateful for his distance—at first. Damien's revelations on that morning after the ball had transformed her return to Scottney Hall into an ordeal surpassing the awkwardness of hedging about her all-night whereabouts. She'd stolen glances at Nicholas during that mercifully brief confrontation—and wondered if she looked at the face of a killer. Her stomach had roiled after only two seconds of the thought, caught between her heart's yearning to believe the best and her head's command to assume the worst. Nicholas's aloofness had been the sole factor saving her from succumbing to the nausea—she couldn't come to *any* conclusion about a person who'd changed into a stone wall.

But over the weeks, the wall began to show a few chips. It began to become a person again, stone by tiny stone. She was certain Nicholas didn't mean for the moments to happen, but they did, here and there . . . and when they did, even Kira admitted herself taken aback. Once it happened when she caught him watching her in the Menagerie, playing tag with Rico and Fred. Another time it occurred when she let a potato fall off her spoon at dinner and ended up with a face full of stew for the faux pas. Many other moments had no incident attached to them; they just *happened.* But each time the marvel occurred the same way. Reluctantly Nicholas would let loose a smile or even a laugh at her—

And in the few seconds he did, she was reminded exactly of Damien's laughter and smile.

That acknowledgment initially prompted her to several days' worth of disconcertment. That she saw the tiniest similarity, let alone these blatant parallels, between the man who'd let her grow up on a separate continent and the man who now lived in her heart, was as unsettling as starting a handstand on a horse that suddenly threw a shoe.

But many times during those precious weeks, she found herself again pondering the phenomenon . . . and amazingly, found herself starting to do so with a smile. She did so as she'd raise her face into a pine-scented twilight breeze; as she looked to the kiss of amber light on the grass fanning out from the road; as she listened to the bleats of sheep and the rush of a creek and the inexplicable "sound" of Yorkshire magic . . .

And she began to realize none of her observations was so bizarre at all. Her perceptions had changed because *she* had changed. Because somehow, sometime within the last three months, she had indeed given her father's land—*her* land—a chance.

In the process, she'd fallen in love.

She'd grown to adore the beauty not just in a lonely man named Damien Sharpe, but in mist across the moors and storms across the mountains; in ancient waterfalls and medieval churches; in the voices of the past harmonizing in the songs of the present . . . and in the whisper of a dream which began to grow in her heart. A dream that perhaps Yorkshire would like a circus troupe to make its magic that much more special.

Simply because of one wonderful word. *Together.*

They would make that word a full reality, Kira vowed. All she and Damien had to do was find a killer first.

No matter how hard the task was turning out to be.

Though she soared to new heights of elation each night because of Damien's loving, she nevertheless found herself battling waves of fresh disappointment each day. No matter how many desks she'd sneaked through, conversations she'd eavesdropped on, and even volumes in the library she'd shaken out, she brought back no new information to her love each night. Concurrently, Damien relayed that his progress among Scottney Hall's servant ranks fared no better.

The only night his gaze did narrow with interest was when she expressed confusion about a letter that arrived one afternoon for Aunt Aleece. The messenger wore no livery, but Kira swore she'd seen the boy the night of the fire at Hyperion's Walk, in the stables when they'd gone to mount Dante. Damien nodded, claiming he knew the lad of whom she spoke, but his faraway tone and even more distant stare prompted Kira's suspicion that his mind had traversed much farther back than the night of the May Day Ball.

Days, then weeks blurred that moment like raindrops filling a footprint in the mud, but the exchange clung to Kira's mind. She pulled the memory back out during her and Fred's walk from the forest ridge to Scottney Hall early one Sunday morning in August. Carefully she examined both her confession and Damien's reaction, especially attempting to decipher the latter.

She took her time about the deliberations. Ally wouldn't venture near her bedchamber for hours yet (now that she'd developed the liking for sleeping in like a "proper lady" should), so she took her time strolling the path to the kitchen, indulging sniffs of the pollen-heavy blossoms and the summer-heavy air while wrapping her mind in theories about Hyperion's Walk stable boys and the purposes of letters they carried to her aunt, of all people. Of course, she reasoned, perhaps the missive had been for Father, and Aleece had merely accepted it for him—

"Kira."

She yelped and jumped back by three feet as the utterance soughed through the kitchen with ghostly implication. By the looks of the long-haired, white-robed figure standing in the dimness made possible only by a hand-carried candle lamp, Kira didn't immediately dismiss that impression, either. She had, after all, been thinking about secret plots and possible murder suspects, a mind-set forming an ideal invitation for a visit from an ominous spirit.

"Aunt Aleece," she at last murmured, trying to hide the fact it had taken her another ten seconds to recognize her aunt in such an informal state. "Heavens, you gave me a fright." She flashed a self-chiding smile as she pulled her shawl from her elbows to her shoulders. "I actually thought you were a—"

"You've been out all night." Again, the words sounded more spectral than substantial, more inquisitive than accusative—not one bit like the *mortal* version of her aunt.

"I—" Kira stammered, nonplussed, "I was—well, I—"

"You're not wearing a chemise, let alone a corset. Your lips are swollen, your skirts are a tangle, and your hair looks like you rode to Scotland and back."

Though swiftly fired, the words again imparted information, not allegation. Baffled deeper still, Kira said nothing. She nervously pressed her fingers to her lips. Erotic warmth rushed to her face at the remembrance of how her mouth got to look this way—

And she instantly realized she'd "said" entirely too much.

"You were with him, weren't you?" This time, incrimination did taint the woman's voice—when she spat the word *him*.

In response, Kira leveled her chin at a regal angle, refusing to convey shame and contrition she didn't feel. "Aunt Aleece," she asserted, "I—"

"You were with *him!*"

"Aunt Aleece, if you'll only—"

"He's a murderer, Kira!"

"He's the man I love, Aunt Aleece."

An interminable silence fell. The warmth of the approaching day now felt more like suffocating humidity. Perspiration trailed between Kira's shoulder blades and breasts; still, she didn't move a muscle. She didn't even yield a lowered eyelash, though as Aleece's glare persisted, she contemplated the terrifying ramifications of her impetuous courage. Worse, she contemplated the price *Damien* would be forced to pay for her recklessness.

I'm sorry, my love. So sorry.

The last situation she expected was her aunt's despondent sigh, followed by an equally hopeless upsweep of a hand. "So," she rasped, "you love him. That's the way of it, then."

Kira swallowed hard, her eyes filling with a sweet, hot sting. "That's the way of it," she whispered back. By the saints, could it be that this softened, vulnerable incarnation of her aunt actually understood what she felt . . . actually understood the incredible, terrible irony of being in love with her family's enemy?

She didn't know the answer to that for certain yet. But she knew she wanted to find out.

"Aunt Aleece," she said, trying to sound humble instead of apologetic, "it . . . just happened. Please believe that.

Please believe I didn't do this on purpose, or to hurt you or Father."

"Of course you didn't," the woman rejoined, though the words were tight and quiet—much too quiet.

On the other hand, Kira debated, perhaps she should be grateful for even this modicum of sensitivity from the woman. Aleece had set the candle lamp on the cutting board and now fixed her eyes to the flame glowing through the frosted glass. The reflection of that gold orb in her unblinking stare also illuminated the conflict of her thoughts: Her niece had just confessed a love affair with her daughter's supposed murderer. *This is impossible,* that stare screamed.

But it was possible. Just thinking of Damien now snapped a torturous band around Kira's heart—a longing not only for him, but for his name; for the honor he so vehemently fought to regain, the honor that was rightfully his. Her love turned his dream into hers, too, she now realized . . . which meant she also shared the pain of battling for its reality.

And the pain of keeping that campaign a secret.

"It's been so hard," she said past her own taut throat then, venturing a step closer to her aunt. "It's been so hard not to tell anyone."

"I know," her aunt replied, still staring at the lamp.

Kira moved all the way to the woman's side now, not looking away from her. "You *do* understand," she murmured, "don't you? You understand what this feels like, don't you?"

"Oh, yes." The reply came swiftly, almost ferociously. But her aunt's voice gentled as she settled her hand atop Kira's. "Yes, I do."

Kira burned to ask the reasons behind this spurt of assurance from her aunt, the reasons why the woman empathized so completely with her frustrated silence. But she also realized she'd just been given the consummate moment to pose her unavoidable question—her all-important supplication.

"Then will you keep our secret, Aunt Aleece?" she asked. "At least for a while longer?"

At that, the woman finally looked up. But her expression affixed to Kira with unguarded perplexion. "Why *are* you keeping it a secret?" she queried, truly without a clue to the answer. "Your father is bound to discover this eventually, Kira, with or without my help, and—"

"Damien didn't kill Rachelle, Aunt Aleece." She let out a huge breath after blurting the interjection, a breath replete with her conviction in the words. Yes, her senses joyously told her, she *did* believe in Damien's innocence. Her certainty was based on the honor of his heart and the integrity of his soul, not the way his gaze mesmerized her or the heat his kisses scorched through her limbs.

"I know you don't believe me," she followed swiftly then, "but for the last two months, I've been helping him gather evidence to prove it. We've been secretive because—"

"You think you can find the evidence *here*." On that final word, the woman jerked away from the chopping block. "That's why you're helping him, isn't it? Because he thinks he can find—"

Aleece cut herself off via a sudden, stunned gape. "*He's* that strange trainer from the stables, isn't he? George . . . that's his name. I knew there was something so familiar about him! He doesn't live here with the rest of the stablemen . . ."

Kira rushed forward until she stood squarely opposite her aunt. She neither lied to Aleece nor confirmed her the truth but leveled instead. "Aunt Aleece, we are on the way to discovering who really killed Rachelle. I am beseeching you now to let us continue, if only to see the monster hang at last!"

As she flung that, her aunt's face contorted in anguish. Kira loathed herself for causing the woman even deeper pain, for inducing the sheen of sorrowed tears, the clenched jaw of rage, the trembling fingertips. She longed to close those three steps between them and take Aleece into a comforting embrace. But a wordless instinct told her the woman would condemn her for the action more than thank her.

Surely enough, when Aleece at last straightened, scooped up her lamp, and smoothed her hair, she clearly showed Kira that though the crinolines and starch weren't back in place, the rest of her primly commanding persona *was*.

"I don't know about this, Kira," she stated with a chilled evenness that directly defied the morning's humidity. "I simply . . . don't know."

At that, the woman pivoted and nearly marched from the kitchen, leaving Kira standing in the dimness of the kitchen—and the terror of her thoughts.

The terror that she'd just made an elephant-size mistake.

For the next two days, she didn't breathe. She slept barely more than that and ate only at Damien's concerned bidding when she saw him on the second night.

"George" had participated in an evening of Scottney stablemen revelry the night before, when they'd all journeyed to York to celebrate the acquisition of a new champion stallion. Needless to say, the first hours Kira had him back in her arms were spent in ample demonstration of how much she'd missed him. When the two of them at last curled up before the lodge's fire for a repast of dark bread, spiced potatoes, and roast beef, she'd fumbled for ways to tell him about her confession to Aleece, but a giant clog in her throat only grew larger through the ensuing hours. It formed as she watched Damien smile more than he ever had, the gleam of hope now transforming his eyes from cloudless midnights to star-strewn summer skies. The clog thickened while he animatedly spoke about the invaluable information he'd gleaned during the York trip festivities.

The danger of posing as "George" for such an extended period had been worth it, he'd told her. The ale had loosened the tongues of his companions enough for him to discover life was not so peacefully "normal" as it seemed around Scottney Hall. Aleece sometimes ordered carriages at strange hours of the evening, but drivers were never requested with them. Every hand in the stable was ordered not to ask questions about the matter, nor did anyone have cause to, as she always returned the vehicles by morning in pristine condition.

The information, Damien believed, was a boon, possibly a large boon. He'd gone on about the matter with such gusto, Kira could only shake her head with amazement at times. So this was what the man looked like when he had a full belly, a well-loved body, and a mind full of purposeful excitement. *This* side of Damien, she decided, she could absolutely get used to loving . . . loving it so much, she also decided she could hold her own tongue for one more day.

When that day dawned, however, she couldn't find that tongue, let alone hold it. She even found herself incapable of forming a protest as Ally breezed into her bedchamber at the stroke of ten.

She rolled over and groaned when the maid pulled back the curtains, letting in hazy sun—a day she should have been happy to greet. She'd been well loved last night, and forty-eight whole hours had passed with little more drama happening at the Hall than Cleo the cockatoo once more disappearing from the Menagerie. Aleece had apparently decided silence was prudent at this time. Their secret was safe.

Life, it seemed, was well.

Kira was not.

"Good mornin' to ya, m'lady!" The maid's cheerful cadence, normally one of the best things about Kira's days, sounded today like fingernails on chalk slates. "Up, up, now! Cook tells me there's berries along with breakfast," she crooned temptingly.

Kira groaned again. "No," she protested, the word drawn out with guttural emphasis. "Oh, no. No berries. No anything."

"Fine. Ya'll starve till tea, then, but be early to lessons. Lady Aleece will pop out of her corset with pleasure."

"*No*. No lessons. Please tell her I'm ill."

"Right" came the sardonic snort over her head. "And I'll also tell her you've received the calling and are taking vows tomorrow." With an efficient grab and snapping *fwoop*, the maid stripped the counterpane and covers away from Kira's curled-up body. "I'm afraid ya've tried to get away with that story one too many—" A startled gasp suddenly interrupted the banter. "Heavens above." A hand pressed coolness into Kira's cheek. "Ya *are* sick, aren't ya?"

Within the next hour, Cook and Aunt Aleece were summoned to confirm Ally's conclusion. While Cook and Ally ruled out an ague or quinsy in favor of more dramatic diagnoses like cholera or consumption, Aunt Aleece gazed at her knowingly and attributed her condition to "a little bug" that would "take care of itself by tomorrow." Kira gave her aunt a meaningful, grateful glance as she was ordered to stay calm for the day . . . which included, the woman strictly added, no afternoon walks to the stables, either.

To her mild startlement, Kira all too happily complied. After sleeping the morning away, she rose and glimpsed at herself in the dressing closet looking glass—and promptly decided it best that Damien not see her wan, tired features until darkness arrived to lend her some useful shadows.

That decision didn't stop her from greedily looking her fill at him, however. She gazed down from the third-floor window of the conservatory as the late-afternoon sun acted like a huge candle over the world, casting alluring amber light over the varied aspects of the Hall. The stable yards were no exception, and the "candle" illuminated her lover's agility as he rode in on a spirited dapple gray stallion.

Damien's own confident spirit was evident in the powerful fluidity of his dismount, every muscle deliciously flexed, and in the smile so broad she noticed its gleam even from this distance. He lavished some strokes to the stallion's neck before passing the reins to a stable boy, then stole some uncomfortable scratches to his "beard," clearly indicating his discomfort with the stage glue and wig he'd been under for several hours now.

With amiable haste, he bid Tom and the others a good day, then departed via the courtyard and the Hall's main portcullis. His next destination, Kira had no doubt, was the forest waterfall—accompanied, of course, by Hamlet and a big cake of Pears soap.

The thought marked her body's turning point toward recovery. Though she'd been feeling progressively better all afternoon, Kira's senses now came alive. Her skin tingled to life as she imagined Damien beneath that cascade of water. Her heart pumped color back to her cheeks as she envisioned his wet hair plastered to the muscled valley between his shoulders, as she visualized the soapy bubbles sliding down the ripples of his torso. And as her fantasies conjured the splendor of his manhood, nestled beautifully between the soaked planes of his thighs, she grew wet without the aid of *any* waterfall.

Dear God, she couldn't wait to see him again.

But the giddy warmth of that thought lasted only half a second. Icy reality vanquished her anticipation. He couldn't see her like *this*!

Kira jolted up from the window seat, scattering the needlepoint over which she'd been laboring. She left the project on the floor; her stitched "roses" appeared more like blood splotches, anyway. She returned to her room swiftly as possible without giving away her sudden spurt of "health," deciding she'd use her extra time to create herself into an especially lovely sight for Damien's eyes tonight.

Occupied thus, the next few hours turned the afternoon into twilight before she realized it. The sun had just dipped beyond the parapets of Castle Bolton when she slipped into one of her favorite items in her closet: a short-sleeved, off-the-shoulder dress with a simple bodice and skirt. What made the ensemble special was the seashell-pink brushed silk of which it was constructed, a color epitomizing utter femininity even before the matching, fingerless lace gloves and patterned silk stockings were slipped on.

She'd turned to where she'd laid those accessories out, on the foot of her bed, when a commotion from the stable yard snatched her curiosity. Kira crossed to her bedroom's corner windows rather than the window seat, in order to push the modern panes outward and get a better peek at the excitement. If the ruckus had to do at all with the new gray stallion, she knew Damien would wish for as detailed a report as she could give—

Unless, of course, the man participated in the action firsthand.

Which was exactly the scene she encountered.

With a scowl falling somewhere between perplexed and dumbfounded, Kira beheld a washed and smiling "George" making his encore appearance at the Scottney Hall stables today. Also on stage for a second time pranced an agitated dapple gray stallion, this time with ears pinned back and a countenance intent on murdering anyone who approached him other than "George."

Kira's frown broadened into a captivated smirk. It seemed "George" had become a valued commodity on Tom's stable staff—a fact she didn't protest in the least. She hitched one hip against the window ledge and took full advantage of this opportunity to witness the combination of firmness yet gentleness expressed so eloquently by that man and his body. That body she desperately ached to touch and caress.

"Well, look who's feeling better!" a voice called amiably from the door. Kira waved Ally further into the room, though she didn't shift her position. The maid bustled over and joined her in perusing the scene below for a minute or two before murmuring "A beautiful beast."

"Mmmm-hmmm," Kira replied. "Seems like a nice man, too."

"I was talkin' about the horse."

"Oh." She flushed furiously as Ally giggled.

"But now that ya mention it, the other 'animal' is quite fine, as well," Ally ventured. "I wonder if he'd like to take some *fillies* around here for walks, too."

"He would *not*."

Again she endured her maid's chortle, but this time Kira joined in the mirth, too. A feeling of peace and rightness suddenly washed through her. Oh yes, her heart concurred with her mind, all of this *did* feel right, in a way she'd not felt during all her travels in America, through all those towns and cities that had never really been *home*.

But here . . . oh, how she belonged right here, in this land that surpassed beautiful, gazing upon the man she loved without limits. If she closed her eyes, Kira determined, her imagination could fill in the few gaps the scene still lacked: Damien would be Damien instead of the mysterious "George," and her love—now her husband—would be down there working with the stallion simply as a favor to Father, before he and she mounted Dante together and returned to Hyperion's Walk for dinner and an evening of lovemaking. She was up here in the bedroom with Ally merely catching up on old news, chatting in the ways old friends did those things—

Her eyes slammed back open as a scream resounded through every room and corridor of Scottney Hall.

"My lord Scottney!" The frantic, shrill wail belonged to Amy from the downstairs staff—and she sounded like somebody had rammed an ax into her belly. "My lord Scottney, he's done it again! Damien Sharpe has murdered again!"

Twenty-Seven

KIRA NEARLY TUMBLED down the main stairway in her horrified haste. But once she stepped onto the floor of the foyer—the floor smeared with a haphazard path of clotted, dirty blood—her legs went cold and stiff as poles of ice.

Still, she forced her stare to follow that crimson trail, until it ended at Amy's crumpled form. The maid moaned and chanted unintelligible words as she rocked and clutched a young woman in her lap. Several gaping wounds dominated the corpse's torso; her eyes stared out at the world in lifeless, pleading terror. Her last breaths had been clearly taken with the certainty she was about to die.

"My . . . God," Kira choked, swaying with dizzying revulsion. She gripped the banister as her legs gave out and she slid to the floor, tears rolling down her face at equal velocity. "Oh, my God . . . oh, Amy . . . who is she?"

The only answer she received from the maid was a raging scream, reminding her of an animal in pain who could express itself no other way. Everybody in the increasing throng gave Kira stares verging on silent accusation, until a strong and reassuring hand curled around her shoulder. She looked up into her father's taut face and strangely, for once, was profoundly grateful for his presence.

"She's Laura Kincaid," Nicholas supplied in a guttural grate. "She's Amy's daughter."

No. No! NO! Her mind shrieked the word, but her throat gurgled out nothing but a string of anguished keenings. Nobody heard her, anyway. Nicholas's statement affected Amy like the crank of a torture rack, and the woman's renewed wails echoed to the end of the Great Hall and back.

"My baby." The maid sobbed. "My baby . . . my girl . . . my little girl!" She wrenched wild eyes up at Nicholas. "This is what that bastard has done to her, my lord! Look at my girl!"

"I know." Her father issued the reply from lips drawn in such a grim line, his mustache hardly moved. But his nostrils flared wide as he inhaled great, furious breaths. "I know," he repeated, "and by God, that beast will *pay* for his evil this time."

"I'm with ye, m'lord," a low male voice interjected then—one of the groundsmen. "The bastard's depraved, and we won't let him go unpunished this time."

"We shouldn't have let it happen the *first* time," another said with a growl.

"Amen," threw in another.

"But the others at Hyperion's Walk will believe us now," the first voice asserted. "And then they'll help us find the bastard."

"Then they'll help us hang the bastard."

"No!"

The foyer fell quiet as Kira's panicked outcry exploded over them all—as she realized they were speaking of doing these things to Damien. Not needing the banister's help this time, she lurched to her feet and swept the mob with a convicting glare of her own.

"Damien Sharpe didn't kill this girl," she stated with conviction that surprised her, considering the foreboding throb of her heartbeat and the way her knees threatened to once more become nothing but packs of weak crumbs. "He didn't kill Rachelle, either."

Some of the glares upon her now turned to stares of stunned pity. Though some of them accompanied those looks with soft *tsks* and sighs, she could hear their thoughts as clear as if they all read from the same loose script. *The chit's barmy . . . can't see the writing on the wall in front of her . . . his poor lordship; just found his little girl and now he's lost her again, if you know what I mean . . .*

"My lady Kira," that same baritone groundsman declared as he waddled forward, "we don't fault your demand for justice—we even admire your American spunk—but we're *certain* about this. The proof—"

"*What* proof?" somebody else interjected, and Kira joined the rest of the throng in looking to James Turnbull, one of the stablemen she'd often seen strolling around with Damien. She flashed the man a fast smile of gratitude, discerning he was probably responsible for helping create "George" as well as now defending Damien.

"He's right," Kira charged, swooping her gaze back over the crowd as she backed up by one step. The action perfectly aided her goal of forceful emphasis; a dozen members of the throng shuffled nervously. "*What* proof?" she reiterated. "You have no proof, do you? No proof but gathered suspicions and rumors!"

Only one voice rasped through the crowd in reply to her then. A voice from the area at their knees. The voice of a mother strangled by the clutches of pure grief.

"Proof," Amy whispered, lips trembling. "You want

proof, yer ladyship?" Somebody had gotten a blanket, draping it across the form in her arms, but now she tore back the covering, revealing once more her daughter's blue-tinged face. "Look at yer bloody proof. *Look* at it, damn ye!"

More sounds spilled from Amy's lips, but the words were a mashing of Gaelic and English and sobbing and screams. Her friends fell to the floor with her, embracing her with tearful croonings of condolence, but the woman's shrieks penetrated their midst just like a killer's knife had gashed open her child. Most of her ramblings were incomprehensible—except for one high, anguished sentence.

"Sharpe has to pay for this!" Amy's body vibrated with the effort; she threw her head back. "Make him pay! Make—him—pay!"

She went limp then, collapsing atop her daughter's body, but the mob guaranteed her labor wasn't spent in vain. Not allowing an instant's pause to diminish the potency of their friend's hate, Amy's friends took up her outcry. The din spurred several men forward. One of them came to stand directly before Kira.

"With all due respect, Lady Kira, get outta our way!" the upstairs butler, a dimunitive man who usually never uttered a sentence of more than three words, bellowed. "We're off to find a killer!"

"That won't be necessary, Roland."

The proclamation filled the foyer more powerfully than a burst of royal drum rolls and snapped every gaze toward the entrance portico. But in the instant after that, only Kira's eyes widened in comprehending horror.

A man walked in with presence nobody disputed, his dark uniform and high boots marking him as somebody governmental and important. Following him were Tom

Montgomery and one of Scottney Hall's carpenters, Sidney Freemont.

The two of them held the horse trainer everyone knew as "George."

"Nicholas," the lawman said with a deferential nod.

"Colin," her father replied, his tone clipped and cold. "I came as soon as Tom found me. During our journey back here, he informed me Laura's death was only the first shock he had to give me today."

At that, the lawman gave a small jerk of his head. Tom acted on the signal, whisking away "George's" hat and head wig.

"No!" Kira yelled, rushing forward. Somebody caught her by the elbow, forcing her back.

Tom ripped away the false eyebrows, mustache, and beard. The throng gasped as one with their concurrent recognition, then realization.

"It's *him.*"

"Sharpe's been lurking among us all this time!"

"Heavenly saints, I fed him apple tarts."

"Heavenly saints, *I* flirted with him!"

"I've been duped by a killer."

"We've *all* been duped by a killer."

"You've all been duped by *yourselves,*" Damien at last said with a snarl. He lunged against his captors, only to be subdued by a pair of thick iron wrist cuffs and a debilitating blow to the back of his knees. As he fell to the marble floor grunting with pain, Kira's body lunged forward again, sheer instinct pulling her.

"For God's sake!" she screamed, wondering how she formed lucid words when savage fury stalked her every thought and breath. "Listen to him! You've got the *wrong man!*"

The lawman swiveled a polite stare upon her. "My good

woman," he stated past a sigh, as if dealing with a sulking child, "will you pray let me do my job?"

"You stiff-spined bastard," Kira spat. "If you were doing your job, Amy wouldn't be sitting here in her daughter's blood!"

"Kira!" came an abashed gasp from behind her—from the person, she suddenly realized, who wielded the hold on her elbow. With new awareness—and the horror halting her heart as a result—she looked to that person now.

And glared with more hatred than she thought she'd ever have to feel in her life.

"Aunt Aleece." Her eyes stung and her throat convulsed. "You're the one, aren't you? *You're* the one who betrayed Damien to them."

She received all the answer she needed in the vacillating moment Aleece took before speaking—a hesitation taken by a woman who never hesitated. "Kira," she said with a rasp, "I—"

"Betrayed him," she lashed, violently wrenching her arm away. "You betrayed *me*."

More like the Aleece she was used to, the woman leveled her gaze and set her lips in a prim line. "One day you shall thank me for this, Kira."

Beyond her control, a lunatic's laugh burst off her lips. The woman spoke as if telling her how to correctly pronounce "destroy" in French, not comprehending she'd done just that to her life.

"Thank you?" Kira said with a snarl on the mirthless remnants of that laugh. "I have no plans of ever *speaking* to you again."

Before Aleece could so much as sputter a reaction, Kira whirled. She did so not only to rid her sights of the face she yearned to pummel but to focus on the fact that two more lawmen now entered and took Damien from Tom and Sidney as if they handled a stuffed mannequin about to be burned at a Guy Fawkes Day parade. On second thought, they'd probably give the mannequin gentler treatment.

Now untethered and enraged, Kira charged at them with bared teeth and tearing hands. "Get your hands *off* of him!" She ripped at their arms, digging at their flesh as much as she could through the wool of their uniforms. "You're hurting him!"

One of the guards relented to her, jumping back with a gritted obscenity, sucking the wrist she'd just gashed with a lucky twist of a fingernail. His comrade, however, only laughed harder as she attempted the same on him.

"Hey," that bastard drawled to Damien now, "ye've got yerself quite a little bird here, Sharpe. Comely little warbler indeed, singin' fer ye like this. I don't blame ye fer keepin' her around instead of slicin' her up."

She thought she'd seen the force of outrage on Damien's features when they'd first taken him into custody. That expression was a lover's glance compared to the glare he drove into his captor now, ordering the guard in an ominous growl "Leave her the hell out of this."

"Ohhhh." The guard lilted the middle of the word in mock fear. "Pardon my humble self fer offendin' ye, Mr. Sharpe. Perhaps I should go place the warmin' bricks in yer coach now? Or fluff the pillows on the squabs? Anything to make ye nice 'n' cozy, Mr. Sharpe."

The guard's taunting sarcasm induced an abundant enough chortle in his comrade that the small injury Kira had inflicted went forgotten. With seething senses and coiled fists, she listened to their shared laughs, fighting the yearning to go at them both again, clawing away every inch of their skin this time. She forced her composure under control, because one shared gaze with Damien confirmed in her heart what she felt in her gut: He'd warned the guard away from her out of more than just masculine protectiveness.

He was determined to keep her out of this mess entirely. Determined her name would not be remotely linked with his, now tainted again by the blood of a murdered woman.

A woman you didn't murder! she screamed at him with her stare, letting her tears brim over and slide unheeded down her cheeks. *You didn't do this, Damien, and I know it. Because I know it, I'm a part of this, whether you like it or not.*

Because you're a part of me, Damien.

Because I love you, Damien.

I'm not going anywhere, Damien.

She watched a leaden swallow vibrate his throat. His jaw was now reddened and raw where Tom had ripped off his false beard—a perfect representation of the way they'd torn away a layer of her heart. Though Damien did nothing and said nothing else, she knew he endured the same torture inside, as well.

But she also knew his heart had heard the declaration of hers. She saw the comprehension in the backs of his eyes before the two guard-idiots twisted at his chains, jerking him away. She knew he truly wasn't happy about her message, but she also saw he'd hoarded every silent syllable into his soul, greedily storing her promises and love like a boy collecting fireflies . . . creating his private supply of light to use in the lightless place for which he was now bound. Behind bars again. In chains again. Heinously mistaken as a murdering beast.

By a mob that far more deserved the name than he did.

Kira cut into that pretentious herd now with a violent outcry. First kindled by fury, the sound was fueled on by despair, a keening that both hated and pitied these people, its echoes resounding with the syllables of one name.

Damien. *Damien.*

The majesty of the word resounded in her head while the lamenting cry continued to pour off her lips, as she chased the prison wagon now clattering out of the Main Courtyard. She watched the contraption disappear from sight through the thick haze of tears.

Slowly her sobs dwindled to exhausted rasps, but she didn't move from the courtyard. Not for a very long while. For hours into the grieving quiet of the night, she stood there and stared at the gate, at the huge amber walls of what was now her own prison, at the empty sky full of cold stars . . . the night sky that had no meaning anymore.

Only then did she pry her lips apart once more and force out from a throat as dry and painful as the wasteland of her heart: "Damien."

"Damien."

She woke him from sleep with the utterance this time, sounding so soft, so sad, so *real*, Damien swore he'd reach out his arms and be filled with her life and passion again. The last twenty-four hours would have been just a hideous nightmare. He would be just a brooding grouch passing himself off as a bloke named "George" once more; Kira would be just a hoyden-nymph who'd barged into his forest and decided to give him dreams for the future once more. They'd laugh and love deep into the night, talking about all those dreams together.

But one of his guards let out an oath then, followed by the frustrated slap of playing cards against a wood table. Another guard snickered—Luke, the tall bastard who'd tempted him to real murder during his arrest—and Damien realized nothing awaited his embrace except a straw mattress, a cup of stale water, and a cell full of even staler air.

And memories. Hours of memories. The incredible moments Kira had given him, each a diamond he'd dismissed at the time as merely a pretty rock, that now plagued his waking thoughts and twisted through his sleep. His heart begged for release from the torment, but his soul pleaded for more like a condemned man cherishing every morsel of his last meal.

Indeed, Damien didn't know what hour would bring the beginning of his end—and this time, he suspected with certainty, the trial would be the end—so he let his soul triumph, forcing his heart to endure the onslaught of every sight, sound, smell, and sensation his mind could remember. He recalled the wet rebel stomping her way up a stream bank at him, the golden-skinned enchantress he'd danced with at a May Day Ball, the lover who gave herself so freely, she had only to glance his way to make him hard for her.

But in his sleep, he had no authority over the images. The nightmare always progressed the same way, not seeming a nightmare at all. First, she came to him wrapped in nothing but her unbound curls, the tresses spiraling around her full breasts and the alluring triangle of her womanhood. But as soon as he'd reach for her, she faded into banks of black smoke . . . into darkness so impenetrable, he could only search for her by listening to her. *Kira!* he'd call, choking from the smoke. *Kira, you've got to help me! Where are you? Where . . .*

That was when she'd answer him. She'd plead to him with her desperate sobs . . . her curse-laden weepings . . . and her screams.

Ah God, her screams.

Please, God, he'd beseech the black void around him, *please help her, because I can't. Please help stop her screams.*

But they didn't stop. Her cries drowned his senses until he'd jerk awake, soaked with sweat. Sometimes even after that, they'd penetrate his mind. Her voice would assault without warning during some stupidly unguarded moment, then echo for hours through his being until he could only pace his cell with frantic speed, warding off the sleep that would make the torment worse.

Pacing. Sleeping. Waiting. As the days stretched on, Damien sardonically ruminated, he was really becoming the animal everyone believed him to be.

Or perhaps this was what the onset of insanity felt like.

He sat with knees to his chin one morning, tugging absently on his hair as he contemplated that theory in any detail his mind could still garner. But the clang of metal against metal brought his head jerking to a semblance of attention.

He watched Luke shove open his cell door with a derisive leer. "Rise 'n' shine, pretty thing," the guard drawled. "Yer day in court has arrived."

Damien surprised them both by laughing at that. "Day in court," he returned in a hoarse croak. "That's a good one, mate. I can go to the gallows now knowing I've heard the joke of the century."

His remark was overwhelmingly justified by the scene they came upon in the courtroom. If half of Yorkshire had showed up for his first trial, then the other half joined them this time. Even a half-dozen steps prior to entering the room, Damien witnessed an impromptu badminton match between opposite sides of the gallery, heard two jokes told at his expense, and spied four separate sets of male hands wandering up an equal number of obliging skirts. Ah, York, he thought while Luke checked the security of his wrist cuffs, a city with traceable history to the seventh century, the onetime center of the Roman Empire, the favored northern outpost of English monarchs throughout history . . .

Now its main courtroom reminded him of a circus.

Especially because it came complete with the most beautiful gypsy performer he knew.

He'd expected she'd come. He'd prayed she wouldn't. But now that he saw Kira wedged in at the front of the gallery, shoulders held straight beneath her cloak and stare directed unswervingly ahead, he surmised it would have been less painful to rip his leg off than wish her anywhere else.

Merely by seeing her again, his body surged with strength . . . and amazement. Amazement at all his feelings for this woman who stood like a goddess among those buffoons . . . and who stood in a part of his heart he never knew existed. A part of his heart filled with all the good things about his life. With happiness and life, with trust and honor, with dreams and—

Love?

"Holy God," he uttered on a throat suddenly too dry for audible sound. God, could it be possible? Could this overpowering, careening feeling be what Kira spoke of when she'd told him she loved him?

When she'd told him she loved him, he reflected . . . so many countless times now. When she'd told him without ever expecting an answer, but always hoping for one.

And he'd never given it to her. He'd never given it to her, and now—

A young woman at the fringe of the crowd caught sight of him and shrieked out her discovery. The news swept across the courtroom like a winter wind across a high moor. Accordingly, the beasts went silent as they waited . . . and watched him. In response, Damien latched his eyes to the front of the room.

The judge entered, his powdered wig and formidable jowls flapping at the same rate. He was Horton Plighton—

the same judge who'd presided at his first trial. *Wonderful*, he thought with a snarl. *Just bloody wonderful.*

Luke shoved him forward, and the farce officially began. Damien paced forward beneath the resounding echoes of his boot steps, the intensity of a thousand stares, and the crushing weight of his heart's all-too-late realization.

Because of that, he didn't allow himself a single glance in Kira's general direction. How could he? How could he pursue the disaster of meeting her gaze once, of subjecting himself to that sienna-flamed magic and not being able to tell her what he felt? Of not being able to stride to her, pull her over the rail, crush his mouth to hers, and profess before the entire bloody county that he loved her . . . *he loved her.*

But he was no fool. He'd slept little and eaten less over the last collection of days. He had few physical stores to aid the depleted mess of his mind, and he knew he'd be annihilated if ever those forces became allies against him. He'd be at that rail inside of three strides, selfishly dragging her name, her reputation, and her honor into the same sludge of shame as his.

He refused to do it. He refused to *think* about doing it. No matter how arduous the ensuing ordeal became, Damien kept his eyes riveted forward, his expression meticulously neutral, and his emotions under painstaking tether. He didn't waver as "witness" after "witness" took their place on the stand against him, most possessing faces he'd called "friend" as recent as a year ago.

Now all those people had their own stories to help the prosecuting barristers unravel the story of how he'd done away with his second victim in eight months—of how "George" had seemed so fond of the young Laura Kincaid, yet how strange everyone agreed he was, not choosing to live at Scottney Hall with the other stablemen. They told how Laura's body had been found in a meadow at the edge of the forest . . . *his* forest.

Finally the barristers called up their last witness. Damien listened for the name with the same curiosity he'd given the previous fifty individuals. He just didn't expect his composure to receive its most shocking beating at this point in the trial.

"Your honor," the barrister announced with knelling surety, "the prosecution calls Rolf Pembroke to the stand."

Kira's gasp sliced through the air behind Damien. Every nerve in his body yearned to second her sentiment with decidely more vehement emphasis, but after he swept a glance over the smug profiles of the barristers, a grim resignation settled over him. He'd seen the phenomenon happen in dying wolves and horses, and now he understood it . . . and accepted it. He was already dead. They'd succeeded at killing him, and now Rolf had been called in just to help them complete the deed with finesse.

He didn't let the bastards down, either. *Very nice work, my friend,* Damien commented via his glare as his "mate" convinced the courtroom his testimony was given only after great personal conflict; that he didn't *want* to tell all Yorkshire about Damien assaulting him the night of the ball, then leaving him sprawled on his back, fearing his skull had sustained lasting damage. He didn't *want* to relay any of it at all . . . which was why he accomplished the feat in such vivid detail.

In the end, Damien let his shoulders sag and his head fall back. The end had at last come, and he was oddly grateful. The illustrious Judge Plighton, adhering to his queen's law, had once more appointed himself as Damien's defense counsel, which, if precedence followed itself, meant nothing. Damien hadn't prepared an argument of his own, either. He knew better this time. As Rolf stepped down, he merely closed his eyes, surrendered to his exhaustion, and waited for his "devoted counsel" to dismiss the court for the day. The prosecution would have the evening to sharpen the nails of conviction they'd drive in to his coffin tomorrow.

". . . and so the prosecution rests," Plighton droned, true to form. He swiveled his jowls and wig in Damien's direction. "Mr. Sharpe, I presume that in refusing to cross-examine any of the witnesses so far, you also do not have any witnesses of your own to present. Therefore, I shall hear the prosecution's closing—"

"Wait!"

Inquisitive murmurs broke out across the courtroom as cold sweat coated the length of Damien's body—pumped by a heart thundering in alarm. Yet unlike every other person in the room, he didn't turn toward the source of the strident shout that had cut Plighton short. He adhered to his vow not to look at *her*.

That, he decided, had been a *good* vow to make. Because right now, he didn't know if he was more tempted to kiss the intrepid hoyden or strangle her.

"Lady Kira?" Plighton's perplexed tone represented the consensus of the crowd's mood. "Do *you* have information to take up with the court about this matter?"

Her reply came as distinct and dulcet as the ring of a crystal bell. "I do, your honor." She cleared her throat with steady purpose. "I would like to call myself as a witness for the defense."

The murmurings erupted into scandalized gasps. A number of people in the crowd chortled, admiring Kira for her "juicy prank." Plighton subdued them by threatening eviction for further outbursts.

"My lady Kira," he stated then, "with all respect, this is highly irregular and usually not done."

"I know, your honor." She was serenely sure of herself. "But I have information that will disprove what all those other people said."

Banned into silence, the gallery could only surge forward as some sort of a strange physical being. Their anticipation formed a nearly visible haze and a very tangible tension.

Damien slid his eyes shut and prepared himself for—

What?

Damn it, Kira, he snarled at her, *what the bloody hell are you up to?*

"Lady Kira," Plighton said ominously, "this court will not let itself be dallied with like—"

"Your honor," she interjected, now shoving into the front section of the courtroom, "is it correct the prosecution has convinced you Laura Kincaid was murdered the night before they found her in the meadow?"

Plighton swept up a hand. "Young lady, your father may be Nicholas Scottney, but I will not tolerate—"

"Damien Sharpe could not have murdered the woman that night, your honor."

"Your ladyship, this is unacc—"

"Damien couldn't have murdered her, because he was with me."

This time the crowd didn't move. Damien didn't think they breathed. *He* didn't breathe. For the first time, Plighton had the courtroom peace he'd demanded, but the man appeared in dire need of a nice, diverting riot while *he* remembered what to do.

Thirty interminable seconds turned into a minute. At last, stroking his jowls contemplatively, the judge asked with quiet calculation, "Do you have proof of this, Lady Kira?"

A light spattering of the chuckles returned—until Kira supplied her equally secure answer. "Yes, Your Honor, I do."

Plighton's gaze narrowed. "Where is it, then?"

"Before your eyes, Your Honor. *I* am the proof."

"You—?"

"I am carrying Damien Sharpe's baby."

Twenty-Eight

KIRA SMILED AS a deafening din broke out around her. At last, she thought, they'd all listened to the *truth*. At last, all these pompous apes in their silly wigs had been forced to hear what Damien was really doing that night— for at last, this very morning, Ally and Cook had confirmed she was carrying the evidence to prove it.

Damien's baby. She was going to have Damien's baby.

That simple knowledge widened her smile to giddy proportions as she now looked to Damien, knowing she'd have no trouble getting him to return her gaze *this* time. Certainly enough, her love's gaze awaited, his stubble-shadowed jaw intense, his eyes in motion with a million midnight hues, yet asking her just one fervent, silent question.

But before she could even nod in answer, Plighton's bellow stormed across the room. "Order!" he charged. "I shall have order *now*!"

The crowd sat back down, but their excitement made their previous silence impossible. Kira glanced at them with gratitude for that. Their enthralled chatterings effectively muffled the maelstrom of her heartbeat, lending her composure she suddenly didn't have in abundance anymore.

But she also turned back from that glance with a twinge of disconcertment. As she'd scanned the crowd, one distinct face stood out along the wall far to her left. She'd instantly noticed the features because they didn't swoon along with everyone else. No, the strangely blank stare on that face was directed at one person in the room: her.

Kira hadn't reciprocated her father's look. She swam in confusion over his presence, not sure whether to be infuriated or indebted by it. She did *not* need this dilemma at the moment, but she couldn't ignore the situation. She couldn't run away from wondering if Nicholas were here to help or hurt Damien's case. How she wished Mama or Sheena were here, with one of their crystal balls nearby!

Crystal ball or not, it seemed she'd have the answer to her confusion soon enough. Judge Plighton stood as he addressed the courtroom now, signaling the importance of his message.

"Lady Kira's announcement has certainly cast a new light on this case," he proclaimed, "which I must review in private before rendering a final decision on Mr. Sharpe's verdict. Therefore, we shall reconvene in precisely one hour."

One hour. Kira shot her sights to Damien again and discerned the words had impacted him with the same double-edged irony. One hour. It could be the longest of their lives. It could be the shortest of their lives.

She thanked every saint she could remember when it seemed his guard comprehended that, too. The bastard might have handled Damien like a slab of meat before, but over the days of the trial, the brutality had given way to a gruff politeness. Now as the guard began to lead Damien back out of the courtroom, he jerked his head quickly her way, too.

Kira followed them eagerly and wordlessly. The three of them proceeded down a long dark hall, until the guard opened a small holding cell. "It's not the palace," he muttered to Damien, glancing around to make certain nobody saw him unlock the wrist cuffs, "and I can't shut the door, but—"

The man interrupted himself with a chuckle. He'd clearly realized neither of them listened to him beyond the instant Kira rushed into Damien's arms, laughing and crying at once. In return, Damien's harsh breaths vibrated through her, his trembling arms crushed around her, his thundering heart pounded against hers.

But suddenly he pulled away. His hands recoiled against his sides. "I'm filthy," he muttered, "and you're gorgeous. Ah God, Kira, you're so damn—"

"Furious!" Kira hissed. She pressed her hands to the sides of his face and wrenched his gaze up to meet hers. "Shut up, you beautiful idiot." She laughed then, kissing him hard, then harder for a second time. "Damien . . . oh Damien, you beautiful idiot, kiss me," she ordered. "Touch me . . . hold me!"

With a surrendering groan, he met, then exceeded her demand. He took her with his mouth and he tantalized her with his hands. He pulled her fichu out of her neckline and teased her sensitive nipples with the tips of his exploring fingers. Kira gave herself over to his ministrations with throaty mewls, her own hands making short work of his shirt buttons so she could feel the bare expanse of his chest.

He felt wonderful. Oh God, *this* felt wonderful. Coherent logic still aided her enough to understand their absence from each other, perhaps both before *and* after today, formed a heady aphrodisiac, but that reasoning still didn't open all the windows of meaning to this moment.

The only way she peered into those windows was by gazing into Damien's eyes . . . especially as his hand moved from her breasts down to her abdomen. Kira swallowed back tears as he flattened his fingers there. But when she saw a discernible glimmer appear in his own gaze, the tears came back.

"Is it true?" he finally whispered. "Kira . . . were you really . . . *are* you really—"

"Yes," she murmured, and slid her fingers into the spaces between his. "Yes. Your child is growing inside of me."

"My God." They laughed together, before he covered her mouth in a long, soul-searing kiss.

During that kiss, even though her eyes were closed, Kira knew she looked into yet another window of this man's soul. Oh yes, she assured herself, something had changed in Damien since they'd dragged him away from Scottney Hall last week; something making his kisses even more delectable and his gazes even more magical.

She beheld that secret force even now, as he drew slightly away. And suddenly, as he softly stroked the crest of her cheek, Kira knew exactly what window had been thrown open inside her beautiful forest demon. Her lips parted on a joyous smile because of that knowledge.

He loved her, too . . . and now *he* knew it!

Surely enough, as Damien continued caressing her with his gaze, he leaned forward and whispered, "Kira . . . Kira, I—"

"Hey, Sharpe shooter." The term was obviously a nickname wielded with amity, but rough regret underlined the guard's interruption, too. "Apologies, Damien," he murmured, looking away as both of them righted their clothing, "but they're ready for ye again."

"It surely hasn't been an hour," Kira said with a perplexed frown.

"No," Damien returned, "it hasn't." Like the face of a mountain subjected to a sudden spring storm, the warmth of his features reverted back to hard, cold angles. As he extended the wrist cuffs for his jailer's key again, he muttered, "Which means the man has either been thoroughly convinced or astoundingly paid."

As they walked back to the courtroom, Kira struggled not to dwell on the certainty with which Damien had leveled the latter conclusion. Or how easy she found it to believe him.

She had to hope. *They* had to hope.

An expectant round of shufflings and murmurings hailed them into the courtroom. Kira tamped the urge to emit an ironic laugh. If she closed her eyes, she would have sworn she entered an arena to begin a performance. She doubted anybody in this crowd would know about the difference in the two spectacles, either. Or care.

The crowd calmed respectfully as Plighton made a production of entering again. Kira scooted her way into the front row of the gallery once more, her heart thrumming in her throat. The judge didn't take his own seat, she noticed. Plighton was ready to give his verdict quickly, then make an equally fast escape from the stand.

But what in tarnation does that mean? her senses screamed.

"Damien Sharpe," Plighton intoned, rolling an imperious glance at the man she loved. "Please stand now." Damien did so, and there in his uncombed and disheveled state, Kira knew she'd never thought him more her dark, proud, remarkable prince.

"Mr. Sharpe," the judge began, "I am faced with a conundrum. You have been accused of murder for the second time in one year—though as civilized members of society, we all know an accusation does not always equal guilt. Indeed, the evidence in your case, along with Lady Kira's testimony, has been"—he glanced to the prosecuting barristers while stalling to select the term he wanted—"compelling; yes, quite compelling. But, I am reluctant to say, 'compelling' does not adequately cover the myriad ways in which a babe can be conceived, nor the equal number of . . . er . . . opportunities necessary to do so, as well. Therefore, your evidence still brings this matter no sufficient resolution."

Kira pressed both her hands over her lips. Much of what Plighton said, complicated by the resonance of his jowls, was a baffling mess of babble to her. She watched Damien's shoulders sag but couldn't discern whether he relaxed in relief or surrendered in defeat.

"It also stands to reason," the judge went on, puffing himself up authoritatively, "that the other evidence in this case cannot be dismissed, either. Two fine women of this county are now cold in the ground because, it seems, of you, Mr. Sharpe. This court cannot, in good conscience, release you from the responsibility of this, nor set you free among the good people of Yorkshire again.

"Therefore, it is the court's decision to deport you to Our Majesty's New Zealand colony at the first possible opportunity. There you will pose a threat only to cows and sheep for the remainder of your days. You shall be transported to London on the morrow's train and remitted to the hands of the prison authorities there for further deportation processing. That is the final verdict of this court in this case. Court is dismissed. God save the Queen."

In an eye's blink, Plighton fled from the courtroom, not pausing to accept the roaring cheer he received from the crowd.

Not pausing to look at the man he might as well have sentenced to death.

In a haze of disbelieving shock, Kira fought her way to Damien and let the guard rush them both out of the court-room, dodging catcalls and rotten oranges as they went. Back in the holding cell, she pressed herself to him again, wishing she could clutch him tight enough to take all of him inside her, then simply walk out of this place without anybody being the wiser. Despite her intense, shaking ef-fort, an onslaught of tears came, drenching his neck. Damien responded with his own embrace, but his arms were slack against her body, defeated and exhausted and battling, she knew, the fear of holding her any closer . . . of succumbing to his own annihilation of emotion.

Finally, with a taut effort, he slid his hands to her elbows and set her away. But she'd barely moved before he yanked her back by framing her face with his hands and kissing her desperately on the lips. In a flash of a second, they entan-gled tongues and moans and souls, grasping each other as if the rest of the world had crumbled away and they stood on the only secure rock left from that catastrophe.

In a way, Kira thought, the image wasn't such a fantasy, either. For in all the wanderings and travelings of her life, she'd never known what a rock could feel like. She'd never known the desire to have a home with big, carved beds and nights by the fire and walks on the moors . . . and a man who saw all that she was and loved her anyway. A man who wouldn't mind if she decided to erect a few circus tents on that rock from time to time . . .

A man they were putting on a train for London tomor-row and a ship for New Zealand next week.

A rasping sob escaped her as she opened her eyes and hungrily drank in the sight of his face. Damien gazed back at her with equal intensity, his eyes fathomless with black despair, his jaw and lips tight with unsatiated fury. He kept one hand upon her face, stroking the curls from her cheek.

"I'm sorry," he at last ground out. "Good Christ, Kira, I'm so sorry . . . for everything . . ."

"Sshhh," she gently reprimanded him. "Sshhh."

They kissed again, lingering over each inch of movement, each shared breath and heartbeat. They had to make these minutes into hours, perhaps months, perhaps years. So many words clamored in Kira's brain, so many promises she had to make to him: *I'll wait for you to send for me . . . I'll come to you after our baby's born . . . I love you, Damien; I love you, Damien.*

But all those words went silent somewhere between her heart and her throat, as she shared his agony of knowing he'd never see his home again or stand on British soil with honor again. He was thinking of his father, she sensed, and the ultimate disappointment he'd at last dealt Kenrick Sharpe. He also thought of their child and the home that little boy or girl would never grow up in . . . the heritage they'd never be able to claim. Kira swallowed back the pain inundating her own soul as she experienced every excruciating moment of his torment—

Until the instant Damien's stare changed.

At first, only the edges of his eyes flinched, and he blinked. But peering closer into his gaze, Kira witnessed a transformation of the thoughts *behind* those eyes—the thoughts that grieved no more but plotted; the mind immersed no more in resignation but decision.

The soul telling her now, in calmly resolved certainty, *I'd rather be dead than deported.*

As soon as her eyes widened in comprehension, Damien prepared himself for anything from Kira, or perhaps nothing at all. He'd just advised her of his intention to become a true outlaw; he couldn't expect or even ask her to join his quest. She would have to come by her own choice.

Elation soared through his heart when she relayed that choice to him via a dazzling, devilish smile.

She didn't give him much time to enjoy her beauty, however. Kira's expression swiftly reverted to a stare of solemn concentration, now directed out into the hall at Luke. After one more moment of contemplation, she jerked back from Damien on what sounded like a pained shriek. The outcry, and her accompanying crouch over her leg, was so distressed that *he* moved forward, not sure what his little hoyden was up to now.

"Yer ladyship!" Luke dutifully dashed in, his eyes fixed solidly on the perfect ankle and shin she now exposed. He immediately dropped to the floor in front of her. "What the bloody blazes happened?"

Kira swung her arm as if in dramatic pain. In reality, she motioned to Damien that the guard occupied a perfect position to collapse gracefully to the floor. "Oh!" She gasped. "I think something bit me! Something big and—and hairy!"

"Sshhh, m'lady; 'tis best to stay calm and—oooog!"

After that short, stunned sound, the guard rolled to the floor like a napping baby.

Damien shook his fists out as Kira shoved Luke onto his back and wrested the ring of keys off his belt. "Sorry about that, mate," he muttered, and meant it. "But this way, at least you're not an accomplice."

By that time, Kira had unlocked the cuffs, which they set gently on the floor, not wishing to disturb Luke's nap— or anyone else still in the building, for that matter.

With equal care, Damien grabbed her hand and led her on tiptoe from the rear entrance he and Luke had used each morning and evening. Only *this* evening he wasn't bound for prison again. He allowed himself a moment's worth of the thought while taking a full breath of the clean twilight air. He was free!

He was also very much still in danger.

They were in danger.

Motioning for Kira's continued silence, Damien pulled her up a steep side street, then down into a narrow alley. The labyrinth of these sparsely populated lanes would have to serve as their escape route—if his memory didn't fail them and take them down an impasse. He concentrated as completely on the task as he could while still listening for any shouts or whistles signaling that their disappearance had been detected.

Steadily they progressed through the city. Miraculously only the sounds of early evening rituals filled the air. Mothers hummed. Teapots whistled. Dogs whined at back porches for permission to enter warm kitchens. Damien's heart gradually began to pump with exhilaration. They were actually going to get out of York without having to run.

"Hey!"

His heart halted as a girl of no more than six suddenly appeared in their path. Where the bloody hell had this child come from, with her nose full of freckles and eyes full of mischief? And eyes full of determination, too. Entirely too much determination.

"Hello, there," Kira said to the imp, though the breathiness of her voice betrayed her own trepidation about this interruption.

"You're a pretty lady." The girl exposed a mouth of healthy white teeth. That aspect revealed her as a child of York gentry, at least.

"Thank you," Kira rushed in return, "but we're in a bit of a hurry, little one, and—"

"I saw you before," the imp went on with rapacious eagerness found only in a child. I saw you in the fancy carriage, with your monkey. You're the monkey lady! Yeah, monkey lady!"

This "rest stop" had just become a fatal mistake. "Let's *go*," Damien commanded, clamping Kira's hand hard. They would have to leave the city at a run, after all.

Thanks to the imp, it now sounded like they were going to have company, too.

Whistles, shouts, bugle blasts, and hound dog howls erupted all around them at once. Damien no longer cared about what streets or alleys they utilized, as long as crowds of lanterns and gleaming police badges didn't illuminate their way. But the police and accompanying bastards seemed to multiply like rabbits, closing in tighter on them—and worse, forcing them back into York instead of away from it. But each time either of them slowed, tempted to give in to defeat, the other took the lead, pulling them on, around countless corners and an endless tangle of alleys.

Kira had just jerked her way into such a lead when shouts erupted behind them, at the opposite end of the alley they'd paused to rest in.

"There they are!" a voice boomed. Lanterns flooded the lane with garish light.

"We've got 'em now!" bellowed a thick Cockney accent.

"Halt in the name of Her Majesty Queen Victoria!"

"Damien Sharpe, halt now!"

"Halt!"

Kira cried out something frantic, but the terror of her voice was drowned by a series of sharp cracks, like a large log popping from extreme heat.

Heat similar to the fire that erupted in Damien's lower right leg.

As the telltale wetness began to ooze from his shin, he squeezed his eyes shut and swore. But he didn't let go of Kira's hand, and he didn't break his pace in keeping up with her. *Keep running,* he commanded himself, *keep running, and pray for a miracle.*

His prayers didn't include a carriage barreling across their path, then stopping. From the vehemence underlining Kira's ensuing curse, the vehicle's interference warranted the kind of rage she usually saved for defending forest does and lion cubs in chains.

With her next words, filled with nothing but disillusionment and hatred, Damien clearly assessed why.

"Father," she cried with a snarl. "Damn you, Father."

Twenty-Nine

"**G**ET IN!"

Kira stood glaring at her father for preciously valuable seconds after he snapped the order, which increased her fury with him tenfold—

Until she realized he'd punctuated the command by motioning to both her and Damien. And that he'd done so clothed from head to toe in the green and gold livery usually meant for his footmen.

Still, she hesitated. "What the hell is this about, Nicholas?" she demanded.

Her purposeful use of his proper name usually stiffened the man's spine to resemble one of the battle lances mounted on the Great Hall walls. But this time Nicholas merely slammed his leather-gloved hands on his livery-clad waist and returned her glare inch for defiant inch.

"This is about saving your arses," he retorted, the salty words tumbling from him with shocking ease. "And perhaps this bastard's leg, too."

Kira whirled at his indicating hand motion. Her eyes

locked to the red stain blooming against the right leg of Damien's breeches. "My God." She gasped. "Damien!"

But no time remained for questions or their answers, for further reluctance or pride. The search party seemed to have tripled its reinforcements, and now bloodthirsty mobs advanced on them from two directions. Kira peered at the dual predators approaching with their undulating yellow lantern eyes.

Then she looked back to her father. She met his gaze, warm and comforting as a deep copper sunset . . . his gaze that suddenly told her everything she needed to know.

This is not easy for me, daughter, those eyes said to her. *But if you love this man, then by God, I'm going to help you save him.*

This time, I'm going to be here for you, Kira.

Kira flashed him an uncertain glance just before she dove into the carriage behind Damien. As the vehicle lurched into motion, bullets pinging against the wheels and thudding against the side panels, the words of one refrain also ricocheted around the confines of her mind. *I'm here for you, Kira.*

"Father," she muttered tautly, "you haven't given me much choice."

Ten minutes later, they clattered out of York with nary a glance from the gate guards who'd been alerted to watch for a man and woman on foot, not a seemingly empty Scottney family carriage. Nicholas still didn't slow their pace, however. He did that only after they cleared Harrogate, and then only by a degree necessary to thank the horses for their outstanding efforts.

"He's already got a destination in mind," Kira deduced. Her tone transcended the darkness of where she and

Damien curled on the carriage floor, amply conveying the scowl she attached to the statement.

She felt Damien's head nod into the crook of her shoulder. He moved with careful economy, the wound in his leg obviously depleting him of the scant strength he still had. "I've got a—good idea—of where—that is," he nevertheless said through gritted teeth.

"Newgate?" she stated wryly.

They both knew she was only half kidding. "Kira," Damien rasped in dispute, "your father—won't hurt—you. Loves—you."

"Sshhh," she chastised, ashamed to admit her exploitation of his injury as an excuse to quell him. "Rest now."

Damien stubbornly shook his head again. "Not—yet. Not—until I—tell you—"

"Damien, you've *got* to preserve your strength."

"*I*—love you, too—Kira."

Her breath caught on a halting cry. She found his face through the near-black shadows and ran the back of her hand along his firm, beautiful jaw. "Damien," she whispered, and leaned to softly kiss him.

Until she realized the dolt had finally chosen to obey her and now snored quietly in her arms.

Eventually, Kira's own eyes slid shut and her head drooped atop his. Exhaustion and slumber consumed her so completely that when the carriage door opened and her father's smiling form appeared, she had no idea how much time had gone by or where they had finally stopped.

Her start of surprise jerked Damien awake, as well. He grimaced when shifting his leg, along with the makeshift bandage formed of her petticoat, but no other expression altered his features as he, too, looked to the moon-illuminated scene beyond Nicholas. His brows didn't leap as hers did. His mouth didn't fall open in stunned bafflement.

As a matter of fact, he looked as if he not only accepted but approved of the fact Nicholas had parked them in the middle of the Scottney Hall stable yard.

"Close your mouth, Kira," her father advised in a stage whisper. "Flies still love stables, even at midnight."

"B-but—" she stammered, "but what are we doing *here?*"

"Last place they'll look," Damien supplied, accepting a grateful nod from her father for the support. Gazing back at her, he quipped, "They may think I'm a killer, my love, but they don't think I've got balls. Not the balls to do *this*."

That comment drew a reluctant but sincere laugh from Nicholas. During that bizarre moment, Kira watched both men, enchanted by what she saw. She witnessed the friendship this pair had once shared as two proud and powerful men . . . perhaps, she yearned, the friendship they'd form once again.

"Besides," her father continued, "here we'll blend in while we take care of Damien's leg. I'll do that while you go fetch your pet and your other valuables. Then we'll move on to Belford."

"Belford?" Damien straightened despite the wince with which he finished.

"Belford?" Kira also echoed, though she pondered why the name sounded so familiar.

"My holdings farther north," her father explained. Again appearing anything but Scottney Hall's formidable lord, he braced both elbows to the top of the carriage door and gave her a sheepish smile. "It's not Scottney Hall," he qualified, "but it can suffice as home to you two until . . ." With that he flicked an ambivalent glance Damien's way. "Well, until we get this whole mess straightened out."

Kira had only to look at Damien to understand the full import of what her father had just offered—not only with the keys to his home but the keys to his trust, as well. On her love's face, she beheld an expression she'd seen only once before: on the afternoon she'd declared her own belief in his innocence.

"Thank you, Nicholas," Damien said. His hand, extended with firm purpose, underlined his appreciation for the Belford home. His voice, rough with emotion, offered his gratitude for the bigger gift Nicholas had bestowed to him.

At that moment, Kira didn't know if she could manage even those brief words. But she told herself she had to try.

Through a gentle haze of tears, she turned to Nicholas Scottney. "Father," she whispered, "you've asked me to try and see 'your' England . . . but tonight you've showed it to me yourself." She paused to smile and press a kiss upon his handsome jaw. "You were right all along," she told him then. "It's beautiful."

She kissed her father one more time—and the tear she found upon his cheek—before promising both men she'd be back within the half hour, Fred and her valuables in tow.

Her material possessions packed easily and quickly. Kira selected only warm, simple garments as her "Belford wardrobe," gladly leaving every one of her corsets and crinolines behind. She also packed the beloved books Father had given her: several tomes of poetry, Mary Shelley's deliciously morbid *Frankenstein*, and an album of color paintings depicting exotic birds. On her reading table, she gleefully abandoned *The Mirror of the Graces*.

Fred, on the other hand, had decided to play a maddening game of late-night hide-and-seek. Calling out his name in as loud a rasp as she dared, she checked the maids' sewing room with the extra ribbons he loved, the music room, and even the kitchens, which usually held no interest for him in their unproductive hours. No mound of rebellious brown fur greeted her in any of those locales.

She snapped her fingers in triumph as she paused on the kitchen stoop. She should have remembered her pet had developed a crush on a new arrival to the Scottney Menagerie, a green vervet monkey from the Caribbean island of St. Kitts. Everyone had taken to calling her Frederika, in honor of her new enamorato. Kira grimaced now as she approached the building, regretting she'd have to break up the happy couple—also dreading her own leavetaking of her beloved wild friends.

"It'll only be for a few months," she vowed with conviction to both her pet and herself. She added in a whisper directed straight toward heaven, "Please let it be only for a few months."

During her walk up the entrance walk to the Menagerie, her scowl deepened. Restless rustlings emanated from the creatures inside, the birds flapping, the monkeys chittering, even the wildcats releasing long *mmmrrrowls* from deep in their throats. At this time of the night, those sounds could only mean one thing: Fred wanted to play, and everyone else wanted to sleep.

"Ohhhh, Frederick." She groaned. "Why do you have to be such a brat, on tonight of all—"

A series of happy gruntings came from the shadows to her right, nullifying her complaint. Sure enough, Kira stopped and welcomed her chimpanzee as he sauntered over from the bushes, proudly showing off his new fur accessories of twigs, leaves, and a fat caterpillar.

"Well hello, my friend," she greeted, though confusion mingled in her tone. While Fred toyed with the ribbon at the neck of her cloak, she turned a puzzled glance back toward the Menagerie—and the animals still shifting uneasily inside.

If Fred didn't provoke their agitation, then what *was* the problem?

She told herself the matter wasn't her concern. She told herself Damien and Father awaited her, and every moment carried the value of an hour right now. She told herself the animals merely sounded restless, not alarmed, and that she always overreacted to intuitions like this.

She told herself all those things as she marched up the rest of the walkway and jerked open the Menagerie door.

That's when her jaw plummeted in amazement.

There on the iron bench before the waterfall, half-clothed bodies twined in a carnal embrace, were her Aunt Aleece and Rolf Pembroke.

Thirty

NEITHER OF THEM heard her open the door over the spattering of the waterfall, which meant she had a long, tormenting look at their lustful gropings before Fred cackled a salutation to Frederika. Kira gladly released her pet to his assignation as the pair on the bench broke apart.

"Oh my God!" Aleece sobbed, yanking her gown back over her exposed breasts and legs.

"Oh my God is right," Kira countered, seeking balance against a building support beam. A wave of dizzy nausea assaulted her, due no doubt to the child in her body, the controlled heat in the room, and most overwhelmingly, the scene she'd just interrupted.

Not surprisingly, the only being in this room unfazed by this confrontation was the man deftly smoothing his hair and refastening his breeches. "Lady Kira," Rolf murmured when he'd finished, approaching her as if welcoming her to a garden gala. "What a pleasant coincidence."

He motioned to the seat where Aleece still fumbled with her clothes. "Won't you please join us?"

Kira blinked up at the man. She peered for the fissure in

his composure, the tiny sign telling her he didn't mean his invitation seriously.

"No," she finally fired, pushing away from the beam and ergo, from him. "No, I will *not* please join you. In case you've forgotten, Mr. Pembroke, you gave testimony today that helped deport the father of my child. I don't wish to 'please join you' anywhere, any more, at any time."

"But I think you do" came the assured reply. Kira should have just kept walking, gladly leaving this silly man and his arrogance to Aleece. But she couldn't. She *wouldn't* let the bastard get away with such suave audacity—

Until she spun back toward Rolf and saw his "audacity" came at the end of a loaded pistol barrel, aimed directly at her stomach.

The panther six feet to her right broke out in a threatening growl. The cat smelled her sudden rise of fear, she comprehended, and for the animal's sake—for *all* their sakes—Kira breathed deeply several times, battling the physical manifestations of having a gun jabbed at her unborn child.

"Well," she stated levelly, reasoning that a touch of humor, however forced, couldn't hurt the effort, "I love a good party."

Not an inch of Rolf's demeanor changed, except he jerked the gun in Aleece's direction. "On the bench," he calmly ordered Kira.

As Kira obeyed, Aleece stared less at her than the shocking incarnation of her lover. "R-Rolf?" the woman faltered, gaping at the pistol with a face vacillating from disbelief to heartbreak to tenuous, desperate hope. "Rolf . . . my sweet . . . what on earth are you—"

"Shut up, Aleece."

Aunt Aleece's chin, still flushed a mortified crimson, trembled. "Wh-what?"

"I said *shut up*." The man still spoke with the mildness of a minister. "I want to hear from our dear Kira right now."

Still conscious of the two pacing wildcats behind him, Kira concentrated on keeping her heartbeat steady. Tarnation, how she wanted to confront the bastard, consequences be damned. How she wanted to find out why, all of a sudden, he now chose to show the reality beneath his gentleman's façade . . . the reality she'd caught glimpses of before, in the moments the man had made her truly shudder.

And what that reality had to do with the necessity of her presence at the end of his gun.

"Really, Rolf," she retorted, "I don't understand what *you* want to know from *me*."

"Everything," he snapped, irritated. "I want you to tell me *everything* you know."

She sighed, equally frustrated. "About what?"

"You *know* what." He—and the pistol—took a slow, sensual step closer. "You were screwing Damien, my *lady*. He told you things, didn't he? He told you about Rachelle . . . and me."

Kira's brows jumped into startled arches, but this time, Aleece bested her by demanding, "What *about* you and Rachelle?"

Rolf snaked up a provocative smile. "Come, come, Aleece," he chided. "I've been honest with you about your special place in my life. But the selection of a wife is different than the seduction of a mistress."

"The . . . seduction of a . . ."

"You *know* the game, darling. And surely you knew what I had in mind toward Rachelle, before you."

"Knew . . . what?"

"Of the intentions I had to court her. Of my intentions

to court her then marry her, then build Scottney Hall into an empire that would dwarf Hyperion's Walk!"

He bared a wider smile at them both then—a smile that stretched too far. In the space of one bizarre moment, his face transformed into the exact opposite of the suave, man-of-ultimate-presence Rolf. Now his face looked wild and weird and demented.

Kira vacillated about what to say to him next. Both the panther and the tiger definitely discerned the threat of an uncontrolled human nearby. They increased their wary pacings, their huge paws *shooshing* across the floor. Her answering animal's instinct exhorted her to turn Rolf's thoughts away from Rachelle, but her woman's heart wrenched her to push him just a little farther, to learn what the man's thwarted plans of years ago had to do with Damien now. With Damien and *her* now.

With one eye fixed on the wildcats, she took the risk of following her heart—for just a while longer.

"But you didn't court Rachelle," she prompted Rolf then, hoping the remark convinced him she "knew" what he assumed she "knew."

"Obviously *not*," the man spat back.

"Because Damien came back," she uttered with slow, dawning realization. Dear God. Perhaps Rolf was right. Between the chunks of information she knew and the chunks *he* filled in, a story began to unfold in her mind . . .

An astounding story.

"Because Damien came back," she repeated, enunciating the words with more conviction, "after you pulled him from that alley in London. You thought Kenrick Sharpe would finally be disgusted with him because of the incident, would disinherit him, but Kenrick didn't. Damien and Kenrick reconciled, and that's when Damien made the decision to court Rachelle himself."

"Right on the bloody money!"

Rolf exclaimed it with a delirious grin, but the words reverberated only with agony. The agony of a man who now gazed up into the aviary behind the bench, looking as if he would shoot every one of those birds down out of sheer malice. "She was the bride that should have been mine," he said with a snarl. "But that was the way things always happened between Damien and me. He *always* got what should have been mine."

Comprehension struck Kira anew—in a single, horrified wave. She didn't know precisely what triggered the epiphany, whether it was the murderous stare Rolf wielded at the birds or the blood-thick bitterness of the words he uttered as he did so, but the realization was thorough in its logic— and heinous in its rightness.

"You," she stated, accepting the calmness of her voice as completely right for this moment. "*You* were the one, weren't you, Rolf? You killed Rachelle because you wanted Damien to feel your hatred, and killing *him* wouldn't let you enjoy the deed at all. You wanted to watch him suffer."

"Damn *right* I wanted to watch him suffer!" Rolf didn't lower his sights from the aviary, but Kira also saw the glazed sheen in his eyes, showing his mind had journeyed to another place, another time. "Yes," he hissed, and a laugh unraveled from his lips the same way his sanity unraveled out of the charming, tragically fragile shell of his mind. "Yes, I killed her. I stole the knife during a dinner party, then I killed the pathetic little thing with it. I also killed that twit Laura Kincaid, and I loved watching Damien pay for every drop of her blood, too. Is that what you want to know?"

Aleece didn't say a word but began to quiver violently next to Kira. She wrapped an arm around her aunt—in truth, needing the woman as much as Aleece needed her.

She fastened her attention on that point of human contact rather than the inhumanity of the monster standing before them—the monster still holding them at the mercy of his cocked pistol.

"A career move, then," she ventured in, unbelievably, a tone that could be termed conversational. She had no idea where her composure came from, but she made a point to thank the saints for it when she got out of here. *If* she got out of here. "Is that what it was, Rolf?"

He rocked back on one heel and nodded confidently. "Mmmm . . . yes," he drawled. "Yes, I'd say so. I like the sound of that. A wise career move."

At that, Aleece jerked tearful eyes up at him. Kira watched in agony as her aunt searched the man's features, frantically looking for the man she'd adored . . . the man who couldn't have possibly murdered her little girl. "And—and me, Rolf?" she rasped. "What about me, Rolf? Was that what I was, then? When you came here after the murder to comfort me, to hold me, to love me . . . was all of that just a career move?"

Rolf considered her question for all of ten seconds before hiking his foot to the bench, then murmuring with a heinously angelic smile, "I think you know the answer to that one, too, my dear."

"Of course," Kira filled in, preventing herself from succumbing to a savage tone only by fixing her gaze to a point in the man's forehead—right between his eyes. "Now that Damien was pushed away into his forest and you were in full possession of Hyperion's Walk, you decided it wasn't enough. If you had Scottney Hall, too, your kingdom would be complete—and Aleece was your key to gaining that. As soon as you'd 'taken care of' Nicholas in one of your 'unique' ways, she'd gladly sell the Hall to you for the price of a wedding band on her finger."

"Well, well, well." Rolf responded to that on an impressed chuckle. "Very nice, my lady. Very nice, indeed."

"Forgive me if I don't return the sentiment," she stated.

"I plan on forgiving you for nothing."

The promise came punctuated by the cold press of his pistol barrel against the base of her neck. "It was truly a shame she didn't behave as we wished her to, eh, Aleece?" he queried. The woman answered with nothing but a pained whimper. "We had great plans before Nicholas surprised us all with your presence, Kira. But Aleece and I weren't going to let that stop us. You would be my Scottney bride, and she would be my Scottney love, and we would all—"

"Love?" Aleece suddenly blazed to life as the word snarled out of her, as she bared a savage, tear-streaked glare at the man. "You never *loved* me, Rolf! Don't you dare tell me you *loved* me!"

The gun tremored against Kira's neck as Rolf sighed his way through a patronizing shrug. "Darling, are you going to quibble with me about semantics *now?*"

If Aleece had claws, Kira suspected Rolf's face would have been slashed into tatters in that moment. Instead, the woman spat, "I don't want to quibble with you about anything, you monster."

"How fortuitous," Rolf returned breezily. "Since you'll soon be dead."

Aleece fell into thick, mortified silence. Kira marveled how she accomplished such, since her own heart pounded against her lungs, screaming for release in huge, panicked inhalations. But she closed her eyes and envisioned Damien, and managed to calm her own composure to a semblance of calm—

Until she felt Rolf lean in at her, his breath now falling on her face, the smell of his previous arousal clogging her senses. "Such a pity," he said, his voice even more melodic as his dementia deepened, "I so would have enjoyed you as my little Scottney bride." Slowly he lowered the pistol's barrel down between her breasts, his breaths thickening. "God, I would have enjoyed giving you some good screws," he said huskily, sliding the gun in and out of her bodice. "But I guess Damien got that privilege instead of me, too."

Abruptly he pulled both himself and the gun away. "Rise, my lady," he charged in a bitter sneer. "*Up,*" he stressed when she didn't move, hauling her to her feet. "I said stand up!"

He didn't ease his hold as he pulled her across the foot bridge, to the other side of the Menagerie. He stopped only when they stood at the door to the panther's enclosure. In sickening contrast to his grip on her arm, he grinned his way through a string of juicy kisses at the big black creature.

"Hello, kitty kitty," he greeted. "Awww, why the sad face, kitty? You say you're hungry? Din-din just wasn't enough tonight?" He yanked Kira closer to him, stroking the side of her face with the pistol barrel. "Now don't worry, kitty. I don't think we can hunt you up a suitable midnight snack."

Kira's senses swam in vertigo as she felt a ring of keys thrust into her hands. "Open it," Rolf dictated, his satiny tone now marred with guttural inflection. But her hands hung cold and numb around the steel pieces forced into them.

"Open—it!" her captor repeated, seething now. He curled her right hand around one of the keys as he shoved cold metal harder against her forehead.

Somehow, Kira's brain surrendered a decision for her. She remembered Laura Kincaid's slaughtered body on the foyer floor and realized this sad but dangerous man would think nothing of squeezing a trigger and exploding lead

into her head. Given the choice between facing his gun or
the wildcat that was familiar with her voice and scent—
    She unlocked the cage door with jerking speed.

As she did so, Rolf began to pepper the air with laughter. The sound grew in intensity until she thought she'd
join him in his lunacy. She glared at him, unsure what she
felt for him now, loathing, confusion, sorrow, rage, or simple pity. Or perhaps all of them. It didn't matter to her. She
was certain it didn't matter to Rolf.

"Come, come, Kira." The man let up from his mirth
long enough to reproach her playfully. "Don't you see the
lovely beauty of this? Don't you see how people will talk in
their salons and ballrooms about you? Why, you'll be *fa-
mous*. 'What a shame,' they'll say. 'What a terrible shame
that darling Kira Scottney died beneath the teeth of those
beasts she loved.'"

He chuckled a few times more but discarded the mirth
when he saw Kira refused to join him. "All right, then," he
said, pouting. "If you insist on being no fun, then I suppose
it's time kitty has *his* pleasure." He shoved the pistol back
where he knew she'd receive his deadly intent the clearest:
at the center of her belly.

"Into the cage," he ordered her. "Now."

"Don't take a step further, Kira."

Damien heard his voice call out the command, strong
and steady in every syllable, but the icy grip of terror
around his senses wouldn't let him believe that intent. Not
for an instant. Not while that madman in the body of his
onetime mate still dug a pistol barrel into the belly of the
woman he loved—into his future child.

Get angry! he ordered himself. He knew anger; he'd been
lovers with anger for months; he craved every hot, invigo-

rating drop of sustenance it would give him now. But he could find nothing but this debilitating ice, this hideous sensation called fear. Real fear.

He didn't know what to do. What to say. How to save Kira. *Dear God . . . Kira.*

But in that instant of frozen desperation, he looked into Kira's face. There, along the planes of beauty he'd fallen in love with, she gave him the answer to his dilemma.

She barely moved her lips, but the two words she mouthed to him were, to his dread, effortlessly comprehensible. *Trust me,* she asked of him.

Trust me.

It seemed, Damien realized within the next minute, he had no other choice. Kira darted her eyes swiftly to his right, where he looked with equal alacrity to see the panther's cage door was still unlocked. But Kira, as the wildcat's intended meal, was the closest of them all to the door.

In order to save her, he really did have to trust her.

Damien looked to her again, hoping she saw his trust in the intensity of his gaze. Hoping she also saw how much he loved her. Christ, he loved her.

But his mooning gaze did nothing to help her situation. The moment Rolf noticed their exchange, he rammed the pistol harder beneath Kira's ribs. "Well, isn't this sweet," he crooned. "And so very convenient." A feral smile curled his lips. "You've picked the perfect time to play outlaw, Damien. Now I can do away with Aleece right here, as well, and let you handle the criminal conviction honors once more. You've made it so easy, my friend. I suppose I should thank you. Forgive me if I don't."

Damien remained still and silent, surreptitiously looking to Kira for a signal of their next move. She gave it to him, pressing her forefinger and thumb together. He had to supply her with more time.

"Bloody hell, Rolf," he muttered. "We were mates—"

"We *weren't* mates!" came the ferocious retort. "Mates get to share things, Damien. Mates means everybody gets to have the same damn things!"

Rolf's voice escalated on the last three words, pitching to a maniacal shriek. Damien forced himself to respond with a long, deep breath—and with that inhalation was filled with a strange, chilled calmness. "Was that what it was about to you, Rolf?" he returned quietly. "The *things* we had?"

The man sneered. "Oh, don't take that high ground with me, Damien. You can stand there and pontificate because you were the one who had it all! You were the one—"

"Who would have gladly shared," Damien stated. "If you'd only asked."

Rolf's reaction to that didn't take the form he expected. Damien steeled himself for another incensed eruption; he even welcomed the man's anger, hoping to goad Rolf into an attack on him. Then Kira and the baby would be safe. For that reassurance, he'd gladly take a bullet in any part of his body.

But Rolf didn't lash out at him again. The man's eyes, assessing Damien's face, seemingly had the power to read his thoughts, too. Because instead of seething or yelling, Rolf now broke out into a savoring laugh as he once more pulled Kira close to him.

"But you see, Damien"—he snickered—"I don't *have* to ask now. I'm simply taking from you, just as you always stole from me."

Damien's icy terror ignited into a fire storm of rage. He twisted every muscle in his body tight to fight the yearning to stalk forward and plant a fist in each of the sockets housing Rolf's eyes. Then he'd take the bastard's pistol from him and use the bullet on the brain that had obviously festered and gone rotten long ago.

"So how does it feel, Damien?" the monster said with a snarl then, gloating and grinning. "How does it feel to see me with *your* possession? How does it feel to watch my hands fondle your woman? To see me enjoy her in the way only you should?"

Damien glared hard and intently—at Kira. With his eyes, he begged for mercy from this torture; he pleaded her to save herself from the gropings Rolf inflicted on her body, to save *him* from the hold Rolf wielded around his mind.

"Now, my good friend"—Rolf's inflection thickened in a sardonic parody of affection—"it's time for you to watch me dispose of your pretty little property, too."

Before Damien could form a reaction, let alone command his body to move, Rolf hauled Kira back and swung wide the door to the cage behind them. The wildcat within released a peeved snarl at their intrusion but held its position atop a mossy log. It dipped its sleek black head toward them, the golden gaze hungrily sizing up the closest piece of warm-blooded meat:

Kira.

"In," Rolf ordered her, emphasizing with a hard poke of the pistol. As Kira hesitated, skidding only a step further, the panther cleared a graceful leap off the log. It strode directly toward her.

Damien watched in agony as the woman he loved and a fifty-stone panther locked gazes just three feet from each other.

But the next moment, he pushed aside the agony to make room for his astonishment. He felt nothing less as he watched her actually extend a friendly hand toward the wildcat. "Hello, beautiful one," she murmured musically. "Are you confused by all this?"

"Confused!" Rolf attempted to hiss it into her ear but missed; he shook too badly in increasing agitation. One of the performers in his scenario wasn't behaving on cue. That performer just happened to be a panther with anxious intent flashing in its eyes. "He's not confused, you little imbecile; he's hungry! Now get into the bloody cage!"

He erupted in raw antagonism as control slipped further and fear pounced into his brain in its place. The distraction occupied Rolf long enough for Damien to act. In two strides he leapt behind the man and snatched the pistol away. Rolf roared, clawing the air for the gun, but when he recognized his effort was futile, he brought that hand down around Kira instead. He curled a vicious and unrelenting grip into her arm, causing her to shriek out in pain.

That cry was the only motivation Damien—and the panther—needed.

Damien pulled her hard against his chest in the moment the wildcat's front paws slammed into Rolf's face. As Kira screamed, he bellowed for Nicholas, who raced in and over to Aleece's side.

The four of them ran out into the night, hurling the doors closed and locking them—though the action didn't completely muffle the mortal shrieks and voracious roars tangling inside, finishing out a ritual of savage death as old as the earth.

Despite the depth of his sorrow for the man who once had been his closest friend, Damien clutched Kira closer and staunchly turned his back on the Menagerie. It was time to think about life now. About starting again now. About hoping and dreaming and being free now.

No, he corrected himself the next moment. He didn't need to learn any of those things—because the woman in his arms had already taught him how.

She'd taught him when she'd ignited his heart with the sweet, wondrous flame of love.

Thirty-One

"**K**IRA," DAMIEN CALLED gently, shaking his head with an amused smile. He supposed he'd have to get used to finding his wife crawling around in stable hay . . . he just didn't think he'd also find her doing so in her wedding gown.

And what a wedding gown, he concluded once again. When she'd appeared at the end of the Scottney Hall chapel in the creation, he'd seen why Nicholas had employed *three* of London's most eminent designers for the task of completing the creation in four weeks. The dress combined present-day feminity with a tribal flair, a perfect representation of the woman who filled it with breath-stopping beauty. He hadn't been the only one who thought so, either, he'd noticed during their intimate ceremony. Enthralled gasps had broken out from every corner of the small crowd they'd invited.

But now the rest of Yorkshire waited on them—while his bride seemed intent, for some reason, on finding a needle in a pile of Scottney Hall stable hay.

"Kira darling," he coaxed again. "Everyone's left for the gala over at the Walk. We're expected. . . ."

"I know," she replied distractedly, "but—ah-ha!"

Her face, framed by an exotic arrangement of white roses, white bird feathers, and her own beautiful curls, beamed him a triumphant smile. With a dramatic flourish, she produced not a needle but a squirming green vervet monkey.

Damien gave up a hearty laugh and heartier applause. "Perhaps you should enroll in the Sharpe Troupe as more than *grande dame du cirque*," he teased. Approaching her— unable to stay more than three feet away from her, actually—he suggested, "Company magician?"

His new bride emitted a musical laugh of her own. She sighed, a light and content sound, while petting Frederika. "Fred refused even to approach the carriage without her. Er—Damien, I'm afraid we're spoiling our children already."

A warm sensation filled him like summer's first breeze. *Our children.* Their children, who would have a heritage now—dualfold. Now that he'd been welcomed back by *all* the denizens of Hyperion's Walk, the two estates would have connecting bonds, after all. It seemed Rolf would indeed get his way, Damien ruminated; he just wondered if his mate could appreciate, from wherever he was, that all it had taken was a bridge built of love. Love he'd almost stopped believing in himself.

They'd have a lifetime of that love, he vowed—and so would their menagerie of children. Boys or girls or a wild mix of both, he didn't care; he only wanted them to have lives filled with adventure and daydreams, of challenges and laughter, of believing they could do anything they wanted simply with the power of believing they could. They would learn how to ride their horses then perform somersaults on them, take up fencing *and* tumbling if they liked; they'd have tigers as family pets and, occasionally, half of England traipsing across their back lawn to view the most spectacular circus and menagerie in the land.

They would all be as amazing as their mother.

He looked at that woman now and subjected his senses to an assault of happiness in the process. And desire. Overwhelming desire for this woman who was now truly his, in all her flowing white gauze and feathers and gypsy baubles—and bits of hay he longed to dispel from her by using his lips.

With an effort, Damien tamped the craving. He turned his thoughts to safer subjects in hopes of accomplishing the same with the hard swell at the front of his breeches.

"Did you check on Aleece?" he asked, plucking a few strands of straw from the "safe" area of her shoulder.

"Yes," she replied softly, and a slight furrow marred her brow. "There's no change. She hasn't said anything since that night. But I think, perhaps, she's in a more peaceful place, even if it is in her mind. I can see she's happy, in her own way."

Damien found himself shaking his head once more, this time in soft awe. "Mrs. Sharpe," he murmured, bestowing a gentle kiss to her forehead, "you're a remarkable and wonderful woman."

He accomplished what he'd hoped with the words. A smile erased the moment of trouble from her features. But as she directed that look directly up at *him*, his position got more precarious. He wanted her again—with unignorable intensity. This time he saw Kira was aware of it, too.

"Damien," she warned—albeit while she released Frederika so she could wrap her arms around his neck. "Aren't we 'expected' somewhere?"

"Mmmm-hmmm." He growled it in the moment before he took her mouth wetly and greedily.

"Oh," she breathed when they dragged apart many minutes later. "Oh, that's what I thought. . . ."

But those were the last lucid words she uttered for a long while after that. For as they sank to the hay together, the beasts around them shifted restlessly, feeling the heat of the fire they emblazoned to celebrate the beginning of their shared life, their shared love.

A fire that now climbed to touch heaven itself.